A Happier Life

A Happier Life

A Novel

KRISTY WOODSON HARVEY

Gallery Books

New York   London   Toronto   Sydney   New Delhi

G

Gallery Books
An Imprint of Simon & Schuster, LLC
1230 Avenue of the Americas
New York, NY 10020

Copyright © 2024 by Kristy Woodson Harvey

First Gallery Books hardcover edition June 2024

GALLERY BOOKS and colophon are registered trademarks of Simon & Schuster, LLC

Simon & Schuster: Celebrating 100 Years of Publishing in 2024

For information about special discounts for bulk purchases, please contact Simon & Schuster Special Sales at 1-866-506-1949 or business@simonandschuster.com.

The Simon & Schuster Speakers Bureau can bring authors to your live event. For more information or to book an event, contact the Simon & Schuster Speakers Bureau at 1-866-248-3049 or visit our website at www.simonspeakers.com.

Manufactured in the United States of America

10 9 8 7 6 5 4 3 2 1

Library of Congress Cataloging-in-Publication Data
Names: Harvey, Kristy Woodson, author.
Title: A Happier Life: a novel / Kristy Woodson Harvey.
Description: First Gallery Books hardcover edition. | New York : Gallery Books, 2024. | Summary: "A young woman discovers the love and family she has always longed for when she spends a life-changing summer at her grandparents' old house in North Carolina" —Provided by publisher.
Identifiers: LCCN 2023029128 (print) | LCCN 2023029129 (ebook) | ISBN 9781668012192 (hardcover) | ISBN 9781668012208 (trade paperback) | ISBN 9781668012215 (ebook)
Subjects: LCGFT: Novels.
Classification: LCC PS3623.O6785 L37 2024 (print) | LCC PS3623.O6785 (ebook) | DDC 813/.6—dc23/eng/20230626
LC record available at https://lccn.loc.gov/2023029128
LC ebook record available at https://lccn.loc.gov/2023029129

ISBN 978-1-6680-1219-2
ISBN 978-1-6680-1221-5 (ebook)

To the Johnsons—
Lee and Tricia, Brooke (Smith), Alee (Halsey), and Ann Rollins—
the best neighbors and dearest friends,
who brought a forgotten house back to life and,
twenty-five years later, inspired a story.

A Happier Life

The House on Sunset Lane: Pioneers

Houses outlive the people they love. When my fellow clapboard houses on Sunset Lane in Beaufort and I were being built by shipbuilders just discovering this port, proud and young and new, we had no idea what our futures would hold. How could we? In 1769, we were the first houses on this street, as much pioneers as the fishermen, whalers, and shipping merchants, like the Saint James family—my family—who made us their homes.

But what we understood immediately was that it was our job to care for the families who lived within our wooden walls—often repurposed from the ships they came in on—who loved us, who filled us with furniture and bedding, crotchety aging grandparents, and howling, beloved infants. It was our job to remember every word spoken, every breath breathed, to store their secrets and successes, heartbreaks and joys, and keep them safe.

Here, on Seven Sunset Lane, the sun still glints on water that slowly, patiently laps the sandy shore. People marvel at us, these structures that have been here since before America was America.

But I alone hold the distinction of still, two hundred fifty-four years after I was first built, being the Saint James House. Other houses on this street have changed hands, been sold, filled with fresh wallpaper, trendy paint colors, and new people who don't care quite so much about the stories their houses hold. That I have been owned by one family should be a point of pride. Only, it has been nearly fifty years since anyone has lived inside of me, since I have swayed with voices singing Christmas carols, vibrated with dog paws speeding down my halls, and cheered with friends blowing out birthday candles. But those aren't the moments I miss most. What I long for is the sound of my door swinging open, the rush of sea breeze through cracked windows, my kitchen filled with the scents of cakes and cookies, roasts and chickens, the simple laughter of ordinary days.

I loved all the families who brought those days to me. But my happiest years, my best times, were with Becks and Townsend Saint James and their children, Lon and Virginia. Sometimes, when I miss them most, I cling to the specks of sand between my floorboards, reminders of when the children tore inside with such jubilance that I would have cried if I had tears. Their mother, Becks, instead of scolding them, wrapped them in towels and kisses and fed them homemade strawberry ice cream on my wide, spacious front porch. I kept them cool in the summer and warm in the winter, a product of facing perfectly south, to the credit of my savvy builders.

I once believed, foolishly, that the parties and dinners, friends and fun—and, most of all, great love of this family, love so big and so pulsating that I could feel it down into my very foundation—would stay forever. For years I have hoped, prayed, wished that they would return, ever since Rebecca and Townsend Saint James unexpectedly met their demise on August 28, 1976. I alone know the real story, have held the truth right here all this time, if anyone had bothered to uncover it.

But that is the plight of old houses. At some point in our seemingly infinite lives, we may be forgotten. And so, we must cling to the joys and secrets forever stored within our walls, until we are remembered again.

All (Are Not) Welcome

I will get this promotion *or something better*," I whisper as I walk down the gleaming, glass-walled hall of All Welcome, the lifestyle brand I have been working for since I was a college intern twelve years ago. Allison, our CEO—and, well, my hero—is big on the phrase. She claims she has used it to manifest her massive success over the last thirteen years, when she started this brand as a recent college grad. Who am I to doubt her? If I'm going to manifest something, now seems like a good time to start.

Casey, one of our interns, winks at me as she passes me in the hallway and crosses her fingers. Her encouragement boosts me as my stomach rolls with the reminder that Jonathan, the head of HR and my ex, is going to be in this meeting about my "future with All Welcome" too. We broke up about a month ago, after eighteen months of dating, but I still haven't told my family. I can almost hear my mother's voice in my head: *I don't like to interfere, but, darling, the man still works for his ex-wife's company. And you work for him. It is unsavory at best, a recipe for disaster at worst.*

Despite my mother's concerns, I had always felt proud that Jonathan—who was *not* my superior when we started dating, I might add—Allison, and I have always been able to work together so seamlessly. Allison and Jonathan used to say it was because their relationship was ancient history. And now, so was ours. Because after we moved in together six months ago, Jonathan and I realized that the single thing we had in common was work. Now the three of us are back to being just coworkers. Coworkers with weird personal histories, to be sure, but just coworkers all the same.

I walk to the end of the hall to the smallest conference room. It is the only one that has solid, soundproof walls instead of glass, so it's the most private. And it's where most promotion meetings take place.

Allison is already there, as I assumed she would be. Punctuality is one of her core values. The others, as I well know, are transparency, honesty, innovation, and excellence. She is a motivational speaker who gets paid in the high five digits each time she flies off to inspire companies and their employees to reach their full potential. She has a huge conference—All-Fest—each year that literally fills an arena, a line of journals and goal-setting notebooks, and has penned four *New York Times* bestsellers. We even decided to publish her last book in-house. We were nervous, but it went so well that we're publishing a handful of other meaningful titles this year by other authors in the space.

It's very exciting. It is also very on-brand for Allison, someone who many, many women aspire to be like. As I open the door, I see that right now—aspirationally—she is walking on the quiet, non-motorized treadmill in the corner of the room. She has exercise equipment in every conference room and her office because she doesn't have time for regular workouts, but this ensures she can still honor her body and spirit each day—her words, not mine. She is *such* a badass. I feel the tiniest twinge of guilt that I can't remember the last time I actually exercised myself.

"Oh, hi!" I say as I spot Jonathan shifting a stack of papers at the head of the table. I thought the breakup would be harder, but since we have had to work together every day since, it already sort of feels like we're back to just coworkers. Even at thirty-seven, he still has ashy blond hair and big puppy-dog brown eyes. He's a good guy. Not *my* guy anymore. But a good guy all the same. He has been letting me stay in the town house we shared while I frantically look for another apartment. Something decent in my price range in New York City is, evidently, hard to come by. And our breakup made me realize I don't have so much as a friend's couch to crash on. My parents' place is a last resort that I hope I don't need.

A glass of water is in front of the seat next to him, so I figure it is mine. I take my seat and am shocked when Allison quits walking. She usually keeps working out, getting progressively more breathless as a meeting goes on. Usually, by the end of an hour, I'm translating because I'm the only one who can understand her. Curiously, though, the woman never sweats.

"Keaton, Keaton, Keaton," she says as she sits down. "Our girl wonder."

I sit on the edge of my seat, keeping my fingers crossed under the table. "I brought you here today to tell you that I'm pregnant."

That's not what I'm expecting to hear, but, still, I gasp and clap my hands. I would know if she was seriously dating someone, so I wonder if she has done in vitro or, knowing Allison, has engineered some new pregnancy procedure that doesn't involve sperm at all. A woman-only pregnancy. She'd be really into that. It would also be great for our brand. I briefly wonder how on earth she's going to take care of a child when she works absolutely nonstop. All that aside, she's obviously telling me I'm promoted because she can't take on anything else in her state.

"That is great news, Allison," I chime in. "And I'd like you to know I'm here for anything you need."

She smiles with an ethereal glow and reaches across the table to take my hand. "I am so glad to hear you say that because there *is* something I need from you."

I feel a grin spread across my face, and I glance briefly at Jonathan. He looks kind of . . . constipated. Which I know he never is because we shared a bathroom in his two-bedroom town house. Maybe he's worried about what Allison's pregnancy is going to mean for his job, which I totally get. But now he'll have me—with my corner office and big, fat salary—to lighten his workload. I try to convey that with my glance, but he doesn't seem to notice.

Then Allison says, with a light squeeze of my palm, "I'm going to need you to move out of the town house."

I look at Jonathan again, not quite comprehending. "Well, I'm looking for a new place, but . . ." I trail off. Some fuzzy atoms are connecting in my brain.

I remove my clammy hand and take a sip of water just as Allison lets out a breathy little laugh. "Oh my gosh. Pregnancy brain. The baby is Jonathan's, and I am going to move back into the house y'all have been living in. My apartment is too small."

I honestly don't mean to, but I choke and spit the water out, spraying it all over Jonathan. He barely moves to wipe himself off; he only looks really apologetic. And kind of sick.

"*My* Jonathan?" I squeak.

Allison smiles in a way that feels very condescending. "Well, mine," she says as she rubs her impossibly flat stomach.

Jonathan barely pipes up. "Well, actually, Allison, I'm not sure I would say I *belong* to you."

She smiles at him in a way that conveys, *Oh, but don't you?*

"I. What? No. You can't. It doesn't . . ." I'm obviously having some trouble with my words.

"Don't worry," Allison says. "We'll have someone pack up all your things and get them moved wherever you go next."

"That is literally the last thing I am worried about." I turn to Jonathan, doing the math in my head. We've only been broken up for four weeks. "How long has this been going on?"

"Well, I'm twelve weeks along," Allison says, batting her eyes at Jonathan.

"What?" I practically scream, realizing *this* is why I'm in the soundproof conference room. I turn to Jonathan. "Are you insane? We only moved in together like six months ago! You're the one who talked me into getting rid of my apartment!"

"I'm really sorry," Jonathan says. "It was so obvious things weren't going to work out with us that I just . . . moved on before it was official. It didn't mean anything at first."

"But then we realized we were still in love," Allison says. "That we wanted to start a family. I truly hope this doesn't hurt you, Keaton, but Jonathan and I think consciously recoupling is the right thing for us."

Consciously recoupling. This can't be real. Anger, which I am usually good at controlling, rises in me. The hypocrisy is too much for me to take. "Do you believe your own psychobabble bullshit?" I ask her, my face turning red. "I mean, do you hear yourself? Oh, *honesty and transparency are my core values*," I say in a singsong voice.

"I'm sorry you feel that way," she says, "because we were here to offer you a promotion to director of marketing. But if you aren't committed to the brand then—"

"You were going to offer me a promotion?" I practically spit. "A *promotion*? So we can work more closely while you and your ex re-marry and start a family?"

"Oh, we won't remarry," Allison says. "Marriage feels so archaic and confining now. But we assumed if the two of us could work so well together after a divorce that surely you could manage . . ."

That's when I know I'm going to cry, and that's the last thing in the world I want to do. I *want* to be archaic and confined. I want to be *married*. I don't want to be married to Jonathan. But the fact that he cheated on me really stings. And, well, explains why he's been so nice about letting me stay in the town house. Guilt is powerful.

"Jonathan, how could you do this to me? All that time we were planning our future together, and you were screwing your ex-wife?" *And I had no idea?*

"I'm sorry, Keaton. I really am."

"You should never be sorry about living your authentic path, Jonathan," Allison interjects.

I take a long look at Allison, and I can't believe that I was so en-amored with her for so long. Yes, she's beautiful in this bird-boned, hippie-at-Woodstock kind of way. And she has this soft voice that you have to lean forward to hear, that makes you want to listen. But she's also selfish. It's always about her. I know this, and yet I've always for-given her for it because I believed she was a good person deep down.

When I got my internship the summer after my junior year at our shared alma mater, UNC–Chapel Hill, I felt like I had won the lottery. Allison and I together felt like kismet. It was clear I would come work for her after graduation. I knew she was going to change the world. And, well, she has. And so that's why it's so hard for me to say, "Why did I buy into this for so long? I did your program to the letter for years, and it's just now occurring to me that I'm not any better, any more enlightened, than I was when I started."

"What do you mean *did*?" Allison asks.

I squint at her. "*Did.* Now, a lot of mornings, I don't even make my bed." *I don't have time since I'm basically running your company*, I add, only in my head.

Allison gasps. "Making your bed is a Vision One, Track One foundation habit. Are you even drinking your eight glasses of water? Moving your thirty minutes?"

"Nope!" I say, crossing my arms, feeling childish. I know she is going to be offended by this admission.

"The foundation habits aren't really that difficult if you're committed," she says. "Keaton, maybe you and I should dive into why you're letting yourself stay stuck."

"Because your entire company is crap, Allison, based on making women feel like they aren't good enough if they aren't as perfect and motivated and successful as you." I know I've gone too far. All Welcome's whole premise is that everyone can find their happiness if they make the time to do what inspires them. And Allison has helped people do that. Even still, I can't help but hit her where it hurts most.

She smiles sadly at me, and I'm torn between regret and hatred. "Keaton, I'm sorry to say, but I think your journey here at All Welcome is coming to an end. I can overlook a spiritually unenlightened reaction in a moment of turmoil, but I can't have people who don't believe in the process be a part of this company."

Jonathan finally speaks up. "Well, maybe it isn't fair to fire her . . ."

I know he's thinking it isn't fair to fire me because in what world am I *not* going to sue the hell out of this company for wrongful termination? "Nope!" I say. "I'm fired."

"Maybe we can discuss a severance package that feels right?" Jonathan says, hesitantly, still trying to smooth over something that has already gotten out of hand.

"Well," Allison says, still with that slick calm voice of hers, "I feel that giving Keaton severance is offensive; it's like saying we don't believe in her or her ability to begin anew. And that simply isn't true. I do believe in Keaton and the power and beauty of her dreams."

I am too nauseated to respond.

"Okay," Jonathan says, standing up. "Allison, we might be making some hasty decisions here."

No severance, bigger lawsuit. For all her preaching, Allison isn't a very good businesswoman. Which is why she needed me. Well, that, and the fact that my role as marketing coordinator had morphed really far from my job description. In addition to handling marketing strategies—like advertising, paid editorial placement, and merchandise—I also oversaw all of All Welcome's social media (which is technically a different department), scheduled all of Allison's podcast guests, the launches for the four books a year (and growing!) the company is now publishing through its publishing arm, sat in on practically every meeting, and on and on and on.

Allison and I worked together nonstop. We laughed together. We dreamed together. I couldn't imagine that it could come to this. And I had no idea what she would do without me. It looks like she's about to find out.

I stand up. "You heard her. I'm fired. No severance. I want all my stuff returned to my parents' place right away. And you damn well better bring my dog."

I'm not moving there, I tell myself. Just staying until I find a new apartment. I have some money saved, and besides, I can always go live with my brother for a while instead.

Only, as I storm out of the building and call said brother to tell him what happened and ask him if I can stay, he flat-out says, "No, Keaton. You cannot come live with me."

I am aghast. "Harris! Are you kidding me? Why can't I live with you for just a little bit? I'm looking really hard for an apartment." I pause, putting the pieces together. My brother is my best friend. There is only one reason he wouldn't want me to live with him. "You have some rando woman living with you, don't you? And you haven't even told Mom and Dad. Or me. What is wrong with you?"

"Well, you won't approve," he says.

"She's like twenty-three, isn't she?"

"Thereabouts."

"Harris! Get your shit together. Break up with her and choose your sister for once in your freaking life."

"I'm not not choosing you, Keat. I love you. But just think about it. How cool would it be to use your severance to get away for a while?"

"I didn't get severance," I say. "Allison feels that would send the message that she doesn't believe in my ability to begin anew."

"O-kay," Harris says. "Well, you still can't live here, but I am hiring you a lawyer."

I enter the code in the keypad to Mom and Dad's building, which is an easy couple blocks walk from my office—well, it *was* anyway—and swing open the door. "Mom told me not to move in with him," I say out loud as I step into the elevator, more to myself than to Harris. "If I had listened to her, maybe I wouldn't be in this mess."

"Oh, Keat. I'm sorry. But, look, I'll help you find a place to live. We'll figure it out."

"Okay," I whisper. "Can you help find me a job, too? *Oh my gosh I don't have a job!*" I am filled with dread. "I have to go." Tears puddle in my eyes, and I literally have to sit on the elevator floor since my legs won't hold me up any longer. I realize that I have given every single part of myself to this job that I just walked away from. I don't have hobbies. I don't volunteer. All my meals are either from a frozen meal delivery service or DoorDash because who has time to cook? I barely have friends because when would I see them? My social life consisted of Jonathan and Allison and my colleagues and now it's all just . . . gone.

The elevator opens, and a woman pushes her walker through. "Hi, Mrs. Ellis," I say with zero enthusiasm.

She starts. "Oh dear. What are you doing on the floor?"

"Bad day," I say.

"Well, a bad day is always a good time to visit one's parents."

I nod, but then another sick feeling washes over me: Worse than getting dumped, worse than getting fired, I'm going to have to tell my mother she was right.

....

Recipe for Disaster

As long as I can remember, my mother has blamed practically
everything that has gone wrong in her life on her parents' un-
timely deaths. She is, in fact, blaming something on their deaths right
now, as I walk into her bright modern living room in her apartment
on the forty-fourth floor of the retirement community where she and
my dad just moved—a fact that everyone in our family finds totally
absurd. But that's Mom: an always-prepared worrier. I had hoped to
find a little solace and compassion at my parents' house, but, instead,
I've walked into a situation between my mom and Uncle Lon that I
don't quite understand.

"I can't go back to Beaufort," she is saying to him as I sit down. "I
just can't."

My mother is dressed in a chic pair of pants and top, always the
height of fashion. She swims forty laps each morning, plays bridge
twice a week, has perfect eyesight, and a memory so sharp she's my
first call when I can't remember something. My father, one year her
junior, still works as the manager of the hedge fund he took over when
he and my mother moved to New York from Raleigh ten years ago,
and he is consistently considered one of the best in his field.

It stunned me that my parents moved to New York and left my hometown not long after I did—not just for my dad's job, but also because they insisted they wanted to be closer to me. My mother wasn't exactly what you would call *involved* when I was growing up. She wasn't on the PTA or planning class parties; she didn't feel the need to be at my basketball games. She taught me to make my own lunch when I was in kindergarten, and by the time I was six, I was in charge of my own laundry. My brother and I were loved, and my dad did most of the parent-bonding stuff with us, but, in a lot of ways, we were on our own when it came to our mom. I used to wonder if it was because she was a solid decade older than my friend's moms, or if maybe she was just tired from working all day. But that was just Mom's personality, I guess. She was independent and wanted us to be too.

"What are you doing here in the middle of the day, sweetie?" Mom asks.

I hoped I would find some sympathy after my terrible day, but now I get the feeling that I have walked into another hornet's nest. I'm fairly certain I haven't heard Lon correctly as he, not waiting for my answer, says, "Well, Virginia, maybe Keaton could fly to North Carolina to put the house on Sunset Lane on the market."

I squint, certain I haven't heard him correctly. "You mean, like, the house you grew up in?"

He nods. "Well, yes."

I shake my head, trying to piece this together. "Mom, I'm sorry. You still own the house you grew up in?" I had always assumed that it had gutted my mother and uncle to leave their parents' house in Beaufort, North Carolina, the mythical house on Sunset Lane Harris and I had occasionally heard stories about but had never actually seen.

She looks as unfazed as I have ever seen her as Lon, who has

Mom's same hazel eyes, long eyelashes, and bow mouth, says, "We never sold it."

"Does someone rent it or something?" I pause. "No. Forget that. How have you had this house my whole life, and I've never known about it?"

"We just—" Mom starts. But then she looks down into her coffee cup.

Lon fills in for her. "Your mom and I haven't been able to bear to go back there since they died."

I'm still squinting, I realize. I try to relax my face. "So, what you're telling me is that you have left this house sitting there, without visiting once, for nearly five decades? You realize it must be a rotting pile by now, right?"

I'm really annoyed, namely because this is a classic Mom move. She managed to almost single-handedly start a domestic violence shelter in North Carolina for women and children who had to flee—often with nothing more than the clothes on their back—and ran it for thirty years until she handed over the reins to a new director and came to New York. She raised the money, hired the staff, and organized the therapists, many of whom volunteered their time. When she wanted to do something, look out world. But what she doesn't want to deal with, she ignores. Her problems. Her small children. And, evidently, a house. But I hadn't recognized that my uncle also shared this trait.

My mother scoffs. "It isn't rotting, Keaton. You're so dramatic."

"We have a handyman who keeps things in order," Lon says. "It's cleaned every now and then. The exterminator comes."

I can't read my mom's expression, but I swear she thinks this is normal. I have so many questions. "Okay . . . so is there a reason you want to sell it now?"

She nods, and her eyes glisten with tears. My breath catches. Is she sick? Is Uncle Lon? Do they need the money to move somewhere else? It isn't until this moment that I realize how much I love having my parents in New York. With me. Where we can have dinner together on Wednesday nights and I can pop by after work and Mom and I can take walks on the weekends. I finally have the family I always wanted. "Well, Keaty," Lon says, "real estate prices have skyrocketed, and with the re-estimation of our tax value, it doesn't really make sense to hold on to it anymore."

I want to say, *But it made sense to hold on to it for all these years?*

Mom picks up: "But, really, the bottom line is that Lon and I aren't getting any younger. We feel like you and Harris co-owning the house with your two cousins would just be so complicated. We don't want any controversy within the family." Her voice cracks. "So we need someone to go down there and get it ready to put on the market. Your dad is so busy with work, and Lon and I just can't bear to do it ourselves. So, we were hoping . . . well, you might be able to step in."

She is clearly very upset. My grandparents have been dead since long before I was born, and, even as a kid, I had this sixth sense not to ask a lot of questions. On the rare occasion Mom mentioned my grandparents—or the car accident that killed them—she seemed so sad that I never pressed. But still, this is a huge ask.

I sigh. "Mom, this just isn't a great time . . . Actually, can I stay with you tonight? And maybe . . . for the foreseeable future?"

She looks at me with a mix of compassion and, well, self-satisfaction. "Jonathan-and-I-broke-up-and-I-got-fired," I say, super fast, like if I don't breathe it won't be real.

To Mom's credit, she doesn't gloat. "I'm sorry, sweetheart," she says.

"Yeah. So I kind of have a lot going on here. What about Harris?"

Mom laughs, as if the idea of my busy, important brother taking a moment off work is simply absurd. Yes, technically, his job—CEO and president of his own celebrity PR firm—might have a bigger title than mine, and, yes, he could get any ungettable ticket or invitation at a moment's notice. But I am also quite successful, which my mother well knows. Or, well, I *was*, I remember with a sinking feeling. I want to point out that Harris, a trained pilot with his own plane, could fly himself to North Carolina and it would take way less time than me fighting lines at JFK. But once she gets an idea in her head, there's no stopping her.

"This is fate!" she says firmly. "You need a place to live. You have some unexpected time off work. Don't you see how perfect this is?"

I shake my head. "Mom, I will go with you if you want some help, but I am not taking this on by myself. No way."

The warm, tingly feelings I get just thinking about that surprise me. Have we ever taken a mother-daughter trip? I know we haven't.

"Fine, darling, fine. I understand. Lon and I will simply have to hire someone to dismantle all that is left of our treasured family memories."

I know what she's doing and it's kind of working. The idea of my grandparents' belongings, any vestige of the people they once were, being packed up and shipped off to the Salvation Army doesn't sit well with me. I'm being given a chance to piece together these people who, combined, are half of me. Am I just going to toss that to the curb?

"Please, honey?" Lon says. "We know you're busy, but you can figure something out, right? Everyone wants a piece of small-town coastal charm. And selling the house for a record price would obviously behoove you too." He pauses. He's a realtor, so he would know. "Look, your mom and I are emotionally ill-equipped humans who can't face our childhood home. If you could get the house cleaned up and organize a few updates, I'll give you ten percent commission on whatever the house goes for."

I raise my eyebrow. Commission. I haven't considered this. It would certainly help ease the transition of looking for a new job. Just the thought of it relaxes me. "What do you think you can sell it for?"

He tells me, and I almost fall off my chair. Even with a ten percent commission, I could start over again, buy myself some time to figure out what I want to do next. But, unlike Allison, I am an excellent business-woman and recognize the need to negotiate here. "All right, commission king," I say, calling my uncle by our family's nickname for him, "I'll consider your offer, but I won't do it for a penny less than thirty percent."

"Fifteen," he counters.

"Twenty-five."

"Twenty."

"You've got a deal," I say, standing and sticking out my hand.

"Keaton, have I taught you nothing?" He doesn't move. "Stand your ground. I would have given you twenty-five."

"I would have done it for fifteen."

He laughs. "Touché." He removes the key from the ring in his pocket and gives me a hug.

"Do you want to have lunch, sweetheart?" Mom asks. "Talk through your terrible day?"

"Forget lunch," Lon says. "The girl needs a drink. But on the bright side, maybe you can take up water aerobics or tai chi while you're here. Get them to puree your food for you. Chewing is overrated."

I laugh. Mom and Dad's part of the building isn't like that, and Lon knows it, but he finds it endlessly hilarious that his younger sister has moved herself two steps away from a nursing home despite even a remote hint of a medical problem.

"Hey, Keat?"

"Yeah."

"Thank you."

"You're welcome," I say as he kisses my cheek. "Love you."

One of our family rules is that no matter what happens in life, even if you're in the middle of a life-altering fight, you don't leave without telling everyone how much you love them.

"Love you. Want me to help you look for flights?"

I scoff. "Yeah. Right." I *hate* to fly. I mean, hate it. Obviously, a thirty-three-year-old who has been places in life has had to fly on numerous occasions. But getting me through requires Xanax for days, cortisone for the welts I get, and visualization meditation—and sometimes, even all that doesn't help. I have been to therapy to try to get to the root of why I am so terrified to fly. But it seems I am one of those special cases where there is no real reason.

"I'll drive," I say definitively.

"It's a ten-hour drive, Keaton," Lon says with an eye roll. Lon knows I'm scared to fly, but he finds it absurd. Now that I know he's never sold his childhood home, I feel a little like the pot and the kettle.

"You *should* drive in case you want to take a few things from the house," Mom interjects.

I highly doubt that I will, but I appreciate that she has saved me. I'll take the vintage Bronco Jonathan bought me as a birthday surprise—the one that, I'll be honest, I was hoping was going to be an engagement ring. Whatever. I'm not giving it back. Severance.

After Lon leaves, I have another thought. "Do I need to get a hotel room in Beaufort?"

Mom looks out the window distractedly. "No. There should be a bed left for you to sleep in." She pauses. "You'll love it, Keaton. It's downtown, right on the water, surrounded by the most beautiful houses and shops and restaurants . . ."

She trails off and I watch her, wishing I could read her mind, wondering why she never went back if she loved it so much. My stomach turns. If my mother could keep a secret as big as a whole house, what else has she been keeping from me? As she turns and smiles with her mouth but not her eyes, a feeling deep in my gut tells me I'm not sure I want to know.

Keaton

....

Wish You Were Here

I'm chatting on the phone with my brother, Harris, as I drive, squinting, over the tiny drawbridge that leads into Beaufort and past the adorable WELCOME TO BEAUFORT, NC, POPULATION 4,789 sign. Yesterday I got up super early to leave and made it all the way from New York to Raleigh, spent the night with one of my cousins, and left around seven this morning so that I could be here early. It's ten fifteen as I cross the bridge, and I am mesmerized by the way the sun dances on the water, illuminating the dreamy marshes on my left and the open water on my right.

"This place is like a postcard," I say.

"I don't know what that means," Harris responds through my car speaker, and I'm annoyed because I can tell, from how distracted he sounds, that he is responding to an email or something. In his defense, it's a Wednesday and some people have to work. I reach over to the passenger seat with one hand to rub my dog Salt's fluffy blond head.

We get—well, *got*—four paid volunteer days per year at All Welcome, and I usually did at least two at the local animal shelter. During a regular day of feeding cats and changing newspapers, a woman came in in tears.

"My son is allergic to dogs," she said, squeezing a little ball of blond fur close to her.

She explained that her family had gotten a mini Goldendoodle for that very reason, because he was hypoallergenic. "But as it turns out," she said, "he's allergic to dog saliva. Any time Salt licks him, he breaks out in hives."

I winced.

"I don't know what to do! I can't find any friends or family to take him." She snuggled him up under her chin. "But I can't put my son's health at risk."

I hadn't thought through the responsibility one bit when I blurted out, "I'll take him."

"Please don't let them put him down," she sobbed, the dog licking her tears.

It was possibly the most heartbreaking thing I'd ever seen. "No, I'll adopt him. He's adorable."

She sniffed and looked up at me. "What?"

I nodded. "I'll take Salt home with me today."

She gasped. "You will? He's so sweet, and he's had all his shots, and I have a crate in the car and tons of toys and food."

She was talking me into something I'd already agreed to. "I promise I'll take the best care of him. Don't worry." I paused. "And I'll write down my address so you can come visit him any time you want."

She took a deep breath and, like it was taking all the strength she had, handed him over to me. She rubbed his ears, kissed his head, and said, "I love you, Salty. You're the best pup in the whole world." She kissed him again and composed herself enough to say, "Thank you so much. I'll leave everything by the door."

I knew then that she couldn't see him again. I snuggled my face into the softest dog fur I had ever felt as Salt whimpered, watching his human mom leave him. I looked into his dark eyes with the longest lashes I'd ever seen and said, "Hi, little guy. We're going to be best friends." As if he knew what I was saying, he covered my face in kisses.

What can I say? It was love at first lick.

I look over at him now, full grown at thirty-one pounds, sitting at attention in the passenger seat. He was the best rash decision I ever made.

"You know," I say to Harris, exasperated, "Beaufort so far is like a 'Wish you were here' postcard."

"Like the ones with the flamingos?" he asks.

"You are impossible," I say, and he laughs. "And you will *not* be getting a postcard from me."

I turn right by a row of white clapboard houses and, when I reach the stop sign, fall instantly in love with the street in front of me. Its ancient trees reach up to touch each other, forming a canopy over the road. The water is only a block in front of me, and, even from a distance, the sun shining on it creates a sea of diamonds.

"Did you know Lon and Mom still owned this house?" I ask.

"No. I had no idea."

"So then why aren't you more surprised it exists?"

"Why are you surprised? Mom and Lon are totally nuts, Keat. Nothing they tell us surprises me anymore."

I kind of get where he is coming from.

"This place is magical," I say, taking in the beauty of the quaint downtown. I love places where you can work and live and eat and shop without ever getting in your car. It was one of the things that always appealed to me about Manhattan.

"I know you're trying to make me come down there, but I'm not doing it," he responds.

I drive slowly and smile at all the double front porches—and the people sitting on them who wave as I pass, as if they are expecting my arrival.

My GPS tells me to turn left onto Sunset Lane, which I do. "I don't need you," I say. "How hard can this be? Clean up a house, put it on the market, sell it in like a day, go home."

Home. Where is home now? Not with Jonathan. Not at my parents', where my mother told me, in no uncertain terms, that I would not lie around and rot. Her exact words. Not at All Welcome where, apparently, I am the only one who is *not* welcome. Well, good riddance. I don't want to be with those sycophants anyway. But even as I think it, my heart breaks a little. I did love Jonathan. At one time, anyway. I am furious that he could have been sleeping with his ex-wife for months while we were together, upset at myself that I hadn't known.

But, even more than that, I am mourning the loss of my life, what's driven me for the past twelve years. They are launching the first book for All Welcome's new lifestyle imprint today—the first book that wasn't penned by Allison, anyway. I spent more than a year working on marketing plans for *Growing with Grace*, a stunning coffee-table-style parenting book written by mommy blogger extraordinaire Grace Collette. And I won't be there to see it launch. I won't be there to oversee the massive pub day party at Serendipity 3, where influencer parents and their impeccably dressed children will sip the legendary frozen hot chocolate while perusing their copies—and, obviously, posing for social media pictures. My stomach grips.

"Okay," Harris says, redirecting my attention back to the task at hand. "I have a sense that this will somehow be more difficult than you think it's going to be."

"Well, I have the whole summer," I say. "As long as it's sold by

Labor Day, Lon says we're good." And then, "Harris . . . I have to find a *job*." I groan.

"You'll be fine," he says. "People will be lining up to hire you."

Brotherly confidence is nice. I peer out the window and stop when my GPS tells me to. Seven Sunset Lane. Like the other homes in the neighborhood, it is a large white clapboard house with a pair of brick chimneys, black shutters, a double front porch, and a white picket fence. It is beautiful.

"Harris," I gasp. "It's perfection. It's a storybook house."

"Write me from happily ever after. I'll be here in New York awaiting your distress calls."

"Haha," I say, hanging up and hopping out of the Bronco.

I can't immediately tell if the brick driveway to the left of the house is mine—or, well, my grandparents'. Am I claiming ownership of this place already? To be safe, I swing into a parking spot by the water across from it. It seems to be the only one left, which surprises me in a town this small.

I walk around to the passenger seat, clip Salt's leash to his harness, and hoist him out of the car.

I wave at a mom pushing a little boy in a stroller as the breeze gently pushes my hair back in the most perfect way. I have to stop myself from thinking how much she would probably love *Growing with Grace*. "Dog!" the boy calls with glee, pointing to Salt, who jumps on the stroller enthusiastically.

"I am so sorry!" I exclaim, but the toddler squeals with delight.

"Oh, no, it's fine," the mom chuckles. "We're very dog friendly."

I smile, corral Salt, and walk across the street to stand in front of my grandparents' house. The paint looks fresh, which is notable given the toll saltwater can take. The yard is newly mowed. Bright red begonias grace a pair of black planters on either side of the front door. I look down at Salt, who is sitting attentively at my feet. "This is going to be a piece of cake," I say. He tilts his head at me like he gets it.

I unclip his leash and open the gate, and he runs through. I close it behind me, making sure it's latched. Salt isn't the escaping kind, but I'm still glad the tiny front yard is surrounded by a sweet white picket fence.

I make my way up the brick walk and the three front steps to the porch. I turn to take in the beautiful view of Taylor Creek in front of me as Salt chases a butterfly around the yard. I am totally taken aback because, when Mom and Lon talked about "the creek" that was by their house growing up, I visualized a shallow, babbling, stone-filled thing. This, instead, is a wide, deep channel that connects the ocean and the sound. It's a thing of beauty. And it is most certainly *not* a creek. There's a little island across the way, covered with green trees, and people are kayaking to it. I want to be one of those people.

I turn to the front door, scolding myself. *You aren't going to be here long. Don't get attached.*

I'm fiddling with the key Uncle Lon has given me, which seems like it doesn't *quite* fit. I finally get it in the corroded lock and, as I turn it, open the front door to find green shag carpet in the entry. Salt peers inside too. Then he looks up at me. "I know," I say. "I'm kind of scared." I take a deep breath. "But we're here. It's now or never."

As if I've inspired him, Salt tears into the house, and I decide to step over the threshold. I squeal as I walk through a spiderweb.

I'm frantically wiping the silk threads off myself, praying there isn't a spider on me too. My dad always says that walking through a spiderweb is good luck, and from the look of this place, I'm going to need all the luck I can get.

The dust floating in the light streaming through the windows is the first thing I notice. I cough. Clearly, the person who has been "cleaning" this house is not doing a great job. I take in the butter-yellow couch, which is flanked by a pair of wood-framed chairs—all super retro. Well, of course they're retro. They're original seventies pieces.

What strikes me even more, though, is the newspaper neatly folded at the end of the couch, the black patent leather pumps sitting by the sofa, the pair of glasses on the wooden coffee table, the small stack of mail in the center.

My heart starts to race. I was expecting to walk into a spartan, nearly empty house. Their shoes are still sitting here, for heaven's sake. I pick up a framed photo on a wooden end table and realize that I have never seen a photo of my grandparents before. It has never struck me as odd until right now. They are probably around my parents' age in the photo, dancing and grinning at each other with such love that it makes my heart feel full. Instantly, I picture them in this house, place them here among the things they chose and loved. I can almost imagine them walking right through the front door.

I put the picture down and open the window closest to me. There isn't much dust collecting on the windowsills, which is a positive. I walk through the den with its plaid couch and huge wooden box of a TV, noting the dead roaches in the corners. I pick up something that looks like a sci-fi ray gun, examining the buttons. "Is this the remote?" I ask out loud.

A glass candy dish sits full of change, a pair of sunglasses hanging on its side.

I step slowly into the dining room, which is less seventies, more classic. The linen tablecloth has turned beige in places, and the Herend chargers—the same ones my mother has—are still on the table.

Is this the aftermath of a dinner party? Or a table waiting to be set? I pick up the place card at the head of the table and trace *Townsend* with my finger.

I keep walking, running my finger along the mantel above the fireplace, watching the dust fly. The kitchen is such a time capsule I have to laugh.

Everything is shades of green and yellow, but what catches my eye is my grandmother's silver in a pile on the counter, turned gray and black with time, but clean and waiting to be put away.

My mind races as I realize the herculean task before me. I don't even want to think about the bedrooms—one of which I'm going to have to clean if I want to sleep here.

I can't resist the urge to text my mother: *Do you think you might have misled me about what I was walking into?*

I am trying to be sympathetic, but *come on.* This is so typical. Just let Keaton do it herself. Why would she need any help? Not at six. Not at sixteen. Certainly not at thirty-three.

Is there a lot to do, darling? I haven't been there in so long I hardly remember.

Uh-huh. Yeah. You don't remember leaving the place like a mausoleum? Sure. The thought gives me the creeps. As I look around the kitchen and peek back at the dining table that looks like everyone just got up and left, I have the distinct feeling that this place must be, has to be, haunted. As if on cue, a cold shiver runs down my spine.

This place is like an untouched crime scene, I respond.

This is actually the craziest thing I've ever seen. I'm reeling as I look around at the wood-paneled walls, the dark cabinets.

It's like everyone walked out of here almost fifty years ago, locked the door, and never came back. Salt—thankfully—bounds into the room. "Buddy, this place is so creepy."

That's when I realize he has something in his mouth. "Salt," I call as he runs off again. "Come here right now!" As I chase him, I yell, "Drop it! Drop it!"

I literally cannot believe it when he does. He's so stinking cute, but he is *not* a good listener. I lean over to pick up whatever was in his mouth and brace myself for something truly horrifying—something of the fur-and-tail variety, perhaps. But instead, it's a beautiful white leather notebook with REBECCA SAINT JAMES'S GUIDE TO ENTERTAINING embossed in gold on the cover. In the bottom right-hand corner, in the same gold, is embossed *1976*.

I hear a noise near the cabinets and, without looking up, run out of there, notebook in my hand, Salt on my heels. Maybe it's a ghost, maybe it isn't. But I can't stick around another second to find out.

It's only as I clip Salt's leash to his harness in the bright morning sun that I realize that, for the first time in my life, I am holding something of my grandmother's. *My grandmother's.* And the only thing that could possibly inspire me to walk back through that front door is the feeling that washes over me, that little voice telling me I want to know more.

Becks

....

Tongue-in-Cheek

AUGUST 28, 1976

Tip: The most important part of hosting any good event, Virginia—whether it's for 5 or 250—is making sure that everyone feels cared for, catered to, and included. Come to think of it, that just might be the secret to most great relationships. Being the person who cares for others is an undervalued role in our society. But it is, I've found, perhaps the very most important role one can play.

Everyone knew that Rebecca Saint James's dinner parties were legendary. They were, in fact, the hottest ticket in the small seaside town of Beaufort, North Carolina. *And for good reason*, she thought as she examined her reflection in the sterling silver cutlery and set each piece back down on the felt polishing cloth, a ritual she undertook before every dinner as women bustled around her kitchen, making lobster salad and her mother-in-law's famous key lime pie. (Her mother-in-law was tricky. But her key lime pie? It was one of the secrets to Rebecca's—Becks, to those in the know—famous dinner parties.)

Her white clapboard house, built by her husband's family in 1769, had air-conditioning now, but Chef Evelyn, who had been with them for decades, who prepared everything based on Becks's exacting recipes and standards, still preferred to work with the windows open, sea breeze pouring in. It made things a bit warmer for the servers, who were dressed to the nines in brass-button blazers with matching slacks and shiny wingtips. But no one argued with Chef Evelyn in her kitchen. Not even Rebecca Saint James.

Any guest in attendance could see right away that being served at a ratio of three guests to one uniformed server was extravagant. Any guest could taste that the food was fresh, fine, and cooked to perfection. They could smell that the flowers were in full bloom, feel that the linens, handed down from Becks's grandmother, were expertly pressed. But only the most discerning guest could describe just why he or she had such a fabulous time. The secret, the magic formula, was the guest list.

Becks spent an exorbitant amount of time dreaming of her weekly "summer suppers." It was a bit of a tongue-in-cheek title, much in the way that the sprawling, three-story, six-bedroom home was the "beach cottage." She planned menus with wine pairings, some fancy, some fun. She chose the tableware and decor for each evening. But she spent the most time curating the perfect twelve people to sit around her dinner table. Becks brought people together who all had a common thread that bound them—one that quite often went unnoticed.

The esteemed twelve of the first summer supper this year had all been raised by parents in politics. The next, they all cheered for the same college basketball team. The one after that, the party varied in age, but they were all from the same home state of Alabama. Even if the guests didn't recognize the commonality, it somehow connected them in an invisible way that made them leave saying, "That was the best dinner party I've ever been to."

That was the enchantment of it all. Beyond the experience, the connection among the guests was paramount. And that was why, as Becks sat at the head of her dining room table with her pencil and slim white leather notebook in hand, she smiled, thinking how perfect the last dinner party of the summer would be.

The notebook was embossed in gold with REBECCA SAINT JAMES'S GUIDE TO ENTERTAINING stamped smartly on the cover. Townsend had been very proud of the gift, and they had had a good laugh over it; only Becks would need an entire notebook to keep her parties in order. But, in her Becks way, she had put it to good use, not only keeping track of her guests, menus, and checklists, as she always did, but also taking the opportunity to write notes to her twenty-three-year-old daughter, Virginia, to pass along all the wisdom she'd gleaned over decades of hostessing. A mother only had so much time, and a daughter could only listen so much, after all.

Yes, all this entertaining could be tricky. Earlier in the summer, for instance, her husband's friend and fellow physician Daniel had sidled up to her by the poolside bar at the house he shared with his wife, Patricia, and asked: "Becks, why is it that Townsend and I fish together every week, that you and Patricia shop and chat on the phone for hours, but we have yet to be invited to a legendary dinner party this summer? Truth be told, I feel like we should be invited to them all."

Ordinarily, asking to come to a party was an automatic cause for blacklisting. But, well, one couldn't very well blacklist Daniel Walker. For Becks, it wasn't because he was the town's beloved physician or because he was widely considered a legend in his own time. It was because he and Patricia were two of her dearest friends. She would have liked to have invited her best friends to every party, it was true. But it was, alas, against the rules.

"Daniel, for one thing, we have only had three parties so far. For the other, you know very well why I can't invite you to every one."

He had sipped the champagne out of the coupe in his hand—they were celebrating the season, after all—and grinned at her. "But see, Becks, that's the thing. I very much do not know why."

Becks sighed. "Because the basis of my dinner parties is that everyone is on equal footing. You . . ." she waved her hand at him like she was scolding a child in mud-stained clothes before church, "suck all the air out of the room."

She loved him, and she was partly teasing. But in every kidding, wasn't there ten percent truth? Being the doctor in a town this size was like being royalty. Combined with the fact that Daniel's family had founded the town way back when, people found him intimidating. Not to mention that the man had more stories than God and loved to dominate a conversation, which was a strict no-no at Becks's dinner parties.

"What if I wear a disguise? A mask? A cape?"

He was teasing her now, but she was actually considering the idea.

"Don't punish Patricia just because I suck all the air out of the room," he continued. "I'll behave, I promise."

"No outlandish stories?"

He shook his head.

"No tall tales? No waxing poetic and enrapturing the guests so no one else gets a word in edgewise?"

He put his hand over his heart in faux offense. "I thought those qualities were what made me a good dinner party guest."

"No," Becks said. "Those things make you a good friend and lend you a fabulous bedside manner. They make you a tiresome guest."

He laughed.

"You have to promise," she said.

"Fine. No tales, stories, poetic waxings, interesting musings of any sort. I shall be dull, drab, and utterly unlikable."

Unlikable the man was not. "Fine. If you can promise, I will consider your proposal."

Becks smiled just thinking of the exchange as she reviewed the guest list for tonight. The last weekend in August meant the last party of the season, which just so happened to be Becks's birthday celebration as well. They would be joined by Daniel and Patricia and their other dear friends Ellen and Milton, along with Becks and Townsend's daughter and her very serious boyfriend, Robert. Their son, Lon, would be there with his girl of the summer. Dear Violet, who had just moved to town—single, if you could even imagine such a thing. She was excited that Patricia had dreamed up a blind date for the girl, if a little disappointed that there would be a total stranger at her table tonight. But, well, these things couldn't be helped. And Patricia— who was the only one with the inside scoop on Becks's dinner party connections—had assured her that her link between guests would be saved: the date was an avid boater, as was everyone around the table. Sure, it wasn't the most inspired dinner party link. But it was passable.

As she stood and placed her notebook and pencil on the antique buffet, Becks considered whether she would dress the table in her favorite handmade lace tablecloth, the special one with details so beautiful it could bring a tear to the eye. Or if something plainer and more modern would be better.

As she walked to the linen closet where her tablecloths and napkins hung, starched and pressed all in a row, she decided that this was a night for special. Because tonight would not just be the last summer supper of the season.

Tonight would be the last summer supper of Rebecca Saint James's life.

Keaton

....

Not a Ma'am

A walk with Salt is just what I need to clear my head. But, never having been to Beaufort, I have no idea where I'm going—or want to be going, for that matter. I feel like I need a drink, but it's only 11 a.m. But I could get a bloody Mary and call it brunch . . . As I'm weighing my options, I turn the corner and Salt jumps onto an older woman on the sidewalk. "Salt, down!" I call. "Sit!" He relents but continues to stare at her.

"I'm so sorry," I say.

"It's okay," she says, leaning down to pat his head. "Hello, Salt."

She looks to be around my mother's age—late sixties, early seventies. She has short, stylish hair that is that particularly gorgeous silver that I imagine only the very, very lucky get. She is wearing a dress that indicates she has just come from a very southern lady event. A church tea, perhaps. Maybe bridge?

She smiles, and the corners of her bright blue eyes crinkle. She is already tan for May. I can picture her being one of those women who dives effortlessly into the ocean as though she is very much at one with nature, like the dolphins pop up and lend their fins for her to hold onto so they can carry her along. I decide right then and there that while I'm in Beaufort I will take up swimming in the sound. I have established, after all, that I need hobbies.

I can tell she is studying me. Intently. And it is making me uncomfortable.

"I'm Violet Scott," she says, as if realizing the way she is staring at me is weird.

"I'm Keaton Smith," I say. "Well," I add, pointing toward the house, "Keaton Saint James Smith."

At that, Violet throws her arms around me, pulling me to her with so much force that I almost drop my grandmother's notebook, which I forgot I'm still holding. I feel like I have to hug her back because it's going to be more awkward if I don't.

She pulls away, wiping tears from her eyes. "You are the spitting image of Rebecca Saint James."

"Really?" No one has ever told me this. But then again, no one has ever told me much about my grandparents.

"Thanks," I say, meaning it. "I'm here to clean out their house, but . . ."

"It looks like they're about to walk right back through the door, and it's eerie?" She smiles through her tears.

I nod. "Oh my gosh. Yes! How did you know?"

"Everyone knows that house has been untouched since the seventies—" Violet's eyes widen, and she points to the notebook. "Is that . . . ?" She covers her mouth, and her eyes fill again.

"What?" I ask.

"It's just that Becks always carried that notebook with her. I'm just shocked it wasn't in her purse when she—" She stops and clears her throat.

I get this tingly sensation all over.

"I always wondered what she was writing in that notebook," Violet finishes. It feels like she was about to say something else and then changed her mind. But that's a mystery for another day.

"Rebecca Saint James's Guide to Entertaining," Violet says wistfully, looking at the notebook like it's her own family heirloom. "Oh, honey, she was famous for her dinner parties. They were the stuff of legend."

"Really?"

She nods. "Oh, yes. Her summer suppers. She had one every week from Memorial Day until the end of August—her birthday weekend—and they were out of this world."

I smile, loving this anecdote about the woman I never knew. "Did you go?" I ask.

Violet nods. "To the last one." She bites her lip, and I realize she wishes she hadn't said that. A chill runs through me.

She touches my arm. "Do you need help? With the house? I'm happy to help you. We all wanted to help after . . . Well, you know. But your mom and uncle asked us to just leave it be, so we did."

I want to say yes and fall into the arms of this kind stranger who knew my grandparents. But I am, by all accounts, an adult. And this is something I should be able to handle. So I stand up straighter, gather my courage, and say, "Thank you, Violet, but I think I'm okay."

She smiles and points to the house behind her. "Well, my husband and I are just right here. So if you need anything at all don't hesitate."

After she says goodbye, it takes everything inside of me to walk back to the house. I remind myself that I am here to do a job: sell a property, get a commission check. There is no such thing as ghosts.

But as I walk back into the kitchen, I hear a distinct scratching sound. Salt's head shoots up, and I scream, which makes him bark. "This place is so haunted!" I shriek.

I gather all my courage and look up, making out the distinct flash of a bushy tail. Salt takes off, barking, and a squirrel scurries up on top of the counters. I shiver, wondering which is worse, a ghost or a rodent. As the squirrel runs across the counters I scream again, throwing the side door open, my eyes never leaving the animal. Maybe a squirrel in your kitchen *is* worse than a ghost.

The squirrel is still. Salt is quiet. They are in a standoff, and I feel myself start to breathe again because surely I can handle a squirrel. But then I turn toward the open glass-paned door that leads from the kitchen down to a side gate and scream again. A little boy—maybe ten or eleven?—with shaggy blond hair and big, inquisitive blue eyes is staring at me, totally still. So still that he can't be human. I look down at Salt, whose eyes are pinned on him. Good. At least he can see him too. But he isn't barking or jumping or doing any of his usual Salt things. And dogs can see the supernatural, right?

"Do you want me to get my pellet gun?" the maybe-ghost, maybe-child asks.

I reach my index finger out and put it on his shoulder. Flesh and bone. Thank goodness.

He looks at me curiously.

"I was making sure you were real," I say. "You know, not a ghost." He smiles, and I wince. "I'm sorry. I'm not really good at talking to kids."

He shrugs. "You're doing all right. So . . . pellet gun?"

"Um, I'm not sure what a pellet gun is, but I think no."

He gives me an indulgent half-smile, like I've said something cute. "It's for the squirrels. It won't kill them, just kind of nudge them along."

I look down at Salt, who is now stretched out on the floral vinyl floor. Some protector. There is a squirrel threatening to destroy the house. There is a strange (but cute!) kid in my kitchen. And the dog is just lying there.

Ghost boy grabs a broom that is standing in the corner. I want to tell him not to touch it. There is something sacred about this place, like it's an archaeological dig, and if I can just leave everything exactly where it is, I can uncover the secrets of a lost civilization. He looks at me. "Um. You might want to go in the next room or something."

"Are you sure? Because, I mean, you're just a child and—"

"I'm a child who's not afraid of a little squirrel."

"Okay!" I shout, running through the door to my right, into the library—for the first time—and shivering all over.

"Come on, squirrely," I hear him saying as I notice all the books in here. "I'm not going to hurt you. That's good. Let's just make our way outside."

I hear the door slam and peek out of the library to see him walk back inside. "Is he gone?"

That indulgent half-smile. "Well, sure, that one is. But ma'am, I hate to tell you: when it comes to squirrels, where there's one, there are more."

"Please don't call me ma'am."

"I have to. Dad will get mad."

"Well, tell him I'm only thirty-three, and I'm not a ma'am."

He shrugs. "Hey, you know no one has been in this house for like a hundred years, right?"

Well, not exactly, but it sure feels like it. I take the broom from him and put it in the exact same spot where he found it, noticing how dusty it is. "Yeah. I know. I'm the granddaughter of the people who used to live here."

"Oh yeah. My dad says they died. Sorry about that."

I'm about to say it's okay, that I never knew them, but as if the aforementioned dad senses we're discussing him, I hear a man's voice calling from the other side of the fence. "Anderson!"

"Are you Anderson?"

He nods.

"Coming, Dad!"

Before Anderson can leave, a man in a rumpled work shirt opens the side gate that leads from his driveway to my porch. *My* porch. How have I already become so possessive over this place? It seems absurd, considering that I didn't even know there was a gate until like three minutes ago. At any rate, it only takes me about two seconds to realize that this man is really something to see. His dark hair—shorter than Anderson's but still just as shaggy—bounces when he jogs up my back steps, and it doesn't take long for me to realize he has his son's same blue eyes—or vice versa, I suppose.

I smile beguilingly, even though he is obviously someone's dad and likely married. And if he's not, he's probably some sort of lunatic, because clearly that is all I have the capacity to be attracted to. Before I can introduce myself with something charming, hot stranger-dad says, "What are you doing with my son?"

I am immediately defensive. "Um, excuse me, your son is practically an intruder in my home." Then I look down at Anderson and realize I might get him in trouble. "But now we're basically friends." Mad dad glares at me as I trail off with, "As one sometimes becomes with intruders . . ."

"I was just helping her with her squirrels, Dad."

He finally looks around and, stepping over the threshold, says, "Oh my God. I thought it was just another stupid urban legend, but people are right. No one has touched this house since 1976." Then, still not really acknowledging my presence, he says, "Come on, Anderson. We've got to go."

He walks out the side door. No *tell the nice lady bye* or anything. He acts like I am a kidnapper. Where does he get off? I am a *ma'am* for god's sake. Evidently. Anderson looks up apologetically. "Well, I better go."

"I don't think your dad likes me," I say, feeling kind of sulky, which is stupid. The guy doesn't even know me. What do I care if he likes me? Only, I do care. I need people to like me.

"Oh, he doesn't like anyone but me, so I wouldn't take it personal."

That is when I notice Anderson's freckles, and I immediately wonder if his dad has those same freckles under his layer of scruff. I give myself a mental kick. You don't wonder things like that about people's dads.

"Oh, I bet he likes your mom," I say, trying to get a hold of myself.

Anderson shakes his head. "I don't have a mom."

I gasp. "Oh, gosh. Did she die?"

"You're right. No ma'am would ever ask me if my mom is dead."

I grimace. "I'm sorry. See, I told you—not great at talking to kids. But I mean . . . You didn't really answer."

He shakes his head. "She left us when I was a baby. Dad and I don't ever talk about her, so it's just like I never had one."

Huh. Well, now, that's interesting. "I'm Keaton by the way," I say, figuring it's past time to introduce myself. "And I'll have lemonade and cookies for you next time. I'm just, um, not quite prepared for company."

We both look around the kitchen, and it is clear that even though he is under five feet tall, Anderson feels my pain.

"Okay, well, I'll come check on you later."

It is so cute and kind, I almost burst into tears.

Anderson starts toward the door and then stops, turning back. "Oh, and Keaton, I'm not a ghost. But just because I'm not doesn't mean you don't have them."

I cross my arms. "Well, that's just a huge help there. Thanks, Anderson."

As he's about to leave, the side gate opens again. "Violet!" Anderson shouts excitedly, running outside.

"My main man," she says, ruffling his hair.

Violet walks in as Anderson waves goodbye. "I don't want to intrude," Violet says, "but when we were talking earlier you just seemed a little . . ."

"Terrified?" I fill in for her.

She laughs. "Like you'd seen a ghost."

She hit the nail on the head. "Turned out to be a squirrel, actually," I say. But I know that's not what she means.

Violet looks around the kitchen, seeming dazed to find herself there. Then, as if she doesn't even realize she's doing it, she wanders into the gorgeous paneled library crammed with books. You can tell by the way it's arranged that this is a real library for real readers. The paneling in here isn't the cheap 1970s stuff either. It's the good stuff, and I can tell it has been here as long as the house itself. "Walnut?" I ask Violet. She's obviously the kind of woman who can identify fine woods with one glance.

"Mahogany."

A crystal rocks glass and a cigar rest on the end table by a leather chair. A leather notebook bearing the initials *TSJ*, crackled with age, is sitting there, face up. She runs her finger over it, as if afraid to disturb it.

"Your grandfather kept journals," she says. "I'm sure you know he was a doctor."

I nod. That, at least, I do know.

"But Townsend was good at everything. A real sportsman, the best-read man I've ever met . . ." She pauses and looks up at me intently. "And no man has ever loved a woman the way Townsend loved Rebecca Saint James."

Suddenly, I feel less overwhelmed by this dark, dusty house than I am by the emotions swirling around inside me.

"Violet, this is insane." I point. "The cigar he was smoking the night he died is sitting here. The chargers are still on the dinner table."

Violet looks around. "Are you planning to take this on alone?"

I nod. I shouldn't air our dirty laundry to a stranger, but I can't help it. I can't keep this inside. "Mom and Lon just left this place like this?"

"Your mom and your uncle had a tough road, sweetheart. We all appreciate that they've kept up the exterior of the house for the town, but none of us blames them for never coming back after their parents disappeared."

Her words stop me in my tracks. "My grandparents died in a car crash," I say definitively, spouting one of the only facts I know about them.

She looks sheepish. "Oh, right."

I have established recently that I am a terrible judge of character, but even I can tell something is off here.

Violet pats my hand. "My dear, you have quite the task ahead. I don't envy you. But just know that you are in a town that loves nothing more than to help. Like I said, we tried with your mom. We'll try again with you." She pauses. "There's a group of us that meets every morning at the Dockhouse, on the waterfront, around eight to have coffee. The Dockhouse Dames. Some of your grandmother's protégées are in our group, and you are welcome to join us anytime."

My instant reaction is to shake my head no. I've gone my whole life knowing very little about my grandparents, and I don't see any reason to start now. "Thank you, Violet. But I'm not planning on being here long."

She shakes her head. "Well, honey, if you change your mind . . ."

As I follow her, she adds, "I can see myself out. I know the way well."

I look around the kitchen again, the china stacked neatly, a bracelet in a dish by the sink, as if someone removed it to wash dishes
and was planning to return for it. Right now, they're just things. But I
already get the feeling that, as the summer goes on, they might start to
mean something to me. They might add up to a story. Only, it's a story
I'm not positive I want to know.

I see movement out of the corner of my eye and spot Anderson
and his dad out the window, throwing a football back and forth. It's
such an innocent, sweet sight that I can't help but smile. And I'm
not thinking about my ghosts at all anymore. Instead, I am wondering what time the Dockhouse Dames end their morning coffee.
Because, after what I assume will be a sleepless night, I might be
too tired to get there by eight. I'd sworn I wouldn't care. I'd promised myself I wouldn't get involved. But now I'm dying to find out
what happened to Anderson's mom. And I can't bear the thought
of leaving without getting to know Rebecca and Townsend Saint
James.

I walk back into the library, wondering about the people who
sat here, who drank coffee by this fireplace, and journaled in this
chair. I can't help but perch myself on the end of this dusty, ancient,
cognac-colored chair and pick up the journal beside me. Before I start
to read, I consider if perhaps I'm invading my grandfather's privacy.
But then again, I am the very definition of lost right now, and I need a
North Star. I need *something* to set me on my path. Don't you have to
know where you came from to figure out where you're going? I look
down at the journal and open it to the first page.

As Salt curls up at my feet and closes his eyes, exhausted from
the morning's excitement, I blink, surprised to see that instead of
1976 written at the top, the date is 1935. I begin to skim the words

and phrases until my eyes lock on "Rebecca Bonner." This must be my grandmother. And I know now that I can't close the journal; I can't look away. Without permission, I begin to hear the voice of a man I never knew. I finally have the concept of *my grandfather*. Of who he was. Of how much I lost never getting to hear his voice.

A Sacrament

JULY 19, 1935

I know my parents have all but given up on their twenty-nine-year-old son finding a wife. My mother told me as much last week in my childhood living room in Raleigh, rosary beads wrapped around her fingers, as they so often are. "Marriage is a *sacrament*, Townsend," she pleaded. "How can you live a life where one of the sacraments is available to you and you just look the other way?"

I wanted to tell her that none of the family had gone through holy orders, nor did I see her jumping in line for last rites. And, also, I wasn't looking the other way. I had worked hard through medical school and was now building my practice. I went on dates; I wanted to find a nice wife. But I wanted real love. I wanted fireworks. I hadn't found that. "If you would just start coming to Mass with us, we know we could find you a nice Catholic girl," she'd added. I had controlled my eye roll and agreed to come to Mass more often, thinking that if it were that easy, I would have found my wife already.

After my mother's lecture, I drove the three hours to Beaufort from Raleigh to visit my grandparents for the weekend. I could have stayed with them, but with their nurses buzzing about, I felt it an imposition. So I decided to stay at the Atlantic Beach Hotel. It was right on the sand on the island dubbed "the summer capital of Tarheelia" and brimming with interesting people. The nearby Casino by the Sea was hosting Borring and Lazur, the famous dancing team from New York City's Coconut Grove Club, and I didn't want to miss their performance. So after a long morning with my grandparents, I felt it was time for all of us to have a well-deserved rest and headed down to the beach.

I set my towel down, feeling slightly uncomfortable about my first time bathing shirtless, as has become the style. I was a doctor; I was comfortable with other people's nakedness. But my own? It seemed so superfluous. Still, as I looked around, seeing that all the other men were bathing shirtless too, I tried to convince myself it was fine. That was when something—or someone, rather—caught my eye.

A woman with shoulder-length blond curls, wearing a belted swimsuit with a blue-and-white-striped bottom, was laughing with an older woman as she flew a kite. She ran, waving to her companion, and the red diamond dipped and dove through the air as it trailed behind her. The sunlight radiated off her body, like it was shining for her, like it rose for her, like it was there simply to make her laugh. And I knew I wanted to make her laugh like that. Who was she? And how would I live without her now that I knew she was in the world?

I racked my brain for how to approach her—feeling nervous, as though I was a child of sixteen afraid to ask a girl to a dance. But the wind intervened on my behalf, as if nature in all her glory also felt that I should meet this effusive woman. Her kite lost wind, dipping and diving erratically before it landed, as luck would have it, directly at my feet.

She jogged toward me, still swathed in sunlight—it was following her, it seemed—looking like the picture of health. "I'm so sorry," she said, laughing. "This kite seems to have a mind of its own."

I picked it up quickly, not wanting to let the opportunity slip away. "I've never been much good at flying them," I said, smiling.

She grinned. "Oh, I don't believe that for a second. But if you insist you have trouble, I am happy to teach you."

"That would be terrific." I paused, seeing my chance. "But I would have to repay you in some way." I pretended to consider the matter a great deal. "With a once-in-a-lifetime cabaret night at the casino, perhaps?"

She smirked, and I felt like my heart might rip at the seams. "What kind of lady would I be if I said yes to an invitation on such short notice?"

Her eyes gleamed.

"A fun one?"

She looked over her shoulder. "I'm with my aunt, but I appreciate the invitation. Maybe I'll see you around. If I do, I can give you that kite lesson."

I sat down on my towel, feeling dejected. See her around? How? I didn't know where she was from, didn't know her name. So that was that.

Later that afternoon, I made my way up the sand to my hotel. As I was fiddling with the key in the door, I heard a peal of laughter that I already knew would come to define my dreams for the future. She stopped when she saw me, that fair-haired woman, now alone. "What are you doing here?" she asked, the smile never leaving her face.

"This is my room," I said casually.

She took a few more steps toward me and pointed to the room across the way. "Well, this is mine."

"I feel it dangerous to go against what fate is so obviously attempting to tell us."

That laugh. "I do have to admit this seems like a fortunate coincidence."

"Or," I said, "a message from the heavens."

"It does seem cavalier to buck such an obvious message," she teased. Then she sighed. "All right, then. I could accept, perhaps, a dinner request on short notice. My aunt is terribly fun and won't mind. But you must never breathe a word of it to my mother."

I put my hand up. "I, Townsend Saint James, do solemnly swear never to tell your mother."

"Then I, Rebecca Bonner, accept."

I smiled. "And it goes without saying that you also accept my invitation to go dancing at the casino afterward?"

She tossed her hair and slid the key into the lock on her door. "I guess we'll see how dinner goes, won't we?"

Later that night, by the time we were finished eating, there was no question that we would be going to the casino together. We practically couldn't stop laughing. It was like we were long-lost best friends—but with an undeniable spark, that chemistry that has come to define literary love.

Borring and Lazur's dancing positively wowed, and every song the orchestra played that night they played for Rebecca Bonner and Townsend Saint James. "Cheek to Cheek," "Sweet Sixteen and Never Been Kissed," "Blue Moon." And when the orchestra, dressed in their tuxedos, switched to "I'm in the Mood for Love," I knew I held Rebecca too close. But she didn't seem to mind.

By the end of the night, strolling hand in hand on the boardwalk and eating ice cream, I knew I was in love. As someone who has often questioned whether he was in love, I now know that when one is *actually* in love, it is quite easy to recognize.

"What are you and your aunt doing in Atlantic Beach?" I asked.

"Celebrating my graduation from teaching school. I start my first job in the fall."

I smiled. "Well, congratulations. That is quite an accomplishment."

"Maybe. But I'm not so sure about it," she said, licking her chocolate ice cream. "I like children fine but keeping up with so many of them seems difficult." She paused. "Do you like practicing medicine?"

"I do," I said. "I think I became a doctor to make my mother proud. But I've found that it suits me. I enjoy the challenge of finding out what's wrong with someone and how to make them well. And Dr. Sweeney, who I'm working with, has taught me so much."

She smiled. "And medicine has come so far. There's so much more you can do for your patients than just a decade ago."

I nodded. "That's what excites me the most. What's to come."

"Soon we won't have to get sick at all!" she trilled.

She was so exuberant I couldn't bear to argue with her.

"And you like Raleigh?" she asked. "I'm excited to move there; it seems time to make a move to a bigger city with my friends. But I'm a little nervous too. I've been in Kinston all my life—and, well, here in the summers. But moving for this job feels a little frightening."

"I like it well enough," I said. "But I have this dream—" I cut myself off, wondering if it was too much to say, if confessing what I'd been thinking might scare her away. Because I was already very clear on the fact that wherever Becks was—we were on a nickname basis already—that's where I wanted to be.

She stopped walking and sat down on a bench, the song of the ocean in front of us so peaceful and steady. "You can't say you have a dream and not tell me about it."

I sat down beside Becks. As I looked into her round eyes, I found myself saying, "It seems impractical, but my grandparents have made it clear that as the firstborn grandson, their house in Beaufort will be mine one day. It has always passed through the generations that way, since the seventeen hundreds. And, well, I'm not sure if there are enough full-time residents in this area for me to make a living, but I would love to move here and become the town doctor, spend my weekends fishing."

Becks gasped. "That sounds simply marvelous."

"It does?"

"Oh, yes. To spend your life where most people vacation? Why wouldn't you?"

I shrugged. "I think it might get lonely."

Becks took the last bite of her ice cream cone, wiped her mouth with her napkin, and did something I hadn't expected in the least: She slipped her hand in mine. "With the right person, I don't think it would be lonely in the least."

Before I could respond, she hopped up off the bench, removed her shoes, and ran down to the water. I watched her, bathed in moonlight. My breath caught in my throat at the freedom of her. "Well, are you coming?" she called.

I took off my shoes and joined her, the water lapping at our ankles. I stepped closer. I didn't want to come on too strong, but with the breeze blowing in her hair, the moonlight making her smile even more radiant, the smell of salt and sand enveloping us, all I wanted was to be closer to her.

"I have to see you again," I said. "Tomorrow. The next day. All the days after that."

The idea of being apart from her ever again was too much. Overcome with feeling, I put my hand on the nape of Becks's warm neck, felt the soft strands of her hair beneath my fingers. I kissed the tip of her nose, then her cheek. When she didn't pull away, I kissed her softly on the lips. When she wrapped her arms around my back, I swept her up in a kiss, which, to my delight, she returned heartily.

When I pulled away, jealous of any man who had ever kissed those lips before, she said, a glimmer in her eye, "I don't know, Townsend. Tonight was fairly perfect. How could we possibly top watching a famous dance duo all the way from New York City?"

My mind raced to an article in the *Beaufort News* I'd seen earlier at my grandparents', and I snapped my fingers. "Why, watching a man set a world record, that's what."

She laughed. "Oh yeah? And how do you suggest we do that?"

I smiled. "Charles Noe is going to drive twelve miles—from Noe Hardware to the beach—blindfolded in the new Ford V-8. He's going to set a world record, and we can't miss it!"

Becks shook her head. "Why on earth would a man do that?"

I had absolutely no idea. "Well, it's the American thing to do. We don't want another country to hold that world record now, do we?"

She smiled. "It sounds needlessly dangerous." She shook her head again. "Well, all right. We shouldn't miss history. We'll go watch the fool man drive blindfolded." She winked. "And then I'll teach you how to fly that kite."

She kissed me again and then, covering her mouth, said, "Look at me out here, a good Methodist minister's daughter kissing a man for all the world to see."

A tiny zip of fear ran through me as she said it, but before I could respond, she ran up the beach, waving over her shoulder, and turned in the direction of the hotel. She left me wanting more. And despite knowing that our religious differences will make things a challenge, I have a feeling she always, always will. There will never be enough of Becks Bonner for me.

I am writing my promise here, right now, so that it will live forever: I, Townsend Saint James, will love and protect Rebecca Bonner for all eternity. Tonight, I had the last first kiss of my life. I have to hope she feels the same way. Because we are meant to be together. I am certain. Now I just have to make her certain too. How hard could it possibly be?

Keaton

....

Immersion

I never truly understood what it meant to clean a house until this trip. I knew I needed to get up and get moving on my to-do list. But sitting in my grandfather's library, reading his words, feeling swoony over—and yes, I'll admit, a little jealous—the way he loved my grandmother, seems so much more appealing.

When I finally motivate myself to get going, realizing that I'm actually going to have to sleep here, I spend five hours getting one bedroom—my mom's—clean enough that I felt like I could inhabit it. I chose hers because it was the only one that didn't have carpet installed over the hardwood floors. With some effort, I roll the bedroom rug up, sneezing as I go. (Salt was a *big* help, let me tell you, growling and pawing at the moving rug.) The bed is tightly, expertly made, as if waiting for someone to come sleep in it. I strip Mom's old pink bedspread and all the linens and put them in the ancient avocado-green washing machine. I decide to toss the mattress pad and pillows, which are easily replaced and not sentimental, and take down the swirling hot pink, orange, and yellow drapery. The drapery is crazy heavy, but I'm not sure if it's from the dust or the thick material. The sun has done a number on it, making the fabric thin and dry in places. I know it can't be cleaned. But I also can't quite bear to throw it away, so I stack the pieces downstairs in the back hallway.

If I can't even get rid of *curtains*, I'm going to be in trouble when it comes time for the sentimental things. I open all the windows and vacuum and dust every square inch of the room, including Mom's typing award trophy, her surfing medals—my mother surfed?—and her photo albums. She had left for college in . . . what? 1970? 1971? I run my fingers along the spines on her small bookshelf. *I Know Why the Caged Bird Sings. The Bell Jar. The Feminine Mystique. The Bluest Eye. Slouching Toward Bethlehem. Play It as It Lays.* On the shelf below sits what I assume is an eight-track player because the stack beside it—little boxes of a variety I had never seen—are labeled Crosby, Stills, Nash & Young, Joni Mitchell, the Doors, James Taylor, Carole King. I pause, holding James Taylor's first, self-titled album, and have a thought that had never occurred to me: Was my mom cool? She had listened to cool music and read cool, feminist books. She surfed. If the guitar in the corner of her room was to be believed, she played the guitar.

I want to know this version of my mom. I also feel a little guilty. I had never considered this person, the girl who had lost her parents so suddenly. But, in fairness, we never talked about them.

One of my very first memories is coming home from kindergarten with a hot pink flyer pinned to my backpack. I could read just well enough to sound out "Grandparents Day." I didn't know what that was, but I knew Grandmommy and Grandaddy were my grandparents.

I remember sitting around our dinner table that night, peas I didn't want to eat on my fork, and saying, "Daddy, are Grandmommy and Grandaddy your parents?"

He smiled at me. I had just caught him feeding his peas to our dog, but, as Harris always said, no one likes a tattle tale. So I kept it to myself. "They sure are, sweetheart."

Then I looked at my mom, piecing things together in my five-year-old mind. Were my parents little once too? Did they have parents who fed them dinner?

"Mommy, do you have a mommy and daddy?"

I had only seen my mom cry once or twice before. But I knew when her face clouded over that she was heading in that direction. She shook her head. "No, Keaton. I don't have a mommy and daddy." She stood up quickly and started clearing our plates. Then she said, "We're expecting a new family at the shelter, and I want to be there to welcome them. Could you finish cleaning up without me?"

I could tell by the way my dad shifted as he watched her go into the kitchen that he wanted to say something. But he didn't. And I filed that away somewhere deep in my memory. I never wanted to make my mom cry. So I never asked about my grandparents again. From then on, on the rare occasions my mom mentioned them, I felt myself storing away every little tidbit about them that I could.

So it wasn't that I was unfeeling or unconcerned. I just didn't have any information. I wondered if every time my mom threw herself into work, into another family at the domestic violence shelter, she was trying to build something she had lost. I respected the work she did, but I couldn't help but be sad that she hadn't thrown that energy into me, into Harris, into *our* family. Her loss led to ours, in a way.

I snap myself out of it, put James Taylor's eight-track down, vacuum again, mop, make up the bed with my clean linens and pillows from home, and flop down on the mattress dramatically. Salt whines until I let him up on the bed too.

I had had Salt about six months when Jonathan and I moved in together, and he convinced me that a dog should be allowed full run of the house—and was a bed-sharing-worthy family member. It only took a couple nights before he was sleeping with us, burrowed happily under the covers. Thinking about that now gives me a pang around my heart. While Jonathan and I—clearly—weren't right for each other, part of me still wishes he were here with me now, helping me wade through this very emotional situation. He took care of me. That was what I really loved about him, more than anything else. But then I think of Allison, of how Jonathan was always hers, never mine.

But there's no use dwelling on what isn't meant to be. I swallow my tears and click on the organization app on my phone that I couldn't survive without at All Welcome to make a list of how to tackle the rest of the housecleaning. It was better, I realized, when I could use it to assign jobs to other people . . . Even still, I add tasks for myself like, buy contractor trash bags, check into the cost of dumpsters, and contact the Salvation Army about donation pickup policies.

I reward myself for all my hard work by flipping through the photo album on Mom's nightstand, dusting each page as I go. I recognize Uncle Lon, of course, and my grandparents, from their picture downstairs. But it makes me sad that I don't know who anyone else in the album is. It is like my mom has just wiped out this entire part of her life. I want to shake her shoulders and be like, *You are a grown-up! You have to deal with things!*

I fall asleep with the photo album open and wake, my cheek stuck to one of the sticky laminated pages, to bright morning sun. I check the time on my phone and am shocked to realize that I slept through the night. It takes me a minute to remember where I am, what I'm doing here. And my first real thought is that I can't decide whether I should go hang with the Dockhouse Dames this morning. On the one hand, Violet seems like she'd know everything about this town, and I get the feeling that her friends will be no different. If I really want to uncover the truth about my grandparents, they might be a good place to start. But do I want to? I couldn't help myself from scanning my grandfather's journal yesterday. I still feel a little icky about reading his private thoughts. But, more than the ickiness, reading his words is like piecing together this man I will never get to know. A man who I am one-fourth of. And that feels like an opportunity I can't give up.

Why I can read his journals and not my grandmother's entertaining notebook, I can't say. But I'm not ready.

"Salt," I say, looking down at my dog. "I think it's time to venture out."

He whines up at me like he agrees. I get ready quickly in my mom's pink-tiled bathroom.

As I walk into the kitchen, I think about the checklist I made for it, which begins with putting away the remains of my grandparents' last dinner party. But I can't help but feel like I will be disturbing evidence. I'll worry about that later. First, coffee.

I open the door and jump, making Salt bark, at the sight of someone sitting on the porch.

"Sorry," Anderson says. "I didn't mean to scare you. I just wanted to see how the ghosts were last night."

I laugh. "You know, no paranormal activity, thankfully. But, my grandparents didn't die in the house."

He looks at me like I'm dense. "Keaton, this house was built in the *seventeen hundreds*. Probably like fifty people have died here." Kid has a point.

I nod. "Hey, shouldn't you be at school?"

"Not until eight," he says. "And it's my last day!" Salt is practically in his lap, licking his face, and it warms my heart. Animals and children have such an instant connection. "But I was going to tell you that if you ever need someone to walk Salt, I can do it."

I smile. "Well, that's very nice. What are your rates?"

He shrugs. "It's just a neighborly thing to do."

I laugh at the grown-up statement coming from under that Camp Rock Springs baseball cap. "No. It's a service. You should charge. Don't you have something you're saving up for?"

He nods. I expect him to say a bike or a Wii or whatever kids are into now, but he says, "A GoPro," and I laugh again.

"Anderson, you are full of surprises. Why do you need a GoPro?"

"I want to start a fishing YouTube channel." He pauses. "I have mad fishing skills."

I nod seriously. "I don't doubt it."

Salt jumps off his lap. "How about five dollars?" I say.

His eyes widen like he would have taken less. I immediately think of Uncle Lon and decide I need a negotiation lesson. "I can help you with other stuff too, you know," he says, looking at the porch disdainfully.

"Squirrel shooting?" We both laugh. "It doesn't seem like your dad would be too big on that. He didn't seem *thrilled* that you were over here the other day."

"Yeah, but he googled you, and you don't seem to be a criminal or a developer so he's cool with it."

"Anderson, you are the most interesting neighbor I've ever had." I pause. "Come by after school, and I'll put you to work. How are you with internet people? Because I need internet, but I hate dealing with them." I'm joking. That is, unfortunately, a grown-up job. But Anderson seems undeterred.

"For five bucks I'll do pretty much anything you want." Anderson gets up. "Bye, Keaton." Salt follows him to the gate, and he leans down to rub his head. "Bye, Salt."

"Have a great day at school!" I call. It's only then that I realize Anderson's dad is watching us from the porch. I wave at him, and he turns and walks into the house without acknowledging me.

"At least we have one nice neighbor," I say to Salt as we make our way down the front walk.

I turn back to look at the front of the house, and as I do, my heart starts to thump. There is a man—well, no, a *pirate*, on the side of the house. A literal pirate. He's wearing heavy brown pants, leather boots, and a red coat trimmed in gold. I squint to see that he has a full-on beard—and appears to be hammering the siding on my house.

Is this the ghost? I watch him. No. Despite the weird outfit, this is definitely a real person.

I decide to call to him from a safe distance, noticing that he appears to have a sword in a holder on his pants. I feel like I should call the police, but what would I say? *There's a pirate hammering my house?* Before I can decide, he notices me, and I freeze.

"Hi," he says, waving and smiling. Despite the lunacy of his outfit, he does have a nice smile underneath his brown leather pirate hat. "You must be Keaton."

Fear grips my throat. He knows my name. What does he want? It's like I'm in one of those dreams where I can't scream or run, so I just stand there, dumbly, as a grown man who thinks he's a pirate walks toward me and opens the gate. "I'm Alex," he says. "I do handyman stuff around the house for Lon."

I feel my shoulders relax an ounce, but I'm still on high alert. Salt, however, is nonplussed. Alex looks down at himself and laughs. "Oh, gosh. Sorry. You probably don't have a lot of pirates in New York City."

I shake my head.

"I do the pirate tours around town."

"Pirate tours?"

He nods. "Yeah. There were a lot of famous pirates who lived in Beaufort at one time or another. I take people around town and tell them about where they came to port, who they killed. You know. The juicy details."

I finally laugh, my panic subsiding. "Oh, wow. That is really fun." I pause. "Unless you were one of the victims. Then, you know, not fun."

"Yeah. Totally unfun," he agrees. "And sorry. I didn't mean to freak you out. But I'm here a lot, just doing little odds and ends." He reaches in his pocket and pulls out a business card. "Call me if you need anything—or, you know, if you find some buried treasure."

I slip the card in the pocket of my dress, laughing.

He points. "I'm going to get back to it. I have a pirate walk at ten."

"Aye aye," I say in my best pirate voice, which is, I realize, abysmal.

He shakes his head seriously. "I can take you on part time, but we're going to need to work on that accent." He points at Salt. "And the dog will need an eye patch."

I'm still laughing as I walk out the gate and onto the sidewalk. It is what I imagine must be a perfect Beaufort day. It is a beautiful seventy-eight degrees with a breeze. Birds are perched on the docks and diving down to catch their breakfasts. "Hey, Alex!" I call across the street. He looks at me. I point. "Is this our dock?"

"Yup! That's yours! Your boat too!"

Lon—or, well, Alex the pirate—must have been keeping up the dock too because it's in perfect shape. And he's right that there's a boat tied to the dock, with a little pilothouse. It is held above the water by these two things that look like tiny cranes, probably to prevent water damage. Even still, it has to be totally rotted by now, right? I shake my head. What a huge waste.

I obviously don't know where the Dockhouse is if I do decide to go. But since there are only a few houses and then water to the right, I go left and assume if I don't pass it, I'll at least find somewhere to get coffee. I walk past a beautiful building, covered in perfectly aged cedar shakes, with thirty-foot-tall doors open on either side. I pause, peering inside. I can see straight through all the way to the water. Inside, two men are sanding the most gorgeous wooden boat I've ever seen. "Good morning," one calls as he notices me.

"Good morning," I say. "Sorry for staring."

"Nah. That's why we keep the doors open. We like witnesses to our hard work."

"I can see why. How long has this place been here?"

"Well, as the Harvey W. Smith Watercraft Center, since 1980."

I smile. "Your boat is beautiful."

The other man, who hadn't spoken yet, says, "We can teach you to make your own if you like. We have classes."

I nod. I can't imagine making my own boat or what I would do with it once I was finished. "I'll keep that in mind."

"You two trying to recruit another member for the splinters club?" asks a voice from behind me.

I turn my head to see my neighbor. Salt jumps on him despite my plea of "Down!"

The neighbor rubs his head and smiles at him. "Hi, buddy." Well, if Salt likes him, maybe he isn't so bad. "Good morning, Bill, Tony."

They wave their good mornings. That's when I realize I still don't know where I'm going. "Um, where's the Dockhouse?"

"I'll walk you there," he says. "I'm Bowen by the way."

"I'm Keaton."

I raise my eyebrow. "Are you following me?"

He rolls his eyes. "I'm on my way to work. See you later, boys."

I smile in spite of myself and walk beside him, my feet tapping the boardwalk. Boats are lined up on docks alongside it, the slips filled with everything from huge yachts and gorgeous fishing boats to beat-up dinghies. "I'm glad someone's living in that house again," he says.

"Well, you could have fooled me."

"Call me when you can't find your kid and he's hanging out with a total stranger."

That makes sense.

Salt has to stop and smell *everything* as we pass a long building with several shops and restaurants. "I won't be here long," I offer. "Just until I get the house cleaned out for my mom and uncle and put on the market." Bowen stops in his tracks, his face clouding. "You're going to sell? That house has been in your family since it was built. Do you know how incredibly rare that is?"

"How do you know that?"

He laughs, his clear blue eyes crinkling. "Keaton, every single time the double-decker Beaufort tour bus rides by my house, twice a day, they mention it to the tourists. But, also, in a town this size, everyone knows everything."

"I'll keep that in mind." I had noticed a red double-decker bus going down the street yesterday—that must have been the bus Bowen is talking about. I make a mental note to take the tour sometime. "My mom and uncle own the house, and they think it's time to sell. And I don't have millions lying around to buy them out so here we are." I pause, now feeling sad that this true family heirloom will be gone. "So, has your house been in your family a long time?"

He shakes his head. "Believe it or not, real estate down here used to be really cheap. My dad bought my house as a rental property back in the seventies, and I bought it from him."

I'm about to ask him about the real estate market here when a dolphin jumps so close to the dock that if I crouched down I could touch it. I gasp. This place really *is* like a postcard. Then I hear, "Kea-ton!" ring out from above me. I look ahead to see Violet practically hanging over the upstairs porch of a place called—lo and behold!—the Dockhouse. She waves. "We're up here!" As if I couldn't tell.

"Well, I guess I found it," I say.

"Good luck!" Bowen gives me a wave and turns off the boardwalk and onto one of the boat-lined docks. I try to see which one he gets on—is he a fisherman?—but I lose him. Suddenly I have meeting-new-people anxiety and, as I walk within easier talking distance to Violet, I call, "I can't come up. I have the dog."

A lady at the table with Violet, rocking round Iris Apfel glasses and hot pink lipstick, laughs. "Honey, you can obviously bring the dog."

There are four ladies sitting on the top porch—Violet and three others—which makes me a little nervous. But, well, they seem friendly, the view should be gorgeous, and I desperately need coffee. I also need to figure out where to eat, grocery shop, etcetera. But eye on the prize: my big, fat commission. Plus, I think, my marketing brain turning on, these ladies seem like the type to bring me a buyer before the house ever hits the market. *Lon's going to have to give me extra for that*, I think.

I walk up the green carpeted stairs inside what is clearly a fun bar at night. The top floor, though, looks like a quaint little café. "So you're sprucing up the old Saint James place, huh?" the woman behind the counter asks. She has pretty brunette beachy waves and is around my age. Her comment catches me off guard, and she must notice because she says, "If you think you're going to keep a secret here, you are very wrong."

I laugh as I eye the pastries in the glass case beside the counter. "That's what I hear. I'm Keaton."

"Amy." She smiles. "What can I get you?"

"I'd like an iced coffee with oat milk please," I say, realizing this doesn't look like the kind of place that has oat milk.

She doesn't bat an eye. "And a cinnamon roll," I add.

"I'll bring it out," she says.

"Do I just pay after?" I ask when she makes no moves to take my money.

"Oh, no. Violet said to put it on her tab."

I smile. Oh, Violet. I'm surprised when I walk out onto the porch that Violet taps the seat beside her, but no one makes a fuss at my arrival. It's a relief.

The lady with the glasses who said I could bring the dog, the one who is clearly the oldest of the group—maybe early eighties to the others' late sixties to early seventies—is saying, "Who died and made her queen of the altar guild? We don't have to have *every* meeting at her house."

"And that dry coffee cake," a woman in a neon sun visor says, shivering.

Violet smiles at me as Amy brings my order. I eat slowly, enjoying the chatter around me, even though I don't really know what it's about. It's like going to a country where you don't speak the language. Immersion is tricky at first, but ultimately, it's the only thing that makes you fluent. My ears perk when the fourth lady, who's wearing a beautiful dress and pearls, says, "Oh, but bless her heart, if that poor girl thinks Bowen Matthews is going to settle down and get serious with a woman . . ."

Bowen. My hunky, kind of rude neighbor who at least now believes me not to be a criminal. Or a developer, which I get the feeling is worse in his estimation.

"What's the story there?" I ask, my mouth full of cinnamon roll. Visor lady gives me a withering look.

"Oh, honey, that is not a tree you want to bark up," Violet says. Salt barks at the word and we all laugh.

"I'm only staying long enough to sell the house, not start a romance, and Bowen has made his distaste for the fact that I'm selling my grandparents' house pretty clear. I'm not barking up any trees. But Anderson said he never had a mom, and I just wondered . . ."

Pearl lady leans in. "It was the saddest thing you've ever seen. Bowen and Kerry brought Anderson home from the hospital, and she just took off."

"She never wanted children, and having Anderson didn't change that. Broke Bowen's heart," glasses woman laments.

Violet brings it home: "But we all chipped in to help care for Anderson, and Bowen is the best dad you've ever seen."

"Anderson is adorable." I can't imagine what it must be like to grow up without a mom. And I wonder how many questions he has about where his mom went. But, I remind myself, I'm not here for long, so my focus needs to be on learning more about my grandparents—since this will likely be my only chance. I want to ask about them now. But being surrounded by the chatter of all these cute ladies is, sadly, the most fun I've had in a while and is taking my mind off the job I need to find and the massive amount of work to be done back at the house and Jonathan *the cheater*. Just thinking his name causes fury to rise in me. Instead of going home alone to grapple with *that*, I sit back, relax, and enjoy their company. As Salt stretches and curls up in a patch of sun, head up as if he's listening intently, I have to think he feels the same way.

I've waited thirty-three years to find out more about my grandparents. One more day won't hurt.

Two Best Friends

JUNE 18, 1976

*Tip: Virginia, women's magazines will spout that early prepa-
ration of food is the key to pulling off a successful event. They
are wrong. With the exception of the Thanksgiving turkey and
a few other marinated dishes, food is almost always entirely
better when made the day of. The key is menu organization. If
you never plan a menu so complicated you can't execute it the
day of the event, you'll never be put in the unfortunate position
of having to serve your treasured guests what are, essentially,
leftovers.*

Mrs. Saint James," a nurse in a starched white uniform with
a nursing cap perched atop her head said, "the doctor will
see you now." Becks placed her pen and small leatherbound notebook
inside her Bermuda bag and clasped the wooden handles. She loved
these new bags and how she could snap on a different cover to suit
her mood or outfit. She had chosen the pink cover today, which was
embroidered with her monogram.

As she stood, Becks glanced at the newspaper, smiling to think of little Tommy Jones who she knew had delivered it. US Viking 1 Goes into Martian Orbit After 10-Month Flight from Earth, the headline read. Imagine. Mars. And only seven years after landing on the moon. What a world.

As Becks followed the nurse down the hall, she wondered if she tired of putting on those hose and white orthopedic shoes. It made her grateful for her comfortable, wide-legged pants—well, *bell bottoms*, she presumed they were—although hers were now ever-so-slightly too big. She had hooked the eye of her gold chain belt one loop tighter today to compensate.

Walking in this office still made Becks so grateful for the lovely life she had had because of it. Townsend's family had found success as shipping merchants in Beaufort, and they had the sort of money that paid for college and medical school, which was a tremendous gift. Townsend's income as a small-town doctor was perfectly suitable—especially for a man who had inherited a house with no payments—and Becks was given the luxury of staying home to raise her children, volunteering, and cultivating wonderful friendships.

Speaking of friendships, Daniel was already waiting for her in his crisp white doctor's jacket, stethoscope around his neck, in the familiar room with the linoleum tile and the table covered in orange pleather that she was to sit on. Ordinarily, she would have waited for him, at least for a few minutes. "Hi, Daniel," she said. She cleared her throat. "Doctor Walker," she corrected, looking at the nurse. Where were her manners today? She must be nervous. As the nurse stepped out of the room, Daniel leaned in to kiss her cheek. "Becks." He gestured toward a chair in the corner and sat down in his own behind a strip of laminate-covered counter, placing his hand on what she assumed was her chart. He smiled warmly.

His smile was familiar, a smile of deep friendship that reminded Becks of all the years they had spent together. When Townsend hired Daniel to go into practice with him—more than thirty years ago now—Becks had, of course, thrown a party to welcome Daniel and Patricia to town. It was the polite thing to do. She never would have imagined how deeply they would have connected, how Patricia and Daniel would become more like siblings to her than friends, filling a gaping hole in her heart. Patricia and Becks volunteered together, played bridge together. And Daniel wasn't just Townsend's dearest friend; he was Becks's too. They read the same books and loved boating. For years, they had all raised children together.

But this new stage as empty nesters had its own merits. Becks was almost embarrassingly happy in her little life with her beloved husband, her now-grown children, and her dear friends. She loved to go on their boat with Townsend, Daniel, and Patricia on Sunday afternoons after a perfect Saturday night dinner party. She loved spontaneous flights with Townsend to Raleigh in their practically new 1973 Beechcraft Bonanza to see their son, or Washington, D.C., to see their daughter. Her husband was an accomplished pilot, after all, and a decorated war hero at that. If he could fly with bombs and guns aiming at him, land in fields and on roadsides during emergencies, he could certainly squire her through blue skies to her favorite cities.

She enjoyed keeping her house just so and weeding the beds in her garden, being at the helm of town affairs, and serving on the altar guild at her church. And while, yes, she did miss having children to take care of, she worked very hard at not pressuring her own kids for grandchildren. That would come soon enough, she hoped.

Becks always reasoned that she was happy because of the life she had created for herself. She wasn't as smart as her cousins. She wasn't as beautiful as her mother. She didn't have aspirations to change the

larger world like her daughter. But what Becks did have was an uncanny ability to read people. It was what made her an exceptional
hostess, a terrific friend, and perhaps the best wife who had ever lived,
in her not-so-humble opinion.

And, right now, it made her all too aware of the bad news that, despite his smile, was written all over Daniel's face. She had been having
back pain and darker-than-usual urine (something she told the nurse
to relay to Daniel because she could *never*), and he had suspected kidney stones. Becks hadn't been too thrilled about getting inside that
newfangled CAT scan machine. Who knew what *that* could do to a
person? But, well, she trusted Daniel, and he was the one who recom-
mended it. She clutched her Bermuda bag tighter. "So, not a kidney
stone?" Becks ventured.

Daniel took a deep breath. "I'm afraid not." That's when the panic
sunk in. This was bad.

She couldn't make Daniel say the words, so she jumped in for him.
"It's cancer, isn't it?" Cancer wasn't even a possibility they had dis-
cussed. But, then again, wasn't cancer always a possibility these days?
It couldn't be breast. He wouldn't have seen that from the scan. So it
must be kidney, she thought. And couldn't a person live with just one?
So maybe they could treat it. Maybe it would be okay.

Daniel sighed. "It's cancer, Becks." He paused. "Of the pancreas."

The room felt as if it was spinning. But she would not faint. No,
she would not. Even still, she knew what her friend had just said: *You
are dying.*

Daniel recovered quickly. "I'm not sure if you've heard, but new
centers are springing up that focus specifically on cancer. I want to
refer you to one that has had decent success with the Whipple procedure, a surgery that removes the head of the pancreas, a portion of the
small intestine, the gallbladder, and bile duct to—"

"I know what the Whipple procedure is," Becks said. She was a doctor's wife, after all. She put her fingers to the bridge of her nose and squeezed in an attempt to dull the throbbing in her head. It was an ungodly surgery that one was lucky to survive.

"And chemotherapy has come a long way in the past thirty years," Daniel added.

Becks had known Daniel for a long time. She had heard Townsend and him many, many times whispering over drinks about the life expectancy of a patient. They were wrong upon occasion, but ninety-nine times out of one hundred, they could call an ill person's time of death down to the week.

Becks noticed how white her knuckles were and willed herself to quit clutching her bag so tightly. "Daniel," she said softly, "I am your friend. Tell me what to do."

To her surprise he got out of his chair and wrapped his arms around her. She wasn't positive, but she thought he was crying. Your physician crying over your diagnosis was never a good sign.

"Be happy and let me make you as comfortable as I can, Becks," he said into her ear. "I'm sorry. I want to help you. I want to fix it. There's a chance one of those treatments could work. Maybe. But it's very, very small. The cancer is very advanced."

"How long?" she whispered.

"Six months, maybe? But if you continue on as you are, with no treatment, at least half of those should be pleasant."

Daniel pulled away, wiping his eyes, and sitting back down in his chair. "I want to consult Townsend on this and send your scans and bloodwork off to MD Anderson for a second opinion."

Becks shook her head. "You cannot tell Townsend."

Daniel looked taken aback. "Becks, he's your husband. He's my best friend. He needs to be prepared for this."

She shook her head again. "I want to give him as much time to enjoy life as usual as I possibly can."

"But, Becks, I really think he'd want to—"

"Is that all?" she cut him off.

He sighed. "Let me drive you home."

She shook her head once more. "You have a waiting room full of patients."

"I have only two best friends, and you are one of them."

"Oh, Daniel, let's not do all that yet. You said yourself we have months."

He half smiled, but his eyes filled with tears again. "You are a wonder, Becks. You always have been."

She squeezed his hand because she knew she'd never be able to respond without breaking down.

Becks felt like she was in a trance as she walked out to the parking lot and climbed into her baby-blue Cadillac Coupe DeVille, a gift from Townsend when their daughter Virginia had graduated college last year—as if Becks had had anything to do with that. Her sobs choked her as she thought of Virginia, who was nearing twenty-three, and her son Lon, barely twenty-seven, both of whom were going to lose their mother at far too young an age. And then she thought of her own mother, whom she had spoken to only twice in the past forty years. She was running out of time. She believed it was too late to make things right. But she also knew she'd never forgive herself if she didn't at least try.

Keaton
....

Reputation

B y my fourth day in Beaufort, I have managed to thoroughly clean
the exterior of the kitchen (the cabinets and drawers seem too
daunting!), the living room, and the dining room of the seventies show-
house. Well, clean is maybe an overstatement, because I have cleaned
around everything but left it exactly as it was, which is driving me insane
because it means I can't fully clear any of my checklists. I don't know why,
but I can't quite bring myself to move anything. The entire house—except
my mom's room, where I am sleeping—has this museum-like quality I
can't bear to disturb. I have only had time to do some cursory digging in
the drawers, which are chock-full of general junk like phone company
notepads from Southern Bell, assorted pens from Security Bank, dried-
out rubber bands, a thumbtack or two, old bills, rock-hard glue, rusty
scissors, and on and on. But the fact that it's all from the seventies or
before makes it so interesting that I can't possibly throw it away. The fact
that my grandparents touched these things makes them treasures. I keep
reminding myself of the commission, that I'm here to do a job. But that is
getting harder with every passing minute.

I'm lying in bed, debating whether to try to go back to sleep or get
up and go get coffee, and I finally reach my breaking point: I can no

longer control the urge to Insta-stalk Allison and Jonathan. As soon as I type in Allison's handle on Instagram, there it is: her pregnancy announcement. The top comment says: *Only a goddess like you could find a way to repair your broken family.* Gag me. She is not a goddess. She puts on a good, good show. In my mind, I hate-message every fan who's written an ooey gooey comment about how thrilled they are for her.

I decide to go back through her feed to see if there were any clues I missed. Um, let's just say there were. TBT photos of when Allison and Jonathan were married, their faces scrunched together in "work trip" selfies. A caption about how Allison didn't know what she would do without Jonathan. Was I blind? When I get all the way down to Allison's posts from three years ago, I realize that this has to stop. It's not helping me to ruminate. I make a deal with myself: If I put the phone down, I will allow myself to do the thing that has felt too hard, too personal, too scary until now. I reach over to my nightstand and pick up the white leather notebook I've been so curious about. I lift the cover and peek inside the inner sanctum of Becks Saint James's life. And I laugh.

I know I must tell the Dockhouse Dames about this, and so I hoist myself out of bed, realizing how sore I am from—what? Vacuuming?

Thirty minutes later, I am telling the Dockhouse Dames all about my inner turmoil with the top secret notebook—how, somehow, peeking into Townsend's life that seemed so vast and intricately detailed felt less scary than lifting the lid on this tiny notebook that Becks carried with her everywhere. They all lean forward as I say, "So I finally looked at the book. And do you know what is on the very first page?"

"Well, what?" Violet asks impatiently.

I grin. "Her chicken salad recipe."

The women around the table laugh. "Well, you'd better share the wealth. I've always wanted Becks's recipes," the woman I now know is named Betty says. She has worn her neon sun visor to coffee all three days I've attended, which is incredibly helpful as it makes it impossible to forget which one she is.

"What else?" Arlene, the pretty one who always looks like she's going to an important function, asks.

I smile, my heart feeling warm. "I haven't made it that far, but it looks like it's her recipes, her guest lists, her conversation starters for each party." It surprises me that my voice catches when I say, "And little entertaining and life tips for my mom."

Violet's eyes well as she smiles at me.

"I don't know if I should give this to her," I say. Now that I'm here, everything just seems sadder and harder. My mother was so incredibly loved. I was never loved quite like that. It hits me hard.

"I think you should," Suzanne in her Iris Apfel glasses says. "It's up to her what she does with it, but I think she should at least have the opportunity to choose."

I look around the table at three other nodding heads.

"Have you found anything else interesting while you've been cleaning?" Violet asks.

I groan. "Don't even get me started on cleaning. I just can't bear to throw anything away. The house is like a living shrine to my grandparents. Who am I to disturb it?" I hand Salt pieces of my bagel, which he gobbles up enthusiastically. "Is any of it *interesting*? I don't know. Because, to me, everything is."

"You should hire a housekeeper to help," Betty says.

I shake my head. "No, I couldn't. What if they threw something away?"

Violet and Arlene share a look.

"What?" I ask.

"Well, it's just . . . Do you think that your inability to throw any of their things away means that maybe you want to know more about your grandparents? That you want to dig more deeply into their lives?"

My entire childhood I felt this weird void. When we were doing family research projects or talking about our family trees, when other kids would share anecdotes about their grandparents during the Great Depression or World War II, I always felt this deep longing. Not only because I didn't have my mother's parents but also because I didn't know their stories. But it wasn't until right now that I realized that, although I'd never get to meet my grandparents, it wasn't too late to learn about the life they'd left behind.

I sigh and take a deep breath, steeling my nerves to ask the question that, for some reason, I don't want to ask. I think it's because, then, I'll have to acknowledge what my mom really went through. But I'm here, and who knows if I'll ever get another chance. "Violet, why did you say my grandparents disappeared?"

The ladies share glances. There must be some unspoken conversation that I am not privy to because Suzanne suddenly produces a manila folder and hands it to me. "We thought you'd never ask," she says.

I open the folder, which, at a glance, seems to contain roughly a dozen newspaper articles. I read the first headline, from August 30, 1976: NEW UPDATES ON REBECCA AND TOWNSEND SAINT JAMES DISAPPEARANCE. I don't read further, knowing I'll want to pore over this later, and, really, what could the newspaper know that these ladies don't?

"My mother Sarah, Ellen, and Laura were Becks's dear friends," Suzanne says. "She saved all of this like she would be the one to find them—or at least find out what happened to them. I never thought she'd recover."

"What happened?" I ask, wanting to read the last page before the whole book.

Arlene shakes her head. "We don't know. They were never found. But my mom and dad—Patricia and Daniel—were also best friends with Becks and Townsend. My mother was devastated, and I've never seen anything tear my dad apart like their deaths."

My stomach clenches. These past few days I am starting to feel like I know my grandparents. I can see my grandmother's face in her pictures, smell the lingering scent of her perfume in her bedroom, stand inside her perfectly organized closet and touch her beautiful dresses, her rows of shoes. I can hear my grandfather's voice in his journal, smell the pipe tobacco preserved in the pages of his books, and almost feel how much he loved the dozens of fishing rods housed inside a stunning glass and mahogany cabinet in his office. A knowing washes over me: My mom and uncle aren't emotionally stunted; they are scarred. Parents dying in a car crash has an aspect of closure: horrible and sad, but a concrete tragedy a person can heal from. But I'm realizing something more traumatic happened here, and I am suddenly filled with love for my mother, who protected me from that. Maybe she wasn't always the mother I wanted. But maybe she was the only kind of mother she could be.

"So why does my mom say they died in a car wreck?"

"That's what the police thought," Betty says.

Suzanne gestures toward the folder. "After their last dinner party in 1976, Becks and Townsend's convertible was found sunk in Taylor Creek. But Becks and Townsend weren't inside."

"What?" My eyes widen. I want to ask them how this large body of water connecting to the ocean came to be known as a creek in the first place, but this feels like the wrong time.

Violet leans over to pat my hand. "Sweetie, how do I put this delicately . . ."

Suzanne, who is not delicate, chimes in. "There are a lot of things swimming in that water that could cause a person to disappear without a trace."

I gasp and Violet smacks her hand on the table. "Honey, we are crazy old ladies with nothing better to do than come up with conspiracy theories. Of course your grandparents died in a car wreck. It has been decades. If that isn't what happened, we would have known by now."

"Yeah, that's true. And surely my mom would have mentioned something about it at some point in our lives if she believed differently, right?"

Suzanne nods. "Absolutely, sweetie." She reaches her hands out. "In fact, you should just give me that folder back. There's no use in even entertaining the mess in there."

But I hold the folder to my chest protectively. "Maybe I shouldn't have brought it up," I say. "But now I can't give these back." I look around at the ladies. "Okay. Someone change the subject!"

They all smile and Arlene says, "Perfect. Because we have a question for you."

I look down at Salt, who has just perked up from his nap, his floppy ears at their version of attention. I want to say, *I know, buddy.* I can tell that whatever these ladies want to rope me into is probably something I'm going to want to run from. Fast. I'm already making a list of polite excuses in my head.

"We want the house to be on tour!" Arlene squeals. Three sets of eyes glare at her. "What?" she says. "Sorry. I was excited."

"But remember how we talked about this?" Violet says. "How we'd ease into it, sell her on the idea?"

I ignore her. "Wait. What? You mean, like, my grandparents' house? Disco central? And what is 'on tour' anyway?"

"Well, I'm chairing the Old Homes Tour this year," Violet says im-
portantly. "It's the single biggest fundraiser of the year for the Beaufort
Historic Site, and people come from all over to step inside beautiful
Beaufort homes and get a taste of its history. It's only three weeks
away, but we thought it would be so special if folks could tour a house
that hasn't been touched since the 1970s."

"What's the Beaufort Historic Site again?" I ask tentatively. I
should know by now, but, um, I do not.

"It's right downtown with the historic houses, the Beaufort Welcome Center, the apothecary, the old jail, the art gallery, the court-
house . . ." Violet pauses. "And you know the Old Burying Ground?"

That I do know because I have walked through there, shocked
at how peaceful it is to be in that tree-shaded, gated cemetery with
headstones dating as far back as the early eighteenth century. It's a
reminder that life is short. "Right," I say. "And we're raising money
to . . ."

"It costs a ton to keep all those things up!" Suzanne exclaims
sharply, as if I've offended her.

"Right. So the Old Homes Tour raises money to preserve the
town's history?"

"Exactly," Betty says kindly, shooting Suzanne a look.

My mind floods with all the reasons it's a bad idea to put the house
on tour. "No," I say. "I'm sorry, but I just don't think it'll be possible. I
can barely get the place clean, and I really don't want to move all the
dishes and stuff in case my mom wants to see the way they left it that
night one last time."

Ohhhhh . . . It isn't until I say it out loud that I realize that to be
true. I feel better that I'm not totally losing it, that my inability to
throw away so much as a rubber band isn't all about me. Deep down,
I just want my family to get some closure.

"Well, that's even better!" Suzanne says. "The chance for people to experience a famous Becks Saint James dinner party one more time."

"We will be your docents," Arlene says.

"Docents?" I ask.

Arlene nods. "You will have people in every room to talk about the history of the house, answer any questions—"

"And make sure no one steals your stuff," Suzanne says wryly.

"Well, yeah," Arlene agrees. "We will ensure that no one touches a thing, and we will tread impossibly lightly."

"And," Violet adds, "think of all the people who will walk through in the two days it's on tour. Buyers, buyers, buyers. You could set a new real estate sales record in town."

My mind darts to all the many, many things in my grandparents' house. Could I use this tour as an opportunity to sell some of it? The idea makes my stomach turn, so I quickly decide I'm not ready for that—and I don't think I'll be ready three weeks from now. But a new real estate record? This does give me, the newly unemployed, pause. And then there's the fact that my grandparents' sad, empty house would be filled with people one last time, just the way they liked it.

When I don't say anything right away, Suzanne says, "Tell her, Violet."

Violet shakes her head. "I don't want her to feel pressured."

"I do!" Suzanne scoffs.

"Well you have to tell me now," I say.

"Well, sweetie," Violet starts, "your grandmother was actually the one who started the Old Homes Tour."

"Her last summer," Betty continues in a tone that is laced with importance. "She wanted to leave a legacy, to know that the historical association she loved would continue to be funded."

I feel my eyes widen. "She did, really?"

They all nod, and I feel my heart swell with pride.

"All our moms were on the original committee . . ." Violet adds.

"And now you can be too," Arlene finishes.

I gasp. "Well, then, I don't see how it could possibly *not* be on tour. It's what Becks would have wanted."

Violet nods in agreement. "She would have."

And Lon will want all the foot traffic. I'm pretty sure about that. And, well, Mom sent me down here without preparing me for what I was walking into, so in my opinion, she had lost her right to vote. "It's only on tour for two days?" I clarify.

"Just two days," Violet says. She appears to be holding her breath.

Two days isn't that much of a setback. "Then I'm in," I say.

Cheers all around.

I leave the Dockhouse realizing I have a lot of work to do if I'm going to get the house tour-ready. I think this is the perfect thing to motivate me to *actually* start going through things. But, first, I'll need sustenance.

Although I have some meager groceries from the Coastal Community Market waiting for me back at the house, I decide to stop by Turner Street Market to grab a pimento cheese sandwich to go because Violet has gone on and on about how good it is. Plus, they give dogs a free piece of bacon, and Salt deserves bacon. I lean down and rub his head. "Because you're such a good boy, aren't you?" He prances ahead of me regally, with perfect posture as if proving my point.

I wave and smile at the half dozen semi-strangers who stop to say "Hi, Salt!" and rub him behind the ears along the way. My dog is already a bit of a local celebrity. He really was designed for small-town life and is loving the attention—and the evening swims we take in the creek. Although now that I know about the allegedly carnivorous beings in there . . . I shiver.

I tie Salt's leash to a bike rack, open the market door, and smile as the woman behind the counter calls, "Hi, Keaton!" Everyone already knows my name. Everywhere. It's hilarious. I've only been here once and I'm already a regular.

I order my pimento cheese sandwich with a side of deviled eggs and sweet tea, put my AirPods in, and say, "Call, Harris."

"Well, if it isn't small-town Suzie," Harris answers.

I roll my eyes. "Um, Harris. Do you know that our grandparents disappeared, never to be heard from again?"

"Well . . ." He breathes for a second on the other end of the phone. "That's often what happens when people die in a car wreck."

"Probably died in a car wreck," I say. "But their bodies were never found."

He's quiet on the other end.

"Harris?"

"Keat, do I need to come get you? I know this has all been a lot on you. The affair, losing your job. You know, let's just hire someone to clean out the house, and you can come live with me. Enjoy the bachelor pad."

"Harris, I'm not . . ." I stop and laugh. "The model dumped you?"

"I never said she was a model."

"But she was, right?"

I say "Thanks!" as I grab my to-go order.

"Hope you enjoy, Keaton!" the woman behind the counter says.

Maybe I *am* small-town Suzie.

"Yes, she was a model," Harris continues. "But that's like being an actress in LA. What does that even mean?"

"You should come to Beaufort for the Old Homes Tour. It's in three weeks, and our house is going to be on it," I say, ignoring his comment as I walk down the street.

"Keaton, who are you? You go to Beaufort for a few days and you're, like, a townie?"

I laugh as I untie Salt's leash from the bike rack and walk toward home. "I think I am. Everyone's just really nice, and we all have to chip in to preserve our town's history. The tour raises tons of money for the Historic Site and *our grandmother started it*." Then I see the internet truck in the driveway. "Crap!" I say. "I've got to go."

"Garden club emergency?" Harris asks.

"Worse: Wi-Fi. Goodbye, loving brother. See if you can keep any models from moving in for like a month to save room for me."

"I don't know that you can hang in New York City now. You're small-townified. Up here, you'll just complain about long lines and traffic."

I laugh as I hang up and run through the front door, which I definitely locked when I left. I can see who I presume is the internet guy standing with Alex the pirate and . . . Bowen? They are all laughing.

"Um, hi?" I say out of breath, restraining Salt from jumping all over the strangers. I have a lot of questions as to why they are in my house uninvited, but, on the other hand, I haven't had to deal with the internet guy, so maybe I should let it go? Before I can decide what to say, I see what they're laughing at. My grandparents' ancient—but no longer dust-covered, thank you very much—wooden-box-on-the-floor television is playing. And in color at that! "No way," I say, perching on the arm of the sofa. "That thing works?"

"It took some doing," Alex says, adjusting his pirate hat.

"But we were up for the challenge," Bowen says.

"Well, ma'am, you're all set," the internet guy adds.

"Oh, but I didn't order cable."

He waves his hand like it's nothing. "Don't worry. It's on the house."

I'm confused. "Wait. What?"

Bowen pats my arm. "Small-town kindness takes some getting used to. You'll assimilate soon."

I roll my eyes at him. "Wow. Well, thanks."

"Internet is running, cable is set up," cable guy continues. "Forgive me for not being able to add your apps to your TV for you."

Now I have to laugh, because the whole thing is so absurd. "Is Lawrence Welk included in my package?" I ask.

That sets us all off again.

As he leaves and Alex follows behind him, I turn to Bowen. "I'm really sorry you had to deal with this," I say. "They gave me a three to five p.m. arrival window."

Bowen snickers. "And you believed them?"

"I guess I did. Silly me." Now I'm kind of annoyed. I look around. "Um, how did you get in?"

He holds up an ancient-looking key on a Texaco key chain. "Your spare is under the planter."

"Ah. Good to know."

He starts to walk out the door, and I say, "Well, thanks for helping me. That was really cool of you, if you ignore the breaking and entering."

He nods and almost, maybe, smiles at me. "Well, you know, it was the neighborly thing to do." Exactly what Anderson said.

I know I shouldn't want him to help me, but the idea that he jumped in without being asked makes me happy. And I have to needle him just a little. "Wait, so are we like friends now?"

He makes a skeptical face and says, "If you feel like you need to tell people that around town, you can."

I'm about to be annoyed again until he adds, "I know you're new here, but those Dockhouse Dames shouldn't be your only friends. They have quite the reputation."

As he leaves, I am laughing out loud. Yeah. Betty, Arlene, Violet, and Suzanne are pretty sketchy. Hang with them too long and you might just get involved in the Maritime Museum. Or worse, the church bazaar.

Bowen's funny. Who knew? For just an instant, he showed me a side of himself I didn't know was there. And, as much as I hate myself for it, I have to admit that a part of me wants to know more.

Becks

....

Let It Go

THURSDAY, JUNE 24, 1976

Tip: Dearest darling, food is love. Flowers are jewels. No good party is complete without both. Come to think of it, no good life is complete without all four.

Becks felt a pang of nostalgia as she made her way down Kinston's Vernon Avenue, thinking of the wonderful childhood days she had here with her mother, her friends, and her beloved, now-deceased daddy. Thinking of him caused that deep pain she'd been trying so hard to keep at bay to well up inside her. Maybe she was procrastinating, but instead of turning right onto the shady, beautiful street she had grown up on, she kept driving straight and turned left into Rider Florist. Wasn't it her mother who had taught her to love flowers so much? She sat in the parking lot for a moment, calming her breath, trying to forget the many days she came here with her mother to get the perfect arrangements for parties.

She pushed open the metal door, its bells tinkling, and was enveloped by the warm, fragrant humidity of the flower shop. Instantly, she was six years old again. The woman behind the counter pulled her glasses down. "May I help you?"

"Hi, Jewell," she said. Jewell, she'd heard through friends over the years, had taken over the shop and put her own stamp on it. "It's—"

"Why, it's Becks Bonner!" The woman rushed out from behind the counter and hugged Becks tightly, as though it hadn't been decades since they'd last seen each other. Becks thought she might cry with relief. She wasn't sure what her reputation around town was like, if her mother had poisoned everyone against her. But the genuine light in Jewell's eyes told her either her mother hadn't tried or she had tried but it hadn't taken.

"What brings you to town?" Jewell asked.

Becks bit her lip. "I'm surprising my mother." Jewell's eyes went wide. The Bonner family feud was big news around the small town, and the fact that Becks was here would be fuel for the fire.

"Well, you'll need the perfect bouquet."

Jewell disappeared into the back and reappeared with a bunch of wildflowers. They were fresh, beautiful, and very trendy.

Becks scrunched her nose. "I don't know, Jewell. For my mother?" Her mother was so traditional that she wasn't sure how wildflowers would suit her, and bringing the wrong flowers to the meeting could start it off on the wrong foot.

Jewell shook her head. "Can you believe it? Your mother loves them now."

Becks could not believe it, and, as she paid for them, it broke her heart that this woman knew more about her own mother than she did. Her mother, who she had laughed with growing up. Who she had cooked with, entertained with, who had braided her hair and tucked her in at night. And then, one wrong move, and it was all gone. Poof! Had Becks realized how tenuous her parents' love for her was, her entire childhood might have been different. She would never have felt so safe. On the bright side, living through what she had had deeply influenced the mother she had become. She would never, *ever* abandon her children. Whatever choices they made, whether she agreed with them or not, she always let her children know that their parents were their safe place.

Becks bid Jewell goodbye and, feeling warm nostalgia wash over her, got back in her car and made her way down the road. When she turned onto her street, the brick two-story Georgian where she grew up was a standout. It was framed by a pair of ancient oak trees and was, in her opinion, one of the most beautiful houses in Kinston.

As she pulled the car up in front of the sidewalk, she admired the way the light shone on the house, like it was being honored by heaven itself. She debated pulling her car into the driveway, between the rows of azaleas in full bloom, but decided against it. She was afraid her mother would feel it was too familiar.

For a moment, she doubted herself. Maybe Townsend was right; maybe her mother didn't deserve this visit. But, as Becks had explained to him, her mother wasn't getting any younger. If she ever wanted to try to make amends, it was now or never. What she didn't say, of course, was that her own hourglass was also running out of sand.

Gathering her flowers, her purse, and all her nerve, Becks opened the door to the convertible—a car, she knew, her mother would deem impractical and absurd—and walked up the uneven brick path she knew so well. Her heart raced as she climbed the two slate steps to the front door. When her mother was home, the big, heavy black wooden door stayed open to let the light in, while the glass-and-wood storm door was closed. The oriental rugs had to be rotated every six months to even out the sun damage, but Becks thought it made them even more beautiful.

The door was open; her mother was home. As she lifted the handle of the huge brass door knocker and tapped twice, she made up her mind that, no matter what happened today, she wouldn't tell her mother she was dying. It would be a betrayal to Townsend for anyone—even the woman who brought her into the world—to know such a thing first. Plus, Becks didn't believe her mother deserved to know the truth. At least, not yet.

She caught a glimpse through the glass of a small, shuffling woman making her way through the entrance hall. In Becks's mind, her mother was still the same auburn-haired beauty she had been when Becks last saw her. But as her mother opened the door, the first thing Becks noticed was the way her white hair—styled with a permanent—had become so thin that you could see parts of her scalp. Age had stolen her crowning glory.

It was only a split second, but her mother looked up into her face and said, "Yes?"

The idea that her mother didn't recognize her seared her heart, but, then again, had this woman appeared at her door, she wouldn't have recognized her either. But once you gave birth to a child, shouldn't you, in the deep-down recesses of your heart, recognize that child as yours, no matter how old they were?

"Rebecca!" her mother finally said with surprise, and perhaps even a fleck of joy.

"Hi, Mother," she said, choking on the words.

Becks hadn't quite been able to wrap her mind around what this moment might be like, but here it was. Both women's eyes filled with tears. Her mother didn't hug her like she'd hoped, but she leaned down anyway to wrap her in an embrace that her mother limply reciprocated. This could easily be the last time she ever hugged her mother, and she felt it best to take the opportunity.

"Come in," Myra said. "I was just warming up some coffee cake."

Becks followed her mother through the house, which was exactly the same as when she'd last been inside it. No trends had touched this place. It was still perfectly traditional, full of antique furniture and knickknacks passed down through the generations.

She smiled, thinking of how after she and Townsend married, even though her mother hadn't attended, her silver chest had still arrived in the mail. Becks had hoped for a letter, but there was nothing. Even still, Becks wasn't confused. In her family, the firstborn daughter received her mother's wedding silver when she married. It was a tradition, and, Becks had hoped, a bridge. She wrote to thank her mother but never received a reply. It was the first of a dozen or so letters Becks had sent her mother over the years. They were all met with silence.

"May I help you?" Becks asked when they reached the kitchen, noticing how slowly her mother moved around the space she had once zipped through with such efficiency and speed.

"I quit needing your help long ago," her mother said pertly as she reached into the fridge for the cream. Always cream. Never milk.

That they had made it a few minutes without her mother making a dig at her was impressive. She had, however, hoped they were past all that.

Myra handed her daughter a cup of coffee and sat down in one of the Windsor chairs that matched a deep walnut pub table. Becks noticed her mother's shaking hand, but whether it was shaking with age or nerves she couldn't be sure. Becks's own hand was shaking too as she picked up the mug. She was filled with so many emotions: sadness for the time that had passed, hope for the reconciliation that could come, nervous that she might make a misstep and ruin the day. "How are you, Mother?" Becks asked.

"Oh, I'm fine. I stay busy. Book club, bridge club, Methodist Church Women." She paused. "Which you would know nothing about, I presume."

Becks wasn't there to talk about church. "I thought you might like to know that I have dinner parties every week during the summer," Becks said, avoiding the implied question. "You taught me how to be a proper hostess so well, and I haven't let you down."

Her mother eyed her warily, and Becks realized her poor choice of words.

"Oh, you haven't let me down. Is that so?" her mother asked pointedly. "Was he worth it?"

Her mother never minced words, but she knew the answer automatically. Townsend was worth every heartache, every little fight, every difficult day. He had been her rock, her provider, the most amazing father to their children. But more than that, he was simply her perfect match. Their last forty years together had been glorious. But she was here to make peace. So she simply said, "Mother, Townsend remains, as he was then, my one true love."

"Grand. So what are you doing here, Rebecca?"

Becks wasn't sure how she had imagined today going, and maybe it was going better than she had feared. But not as well as she had wished. She had wanted a real conversation. Apologies all around. Tears. Hugs. She knew this woman nearly as well as she knew herself—or, well, she had at one time—and she felt that she could break down those walls around her heart if she tried. But would that be fair?

Because Myra Bonner had mourned the loss of her child for forty years. She had come to terms with it. Would it be right for Becks to come back into her life knowing that she was dying—knowing that, even if they had the reconciliation she dreamed of, she would inevitably cause her mother such tremendous sadness all over again? She knew it wouldn't be. And so, Becks decided to be content with knowing she got to see her mother one last time. Still, there were things she knew she had to say. "Mother, I only came here to say that I love you. And that I forgive you."

Her mother laughed. "*You* forgive *me*? Now that's really something. I believe I'm the one who would need to forgive you."

Becks nodded. "Maybe so. But in case there ever comes a time when you wonder how your daughter felt about you, I only want you to know I've put it all behind me—and I understand you a little better than I once did. I know you only wanted what was best for me, in your way."

A wave of recognition came over Myra's face, and, for a split second, Becks thought that maybe she knew her daughter was dying; maybe she could intuit, in that way mothers do, that this was a making of amends before the end. But if that was what Myra understood, she didn't let on. Instead, she put her coffee mug down. "I have tried to be cordial, but I think you should go."

Becks shook her head, fully intending to do so. But she couldn't help herself from saying, "Mother, really? Forty years and you still can't let it go?"

Myra stood up from the table, gaining a burst of strength. "Let it go?" she asked. *"Let it go?"* She pointed at Becks. "You killed my husband, your own father, a man of the *cloth*. And now you want me to *let it go*? I will never let it go."

The worst-case scenario Becks imagined had come to fruition. She stood, noticing the tears running down her mother's face. Was she still really that angry? Or was this a remnant of an old hurt? Becks didn't know. Suddenly, she was overcome with so much anger at the mother who abandoned her that she knew she had to leave. But as she began to exit, her mother said, "Rebecca" softly.

Becks turned and held her mother's gaze for a few moments, in which she was filled with hope. But Myra remained silent.

Becks walked into the foyer, hands trembling, she turned to look around the house she once loved so very much, at the place that once meant warm hugs and happy Christmas mornings. She knew that those joyful moments were a thing of the past. Maybe they were never really real to begin with. But, either way, they were her memories, her childhood.

As Becks took one last deep breath of the smell of pipe tobacco and furniture polish, fresh cake and real wood fires—the mingling scent of "childhood home" that her brain had filed away long ago—she put a shaking hand to the brass knob, worn smooth with time and use. Her heart beat rapidly, her eyes filling with tears. Rebecca Bonner, now Rebecca Saint James, knew she would never walk through her own front door again.

The Popular Table

I am fully aware that I have been a workaholic over the past few years. Maybe that's part of what made my relationship with Jonathan work while it did: We were both married to our jobs. Now that I've had a little time away I know I don't want to go back to a job that I eat, sleep, and breathe, but I also don't want to get totally off schedule. Which is why I'm in the dust-and-cobweb-filled detached garage poking at bicycle tires at six forty-five in the morning. Everyone here— like, seriously, everyone—rides bikes. And, as I'm trying to embrace life more, I think I'd like to try it out, see what it's like. Anyone could see that these bikes are mostly dry-rotted, but I select a pink one that seems the least rusty, locate a dust-covered pump, and attempt to put air in the tires while Salt looks at me skeptically.

"This is going to be fun!" I say. "I'll put you on your leash, you can get a good run in, and we can ride over to Les Ciseaux and get fresh pastries."

He tilts his head and wags his tail when I say "leash." It's his second favorite word after "chicken." Ten minutes later, I have wiped the bike down, wrapped Salt's leash around my wrist, and we are making our way down Sunset Lane. I'm a little teetery from a combination of my less-than-ideal bike and the fact that I haven't ridden one in ten years. I was nervous about how Salt would do, but this is working out pretty well overall. He is matching the bike's pace as I admire the sunlight gleaming on the waterfront. Horses graze on the Rachel Carson Reserve, which I have a beautiful view of from the Dockhouse each morning with the ladies, and, as if putting on a show just for me, a pod of dolphin swims my same path down Taylor Creek, jumping every few minutes. They seem to be playing—or dancing. And I wonder if I am actually in heaven. "Look at us, Salt!" I exclaim. "Riding a bike is kind of a hobby, right?"

I turn left onto Queen Street and join the line for the small bakery that produces delicious authentic French pastries. The man in front of me, who I do not recognize, leans down and says, "Hi, Salt!"

It's uncanny. Everyone in town knows his name. He smiles at me and says, "I hear there's pain au chocolat today."

"Yes!" I say, feeling an anxious bubble rise. There are four people in front of me so they could easily run out of my favorite pastry by the time I get there. Fortunately, they don't. As I take my place inside the small vestibule in front of the counter, inhaling the scent of coffee and fresh bread, I order two pain au chocolat—one for me and one for Anderson, obviously—two croissants for Salt and me for breakfast tomorrow, and a baguette. Because what is chicer than a baguette peeking out of your bike basket? I mean, honestly.

The man behind the counter who I know is also the baker says, with a heavy French accent, "All of this for today?"

I feel so ashamed that, for a moment, I can't answer until he adds, "I do not like anyone to eat day-old bread" and winks at me.

I laugh and pay him.

As I get back on the bike, situate the leash loosely around my wrist, and turn toward home, I make a note to ask Anderson where

I should get new bike tires. I am pedaling like I'm riding through sand.

Despite the slow going, I manage until, less than a block from the house, a squirrel leaps out in front of my bike. I slam the brakes hard, stopping abruptly, and miss the squirrel. At the exact same time, Salt practically leaps in the air and starts running toward it at top speed, yanking my arm and almost pulling me off the seat in the process. "Salt, no!" I yell, pedaling again because my balance is too precarious to pull on Salt's leash and make him stop. "Salt, no!" He's zigging and zagging, and I almost topple over more than once. Everything but the baguette is tucked down in the basket, and I'm perhaps more preoccupied than I should be with trying to keep my chic bread from meeting its demise on the asphalt.

Even in my panic, I could *swear* this is the same squirrel that tried to give me a heart attack in my kitchen.

I hear Bowen's voice yelling, "Drop the leash!" before I see him emerge from the cluster of trees that line his driveway. "Keaton! Drop the leash!"

Drop the leash. But I can't drop the leash. What if the dog gets hit by a car?

"I'll get Salt!" he yells. At what feels like the last second before I am going to flip over the handlebars, I manage to unloop the leash from my wrist and right myself. With that, Bowen sprints into the street and steps on Salt's leash, yanking him back from the squirrel. I am sweating, my heart is pounding, and now I'm worried all the force has hurt the dog. But the second Salt sees Bowen, he jumps on him like the squirrel never existed. I lay the bike on the sidewalk, tucking my baguette under my arm and retrieving my bag of other goodies, still panting.

"Keaton," Bowen says, "are you kidding me? You don't ride a bike with an animal."

I am sheepish, but, gosh, this man loves to scold me. He wraps the leash around his wrist, and I'm surprised when he puts his arm around me and pulls me to his side. I realize I'm shaking as he squeezes my shoulder, steadying me. "You're okay," he whispers.

I look up at him, into those eyes that I could swim in. I'm shocked by how comforted I feel by him right now. I'm surprised that I don't want him to let me go.

"Dad!" comes a yell from the direction of his house. "Dad! Where are you?"

Bowen releases his hold on me—physically, but maybe not mentally—as Anderson, who I have really adored until this particular moment, appears at the end of the driveway. "Salt!" he yells.

Bowen drops the leash, and Salt bounds toward Anderson in that friendly way that brings out his golden retriever side. (I have to think the pain in the ass that nearly killed me earlier is his poodle side.)

"Thank you," I say to Bowen. "I don't know what I would have done if you hadn't been there."

He smiles. "That's what neighbors are for."

I shake my head, trying to calm my still rapidly beating heart. "Can you believe I could even get one of those old bikes to go?"

He shakes his head. "That was one of my old bikes. I stored it in Becks and Townsend's garage since I don't have one. I hope that's okay . . ." He pauses. "Trust me, 1970s tires wouldn't pump." He walks back across the street, toward Anderson. "Let Salt in the fence," I hear him say.

I can't help myself. I watch him walk away. And my pulse picks back up when he looks over his shoulder at me one more time. "Oh!

Oh! Anderson!" I run up behind him and he turns. I rummage through the paper bag, and his eyes widen because he knows something good is inside. "Pain au chocolat," I say, grinning as I hand it to him.

"Yes! Keaton, you're the best!"

Bowen smiles, and he's so cute I nearly drop my baguette. "You sure know the way to a man's heart," he says.

Although I know he was talking about Anderson, I can't stop thinking about Bowen all day, as I scrub cobwebs out of kitchen cabinets and even manage to put an entire box of items in the "giveaway" pile. Somewhere around organizing the Tupperware cabinet filled with mismatched pieces in orange, green, and mustard yellow, it occurs to me that Bowen's "old bike," the pink one with the banana seat and the basket, must have been Anderson's mom's. I wonder what it means that he hasn't given it away, that he has kept it in storage all this time. I decide it's a good time to break for dinner, so I can take my mind off it.

I haven't cooked in years, but ever since I started flipping through Becks's notebook, I've had the urge to try. And her first recipe for chicken salad looks pretty easy, even for a total novice like me.

Earlier in the day, I went down to Beaufort Ace—in the car, lesson learned—where a very friendly woman helped me. "Do you have a 'large fryer'?" I asked.

She led me over to a shiny deep fryer. I looked from the machine to her and back again. "This not what you want?" she asked.

"I don't know," I said. "I'm trying to make my grandmother's chicken salad, and it says you need a large fryer."

I handed her the notebook, and I'll give her credit, she tried really hard not to laugh. "Sweetheart, a large fryer is a chicken." She paused and said, gently, "But maybe you should just substitute with two pounds of chicken breast."

I wanted to be offended that she didn't think I could handle a whole chicken, but, well . . . I was Amelia Bedelia. So I took her advice. The part about boiling the chicken and removing the skin and bones was just too much for me, anyway. So, instead, I dump the pack of chicken into an ancient silver pot with worn black handles, water sloshing everywhere, wash my hands, and cut up the two "ribs" of celery and one small onion with a knife that is still surprisingly sharp. I also presume that Becks made her sweet pickle cubes from scratch. Mine are from a jar. I smile when I read Becks's note at the bottom of the recipe: *I do not use hard-boiled eggs, for it takes away from the taste of the chicken. Most people use eggs, but I have found it tastier without them.*

I wash my hands again, clean up my area, and wait for my chicken to boil. I realize that my growling stomach is not going to accommodate the time it's going to take for this chicken to cool. The idea of mixing mayonnaise into hot chicken makes me want to gag, so, instead, I cut the chicken up once it's cooked, mix the veggies in, and decide to put it in the fridge and finish it tomorrow. Chicken salad is really a better lunch anyway, right? So, no, this didn't go perfectly. But it was a start and, regardless, I feel very accomplished.

I opt for a bowl of cereal for dinner instead and am sitting at the breakfast table, thinking how very different my life is here than my life back home. Well, my life in New York. Did it ever feel like home? Thinking about New York makes me think about Jonathan . . . And my phone is right here, so I decide to just check his Insta profile, super quickly, even though I know he barely ever posts and that, if he does, there is like a ninety percent chance Allison or one of her minions has done it for him. I kind of feel sorry for him. She sucked him back in, and he'd gone willingly. But I'll give it to the woman: She has that power over people. And not just over the ones she is having sex with.

As if he senses me stalking him, my phone lights up with a message from Jonathan for the first time in three days. I have yet to text him back. But how does one even respond to an apology text from her ex about impregnating his ex while you are still dating? I mean, it's too absurd. And mortifying. I have felt too furious and embarrassed to even formulate a response. Plus, honestly, I haven't forgiven him. Not yet. I raise the spoon to my mouth and then set it back down. I am angry, sure. But not raw, vulnerable, or heartbroken.

And, well, that makes me sad. Where was my *heartbreak*? Had I felt devastated when our relationship ended, even before this fiasco? Sad it hadn't worked out, sure. Wallowing in my faults and flaws, maybe. But never devastated.

I sigh and read Jonathan's text: *I'm going to give you your space because I know it isn't fair for how we proceed to be on my terms, but please know I'm here when you want to talk. I really am sorry. I know it didn't work out between us for other reasons, but there is still no excuse for what I did.*

It's a nice text. The next one is something closer to comical.

Allison and I would really like to fix this. Please let us know how we can accommodate your best transition back into us all working together.

"Fat chance, buddy," I say out loud. That is when I realize Salt isn't at my feet. And I haven't left him in the yard. As if on cue, he starts barking in the living room. "Salt!" I call.

He is sitting at the foot of the couch, looking directly at its center, barking furiously. A creepy feeling washes over me.

"What's the matter, buddy?"

I look under the couch, on it, behind it, over it.

"Salt," I say, "there's nothing there."

"Nothing you can see," a voice behind me says, making me scream.

I turn, hand on my heart. "Anderson, you are going to give me a heart attack. You have to knock!"

He looks confused. "Why?"

"Because in New York someone who randomly walks in your house is probably there to strangle you."

I realize this is another thing on a long list of things one should not say to a child.

"Sorry," he says sheepishly, standing just inside the doorway. "I'm just going to my sleepover, and I wanted to see if you needed anything before I went."

Now I feel bad because that is so adorable I can't stand it. "Hey, want some cereal before you go?"

"What kind?"

"Lucky Charms." I make a mental note to buy something green the next time I hit the store.

Anderson looks down at my full bowl. "Wait. Are you having Lucky Charms for dinner? Aren't you supposed to be a grown-up?"

"Supposed to be," I say as I fill a bowl for Anderson, who starts eating so ferociously it's somewhat alarming. "But it hasn't quite taken." He shoots me a thumbs-up as he slurps.

"Hey, does your dad know you're here?" I ask between his crunches.

He points to his mouth like it's too full for him to answer, which is a hard no.

"Anderson!" I scold.

A light rap on the back door is followed by Bowen's voice. "Keaton!"

"Come in!" I call.

I raise my eyebrow at Anderson, and he looks guilty.

"Oh, hi," I say. "I was just asking your son if you knew he stopped by."

He looks at Anderson. "Why aren't you at your sleepover? I thought when I said you could walk that meant you were going straight there."

He gives Bowen a knowing look and gestures toward me like, *Duh. Someone has to check on her.*

"I'm okay, Anderson, but thank you."

He sighs dramatically as he gets up. "If you need help with the ghosts, you know where to find me."

Bowen looks at me curiously as Anderson walks past us. "Hey," Anderson says, picking up the notepad by the phone. "What does this mean?"

"What does what mean?"

I turn as Anderson reads, "There's a place that I know, it has called out to me, where the sea meets the sky, and the sky meets the sea."

I look down at the notepad in his hands, resisting the urge to tell him to *put it down*. "Huh. I don't know." I've read enough now to know that it is my grandfather's handwriting. "My grandfather liked to write. Probably just something he scribbled." *Before he died in a tragic, unsolved accident.* But before I can ponder further, the phone on the wall rings, Salt starts barking again, and Anderson says, "See you tomorrow!"

I'm not going to answer the phone with Bowen standing right there. It is certainly a spam call, right? But, well, it is so insistent, and I want to feel what it's like to talk on an old-timey corded phone. I put my finger up to Bowen and answer, "Hello?"

"Wow! I haven't called this number in forty years!"

"Hi, Uncle Lon," I say, smiling at his voice.

"How's it coming?"

"Well, kind of slow." I wrap the phone cord around my finger and smile at Bowen. "But I'm putting the house on tour."

"You're doing what?" Lon and Bowen ask at the same time.

"Yeah, I thought it would be good to get some foot traffic before we put it on the market. I thought you'd be thrilled."

Lon says, "Keaton, you can't show people the house before it's in perfect shape. That's a terrible idea," right as Bowen says, "You let those ladies talk you into that? Come on, Keaton. Be smarter. Next thing you know you'll be chairing the parade committee."

"Who is that?" Lon asks.

"My neighbor," I say, taking in Bowen's jeans, cowboy boots, and button-down. He is freshly shaven, and his hair is clean but tousled. *My hot, hot neighbor.*

"Is this tour thing going to stop your progress?" Lon asks. "Are you throwing things away?"

"Honestly, Lon, I'm not making much progress. I can't bring myself to do it. But I can't think that the tour will be a problem. There's so much to do here. It might actually help bring in potential buyers." I look at Bowen. "Hey, I'll call you later, okay? We can go over the plans for the house when I'm less . . . busy."

I hang up. "Sorry. My uncle."

"Keaton, you can't just say yes to everything everyone wants from you all the time."

This strikes me as funny since this man doesn't know me at all. He looks down at my cereal bowl. "That's not a proper dinner." He pauses as if considering something. "I'm going to get wings at Stillwater. Come with me."

I want to be cool, to be less eager to follow him basically anywhere, but, well, here we are. "Okay," I say.

"What did I just say?" he says. "You can't do everything everyone wants all the time."

I smile. "I heard you. But wings trump cereal. So . . ."

He smiles too. Salt rushes to him, jumping up.

"I'm sorry," I say. "Down, Salt!"

He listens . . . Well, not at all. Bowen rubs his head and his ears. "Hey, buddy. You're just excited to see me, aren't you?"

I kiss his little furry head and say, "I'll see you soon. Be good. Don't eat the couch. Do scare away the ghosts."

We walk across the street and get situated at the outdoor bar under the covered porch area of a restaurant right across the street labeled "Front Street Grill." I make a note that, to the locals, this is "Stillwater." I order wings and champagne. Bowen orders wings and beer.

"Wings and champagne?" he asks when the bartender leaves.

"Everything and champagne," I say.

He nods. "So what brings you to Beaufort?"

"Well, the house," I say, as if that's obvious.

Bowen eyes me. "So what brings you to Beaufort?"

I laugh. "Am I that transparent?"

"Nah. It's just that house has been empty for almost fifty years, so . . . Forgive me for assuming you're fleeing, but, well, I get the feeling you are fleeing."

"Just the vibe I was hoping to give off."

I fill him in on Allison and Jonathan and my job and the whole sad story. I don't know why I'm spilling my guts to this stranger, but I guess it's mainly because after the house is sold I'll probably never see him again.

Our drinks arrive and he says, "Well, cheers to fake assholes getting their comeuppance."

"I like that. Cheers." We clink our glasses and each take a sip. "They want me to come back," I say. "Which makes me happy, because I feel like they probably can't run the company without me."

"And will you go?" Bowen asks.

"The obvious answer is of course not, but the honest answer is that it wouldn't be completely off the table. I love my work there; I love my team. I'm mad at Jonathan for cheating on me, but we broke up a month before I knew anyway, so do I even have a right to be mad?"

Bowen stops, his beer inches from his mouth. "Uh, yeah. He impregnated his ex-wife while you were together. You get to be mad about that."

I smile. "Okay, thanks. But I'd already come to terms with the fact that, as much as I wanted to, I didn't actually love Jonathan. He is, like, the guy I *should* want to marry."

"But you don't want to marry him."

I laugh. "Well, certainly not now."

"No, I get it," he says. "Which is why I haven't dated much in the years since my ex split—"

"Your ex split?" I ask casually.

He shakes his head. "Don't do that. You have breakfast with the gossip squad every morning. I know you know about my ex. I know you know every person in this town's entire bag of dirty laundry."

The champagne bubbles tickle my throat, and I give him my most gleeful expression. "I do! I totally do! It's so awesome to be at the popular table."

"So I don't need to tell you about my sparse failed dating attempts. You probably already know."

I shake my head, wondering how he has failed relationships. I mean, he's stony. But, after Jonathan the king of feelings, I don't hate that about him. Not that this is a date. Obviously not. "I actually don't know, but how about this: I won't show you mine if you won't show me yours."

He laughs. "That sounds like a really good plan."

The bartender sets down the wings, and Bowen orders us two more drinks. I'm kind of self-conscious that my hot neighbor is going to see me with sauce all over my face, but he dives in with such gusto I decide I don't care.

"You have the cutest kid in the world," I say, changing the subject.

He wipes his mouth with one hand, holding a wing in the other. "Yeah. I'm pretty sure he has already met his first great love."

"Aw, really. Who?"

"You!" he says, laughing.

I laugh too. "No. He's just really protective of me. It's so sweet. He's going to be a very good man. You can just tell."

"Well, thanks for saying that, because sometimes it feels touch-and-go. I'm sure you know that I've had him alone since the day he came home from the hospital. I wouldn't have survived it without Violet, Arlene, Betty, and Suzanne."

I take a sip. "Bet they don't let you forget it either."

"Not for a minute. But my parents were both working at the time, and I obviously have a job, so I don't know what I would have done without them during Anderson's early years."

It occurs to me that I don't know what his job is. From the build and look of him, he seems like he'd either be a hot fireman or a hot handyman—although I guess neither of those involve a boat and I know he works on a boat. Or a boat handyman or water fireman. (Was that a thing?) I almost don't want to ask in case he isn't one of those things. I don't want to ruin it. But now it seems weird not to ask. I sigh. "What do you do?"

He examines me. "I don't have to tell you if it's so odious to uncover my basic life details."

I roll my eyes. "You don't have to be so dramatic."

"I work for UNC Marine Sciences. I'm a marine biologist."

"That's a real thing?" I ask, only half kidding.

"What?"

"Well, you know, it's like every kid's dream. They either want to be a ballerina, an astronaut, or a marine biologist. It's almost like it isn't a real job."

"Well, then," he says, taking another big bite of wing, "I guess you could say I'm living the dream."

He grins, and I raise my thumb to the corner of my mouth, indicating that he has a huge blob of sauce on his.

He reddens slightly and wipes his mouth. "Note to self: Never eat wings in front of a beautiful woman."

It takes me a minute to realize he means me. He thinks I'm a beautiful woman?

I shake my head. "Let me tell you, Bowen. The trick is to be who you are, eat what you like, laugh too loud, have opinions too big, from the very beginning. Then people know what they're in for from the jump."

"So that's the trick, huh?" he says.

I nod.

"So, Keaton, what's your biggest, most controversial opinion these days? Lay it on me."

Without even thinking, I say something I haven't even realized yet—at least, not consciously. "I have this weird feeling that my grandparents' death wasn't an accident."

It's only once I say it out loud that I start to believe it's true.

Becks

....

The Truly Lucky

JUNE 24, 1976

Tip: Champagne is a hostess's best friend. It pairs well with practically every dish, adds a general air of celebration to an evening, and tends to produce happy but not overly inebriated guests. I always have a case on hand. You never know when you might have something to celebrate. Or, more to the point, you never know when you might want to turn an ordinary day into a party.

When Becks got home, Townsend was ready and waiting to take her to the airport for a quick flight in their plane, as was their several-times-a-week routine. As she sat beside her husband in the cockpit, so close that her arm touched Townsend's, she said, over the thrum of the plane's propeller as they took off, "Do you remember the first thing we did when you got home from the war?"

Townsend laughed. "Remember? Of course I remember." He raised his eyebrows at her, and she swatted his arm. "Not *that*. After that."

The yoke was pulled toward Becks and Townsend and, even though it was close enough that she could fly too, she sat back and relaxed, watching as Townsend used the control wheel to bank left. She loved to be up here with her husband, a world away from any earthly problems. And, even though she could do it herself, Becks still loved it best when Townsend flew her.

"We went to the airport," he said, reminiscing. The Beaufort airport was four blocks from their house.

"That was when you told me you were going to teach me to fly."

He kissed her hand. "And now, Becks, I think you might be a better pilot than I am."

Becks rolled her eyes. Now *that* was absurd. Becks understood how to read an altimeter, an air speed indicator, the artificial horizon, and directional gyro in a functional way that allowed her to fly a plane. But Townsend was masterful in the air. He was a part of it in a way that Becks simply would never be.

She smiled, gesturing toward the clouds surrounding them. "And this is where you brought me that day."

Becks gazed out the window at her favorite part of the southern sky, where the clouds and the water became one. There was nothing around them. No people. No land in sight. They were truly one with nature. Before she flew herself, Becks often wondered how Townsend kept it straight, this vast expanse of blue, how he didn't become disoriented when it all united into one seamless being.

"Where the sky meets the sea," Townsend said, speaking her thoughts out loud, just like he had more than three decades ago that night he came home.

"Where the sky meets the sea," she whispered, trying not to get choked up, suddenly overcome with emotion. How many more times would she see this spot with her husband? How many more good days did she have? "I love you, Townsend," she said, squeezing his hand.

"I love you too, sweetheart," he replied.

When the summer was over, she knew, her bad days would likely outnumber her good ones; her illness would be impossible to hide. That was when she would tell Townsend. But not a minute before. She wanted their last summer together to be perfect.

Looking at the horizon line, so blue, so cohesive, she said, "It makes you feel small, doesn't it? The endless everything of the sea and sky and no land in sight?"

Townsend kissed her hand. "You could never be small. And it would take all the infinite everything of the sea and sky to hold the love I have for you." He sighed. "Becks, I live for this."

"For what?"

"For flying."

"I know, sweetheart." She knew Townsend had worried lately that he was reaching the age in which it was no longer responsible to fly. "Don't forget fishing and hunting. You live for those too," she half joked.

He nodded in agreement.

"Oh, Townsend, there's so much more to life than sport."

But even as she said it, she knew that, for her husband, life without sport wasn't life at all. And the unfortunate reality was that age would likely steal so much of what he loved from him, including her. She had imagined a world in which she could help him through that inevitable transition period as they both got older, would be by his side as they took up golf, maybe. But now she wouldn't be here to do that.

"Oh, I suppose you're right," he said. "Speaking of, who's coming on Saturday, my dear? And do you tell me the theme now or do I guess?"

Becks's melancholy was replaced by an electric zip of excitement. This was the best part of her week. She ignored that she had already told Townsend both the guest list and their connection. He'd probably been reading the paper and not paying attention.

"The Dodsons from Kinston, the Taylors from Goldsboro, the Corletts from Asheville, the Willises from here, and the Tylers from Bethel."

Townsend furrowed his brow. "I don't know the Dodsons from Kinston."

Becks peered at him. "Townsend, of course you do. Sammy Dodson shadowed you the summer before he went to medical school."

He paused a moment, then laughed sheepishly. "Oh, of course he did. I'm sorry, love. Seventy isn't as sharp as I'd like it to be."

It was an easy mistake to make. They did know an awful lot of people. "Guess what links them."

"They all went to the same college."

"No," Becks said. "But you're warm."

"Warm? How can I be warm?"

She laughed. "Just keep guessing."

"They all have the same profession? They all have children?"

Becks laughed again. "Well, yes, but I'd hardly call that a dinner party connection. That said, you are very, very hot now."

"Why, thank you."

Becks rolled her eyes and gestured for him to keep going as the plane made its descent back to the Beaufort airport. She heard the landing gear release and, as was her habit, felt a sigh of relief that they were landing safely.

"I was warm with college. I'm hot with them all having kids . . ."

As the wheels touched down on the runway with one of Townsend's signature, flawless landings, he exclaimed, "After this summer, they will all be empty nesters!"

Becks cheered over the roar of the plane skidding to a stop. "You are a genius!"

He leaned over to kiss her. "No. You, my dear, are a genius. Everyone thinks so."

"Not my mother," she muttered.

Townsend examined Becks's face. "I wasn't sure you'd want to talk about it, so I haven't asked. But . . ."

Becks shook her head, and Townsend said, seamlessly, "I thought maybe we could pick up some friends and go for a sunset boat ride? Take the good champagne?"

Perhaps that was the true glory of forty years of marriage, of knowing someone as deeply and intimately as you knew yourself: You knew when your spouse wouldn't want to talk, so you did something fun instead.

Becks was absolutely exhausted—something she was feeling more and more lately. But she could pretend. For Townsend. And she wondered if perhaps the pretending could help make it so; if she pretended to be well, she would continue to be well.

She kissed him. "I think that would be absolutely perfect." She lingered for a moment, pulled him close, breathed in the scent of him. Because how many more kisses would she get? How many more days would she have in the arms of the man who had stolen her heart from the moment she had met him?

Half an hour later, walking across the street to the dock, she laid eyes on one of the best things that came along with loving Townsend: Virginia. "My girl!" she squealed, suddenly energized. She raced across the street quicker than she thought possible to wrap her daughter in a hug. She pulled back to look at her, a vision of youth in rolled-up jean shorts paired with a tucked-in T-shirt, a long, sleeveless crocheted vest over top, and high-heeled clogs. Virginia wore the fashions right now so very well. "You look sensational," Becks said. *If there was ever a moment I needed my daughter, it was this one.*

Virginia smiled. "I just thought I'd come home for the weekend."

That, Becks knew, was code for she needed her laundry done, possibly some clothing alterations, and was also, in all likelihood, hoping that Becks would find a new coffee table for her apartment in D.C. But she would, of course. Anything to have her daughter home. Plus, Becks liked to be needed.

Townsend walked up the dock, waving. "Oh, good!" he called. "I was worried about how we'd possibly drink all this champagne."

Virginia walked to him, her clogs clonking along the dock, and scooted up under his arm. Patricia and Daniel arrived moments later, giving hugs all around. Virginia took off her shoes and held them in one hand as Townsend helped the ladies, one by one, on board.

On the boat, a shining display of polished teak and perfect craftsmanship, with her friends and daughter, Becks smiled, settling with Patricia at the front, Townsend driving, Virginia beside him on the captain's bench, and Daniel standing, holding on to the console. Townsend had poured them all a hearty glass of Taittinger before pulling away from the dock, and the champagne now bubbling in Becks's mouth gave the tiring day an exciting edge. She took a deep breath, inhaling the cooling night air out on the water. The hot summer day had given way to this crisp beauty, like it did almost every night. Patricia took a sip from her own glass and said, "So, Towns said you were going to see your mother?"

Becks grimaced. "Let's just say it didn't go well. It appears she still hasn't forgiven me."

Patricia sighed. "I can't imagine. I just can't imagine that my child could do anything that would make me stop speaking to her."

"Neither can I." Becks shook her head, turning to look at Virginia and thinking of Lon, her two miracle babies, who she loved with all her heart. It made her feel sorry for her mother because she had missed so much; she had sacrificed the magnificence of her grandchildren for a grudge. After leaving her mother's house, Becks had cried the entire car ride home. And then she had promised herself that in the short time she had left she wouldn't shed any more tears over the parents she had lost long ago. They had made their choices. She had made hers.

"Forty years later she is just as stubborn as she ever has been."

She silenced as Virginia approached. "You look radiant," Patricia said.

Virginia pushed the long, dark hair from her face. "I've been wanting to tell you ever since I got here: I have a *boyfriend*," she said, somewhat breathless.

"So, you mean, some lucky soul made it to the second date?" Patricia joked.

Virginia was very, very particular, and quick to find fault. She had plenty of first dates, but very few seconds.

"Is this the same boy you were telling me about last week?" Becks asked. She tried not to get attached to these poor men.

Virginia's eyes lit up as she turned to her mother. "Mom, you'll love Robert. He's handsome and smart and enlightened and everything."

Enlightened. Becks smiled, thinking at how this world had changed, at how this daughter was so different from her. She was so brave and forward-thinking—and searching for a man who was too. Becks was proud she'd finally found one.

"When can I meet him?" Becks asked. Her heart raced uncomfortably. Would she live long enough to meet her daughter's new beau? What if they ended up marrying? How would Virginia plan the wedding without her? She shook her head, as if physically shaking off those thoughts.

"It might be a little early," Virginia said. "But his family has a house in Atlantic Beach, and they've invited us to stay for an engagement party for one of his cousins in August. Could I bring him to a summer supper that weekend?"

Becks lit up. "That would be absolutely marvelous."

"Does he know what he's in for?" Patricia asked. "And do you know how you're setting yourself up? Once he's been to a Becks Saint James dinner party, that's what he'll expect from you."

Virginia smiled, taking a sip of champagne. "Well, whatever it takes."

Patricia and Becks shared a gleeful look before returning their attention to Virginia. "How are Mimi's wedding plans coming?" Becks asked.

Mimi was Virginia's friend, one of the first she had met when she moved to Washington. She had recently become engaged to a handsome young doctor, and her impending nuptials were all the buzz. Virginia's eyes went wide. "Well, they aren't actually. She called it off."

Becks tried not to look shocked. These things happened, of course. Not so much in her day. But maybe it was better to cancel than to endure divorce, which was becoming more and more common.

"Oh my goodness. Why?" Patricia asked.

Virginia leaned in, as if anyone could hear them over the rush of the wind. "Well, I'm not sure what will come of it—or if this is even true—but rumor has it that he killed a patient."

Patricia and Becks both gasped, and Becks said, "Oh, how awful. She would leave her fiancé over a medical mistake?"

Virginia scrunched her nose and said, conspiratorially, "Well, see, that's the thing: It wasn't a mistake."

Becks felt her own eyes go wide. "What do you mean, it wasn't a mistake?"

Virginia waved her hand. "Oh, it would be impossible to prove that he purposefully administered a lethal dose of morphine, of course. But I guess Mimi felt sure . . ."

Patricia's hand was over her mouth. Through her fingers, she said, "Will he go to jail?"

She shrugged. "I don't think so. For some reason, the family decided not to press charges, so there's not much to do. But all I know is that she broke up with him and he left town."

"Well, that is a real shame," Patricia said. "So he could be out there hurting other patients and no one would be the wiser."

The thought made Becks's heart race, but she took a deep breath. None of this affected her. Getting caught up in other people's dramas wasn't exactly the best use of her time these days.

Virginia pursed her lips. "Well, we all think Mimi is crazy. It might not even be true." She leaned in again. "And even if it is, he is so handsome it'd be worth the risk. He has these eyes that are literally the color of ice crystals, the clearest blue I've ever seen."

"Virginia!" Becks scolded.

"Maybe we don't know the whole story," Patricia said. She always worried that one day her husband could be accused of making a medical mistake. It was scary, when you thought about it, to have people's lives in your hands. Doctors were only human, after all. "I feel badly for him if this is all just gossip."

Virginia shook her head. "He'll be fine. He's from a small town in Kansas, and I'm sure he just went back home to the farm." She paused. "Although he once mentioned he hated that farm. He had this bat-shaped scar on his hand from a farming accident." She giggled and took the last sip of her champagne. "We called him Batman because of it. Hopefully he doesn't start killing off the local farmhands to avenge his injury."

Becks rolled her eyes at Patricia. "Great. My daughter has a crush on a murderer."

Virginia laughed and stood up. "Oh, mother, I'm only teasing. Refills?"

"I'll join you," Patricia said, walking with her to the back of the boat as Daniel met Becks on the bow. "MD Anderson has agreed to see you," he said, his voice slightly muted by the roar of the engine.

Becks sighed, sipping her champagne. "You can't just let a lady die in peace, can you?"

He gave her a withering glance. "Becks, please. At least tell Townsend soon. I can hardly be around him knowing this huge thing he doesn't know."

Becks crossed her arms. "Daniel, I'm not keeping things from Townsend. I'm protecting him."

Daniel laughed. "He's a grown man. He doesn't need your protection."

"Well, he will know soon enough, because I won't be able to hide it. Until then, let him be happy."

They both turned to look at Townsend, who was driving the boat, in his element, Virginia cozied up next to him on the bench seat once more. God, she loved those two. At least they'd have each other.

"He is a happy son of a bitch, isn't he?" Daniel remarked.

Becks teased, "And you, his best friend, want to take that away from him."

Daniel looked at Becks solemnly. "I think you know that I, his best friend, and a best friend of his wife, only want to soften the blow." He paused. "No. What I want is to find a solution, a miracle, a cure. I hope you know I would go to the ends of the earth to save you, Becks. The absolute ends of the earth."

Becks didn't want to cry again today. She felt quite out of tears at this point. So she just whispered, "I know that, Daniel. I know. If there was anything to be done, we would do it." She smiled. "I don't want to leave him. It's the worst part."

Although she knew her children would struggle in their own ways, Virginia was really coming into her own now. And Lon was his father's child, an avid sportsman, an outdoor enthusiast, fiercely independent. They both loved her, of course. They had good laughs and great memories and she had made taking care of them her life's most important mission. But they would be fine. They had busy lives and bright, shining futures. In the midst of living, they would forget that their mother had died too soon.

Still, she wasn't so sure about Townsend. She was his beating heart inside his chest. She knew it because he was the beating heart inside hers. He would often say that he was so grateful to be older, so happy that he would never have to live a single day without his true love. The idea of him going before her had always made her feel as though she would break in two. But, as women so often do, she knew she would rather bear that pain than make him feel it himself. So to know that their roles had now been reversed made her feel terribly guilty.

"Please take care of him, Daniel," she said to her friend. "Please take care of my love when I'm gone."

"He won't make it long without you," Daniel murmured, in a manner so succinct it took Becks's breath away. When he saw her tear up, he patted her arm. "Don't worry, Becks. It's a good thing."

She gave him a questioning look.

"Only the truly lucky are given the gift of dying from a broken heart."

It was the most beautiful thing Daniel had ever said.

....

Time Capsule

I am ashamed to admit that my progress on the house has slowed to a halt. Sure, I've managed to get it clean—or, at least, as clean as it can be. But it seems like every time I turn around, more dust has fallen despite my best efforts.

Between tearing through my grandfather's journals, slowly sifting through Suzanne's newspaper articles, replaying my night with Bowen in my head, and meeting the ladies for morning coffee, I've done very little in the way of actually clearing out the house. Plus, every time I attempt to sort through a drawer of photos or mementos, I get lost in the moment and end up putting everything back. Notifications from my organization app are clogging my email, but I—very unlike me—feel powerless to move forward.

Anderson has been a great distraction, coming by every day after camp to play with Salt and hang out with me. And, I have to admit, it seems like Bowen is making more excuses to come by too. But it has been nearly two weeks since our dinner, and he hasn't expressed any real interest in me since. I'm starting to wonder if our connection is one-sided.

So I am distracting myself from all this by continuing my culinary education. I have Becks's notebook open on the counter opposite from where I'm doing my mixing because I'm so afraid I'll get something on it. I've decided to make some cookies for Anderson (and, okay, yes, maybe Bowen) and have gathered the butter, brown sugar, white sugar, eggs, all-purpose flour, baking soda, vanilla, oats, and pecans I need for the recipe. I'm at the first step, and I'm already mystified. *Cream the butter.*

I rack my brain and look over to see Salt doing this adorable thing he does when he is stalking something and jumps with all four feet at the same time, looking like a little goat. "Okay," I say out loud, smiling when I realize he is pouncing on a pecan that has escaped from the counter. "What could it possibly mean to cream butter? Melt it? Like turn it into cream?"

I'm about to google it, but when I hear a knock and "Keaton!" I sigh. "Oh, thank goodness," I say as I make my way to the living room. The front door opens, and Violet pops her head in. She sticks an arm holding a Swiffer duster through the door. "I'm here!" she calls. "And I have reinforcements!"

"Please, come in!" This morning at coffee I was complaining about my ever-falling dust. I'm surprised that I feel relieved, not inconvenienced, at the sight of Suzanne, Betty, and Arlene filing in behind Violet. I have been leery of letting anyone in here, but these women knew and loved my grandparents—or, due to their age difference, at least looked up to them. They will handle their possessions with kid gloves. I put my hand to my heart. "Ladies, you don't have to clean my house," I say.

"Honey," Arlene says, "this house will be the biggest attraction on the Old Homes Tour by far. We are not cleaning for you; we're doing it for us."

"Exactly," Betty agrees. She is still wearing the sun visor. I'm beginning to wonder if it's like the story about the girl who always wore the ribbon around her neck and when her lover finally unties it, her head falls off. Does the visor somehow keep Betty's scalp intact? I make a mental note to ask Bowen. Just the idea of his laugh makes my stomach erupt in an ocean of butterflies. That's why, I suspect, my job hunt has been completely nonexistent. Every time I open my laptop to search for openings or polish my résumé, I'm consumed by thoughts of him. What if he had tried to kiss me after our dinner? What if, Anderson-free, he had ended up here? Although, I am sleeping in my mother's childhood bed, so, ew. Maybe I could have ended up there? It's just now occurring to me that I haven't actually seen the inside of his house. So, okay, maybe I'm not living the great love story my mind is playing after all.

All four ladies are staring at me expectantly. "You can feel free to get started if you like; I just want to get these cookies finished. But first, um, how does one cream butter?"

All the ladies laugh, and Arlene begins poking around inside cabinets as Betty looks over my shoulder at the open notebook. "Oh, you're making Becks's famous oatmeal cookies."

"She always kept dough in foil in the freezer," Violet says, "and if you dropped by unannounced, she'd cut a few slices and make fresh cookies."

I want to be like that. If only I knew how to cream butter. Arlene emerges from a cabinet holding a yellow hand mixer. She plugs it in and motions for me to step aside. She puts the two sticks of butter in the bottom of the metal mixing bowl and that million-year-old mixer roars to life. I'm amazed. Not one thing in this house has been broken except the now-fixed TV. The sound of the metal beaters clanging against the sides of the bowl isn't the best, but I go with it. "Honey, start pouring in the sugar a little at a time," she says over the noise. She moves the mixer to the side. I'm a little afraid the thing is going to chop my hand off, but Arlene is a pro and, a minute later, we have perfectly "creamed" the butter with sugar. I add the eggs and then the rest of the ingredients as Arlene mans the mixer. When she turns it off, I clap my hands. "Arlene! We have dough!"

I hear a thud at the back door followed by an impatient-sounding Anderson calling, "Keaton!"

"Come in, bud!" I call to him, and he appears in the kitchen.

"Did you hear the knock?"

I laugh. "I did!"

"You're baking?" Anderson asks. "I thought I was helping you organize today. My GoPro isn't going to buy itself, you know."

"Anderson, these cookies were going to be for you, but if you're that impatient . . ."

"Wait, wait!" he says. "I didn't know that!"

Arlene laughs. "I'll put these in the oven. You two get going."

"Okay," I say, taking a deep breath. "Anderson, you and I are going to start on the library today. We need to dust every book and shelf and dispose of anything moldy or disintegrating." We should donate the books in good condition to the library, but I can't bear the thought of dismantling all I have left of my grandfather quite yet.

"Ladies, maybe you could start on the dining room?" I say, turning to these four who I now actually consider my dear friends. I pause and bite my lip. "Because, well, I have a true confession."

Violet grins. "We don't judge."

Suzanne laughs. "What Violet means is we judge terribly harshly, but only behind your back."

They all laugh, and I join them. "Well, you might change your mind when I say this." I look sheepish. "I have never polished silver." It's kind of surprising, since my mother raised me to do everything by myself. But she didn't entertain much, and when she did, it was more of the paper-plate variety. I never gave polishing silver much thought but now, knowing that she was raised by Rebecca Saint James, queen of entertaining, I can't quite understand it.

Suzanne doubles over in laughter, as Betty guffaws. "Who raised you, child?"

"Can't cream butter, can't polish silver," Suzanne says. "This is Becks Saint James's granddaughter?"

I ignore her, but it does give me pause. How was my mother raised by this incredible hostess, yet she never hosted anything herself? And, furthermore, did that mean that the way of life my grandmother cherished so, that these women still practiced, was dying out? The thought filled me with sadness. "The dining room obviously has a lot of silver displayed," I say. "And Becks's dressing table has this pretty tray and crystal perfume bottles with silver tops."

"Oh, and that monogrammed cotton ball holder I positively covet," Arlene says.

I nod. They know this house better than I do. I think for a moment before I say what I've been contemplating, but then I decide to go for it. I can always change my mind. Becks's notebook is so detailed, and every time I read her handwriting, it makes me want to emulate her more and more. Plus, I mean, come on: I'm a marketing pro. And if I'm here to sell a house, this is marketing, plain and simple. "I was thinking that it might be really fun for the tour if we set the dining room table and decorate the house as though it's ready for one of Becks and Townsend's dinner parties."

Violet gasps, and I'm surprised to see her eyes fill with tears.

The other three nod in unison.

"That would be the loveliest tribute," Arlene says, seeming emotional too. "Your grandmother would be so proud."

My heart swells. I guess people like to make their grandparents proud, even in absentia?

"I have all the details in Becks's notebook, but you ladies know how to make this happen better than I do. I think polishing the silver might be the first step." I pause. "Oh, and, obviously, if you come across anything that seems pertinent to Becks and Towsend's disappearance while you're cleaning . . ."

They nod. I have a feeling my grandparents mean as much to them as to me, so I wipe my worries away that they will somehow destroy the evidence of my grandparents' lives . . . or deaths.

"Okay, Anderson," I say. "You and me, buddy." He follows me to the dark-paneled library and I inhale, relishing the scent of leather and tobacco and, now that I have done more cleaning, Old English. "How was camp today?" I ask.

"So cool! We went surfing. I can totally shred, you know," he says seriously.

"I never had any doubt."

He picks up one of a small pair of antique samurai swords. They are encased in beautiful ebony sheathes, each adorned with a red tassel.

"Do you have a best friend?"

He nods absentmindedly while examining the sword. "Three of them. Two in my class. They all go to camp with me. We call ourselves the brother boys because none of us have a real brother."

"That's cool," I say. "I have a brother."

"I'm jealous," he says. "I wish I had a brother."

"Friends can be so good they're like family," I say. "So maybe the brother boys kind of are your real brothers, after all?"

Anderson shrugs. "Yeah, I guess so." He slides the cover off the sword, and, as the blade gleams in the light, I scold, "Anderson! That might be sharp. Put that down."

Not listening *at all*, he touches his finger to the point and sucks in his breath, wincing. "Oh my gosh," he says, holding the sword up to the light. "There's blood on this."

"Oh no! Did you cut yourself?" I move closer to him, and he hands me the blade.

"No, I mean, it's really old, dried blood."

I squint at the sword and find it unsettling that he appears to be right. But, to ease his mind, I say, "No way. That's just rust."

He raises his eyebrows skeptically as I put the cover back on and change the subject, more for me than for him. I point to a large book-shelf to the right of the fireplace. "This is going to be your shelf to go through, okay?"

He nods. "Okay."

I pull the first book out. "You're going to check this." I turn to the copyright page. "Wait. You can read, right?"

He rolls his eyes. "Kea-ton."

I laugh. "Okay. So right here it says if something is a first printing or first edition. Those you want to keep even if they're moldy. Or if there's a signature."

"Wow," Anderson says, looking at the copyright page. "So does this mean that this book was printed in 1932?"

I smile. "Yeah. Pretty cool, huh?"

"Really cool," he echoes.

"And, sometimes, the book might not be signed by the author, but someone wrote a little message inside for Christmas or something. We want to keep those too."

"Okay," he says. "So I'll take the whole shelf out, sort it into keep and throwaway piles, wipe the keep books down, clean the shelf, and then put them back."

My eyes widen. "Dang, Anderson. That's impressive. That's exactly what I want you to do."

"I'm ten, Keaton. I'm not an idiot."

A couple hours into our work, Anderson and I are really getting into the swing of things when I hear a knock at the back door, and I hope I yell "Come in!" loudly enough that whoever it is can hear. And I laugh at myself, at how quickly I'm assimilating. But with Anderson here all the time, the ladies here now, and Alex the pirate always doing whatever he does to keep this ancient house standing—never mind the general fresh air, open-door, friendly vibe of this whole town—I'm becoming less and less concerned about random murderers walking in.

"Hi, honey," I hear Violet say. "Are you here to vacuum?"

A moment later she and Bowen are in the library. He smiles, and my heart thumps. *Stop it*, I tell myself. *You're in Beaufort to get in and out, no complications.*

"Anderson, Dr. Scott is grilling steaks tonight. That okay?" Violet asks.

"Yes!" he says, jumping up off the stool he is standing on in what looks to be a death-defying leap. But he lands with little fanfare.

"Anderson has dinner with Violet and Dr. Scott every week," Bowen fills in for me.

"So Dad can drink beer with his friends," Anderson says matter-of-factly.

I laugh and Bowen says, "Exactly. We have a big group, but we're a little low on ladies if you want to join us? I think Amy would appreciate it."

"Amy, like Dockhouse Amy?"

"The very same one," Violet says. "Although she's kindergarten teacher Amy too. The Dockhouse is her summer and weekend job."

"A night out sounds fun." I look seriously at Anderson. "I think our work here is done for the day. Enjoy your steak."

I corral the ladies and tell them goodbye, feed Salt his dinner, and Bowen and I walk out into the night air. "It's amazing how every night is cool no matter how hot the day is," I say.

Bowen chuckles. "You haven't been here in August yet."

"Lucky for me, I won't be."

I look up to see his face cloud, which surprises me. I wish I could take it back—I don't really believe that I'll be lucky to leave here. It's moments like these, the small ones, that I realize how much this quirky little town has embraced me, made me feel so included. The realistic part of me knows that there's no job for me here, no future. But the romantic part of me is wondering how I will possibly ever leave.

Especially now that Beaufort is hitting its summer stride. The docks are full tonight, with huge fishing boats, sailboats, and a powerboat or two. More sailboats are moored in Taylor Creek, between the boardwalk and the island. The setting sun colors the calm water pink and orange, and I have the most overwhelming urge to dive into it, to be a part of all the colors nature can make. It's pure magic here. The breeze blows and horses graze on the island across from us. People meander up and down the boardwalk, walking in and out of stores, eating ice cream. No one is in a hurry. Everyone is happy.

"Is this real life?" I ask. I take a deep breath, wanting my lungs to fill with this fresh air, wanting to make a memory I can carry back to crowded city streets, honking taxis, and . . . a life that's fallen completely apart. Before I can ruminate on the job I haven't found, the apartment I haven't looked for, and all my other stressors, I make myself stop. *Be in the moment.*

"My parents thought I was crazy when I moved here from Charlotte," Bowen says. "They told me I couldn't raise a kid here. It was too small. There weren't enough opportunities." He pauses, looking out over the water. "But I guess the longer I've been here, the more I realize that getting to live a life on the water is an opportunity in and of itself. I mean, no, Anderson doesn't spend his summers at STEM camp. But he can call the birds by name. He knows every fish. He paddleboards after school."

I smile. "I would call those opportunities. For sure."

"Not Kerry," he says. Although the Dames have mentioned her, this is the first time I've heard him say her name. "She wasn't happy here. But, looking back, I don't think she would have been happy anywhere back then."

Before I can ask him anything more, "Keaton!" rings out in the night air. I look over at Black Sheep, a gourmet pizza place on the water, and see Alex the pirate—miraculously not wearing pirate garb—Amy, and two men I don't know sitting at a big outdoor table.

I wave, and Amy jumps up and hugs me. "Finally! Another woman!"

Bowen introduces me to Jimmy, whose paint-covered hands tip me off to the fact that he's an artist, and Clayton, a chef at an upscale restaurant called Aqua the ladies have raved about but I have yet to visit. "This is my night off," he says.

I nod. As we all sit down, Bowen makes eye contact with the waitress and mouths *champagne* as he points at me. He turns. "That's what you want, right? You did say 'champagne and everything.'"

I smile, thinking of my grandmother and her proclamation that champagne turns an ordinary night into a celebration. And a warmth washes over me that Bowen remembers this detail.

"So what do you do?" Clayton asks.

I feel a stab in my heart. Even in a town of interesting, eclectic people, this is still a question I have to answer. "Right now, I'm getting my grandparents' house ready to put on the market," I say.

"The Saint James place," Amy fills in.

"Oh, cool," Jimmy says. "Alex is always talking about that house. I did a painting of it once." He puts his finger to his mouth like he's thinking.

"He loses paintings all the time," Amy says, rolling her eyes. "Fills rental storages with them and then loses track." There's an affection in her voice that indicates there's something between them.

"Well, if you find it . . ." I trail off. If he finds it, what? I probably won't have a place for it, and my mom won't want the reminder.

"Keaton was in marketing with All Welcome before coming here," Bowen says, and I nod.

The guys look confused, but Amy brightens. "Damn. Really? I've read all of Allison's books. What was working with her like?"

"A disaster," Bowen says under his breath.

But I find myself smiling. "Nothing's perfect," I say. "Allison is like everyone else. I mean, she has flaws and insecurities."

"And deep, diagnosable narcissism," Bowen says, taking his beer from the waitress. I shake my head at him in irritation, but also, I feel that warmth again. It's sweet that he's so protective of me.

"I can look back and think that I kind of helped create her, you know?" I say. "I worked with her for years, even before Allison was . . . well, Allison. Making a person into a huge brand like that is really rewarding, super fulfilling." I can feel the grin on my face. I should have bad feelings about all of it, but, no matter how it happened, I know how good my work was there; I'm proud of what I accomplished.

I take my glass from the waitress when she brings it over, and Alex says, "Damn. You feel the same way about marketing that I feel about pirate tours."

Clayton nods. "You're all lit up."

I look down into my champagne, realizing how much I miss the rush of creating something new, of building something great.

Jimmy raises his glass. "To Keaton finding her next great thing."

"To a woman in the group!" Amy enthuses.

"To opportunities," Bowen says, locking his eyes on mine. "May we be brave enough to pursue them."

"Hear hear!" I say.

We all clink glasses, and I take a sip, the bubbles filling my mouth, as Clayton says, "While we're waxing poetic about our dream jobs, let me tell you about mine. So last night, this lady sent her meal back three times. When I came out from the kitchen after the third time to find out what was wrong, she was like, 'Young man, I'm going to teach you how to prepare a proper steak.' And I was like, 'Ma'am, you ordered duck.' "

We all laugh, and I look over at Bowen and then the water. It is a perfect summer night. I haven't felt this good or this free in quite some time. I'll probably never meet Bowen's ex, but as I look around at the smiling faces at this table, I have to think that she must have been crazy to have left all this. His eyes glint as they catch mine, and I can't imagine ever walking away.

Final Destination

FRIDAY, JULY 2, 1976

Tip: Virginia, I hope you've seen this through example. But your dinner table is where you share your values. It's the perfect place to prove that, at our core, we are all very much the same. Every time you host, you have the golden opportunity to bring someone in who might ordinarily be left out. It's a simple thing, but it does change lives. I have seen it with my own eyes. I believe it with all my heart.

Becks's favorite day of the month was book club day. She and her friends Patricia, Ellen, Sarah, and Laura met once a month to talk about great classics, new reads, and town happenings—obviously. They'd been doing it for the past fifteen years. Becks loved being immersed in a novel and today's read, *Ordinary People*, was no exception. Laura had gotten early copies for them from her brother in publishing, making it all the more exciting. As Sarah was saying, "I just didn't respect the dissolution of Beth and Calvin," and Laura countered, "But, Sarah, they weren't in *love*; this was a happy ending,"

Becks's mind wandered to her own love, to October 1935, when her life had suddenly, agonizingly changed.

After a whirlwind few months of dating, Townsend had broken up with her with no warning at all. Becks was not only heartbroken; she was mystified.

Becks knew she wasn't the only woman in the world to ever be broken up with. Even still, she found it nearly impossible to get up and go teach every morning, to stand in front of a class of kindergarteners and draw letters and talk about a butterfly's metamorphosis, to read fairy tales of love and redemption when, as she now believed, love did not exist. She was only twenty-two years old and, already, she felt like her life was over.

Every day after school, she went to her parents' house and cried to her mother over the man she loved, who had discarded her like an out-of-fashion sports coat.

"I just don't see how it can possibly work," was all he had said after he unceremoniously told her he thought they should stop seeing each other. She was sitting on the back steps of the house she shared with three other single female teachers, getting some fresh air after an entire day in the classroom. Townsend was coming to take her to a new film that had just been released. She had been expecting a proposal any day. To say Becks felt blindsided was an understatement.

"Why?" she had asked, immediately on the defensive. In that moment, their love story flashed before her eyes. She could feel Townsend's arms wrapped around her on the beach as they sat under an umbrella, only days after they had first met. He had kissed her for all the world to see, unafraid of the appraising looks of strangers, whispering, "All this time, Becks, I was only waiting for you."

But he hadn't been waiting. He had been—just like everyone warned—having a good time until he tired of her. *Do you really think a twenty-nine-year-old man wouldn't be married by now if he wanted to be?* friends asked. But she had been so sure that he was her destiny, that he was the one her heart had been waiting for, she couldn't even hear their warnings. She heard them loud and clear now.

"Becks, I'm sorry," Townsend had said. "I think the differences in our religious beliefs will just be too big a hurdle for our families to cross. And I know this is my fault. I should have told you from the beginning I was Catholic. I kept it from you because I wanted you for myself, and that was selfish."

Well, yes. Yes, it was. And, sure, when Townsend revealed this truth to Becks on their fourth date, she had been shocked and worried. How would she tell her Methodist minister father? But Townsend had been the one to convince *her* that it would be okay, that they could weather this storm. He had been the one to convince her to take a chance on them. And she had; she did. The truth of the matter was, it was too late now. Becks's heart already belonged to Townsend. "Sure, maybe," she agreed. "But, Townsend, none of that matters now because I love you."

She stood so that she could be eye level with him, so that she could reassure him over whatever crisis of confidence he was having. She kissed him softly, not letting him pull away when he tried to. "This is me, Towns," she said. "I can see in your face you don't really want to do this."

He looked her in the eye, finally. "I don't want to do it," he said. "But, Becks, it's the only way you'll be happy."

"It is certainly not the only way!" she protested. "We tell our families the truth, and they can support us or not!" The idea of losing her family terrified her. But the idea of losing Townsend terrified her more. "I can only really be happy if I'm with you."

He kissed her hand. "I will always love you," he said. "In fact, I love you enough to let you go. I know it hurts now, but it's for the best, before we can't turn back. You'll see."

Looking into his face, Becks felt that this wasn't Townsend at all, that this wasn't coming from him. As he turned, she wanted to call after him, but she felt too weak, like her voice had simply disappeared, just like the Little Mermaid her students loved so much.

Months of love had all boiled down to this one sad, unexpected moment. Lying on the couch the next night, her head in her mother's lap, she said, for what felt like the millionth time, "I know something happened, Mother. I know it did. Townsend didn't just change his mind. Someone or something *made* him change his mind."

"There, there," her mother had said. "The reason doesn't matter, darling. What matters is that it's better you know now. If he wasn't serious about marriage, he wasn't the one for you. He did you a favor."

"This does not feel like a favor," Becks said, tears soaking her mother's skirt.

"I know it hurts now, sweetheart, but every day will get a little better. And then you'll meet someone new, have a new love in your life. And you'll look back and realize that this was all meant to be, that Townsend Saint James was merely a stop on your journey, not your final destination."

Becks wanted to argue that she didn't want another man, that Townsend was her one and only. Her friends came over to try to cheer her up; her mother made all her favorite foods in an attempt to rekindle her appetite. And while she was grateful, none of it particularly helped.

In fact, she was surprised that it was her father who finally gave her some clarity on the situation. Almost a month after the breakup, Becks, who was convinced that time would never heal this wound, was helping her mother dry the dinner dishes. She knew she needed to go back to her own house tomorrow—to school, to her job—but she was tired, and driving all the way back to her house seemed too hard. Plus, staying in her childhood room was such a balm to her aching soul. She wasn't so alone here.

Her father came back from his after-dinner walk, kissed her mother, who was going up for her bath, and said, "Rebecca, why don't you sit on the porch with me."

Her father had been tight-lipped about her breakup, but she had only assumed that fathers weren't really made for soothing their daughters' heartbreak.

She followed him outside, and he sat down in one of their rocking chairs and lit his pipe. She sat beside him, taking in the warm scent of tobacco that would always remind her of home, of him. "Daddy," she scolded, "you aren't supposed to be smoking with your heart."

He waved his hand. "Do you think if smoking were bad for you so many doctors would do it?"

Becks did suppose that was true. But still. Her father had been having heart trouble, and she wanted him to take any and all precautions.

"Becks, Townsend came to see me."

She gasped and sat up straighter, turning her body toward him. "When? Today?"

He shook his head, fiddling with his pipe. "No, sweetheart. About a month ago."

Becks felt light-headed. She knew instantly her father was the cause of their breakup. She could already feel the anger rising in her. But this was her father, her minister, too, and she must be respectful at all costs. "What did he say, Daddy?" she whispered.

He turned to look at his daughter and put his large, worn hand over her much smoother, smaller one. "Becks, sweetheart, did you know he's a Catholic?"

Her face reddened. She had been raised not to date a Catholic, and certainly not to marry one. Theological texts—and even a popular novel, *Mixed Marriage*—had warned of the dangers. But then, she began to think: *Why* was that the rule? She understood bedtimes and vegetables at dinner. But why couldn't she love a Catholic man? Or speak her mind? Or stand up for herself, for heaven's sake? What kind of rules were those? "Well, I do now, Daddy. I didn't at first. But now I love him. I want to marry him."

Her father chewed on the end of his pipe. "Becks, honey, I know you think that now. He's a handsome doctor, and he's tricked you into thinking he can give you some sort of life that you want."

Now she was furious again. *Tricked her?* Like she was a child who didn't know the difference between true love and a silly game?

"But you don't understand how life would be for the two of you in a mixed marriage," he continued. "You'd have to raise your children in the Catholic church and your marriage would be a civil one, never blessed in the eyes of God. Not to mention what people would say."

In that particular moment, Becks very much did not care what people said.

"No, sweetheart," he went on, "you haven't seen what I've seen. These marriages, the few of them I've been privy to, have been doomed from the start. Marriage is hard under the right circumstances. Why would you want to make it any harder?"

Rebecca Bonner had never talked back to her father in twenty-two years. This was the moment when all that changed. "Daddy," she said, "you stand in that pulpit every week and preach that we should love our neighbor, that we should love our enemies, that we should try to bring others over into the right ways of the Lord. You stand there and tell us to be kind and inclusive, to invite the poor to dinner and minister to the sick, the imprisoned, the widows, the orphans. And now you're telling me that the man I love isn't suitable for me because he's *Catholic*? Is that the real message here, Daddy? Love everyone but the Catholics?"

He looked stunned. But also disappointed. "Rebecca, I am not getting into a theological discussion that will be over your head. But I will tell you that if you think it's bad on our side, it's a million times worse on the other. Protestants aren't wild about intermarrying, but Catholics prevent it at all costs. Do you think Townsend's parents would ever approve of this?"

She presumed they would not.

"Sweetheart, I don't want to strain your relationship with your mother, so I'll let this be our secret. She would be very disappointed."

Becks stood. She couldn't continue this conversation. It already felt like the whole world was against her and Townsend, but that felt like nothing compared to the disapproval of her father. Her view of her father, who had always been the pinnacle of wisdom and kindness, understanding and trust, had changed in this moment. She knew that society looked down on mixed marriages. But what about real, true love that you knew you couldn't live without? That made you both better people? Isn't that what God really wanted?

Becks drove home that night feeling a mixture of sadness, anger, and relief. Townsend wanted to marry her. It was her father who had stopped it. She wanted to go to him, or, at least, call him. But it was terribly improper for a woman to call a man. And she couldn't very well just show up at his house. But then Becks had an idea.

The next morning, she called in sick to school. She put on her favorite blue polka dot dress with the white collar, which had three buttons down the center, and a belt that cinched her waist. She applied her makeup just so, fixed her hair, and spritzed perfume on her neck. She buckled the Mary Janes with the little bow and the kitten heel she had purchased with her first real paycheck.

She sat in a small waiting room and was then led into a room where, even though she wasn't sick, she still sat on the table. When Townsend walked in, handsome and confident in his doctor's jacket, he stopped in his tracks. Then he ran to her.

"Becks! " he exclaimed. "Are you okay?"

He was close enough that she could hold the end of his stethoscope, place it on her chest. "Do you have anything for a broken heart?" she asked.

He looked at her sadly. "If I did," he whispered, emotion lacing his voice, "I would already have given it to myself."

"My father told me about your visit," she said. "And I'm here because I don't know if you still love me—"

"I do, Becks!" he interrupted. "I love you with all my heart."

She smiled. "Well, in that case, I'm here to tell you that I choose you."

"What?"

"I choose you. Over my family. Over my church. Over any other life I might have had. Because I don't want to be in a world that you are not in. I want to be with you and that is that."

It was the bravest thing she had ever said, and certainly the most forward. Women weren't supposed to speak their minds, announce their feelings. They were to wait coyly while the man said what he wanted. But the last eighteen hours or so had changed Becks's mind about pretty much everything she had ever known.

"Becks," Townsend said, breathless, "I can't ask you to choose me over your family. I would never make you do that."

"You didn't ask me," she said. Plus, no matter what her daddy had said, Becks believed her family loved her enough that this would be forgiven.

Townsend shook his head. "Becks, you don't understand what you're getting into, not really. I broke up with you to protect you. Nothing has changed."

"The thing that has changed," Becks said, resolutely, gathering all her courage, "is that the month we've spent apart has given me time to realize that I don't want to live without you. That's the bottom line. The rest we'll figure out." When he didn't say anything she whispered, "That is, of course, if you still want to be with me."

Becks held her breath, waiting for his response. Townsend just stood there, looking at her, searching her face as though searching for an answer. Just as she'd resolved that it was all over, he reached for her hand. "Becks," he said, "the day we broke up, I took all my savings and bought the best, most beautiful diamond that I thought you would love. It was my sign of faith in us, my good luck charm. I've kept it with me every minute since in the hopes that you would come back to me. And if you didn't, I knew I'd be alone forever."

She smiled, so overcome that she wasn't the only one who felt this deep, poignant love. "So what are you saying?" she whispered.

"What I'm saying is that I have kept that ring in my pocket just in case." He got down on one knee. "What I'm saying is that the last few weeks have shown me that I don't ever want to live without you, Rebecca Bonner. I knew from the moment I laid eyes on you that there was something about you that completed something in me, and you have proven that every second since. I want to take care of you. I want to love you. I want to have children with you, and I don't give a damn what church pew they sit in on Sunday mornings. All I care about is that you're their mother, that we make a life together, that I get to be by your side until my dying breath."

He pulled the ring out of his pocket and Becks had to cover her mouth. It was the most beautiful ring she had ever seen—and certainly the biggest. A large, sparkling center stone set in a filigree setting with diamonds inside it, and a small row of rubies lined the top and bottom.

"I didn't know diamonds like that existed."

"I didn't know women like you existed," he said. "Becks, until I met you, I was content to be alone forever. But now that I know you, I have to be with you. So please, please, Becks Bonner, be my wife. Will you marry me?"

How concerned he looked about her answer made her smile. "Yes!" she practically squealed. "Yes, I will marry you! I cannot wait to marry you!"

Townsend slipped the ring on her finger, and she wrapped her arms around his neck as he stood. He lifted her into the air and spun her around, kissing her before setting her down. "I love you, Becks," he said. "I wanted so badly to fight for you, but I couldn't. It wouldn't have been right. I knew this had to be your decision. I prayed every night you would come back to me."

"I love you, too," she said. "And I prayed the whole way here that you would still choose me."

They kissed again, and, while Becks knew she wouldn't get her dream wedding in her hometown church, that she wouldn't dance with her father or cry with her mother if she made this choice, none of that was as important to her as being with Townsend. And it struck her that God didn't seem to care that she was a Methodist and he was a Catholic. She and Townsend had prayed for the same thing, and

He had answered them. If that wasn't a sign that their marriage was meant to be, Becks didn't know what was.

Forty-one years later, it was still the best decision she'd ever made. And that was why, now that she knew the end was coming, she also knew she had to do everything she could to make sure Townsend was taken care of after she was gone. Townsend, and the community they both loved, the place that had loved them and become their family when she had lost hers. This town was part of Townsend's family's history, for generations and generations, and, once they had married, it had become part of hers too. She took her commitment very seriously.

Surrounded by women and cigarette smoke, Pink Squirrels in hand, Becks was trying not to listen too intently as her book club discussed *Ordinary People*'s themes of overcoming loss—and the desperate toll such a thing can take on families. That was hitting just a little too close to home. So close, in fact, that she reached over and took a cigarette out of Patricia's pack, lighting it with the mother-of-pearl lighter on the end table.

Patricia raised her eyebrows at her friend, but didn't say anything. Becks hadn't smoked for a dozen years, quitting in 1964 when the surgeon general released a statement that smoking caused lung cancer. But she was dying anyway. Why not enjoy every moment?

Becks shrugged at her best friend as Ellen, the optometrist's wife and Becks's first friend in Beaufort, said, "Okay, well, I don't have anything else to say about the book. Anyone else?"

"I think we've covered it," Laura said.

Sarah nodded. "Well, then, on that note . . ." She leaned in closer. "Has anyone heard that the Historic Site might be selling off one of its houses? I hear they're in financial straits."

Becks snapped to attention at that. "No!" she said. "That can't be!" The Historic Site was her favorite spot in town—and Townsend's.

They had raised their children running through the boxwood maze, and she couldn't count the hours she had spent volunteering when school groups came through. "We have to do something!" she said, inhaling from her cigarette with more passion.

"I love the Historic Site as much as the next person. But I don't see a way to raise the money to keep it up year after year. Everything in this town counts on the same handful of us to donate. We can't save absolutely everything."

Becks loved Ellen, but the woman was a bit of a pessimist—and, well, perhaps she shouldn't be on the board with her and the rest of the book club if that was the way she felt. "Well," Becks piped up, "we'll just have to find a way to broaden our fundraising reach, get tourists involved in an event that will knock their socks off. Something that will make them want to come back year after year."

"Are you going to host a party for tourists, Becks?" Sarah asked.

Becks shrugged. "Who said anything about a party?"

"Well, how else does one raise money?" Laura chimed in, swaying slightly. Patricia got up to refill Laura's glass even though, in Becks's opinion, Laura had had quite enough to drink already.

"I would open my home to tourists if it would help," Patricia said. "I think we all have to do our part."

It made Becks think of the war. She looked around Patricia's beautiful, cozy home that, only two doors down from her own, had existed on this street since the mid-1700s. Becks and Patricia often discussed that one could never really *own* a home like this. No, they were simply its caretakers until the next generation came along. Maybe it was the Pink Squirrel, maybe it was the cigarette, or maybe it was that thought. But, whatever the inspiration, Becks was struck with an idea. She sat up straighter and snapped her fingers.

"Rebecca Saint James has an idea," Ellen said.

"Look out, world!" Sarah added.

Becks smiled and said, "I do indeed. Ladies, vacationers, and locals alike would certainly pay a hefty ticket price for the chance to explore inside these pieces of history."

"What pieces of history?" Sarah asked.

"Our houses," Becks clarified. "The old homes that make Beaufort, well . . . Beaufort."

"I don't like it," Ellen interrupted.

"Oh, Ellen," Laura scoffed. "You don't like *anything*. Let the woman talk."

Patricia laughed, lighting another cigarette and sharing her light with Ellen as well.

"We could band together," Becks continued. "Open up our homes for a tour of sorts. Sell tickets to view them. That way, we wouldn't be asking locals for more donations. Instead, we would be selling tickets to anyone who wanted them, and the money could go to the Historic Site."

Patricia gasped. "I love it! I absolutely love it!"

"Strangers traipsing around our *homes*?" Ellen said. "You can't be serious, Becks. Think about our children. You want a bunch of potential criminals in the rooms where Virginia, Lon, Suzanne, Arlene, and Betty *sleep*? Milton would never stand for that."

Patricia and Becks shared a look. "Ellen," Patricia said with that Mississippi drawl Becks loved so much, "Milton will do positively anything you want. You can't play that card with us. Plus, I believe our children would survive."

She rolled her eyes.

"I'll do it, Becks," Sarah said. "If you'll do it, I'll do it."

"I'll do it!" Patricia chimed in.

All these new-age psychiatrists were writing and talking about peer pressure and how to keep your children from experiencing it.

But, Becks was realizing, it could still strike at any age. And, if you asked her, it could be quite useful under certain circumstances.

"Well, you know I can't be left out," Laura said.

Ellen mashed her cigarette in a silver-rimmed crystal ashtray. "Oh, for heaven's sake. What's next, taking in boarders?"

Becks smiled. She could tell by Ellen's tone that she was relenting. That was five houses right there. With any luck, she could arrange five more. "This might not take off, you know," Ellen warned.

But Becks just smiled. Because she knew in the very marrow of her bones that it would. Who didn't want a chance to try on someone else's life, just for a few minutes? As Becks put out her cigarette, she remembered her plight. She remembered that, even if she pulled this off, even if it became an annual tradition, this would be the only Old Homes Tour she would ever see. And it made her wish that, just for a moment, she could try on someone else's life too.

Ad Nauseum

I 'm not saying we aren't happy that you are having so much fun on your nights out with your cool, young friends," Violet says as she sips her coffee on the Dockhouse deck. "But are we being replaced?"

I laugh. "No one could *ever* replace you four!" I spot Bowen walking down the dock and desperately want to get his attention, but I don't want to seem too eager. Fortunately, Arlene calls, "Bowen! Come have coffee with us!"

"I have to get to the boat," he says, pointing to the huge steel Marine Sciences vessel at the dock. "We're shark tagging today." He grins at me.

"Just one cup!" Violet calls. "The sharks can wait."

I can tell Bowen is about to say no, but then he looks up at the deck, and his eyes lock on mine. "Well, maybe just one cup."

Violet looks self-satisfied, but Betty scoffs, "He didn't say yes because of *you*, you old bird. He said yes because of *Keaton*."

Four sets of eyes are on me. "What's going on there?" Suzanne asks.

"Nothing," I hiss. I shush them as Bowen appears on the porch.

Salt jumps on him, tail wagging furiously. "Salt, down!" I say. But Bowen hands me his coffee and takes both Salt's ears in his hands, rubbing them playfully. "It's pretty gratifying to have someone love you like this."

"Oh, I know. I didn't think I was a dog person, but now I can't imagine coming home and no one freaking out at my mere presence."

"I keep thinking that Anderson should have a puppy, but then I'd have to find someone to let him out in the afternoons, and it doesn't seem fair to keep a dog cooped up all day when no one's home."

Amy walks out with coffee for Bowen and refills for the rest of us, just as Violet asks, "Bowen, honey, are you coming to the opening-night party for the Old Homes Tour? I can put you on the list."

Amy laughs, but I'm not sure why. I am so excited about attending a party with all the amazing townspeople I've gotten to know here, under a tent on the grounds of the Historic Site with music playing in the background. The breeze will be soft, the wine will be cold, and there will be a dance floor. Not that I have anyone to dance with . . . I look at Bowen and try to ignore the thud in my heart.

"Thursday night, right?" Bowen asks.

Violet nods.

"Opening-night party on Thursday, prep all day Friday, and Saturday and Sunday the touring magic happens," I say, more to myself than to him. I can't believe these events are almost here and am trying to ignore my nerves.

"Team Keaton will be there," he says, smiling. He looks at Amy. "Can I get my refill to go? I've got to run."

She nods. "Sure thing."

"Bye, ladies," he says, standing and following Amy inside.

For a few seconds, all the ladies are quiet, which is unnerving in that it has never happened before.

"What is going on?" I whisper as the door opens again and Amy reappears. We're the only table at the restaurant this early, so she sits down with us.

"Well, I never thought I'd see the day," she says, almost as if in awe.

"What day?"

"Bowen has never, not once, attended an Old Homes Tour event," Arlene says with a wink.

My face gets warm, but I try to play it off. "Well, maybe he's maturing, getting involved in town activities."

Amy shakes her head. "Jimmy, Clayton, Alex, and I have been discussing the possibility of this . . ."

"The possibility of what?"

Suzanne shakes her head. "It is indeed as we have suspected."

Betty nods. "Yup. I knew it."

"What are you talking about?"

They act as if I haven't spoken. "He is indeed in love with her," Violet says.

I laugh. "He is *not* in love with me. Are you guys talking about this behind my back?"

"Oh, yes!" Violet says. "Ad nauseum."

Movement inside the restaurant startles Amy out of her seat, but as she goes back in she whispers loudly over her shoulder, "Keaton and Bowen sitting in a tree!"

"Mature, Amy," I call behind her.

I look at the ladies. "Enough. Bowen is being friendly. And I'm leaving soon. There's no need to go down this road."

Arlene nods, getting the hint. She points at the book sticking out of my bag. "I love that you carry Becks's notebook with you."

I put my hand to the worn leather. "Do you think she would mind that I'm reading it?" I ask, sheepish.

"Mind!" Violet says. "Becks would be thrilled! It's the one thing she always had with her," she says.

"Well, that and that huge honking diamond," Suzanne adds.

I smile even though this makes me a little sad. "Her engagement ring?"

"It was magnificent," Violet says wistfully.

"I wish Mom had it. But I guess wherever Becks is, the ring is."

Betty squeezes my hand and I shake off my sadness, thinking of what I *do* have of Becks's that has given me more than any ring ever could. "I love the notebook. I love getting a feel for what she loved, and, let me tell you, I'm becoming quite the cook. I made her heavenly biscuits last night, and it only took me three batches and one smoke alarm to get an edible dozen."

Arlene pats my arm. "Bless your heart, honey."

Betty gasps. "Do you know what I just realized?" We all wait. "Keaton is to us what we were to Becks."

They all nod knowingly. "What?" I ask, feeling like I haven't been invited to the party.

"We were Becks's young friends, and now you're our young friend."

I'm shocked by how much I'm going to miss them when I leave.

I pause, feeling a tightness in my chest over how sad I'm going to be to lose my foothold here. "Maybe when we sell the house, I can use my portion to buy a little condo here or something, so I can visit during the summers."

Violet looks aghast. "You will not buy a condo!"

"What's wrong with a condo?"

"Nothing," she says. "But why would you buy a condo when you could stay with us?"

I smile and reach over to squeeze her hand. "Okay," I say. "Back to the salt mines."

I must, must, *must* make some real progress on cleaning things out today. I am going through a list in my head as I walk back up to the house and spot Alex on a ladder. He isn't in his pirate garb, which makes me happy because I always worry he's going to pass out from heat exhaustion when he is. "Hey, Keaton!" he calls. "Getting these gutters all sorted before the Old Homes Tour. We need to make sure you're looking right!"

He climbs down the ladder and walks toward me, his shirt stained with sweat. "Well," he says, "looks like I am officially on your docent team."

We will have six docents, a.k.a. tour guides, at the house. Each is assigned a room to talk about its history and stories—and, well, keep an eye on all the people wandering through.

I clap in excitement. "Really? What room are you doing?"

"I'm going to be the outdoor greeter, and I'm going to tell a great pirate tale."

I raise my eyebrow. "Is it true?" We have established that some of the lore from Alex's pirate walks is . . . stretched a bit.

"True enough," he says, wiping his brow.

"Come inside! Cool off. I'll get you some water."

He follows me in, and I pour him a drink. "Hey, how many tours do you do a day?" I realize that, despite seeing him on an almost-daily basis, I've never asked him this.

"Well, three a day in the summer, one or two the rest of the year. I take groups of ten to fifteen."

I know he charges twenty-five dollars per person, and, doing the quick math in my head, I gasp. "Alex! Are you serious? You have a gold mine!" My marketing wheels start turning. "Do you have a waitlist or anything?"

He shrugs. "Oh yeah. I mean, I could easily add another tour or two a day. But three hours of tours and a handful of handyman jobs keep me as busy as I want to be."

"Right. But you could hire someone else to help you! We could get you a website, some social media, advertise a little. You could have this whole huge business and—"

He laughs. "Keaton, sometimes enough is okay, you know? I don't need more money. And I can't make more time. I want to work a little during the day, have drinks with you guys to end the night. Fish in the mornings. Swim in the afternoons. You can't take it with you."

I study him, suddenly embarrassed. I have spent my career worrying so much about growth and profits and strategies and bottom lines that I sometimes forget that happiness is what really matters. Alex is reminding me of that. I nod. "Sorry. Old habits."

He hands me his empty glass and squeezes my arm, looking around. "I'll get the paint touched up in here before the tour."

"Thanks," I say. "Just let yourself in whenever. I might not be here."

"So you won't be walking around naked in the kitchen or anything?"

"Since the people in the houses on either side of me can see directly in the windows, I'd say that's a safe bet."

An hour later, Salt and I are in my grandparents' bedroom. I sit down at the vanity—where the silver gleams, I might add—and take a deep breath.

I have just hung up with my brother, who hopes we sell the house quickly so I can get back to New York. "Then I won't have to worry about you roaming around that house in our grandmother's dresses," he said. I'd laughed, but, sitting at Becks's vanity, I can see his point. It has been easy to get sucked into her world.

I pull the little Victorian handle on the middle drawer. Inside is neat and organized, which is why it's so easy to spot what is right smack in the middle: a huge diamond ring with rubies lining the top and bottom, and diamonds set in filigree all around the center stone. I gasp, and, ignoring the thought that maybe I *am* morphing into my grandmother, slip it on my finger. It's the perfect fit.

Underneath, a yellowed envelope sits, bearing my mother's name. I flip it over and see that the back is still sealed tight. I hold it up to the light to see if I can read through it, but I can't quite bring myself to open it. It would be wrong, wouldn't it? Still, this is the sign I needed to try to persuade my mom to come here, to unearth what is left in this house. This is her childhood, her history. There are things here that mean something to her that I will never understand.

As I hold my grandmother's diamond out to admire, I say "Wow" as the light catches the ring. It is truly the most spectacular thing I have ever seen.

But didn't the ladies say my grandmother never took it off? Chills run down my spine, and I suddenly get the creepiest feeling. Her diamond is here. Her notebook. I think of Anderson and the library. Why was there dried blood on that sword?

I open the left-hand bottom drawer, curious to see what's inside. I am shocked to see that it's cluttered with jewelry. I touch a double strand of pearls with a jeweled clasp, a simple single strand of bigger pearls, a sapphire cocktail ring, a pair of emerald earrings, and a tiny gold baby bracelet that I recognize as my mother's. She's wearing it in the framed picture of her and Lon as small children, which sits on the vanity.

These are valuable things, things that certainly would have been stolen if there was some sort of foul play involved, right? I resist the urge to play dress-up with my grandmother's jewelry and open the top left drawer to do more exploring. Inside, makeup brushes sit in a straight line as if they were organized yesterday. The right-hand drawer reveals rouge, powder, lipstick, and mascara. I know I should throw them all out. What good is makeup from the seventies? But I can't shake the feeling that maybe my mother should be the one to do that, that she should have one last moment in time at her mother's vanity.

I decide that I should keep the ring on—for, you know, safe keeping. It is the perfect fit, after all. I decide I have to call my mother. I know it hurts, but this is her last chance to say goodbye to her parents. Not to mention the fact that there is a letter waiting for her.

I could call her on my cell, but for a reason I can't quite explain, I feel like I want to call her from the kitchen phone—like somehow seeing her old phone number on the caller ID might convince her to come say goodbye. This is the closest to closure she is ever going to get, and when it's gone, it's gone.

As I make my way down the back stairs, I hear a voice saying, "Good boy, Salty! Good boy."

Bowen.

I smell him before I see him. The distinctive odor of fish and salt-water seems to radiate from his general direction. His hair is disheveled, his clothes are damp, grime and what I assume is fish or shark blood is on his clothes and splattered a little on his legs. It appears he hasn't even noticed.

"Do you smell the fish on me?" he asks Salt.

"I do," I say, and they both look at me.

He smiles. "Sorry, I'm gross."

I walk a couple steps toward him. "That's okay."

He walks toward me with purpose, and my face flushes with the remembrance of my conversation with the ladies this morning.

At that exact moment, there's a banging at the front door followed by, "Keaton! If you're naked in the kitchen, I'm coming in with the paint!"

Bowen looks horrified, and I laugh. "No! No!" I say. "It's a joke. Because, you know, no privacy in Beaufort."

"Tell me about it," Bowen says under his breath as Alex enters the kitchen, once again in full pirate garb. "Oh, hey man." He looks from me to Bowen and back to me, and, instinctively, I take a step back. "Am I interrupting something?" I hate the knowing way he says it and am immediately embarrassed. I feel like a teenager who has a crush on a boy and everyone knows it.

"Feel free to stay—I was just heading out, actually," Bowen says. "Got to wash off these fish guts."

He gives me a nod as Alex heads off to the library, and, just like that, I'm alone in the kitchen, alone with my thoughts, trying to decide if the spark I just felt with my neighbor is all in my head. And as I watch him out the window, as he makes his way into his house, I realize I decidedly hope not.

A Happier Life

MONDAY, JULY 12, 1976

Tip: Food is not a trend. When planning a menu, ask yourself:
Will people still eat this in ten years? Did people eat this ten
years ago? If the answer is no, for heaven's sake, do not serve
it. I know that I sometimes bend to your father's will on these
matters. But, do as I say, not as I do always applies. Trends
come and go; the simplicity of timeless meals with the ones you
love is forever.

Telling Townsend's parents about the engagement had not gone
well. There had been a lot of dramatic crying and "Where did
I go wrong?" on his mother's part, a lot of silence from his father, and
plenty of "You'd better hope I'm still around to pray you out of pur-
gatory" from his youngest sister, who was fourteen. To his family's
credit, though, they never once mentioned disowning Townsend or
not being a part of their lives. (They did, however, give Becks—whom
they had not even known *existed* until this announcement—the third
degree about how they would raise their children.) Becks was glad

that Townsend's family at least heard them out, although she privately thought he could have done a slightly better job of easing them in by at least mentioning that he was dating someone first. *Men.*

While the Saint Jameses had begrudgingly consented to their so-called mixed marriage (it made her feel like they were part of a pie, wet and dry ingredients poured in the same bowl to disastrous results!), Becks had not confirmed she would raise her children Catholic and knew that was highly unlikely. Although she wasn't terribly keen on Methodists at the moment, either. She wondered if she could see herself stepping foot in any church after all this.

Townsend took her hand as they drove away. "Well, my darling, that went better than I thought it might."

Incongruously, she burst out laughing as if she were an overfilled balloon that could no longer take the pressure and had finally popped. Townsend laughed too. "One down, one to go."

He squeezed her hand as they pulled into her parents' driveway. Becks felt ill. She shook her head. "I don't think I can do this, Townsend. Twice in one day?"

"I know. But once we get this over with, we can go on about the business of being happy. Not telling your parents doesn't change the truth of the matter at hand, and the truth is that we are getting married."

"Well, I can't argue with that, now can I?"

Becks knew her parents would be home. Wednesdays were for church, Thursdays for bridge, but Tuesday was for family.

When she walked through the front door, calling, "Mother, Daddy," her father saw them first. The look he gave her caused her to drop Townsend's hand. "What are you doing here?" he asked Townsend, glaring daggers at him.

"Well, sir—" Townsend started, but Reverend Bonner cut him off.

"Did I not make myself clear in my office?"

Townsend looked at Becks, who was very grateful that her mother bustled in, perfect in her heels and pearls as always. "Now, dear," she murmured, "that's no way to greet company—or your daughter."

"That boy is not company," he seethed, which Becks found rather funny, since Townsend was twenty-nine years old and very much not a boy.

"Children break up, darling," her mother soothed. "And they come to their senses."

Becks didn't know what came over her, but she blurted out, "We're here to say that we're getting married and there's nothing you can say to stop us!"

Her father's face got very red, and he coughed.

"Oh, my good Lord," her mother said as she examined her daughter's left hand, noticing the ring for the first time. "How will you manage to hold up your arm?" She paused. "You're a grown woman, Rebecca, and Townsend is a gainfully employed physician. Why would we try to stop your marriage?"

That's when Becks realized her father had been true to his word: He had not told her mother the truth about Townsend.

"Because he is a . . ." Reverend Bonner pointed at Townsend and managed to exhale "Catholic" before he fell to the floor, clutching his left arm.

"Call emergency services," Townsend ordered to Becks as her mother screamed. He immediately started chest compressions. Even as he found his rhythm and performed mouth-to-mouth resuscitation, Becks could tell by Townsend's stricken expression that he knew Reverend Bonner wouldn't pull through. Still, Townsend was the one who rode in the back of the ambulance, who underwent the task of admitting him even though he would later tell Becks he knew it was useless.

After Becks and her mother arrived at the hospital, Townsend sat with Becks all night in the waiting room while her mother sat vigil at her father's bedside. They prayed for a miracle. To the same God, as it were. When Becks's mother called with the worst news of her life, she was no longer hysterical; she was eerily, hatefully calm. "I hope you're happy," she hissed at her daughter. "You killed your father."

Becks dropped the phone and burst into tears. All Townsend could do was hold her.

Forty-one years later, it was still the worst moment of her life, even worse than finding out she was dying herself. Your own demise was nothing compared to the cruel knowledge that you had caused someone else's.

Becks hadn't been welcome at her father's funeral.

Now, all these years later, she wondered what that funeral was like as she sat in a sliver of sun on the front porch, writing out her wishes for her own funeral in her notebook. She had been trying to hide how wretched she was starting to feel as best she could, napping when Townsend was out on the boat, begging off their flights or lunches and blaming her newly busy schedule on bridge or book club or Old Homes Tour preparations whenever she had a doctor's appointment. Daniel had been a lifesaver, keeping her pain in check by delivering these lovely little shots of a drug called Numorphan. She had read articles about how people got terribly addicted to it, that many addicts preferred it to heroin. But, as Daniel argued, "Becks, I wouldn't really worry about rehab in your future." So she didn't. She instead felt grateful that, for days at a time, she could ignore the fact that everything in her body hurt.

There was, however, still the issue of telling Townsend, which Daniel hounded her about daily. She could feel death tiptoeing in, creeping around the edges of her life. There were plans to be made, nurses to be hired, hospice to be arranged. A funeral to be planned. Becks wasn't the kind of woman to leave any of that to chance, so she would handle it. She would handle it all. Which is why she was making lists of all that needed to be done when she was gone. But, for now, finding the entire exercise far too macabre, she decided to focus on the guest list for her last dinner party of the summer. This would be the last summer supper she would ever throw, so she wanted to take the extra time to make sure it was perfect.

Her children would be there, Virginia and Lon, with their significant others. She had met Lon's girlfriend once, briefly, and she was just dying to meet this Robert fellow. Townsend was too. Virginia seemed truly happy with him, and there was nothing that made Becks happier than imagining that her daughter would be well taken care of.

She would invite that darling Violet who had just moved to town because, on the off chance Virginia ended up moving here, she knew Violet would invite her into the fold, introduce her to everyone. Daniel and Patricia would be there too, of course.

She glanced at the checklist that always guided her:

Place cards

Flowers (from her own yard, arranged by her own hand. Oh, she did adore summer!)

Welcome champagne

Full ice bucket

Ice tongs polished

Linens ironed

And on it went, a seemingly endless list of details that a good southern hostess like Becks knew by heart. It wasn't unlike the checklist she undertook before flying. Altimeter—set. Flight controls—free and correct. Fuel gauges—checked. Instruments and radios—checked. Propeller—exercised. In the plane or in her home,

Becks could identify at practically a glance whether she was prepared. Even still, you had to work the checklist.

It occurred to her that this cancer was something she didn't see coming, couldn't have prepared for even with a checklist. A woman who was always prepared had met her match, and it felt like a cruel joke.

The sound of one of those insistently loud—and way too fast to be safe—Oldsmobiles rumbling down the street gave Becks pause. She was shocked when it turned into the driveway of the house next door, which was almost always empty. Her neighbors had sold it to a man who made it a *rental*—of all the dastardly things to happen to a proud and elegant street like this, where houses were passed down through family lines.

She watched through a gap in the bushes as a man got out, stretched, and retrieved a small bag from the front seat. He used a key to open the front door of the house. Becks sighed. Well, it was starting. Here he was, a renter. She didn't love the idea of a single man living next to her, especially one with a noisy car. No family. Becks went back to her notebook, but, moments later, had the uncomfortable feeling of being watched. She looked around and gasped when her eyes caught the man, in an upstairs window, staring at her. He didn't wave but also didn't look away, his gaze on her firm. A shiver ran down her spine. She looked away, uncomfortable, and, when she looked up again, he was gone.

The door opened, causing her to jump, and Townsend walked out onto the porch and kissed his wife, who sat up straighter. She closed her notebook and slowed her breath. She was so on edge these days.

"What are you doing, my love?" he asked.

"Just making a list for the last dinner party of the summer." She smiled brightly. "I thought it might be fun to have the kids."

"Now, that would be fun!" he said.

"Who knew grown-up children would be such a joy?"

"I know," Townsend said, bringing his coffee to his lips. "We should have had grown-up children first." He paused. "Can you imagine how fun it's going to be to have grandchildren?"

Tears, unbidden, sprang up in Becks's eyes, and she looked out over the water so Townsend couldn't see them. She couldn't imagine grandchildren, actually, and that was just as well. Because what use was it to dream of something she wouldn't live to see?

"Speaking of our future grandchildren . . . Since Virginia and Robert will be here I thought I might invite Violet so she can meet them."

"Robert?" Townsend questioned.

Becks looked at him incredulously. "Robert? Your daughter's boyfriend whom we are dying to meet?"

Townsend laughed. "You know I always want to forget Virginia's boyfriends," he said, covering his gaffe.

Becks had been so preoccupied with her own health lately that she perhaps hadn't been as attentive to Townsend's as she should have been. He was very forgetful lately. That was normal at seventy, wasn't it? But what scared her was, when they got in their plane to fly last week, he turned to her, his face stricken, when it came time for his flight checklist. She could tell he couldn't remember what to do. As soon as she started the list for him, he rattled the rest of it right off. So maybe it was nothing. But if it was something . . . She opened her notebook and scribbled, *Get Townsend appointment with Daniel.* Either way, she needed to make sure he was taken care of when she was gone.

"Who should our last couple be?" she asked. She tapped her pencil to her chin. "How about Ellen and Milton?"

"That would be fine," Townsend said.

Ellen and Milton were their closest friends besides Daniel and Patricia. Plus, she was calling on Ellen quite a bit outside of book club to help her organize this Old Homes Tour—which, she was learning, was quite a bit more work than she had perhaps originally imagined. At least it meant that some of her excuses to Townsend were legitimate ones.

Townsend looked at her lovingly. "May I request Chef Evelyn's cheeseball for an appetizer?"

"You may request whatever you like," she said, making a note. "We won't be having a trendy cheeseball at my last dinner of the summer, but you are free to ask."

Townsend laughed. "All right then. It is your birthday, after all. Whatever you like is what shall be."

"Ten-layer chocolate caramel cake?" she questioned. She knew she wouldn't live to see another year after this one so, at this party, she'd have her last slice of birthday cake to celebrate for the last time.

"Pulling out the big guns," Townsend chuckled. "Could we have that salmon loaf I love so much?"

Becks wrinkled her nose, and he laughed. "Townsend!"

"So no Watergate salad?"

Becks smiled warmly at her husband. He was still so handsome, even after all these years, and he had such a strength about him. He was in excellent shape from fishing every day the weather allowed—and some the weather didn't—hunting, and his daily walks around town. When they first married, she spent so much time worrying when he was off on his adventures. What if he was caught in a storm? Or by a stray bullet? Or by a rogue wave? She wished she could take the worry back now, give herself the gift of unencumbered happiness.

Townsend had a tanned and ruddy complexion that made him look younger than he was—younger than she, she suspected, since she was having trouble keeping her weight up now. The rapid weight loss was making her face more wrinkled and saggy, no matter how much Oil of Olay she applied. Yes, aging was a tricky animal. But she'd never really reach the true ravages of it. And she was, she had to admit, a little bit okay with that.

Becks, if she was honest with herself, had never really wanted to grow old. Yes, it broke her heart that she would never see her children marry or have children of their own, that she wouldn't be the one to sit by Townsend's side as he took his last breath. But she also didn't want to have to slow down, use a walker, lose control of things one should never lose control of. She didn't want dimming eyesight or damaged hearing or a befuddled mind. And, in the vainest way, she didn't want to *look* old. So if someone was going to have to die before their time, it was okay that it was her. She could handle it.

"Watergate salad," she said in response to Townsend's question, "is an aberration. Jell-O pudding, whipped cream, and marshmallows do not a salad make."

"Yes, but when you add the walnuts and cherries and pineapple, it becomes a veritable health food."

Becks laughed and relented. She wasn't going to deny her husband the wishes of his heart—or stomach. "We will have Watergate salad this week," she sighed. "But not for the last dinner party of the summer."

"Hooray!"

She made a few more scribbles in her book. They would do fondue with the younger group this week, too. It was always nice to have something to do with one's hands, especially for those less trained in the art of conversation.

Townsend sat beside Becks. He kissed her and, as he pulled away, studied her face, frowning slightly. Self-conscious, she tried to look away. "Becks, is it my imagination, or do your eyes look a little bit . . . yellow?"

Jaundice was a symptom of pancreatic cancer, one of the only visible ones. She had tried to hide it, but how does one hide yellowing eyes?

She waved him away. "It's probably just the sun."

He studied her again. "Are you sure? Because you look jaundiced to me. Maybe we should call Daniel. Or I could take you in myself and do an examination?"

She smiled at him brightly. "Darling, you worry too much."

He kissed her again. "All right, then. But keep your eye on it, and let me know if you change your mind. I'm off to conquer the seas."

She held up her book. "I'll be right here conquering home economics."

They both laughed. Townsend got up and then turned back to her. "A flight before dinner?"

"A flight before dinner," she agreed, already imagining the quiet of just the two of them, up in the air, a world away.

"Becks?"

"Yes?"

"It has been worth it, right?"

"What has been worth it, my love?"

"Our life together. Was it worth the pain it caused you, the separation from your mother? Because I've been doing some thinking after your visit. I worry sometimes that—"

"Shhhh," Becks said, standing up and walking to Townsend. "I could not possibly have had a happier life."

He nodded. "Me neither."

She thought he seemed choked up, but he recovered quickly. Townsend kissed Becks then, wrapping his arms around her, their bodies radiating in a perfect sliver of sunlight. If anyone had walked by, they would have believed them to be much younger, lost in each other's embrace, savoring the feel of each other like they always had.

In that moment they were ageless, weightless, timeless. *And that's,* Becks thought, *what true love can do.*

Keaton

....

The Flashlight

I know, Mom," I say as I balance the phone between my ear and shoulder and pour Salt's food into his bowl. "But I'm just saying that this house is going on tour, it's probably going to sell, and you might want to go through some of this stuff before we have to clear it out for a buyer. I mean, there's your dad's journals, your mom's jewelry, chests overflowing with family photos and Christmas cards . . ." I pause dramatically for effect. "And, Mom, Becks wrote you a letter."

I never knew what to call her. It was weird to call your grandmother by her first name, but I never got to be that little kid who sounds out Gigi or Gaga. Suddenly, that makes me feel very sad. I'd always thought you couldn't miss something you never had. But maybe I'd been wrong about that.

"A letter?" Mom asked.

"Yes. In her dressing table. And her ring, Mom."

I could almost hear her perk up. "Her engagement ring?"

"Yes," I say.

"That is so odd."

I still haven't been able to bring myself to talk to Mom about the idea that maybe her parents didn't die in a car wreck. Somewhere deep down, I'm still that little girl who's worried about upsetting her just by mentioning them. And things have been so good between us lately that I don't want to ruin it. "Have you told Lon?" she asks.

"No. I haven't talked to him in a few days. Want me to just snatch up all the jewelry for us and not tell him what I found?"

She laughs. "No, you can tell him. I don't care. I could never wear my mother's jewelry anyway."

I hold my hand out and admire the ring. "Mom, you have to be kidding me. Do you remember her ring? It's insane."

"Oh, I know. Her jewelry was beautiful. But it's just too sad."

I can see how it must be hard. "You take it please, sweetheart," she continues. "And whatever else. Tell Lon what you want, and I'll settle up with him when the house sells."

I gaze down at my hand. "Oh, no, Mom, I really couldn't," I say, but only because it's the polite thing to do.

"I insist," she says. "I want you to have it." I want me to have it too.

"Mom, you know the Old Homes Tour is tomorrow and Sunday, and the house looks so good. I think you would love—"

She cuts me off. "You are doing *such* a fantastic job without me, sweetheart. I can't thank you enough. Plus, I couldn't possibly get away."

We say our goodbyes and I think, *So that's a no, then.*

When I get to coffee with the Dames around ten (they stay at coffee for *hours*), I plop down, frustrated. "I can't get Mom to come to the tour this weekend," I say. "She just can't do it."

Violet reaches over to pat my hand. "We'll help you, sweetheart. We've all been through this, and we're in a good place to know what to save and what to throw out."

"Throw it all out," Suzanne grumbles. "You'll never look at any of it again."

Arlene shoots her a look and then screams, "Holy Mother of God!" as she grabs my hand. "It's the flashlight!" I had ultimately decided it wasn't right to wear the ring until I talked to my mom about it. But now that I had her blessing . . .

I laugh. "The flashlight?"

Betty nods. "That's what we used to call Becks's ring because, well . . ." She pulls my hand into the light and we all have to cover our eyes.

"Wait, wait, wait," Violet says. "Becks wasn't wearing her ring when she died?"

"Weird, right?" I ask. "It's been sitting in her vanity for all these years."

"Weird," Violet agrees.

"Want to know what's weirder?"

They all nod in agreement.

"My mom doesn't want the ring."

Betty slumps back in her chair. "Well, that settles it. She is certifiable."

I nod. "I agree." I see Bowen walking down the dock then. He stops, shades his eyes, and grins when he sees me. He waves, and I wave back.

I realize maybe my wave was a little too enthusiastic because all eyes are on me. I bite my lip but say nothing. I'm trying not to get my hopes up.

"So," Betty says, raising her coffee mug, "cheers to Violet for pulling off the most spectacular opening-night party in Old Homes Tour history last night."

We all clink our mugs.

"Cheers to Keaton for getting Bowen to come to an Old Homes Tour event," Arlene adds.

I hate how girlish and smitten I sound when I laugh. Bowen had scarcely left my side the entire night, introducing me to most of the people in town I hadn't met yet. Just thinking of his hand on the small of my back as he led me through the party gave me butterflies.

Suzanne taps her pencil on the table. "Not that I'm not incredibly interested in the dramatic love story unfolding here, but can we go down to your house? We need a final walk-through before the tour tomorrow."

My eyes widen. "I can't believe it's here already. And you're sure it's okay to let people inside in its current state?"

"Absolutely," Violet says, which is expected because she's in charge of this thing and where would that leave her if I backed out at the last minute?

"Lon told me when I first got here that he really thinks we need to redo the kitchen and bathrooms, strip the shag carpeting, get rid of the furniture, and give the interiors a fresh coat of paint before we put it on the market and, well, show it to anyone. He's, um, not super happy that we are putting it on tour in this state." Harris found this further proof that I was getting way too sucked into Beaufort life, and that it was getting me offtrack. Maybe it *was* getting me offtrack. But I honestly couldn't remember the last time I'd felt this happy. And shouldn't happiness be worth something?

"You don't have to put it on the market now," Violet says. "You might want to keep it a while . . ." She winks at me, and I shake my head. But she isn't wrong.

The ladies and I walk the two blocks toward my house, chattering and laughing along the way. The most fun thing about participating in the upcoming tour is that I have learned so much about the house from the docent training, and its stories both excite and unsettle me. According to Alex's lore—which, I mean, a person has to take with a grain of salt—a famous pirate was killed right in the living room, which makes the fact that Salt goes in there and barks at "nothing" for like twenty minutes at least once a day even more disconcerting. But I also know that my great-great-great-great grandfather built this house for his daughter and her husband as a wedding present—that, in the old days, it sat right on the water instead of across the street. The street was added later in front as flood protection. I also learned that my grandparents, only weeks before their deaths, hosted the kickoff party for the first-ever Old Homes Tour, which was attended by most of the town, right here.

We walk through the front door and, since the ladies are still chattering around me, it takes me a second to recognize that there are voices coming from the library.

As I make my way toward them, I hear Anderson saying, "This thing must be worth a fortune, right?"

A man's voice—one that takes me about a half second to recognize—replies, "Oh, yeah. A fortune. But you know *someone* will never let us sell it."

"Harris! What are you doing here?" I squeal as my brother turns, and I run to hug him. Even though I didn't know he was coming, I'm not actually surprised he's here. My entire life he has acted cool and detached in that big brother way. But he is also the one who skipped his own classes on more than one occasion to go home and get homework I forgot so I wouldn't get in trouble. He is the one I cried to over breakups and skinned knees. Harris has always taken care of me. Always. And given how concerned he's been about my small-town Suzie life . . . well, I should have known he'd show up eventually.

"I wanted to fly a little this morning," he offers in terms of explanation. "It was such a nice day. And then I figured I could use a few days' vacation. So I figured why not fly here and make sure my sister isn't dressed in colonial wear?"

"Aw," I say sarcastically. "You missed me."

"Get a load of the brother," I hear Violet say from behind me. I turn to her and point my finger. She is so bad.

Wow, Betty mouths at me.

Harris is rather handsome, I suppose, in a fitted-khaki five-pockets and button-down kind of way.

He pulls back and looks at me, turning me around. "Good," he says.

"What?" Arlene asks.

"She isn't wearing our grandmother's clothes."

"Oh, but she should!" Betty trills. "They are spectacular!"

Harris shakes his head and pulls up my hand, eyes wide at the ring I'm wearing. "Whoa."

"Sorry," I say. "I am channeling her a little, I guess."

"Don't be sorry," he says. "I approve." He smiles. "You wouldn't shut up about this Old Homes Tour thing, so I thought I'd better be here to check it out for myself."

I smile and hug him again. "I'm so glad you're here."

I introduce him to the ladies, who, well, fawn. As if Harris needs any more women fawning over him. "And I see you've met my neighbor, Anderson."

"I have indeed," he says. "And Anderson has made a shocking discovery."

Anderson, in his Patagonia swim trunks and Aftco fishing shirt, points to the books on the shelf. "See all these Hemingways?"

I nod, and he hands me one. "They're all signed to your grandfather. All of them. And they have notes in them about fish they caught and stuff."

I'm taken aback. "Really?"

He hands me *The Old Man and the Sea*, and I read the note scribbled on the title page out loud. "Dear Townsend, a man among boys: the Key West waves might try, but they can never defeat us. Here's to many more days on the open water with a true sportsman. I look forward to our next battle in Beaufort one day. My best, always, Ernest.

"Wow. But really? Our grandfather fished with Hemingway?"

"According to this he did," Harris says, handing me an open journal. "In Key West on his and Becks's honeymoon." I can see the empty spot on Townsend's journal shelf in the bookcase where he got it.

Now I am incensed. "Harris!" I scold. "I have a system here. I'm going through these in a very specific way and now I've lost my place."

Violet points to the ladies. "We're going to go practice our docent lines in our assigned rooms," she says.

"What she means is," Arlene adds, "we're going to leave you two to your family drama and stay out of it."

Suzanne leans against the wall. "Speak for yourselves. I'm staying right here." But Betty pulls her arm, and they are gone.

"Who are they again?" Harris asks.

"They're my besties," I say.

He laughs, and Anderson, who is back on his stool dusting an empty shelf, adds, "She's serious, man."

Harris points at Anderson. "That kid is a trip." *If you like the kid*, I think, *you should see the father.*

Surrounded by all these people who have given me such purpose over these last few weeks, I pause. Have I ever, in my adult life, felt this happy? I was up half the night stressing about getting my résumé together and applying for jobs and going back to New York, but is that how it has to be? Bowen loves living here. Alex, Jimmy, and Clayton have all found ways to pursue their passions. Amy is the cutest kindergarten teacher slash barista in the known world, and she has found her place. What if I was meant to come here? What if this was always how my story was supposed to unfold?

"Keaton." Anderson turns to me, breaking me out of my thoughts. "Is my dad taking you on a date tonight or something?"

I wish. "What? No! What would make you say that?"

He shrugs. "I don't know. He asked me to help him pick out a shirt, and it seemed weird."

Harris and I exchange glances. "So is that what your dad does when he goes out on dates? Asks for your help picking out his clothes?"

"I don't know." He shrugs. "My dad never goes out on dates."

Harris covers his laugh with his hand. The butterflies in my stomach are multiplying. I mean, we usually walk to Black Sheep together on Fridays now to meet Amy, Alex, Jimmy, and Clayton, so I figured I'd see Bowen tonight, but . . . I have to calm down.

As I'm trying to get my mind off it, I realize an extra perk to my brother being here: I would very much like to know what happened to my grandparents, and I've wondered if Townsend's journals hold any clues. I've only read the early journals, the good, sweet, love-conquers-all ones. I haven't made myself look at the later ones yet; I'm a little afraid of what I'm going to find there. So I pull the last two—from the 1970s—from the bookshelf and hand them to Harris. "Your assignment," I say. "These are our grandfather's last two journals. I can't bring myself to read them."

"Like mother, like daughter," he says, smirking. Then he leans over and kisses my cheek. "I'm really glad I came. I missed you, sis."

I'm glad to hear him say that, because I have done exactly zero in the way of looking for a place to live after Beaufort. It's becoming likelier by the moment that I will have to live with him for at least a short while when I get back to New York.

"Sure, sure," I say, crossing my arms. "But I'm glad you're here for immersion therapy. Want me to get you a strand of Becks's pearls to wear too?"

"Maybe," he says. "But for now, which room should I sleep in? Doesn't this place kind of give you the creeps?"

"No!" I say, offended, which makes no sense since, yes, I was also creeped out at first. But now I'm over it.

"Have you been in Mom's room yet?"

He shakes his head.

"Harris, I have something shocking to share."

He looks like he doesn't want to hear it.

"I think our mom might have been cool."

He shakes his head again. "No way."

"No, her room is, like, very cool."

"Everyone was cool in the seventies," he says. "But I'm cool now, and we don't have to stay in the seventies. Maybe let's just stay at the Beaufort Hotel."

"A hotel?" I turn to see a fish-gut-covered but slightly less smelly than yesterday Bowen leaning against the wall.

"Ah, this must be Casanova," Harris sighs. I shoot him a *stop it right now or you will be sorry* look.

"Bowen, this is my brother," I start, as Anderson exclaims, "Dad! Signed Hemingways!"

He nods. "Oh, yeah. I remember Violet's husband Dr. Scott telling me that your grandfather fished with Hemingway."

That pang again, that all these people have all these stories about my family and I don't.

"I just wanted to make sure Anderson was here. I shouldn't be surprised. I was going to swing by and pick you up tonight to go to Black Sheep." He pauses. "Unless you wanted to hang out with your brother?"

"If it's okay with you, I think Anderson and I can make plans for pool and burgers at the Royal James."

Anderson nods. "And beers."

Harris ruffles his hair like they're old friends. "How about root beers?"

Anderson chimes in, "Violet has so much to do for the tour tomorrow that she wouldn't have time to babysit me." He pauses. "Please, Dad?"

Bowen looks from Harris to Anderson to me. I nod my approval. "He's a competent babysitter for a child who is completely self-sufficient."

A knock on the front door stops us all in our tracks, and I think we're thinking the same thing: *Who knocks?*

Harris goes to answer the door, which is good because I can't quite seem to physically pull myself away from Bowen's general vicinity. I hear a voice that, for a split second, I think I recognize. But it couldn't be. "Oh, Harris, you just get more handsome!" I freeze as I hear a pair of footsteps coming through the house and into the kitchen.

"Who is it?" Anderson asks, clearly sensing my change in mood.

"Allison?" I say, tentatively. I step toward the kitchen, thinking I must be mistaken. This must be a dream. But as I enter the room, she's looking around and Harris is standing behind her, shaking his head with a truly unhappy look on his face.

"This is a trip," she says, mystified. "I mean, it's like a museum of the seventies."

The way she's acting like it's so normal that she is here unnerves me. She hugs me, and I feel like an idiot because I let her. What feels worse is that I'm almost relieved to have her hug. I haven't admitted it to myself, but I've missed her. For better or worse, we became really good friends while I worked for her. And suddenly I have this notion that she's a little bit right. Jonathan was her husband before he was my boyfriend. I had always felt like I crossed a line by being with him, but they both seemed so okay with the whole thing that I blamed myself for being terribly provincial.

She has the tiniest bump under her linen maxi dress, but her face is as narrow and her arms as toned as ever. She is the picture of glowing good health. "Um, hi," I say. "How in the world did you know where I was? And what are you doing here?"

She smiles like that's a quaint question, like she has the FBI on speed dial. "Just did a quick google search, sweetie. Since the Saint James House is on the Old Homes Tour website, it was a pretty easy find." I can't believe she's here; I feel ambushed. And I realize this is what she wanted. Allison is the absolute master of shock and awe. Prepared people can tell her no. She's catching me off guard on purpose. Only, I don't quite know why yet.

"Oh, I'm so glad I came," she says. "I missed you. I needed to lay eyes on you, make sure you were okay. I ran into your mom and she told me what you came to do, and it felt like . . ." She looks around at her audience.

Thanks for telling me you ran into Allison, Mom, I think, trying to control my eye roll. Although, in her defense, maybe she just didn't want to bring up sore subjects.

"This is Anderson," I say, gesturing toward him. "And this is Bowen. You obviously know Harris. Anderson and Bowen, this is . . ." *My old boss? My ex-mentor? The third angle of my equilateral love triangle?*

"I'm Allison." She sticks her hand out, and Bowen gives me a disapproving look. He doesn't offer his.

"I see my reputation precedes me," Allison says, laughing lightly. "But it was all a misunderstanding, and I'm here to clear it up."

Bowen's face says this is above his pay grade, and I don't want him to think I'm some drama-fueled, immature woman.

I shoot a pointed look at Harris, and he seems to get the picture.

"Oh!" Harris says. "Does this place have internet?" he asks Anderson.

"Oh yeah," Anderson says. "And you won't believe what TV on that big box in there looks like. Can you believe it isn't flat? Dad, we've got to show him."

Harris laughs, and I smile. I've never seen this side of my brother, and, I have to admit, I kind of like it.

Bowen eyes me warily but follows them out of the kitchen.

Allison pauses, her eyes fixated on Bowen. "Who is *that*?" She squeezes my forearm, raising her perfectly shaped eyebrows. I can't help but smile and I *want to be mad at her*. This is how cults begin. Impossibly charismatic people like Allison start them and they have some mystical ability to trick innocent humans into following them even when they act terribly.

"Want to sit down?" I ask Allison, pointing toward the breakfast table in the corner of the kitchen. "Can I get you anything?"

"I don't suppose you have any chilled ginger tea?"

"Um, no."

"Well, then I'm fine," she says, sitting down. "Just a little queasy."

I smile tightly, annoyed by her mention of her love child with *my ex-boyfriend*. And then I smile for real, because what's more seventies than a love child?

"Look, Keaton," she says, "I know Jonathan has been texting you, and I get why you haven't responded. I wanted to come here in person to say that I'm sorry. I didn't handle our meeting well; I haven't handled the past few months well. I treated you badly, and I feel terribly about it. But I'm here because I want to fix things between us. I'm here because I want to beg you, on my knees if I have to, to come back to All Welcome."

I hate how happy I am that things are clearly falling apart without me. I am the type-A, controlling counterpart to Allison's hippy-dippy, I'm-the-ideas-you're-the-execution management style. And, if I'm honest, what I'm going to do once the house has been sold has been keeping me up at night. I've barely even started looking for a job, and every time I do, nothing seems to fit. I'm either underqualified or overqualified for everything. And, while I don't want to go back to All Welcome, I have to think that if I take the promotion and eke out even six months, I'll be launched into any job I want next. Plus, I miss being so close to my parents and brother.

Then it hits me all at once: My relationship with Allison is a lot like my relationship with my mother. I take care of her. I do her dirty work. Maybe it's dysfunctional, but this is what makes us work. This is a role I know how to play. Maybe I do want my job back; it'd be easier than starting over. I can't stop myself, every day, from thinking about campaign launches or books we're publishing, all the new projects I had lined up and waiting. And as much as I hate to admit it, I've missed that. All Welcome wasn't just a job for me. It was a relationship, complete with a breakup that I didn't want to happen.

But I'm not just going to fall at her feet and thank her for a second chance. "You know, Allison, I've got a lot going on here."

She looks around. "Uh-huh. Yes. The Old Homes Tour seems very taxing." I smirk. "Well," she continues, "I was thinking that if you came back right away—"

"Anderson's school play," I hear Bowen's voice say behind me. I hadn't realized he had come back.

"What?" I ask.

Anderson appears beside his dad. "I have my school play next week, Keaton," Anderson says. "You promised you would come."

"You promised," Bowen repeated.

I have no recollection of hearing the first thing about any sort of school play, and, for a split second, I'm afraid I'm losing my mind. But then, as I look into Bowen's face, I realize this is a made-up play. Or, at least, my participation in it is made up. He's protecting me.

I turn back to Allison. Bowen is private and damaged and hasn't seriously dated in like a decade. I am lonely and in a weird place. Am I just projecting my feelings onto him? Allison is offering me a real chance at a real job. In my mind, I walk upstairs and pack my bags because what am I doing here anyway?

"It's, um, the end of June," Allison says. "Does Anderson attend year-round school?"

Good plan, guys. Really smooth.

As if summoned by Bowen's obvious lie for corroboration, Violet, Arlene, Betty, and Suzanne trail in, clearly having overheard. "It's part of the Old Homes Tour festivities," Violet says, so seamlessly that I start to believe that maybe there *is* a play.

"Oh, yes. It's very good," Betty chimes in, giving Allison a look that dares her to ask more questions.

Allison smiles and says, earnestly, looking from Anderson to me, "Okay, then. We will work around the play. And I'll move Jonathan to another department. You won't even have to see him. It will be just the two of us at the helm," she says.

I study her for a moment. "Wait. I thought you wanted me to come back as director of marketing."

She shakes her head. "I want you to come back as VP of Operations, which, as you know, means stock options, six weeks paid vacation, paid volunteer days, votes in how we disperse foundation dollars—really, anything else you can think of. Just ask. I want you as my number two, Keaton."

"But isn't that Jonathan's position?"

She shrugs. "He wants to be home with the baby some. I will create a new position for him."

I know I shouldn't worry about Jonathan; he certainly didn't worry about me. But I do. I look at Bowen and Anderson. I look at Violet, Arlene, Betty, and Suzanne and think about our mornings at the Dockhouse. I look out the window at the water rolling by. I have been so happy to get a peek into another life. But could this be my real life? Or has it just been a respite?

As I think about the years I've spent climbing the ladder, building my career, the idea of going back seems so much easier than starting over. And I have to wonder: Has Allison just made me an offer I can't refuse?

Becks

....

A Little Something Extra

FRIDAY, JULY 16, 1976

Tip: I know it is overdiscussed to the point of cliché, but, my darling, the saying is true: the way to a man's heart is through his stomach. And, well, most women's too. I have found that anything I need to accomplish can be done with a basket of muffins, a warm chicken potpie, or a delicious dinner party meal. A woman must use every tool at her disposal.

Becks pulled two tins of perfectly plump, browned-on-top blueberry muffins out of her oh-so-chic green oven and inhaled their fragrant scent. She didn't cook that much anymore, thanks to lovely Chef Evelyn, who did most of it now. Evelyn's weekday meals were simpler than her extravagant summer suppers—usually casseroles or things she had frozen ahead of time. But when the mood struck, Becks would still whip up a batch of chicken salad or pimento cheese, her famous chicken potpie, and she did enjoy baking ever so much. Of everything she made, she thought her blueberry muffins might be her most popular treat. Everyone asked for her recipe, but a lady had to have a few secrets, didn't she?

Still, the first secret was a little obvious—at least in Becks's mind. Each summer on their annual trip to Maine, she and Townsend shipped home buckets of wild blueberries. They were small and sweet and a little firmer than the local blueberries. She hated biting into a muffin and an over-juicy berry bursting in her mouth. Now, she couldn't resist the scent of those warm muffins, which made her happy; she had so little appetite these days. She closed her eyes and took a bite so warm it almost burned her tongue.

The sound of Townsend's footsteps down the stairs made her turn. "Blueberry muffin day! My favorite!"

Becks smiled as Townsend kissed her cheek and reached for one of the muffins. He made a noise of pure delight as he chewed. He swallowed and paused, as if thinking and savoring at once. "Oh, Becks, that fresh zing at the end is just heavenly!"

As Townsend wrapped his arms around his wife's waist from behind to plant a kiss on her neck, Becks turned and looked out the window at the Meyer lemon tree on the far side of the gate that Townsend had planted when they first moved into the house. It was so overwhelmingly thoughtful that Becks knew then and there she would always be happy with Townsend.

"Those lemons, darling," she said softly, gesturing outside, "are the best gift you've ever given me."

He smiled and pulled away when a knock sounded at the front door. "Are you expecting company?"

Becks bit her lip. "The girls and I are going canvassing for Old Homes Tour houses, dearest."

She didn't ask him if he remembered because he obviously did not. "Oh, right," he said. "Of course." Muffin in hand, Townsend walked toward the front of the house. My, he was getting forgetful lately. Becks pushed her worries aside and divided the muffins between three white wicker baskets with perfectly pressed linen napkins lining them.

"Your wife is truly insane," she heard a voice say from the living room. Oh, Ellen. "If she thinks she is going to make a go of this homes tour, she has really lost her marbles. I agreed to be nice, but . . ."

The voices were drawing near the kitchen as Townsend said, "Well, Ellen, I think we both know that one should never count Rebecca Saint James out."

Then "Yoo-hoo! Becks, dear!" rang from the back door. Patricia, right on time.

"Come in!" Becks called, wiping her hands on her apron and leaning over to kiss her friend as she entered the kitchen. She was wearing a darling, floral print A-line dress in shades so happy Becks couldn't help but smile. She was similarly clad, and grateful that the style hid her dwindling frame. And with colors so vibrant, who would even notice a woman's sallow skin?

"It has happened!" Patricia exclaimed. "After more than a dozen interviews, Daniel has finally found a doctor he believes is competent to serve the town of Beaufort."

Ellen and Townsend entered the kitchen and, Patricia amended, "He's no Townsend Saint James, of course. But he will do." She winked.

"Well, I cannot wait to meet the fellow," Townsend said.

"He starts next week, so I'm hoping Daniel can get some much-deserved time off," Patricia said.

Becks wanted to ask more, but Ellen chided, "Come on, now. The day is wasting." So she handed each of her friends a basket and kissed Townsend goodbye. As they walked out into the bright morning sun, the birds were chirping, the sea alive, and everything felt fresh and new—even Becks, if only for a moment.

Ellen lit a cigarette as they walked and looked over at Becks questioningly. "Well, just one wouldn't hurt," Becks said, taking the cigarette her friend offered.

Patricia shook her head disapprovingly, but Becks ignored her. She was confident that if her friend knew the truth she would allow her this indulgence, and so she made her peace with that. Plus, Becks felt quite certain that the diet pills Patricia downed like Tic Tacs weren't particularly healthy either.

"Becks," Ellen said, "I do agree that Sarah and Laura will likely be able to talk the Morrises and the Henegars into including their houses on the Old Homes Tour, especially with this blueberry muffin bribe. But if you think Walter Allen is going to agree . . ."

Becks only smiled as she inhaled her cigarette. No one would tell her no. She walked through the world with a supreme confidence that usually got her what she wanted—well, until this dreadful cancer, of course. Becks was working very hard to ignore it as best she could and hope it would go away. As of yet, very little luck.

As they reached the home of Mr. Walter Allen, Becks paused for a minute to admire it. It was a huge white house with the most imposing columns in all of downtown Beaufort.

"I can't believe this came in a kit," Patricia whispered.

The reason Becks was so dead set on having this home on tour was because it was one of the original Sears kit houses, which was hard to believe. With its beautiful widow's walk, stunning glass sunroom, and gracious porches, it did not seem possible it had been shipped here in boxes and assembled on-site in the early 1900s.

Becks took a deep breath and opened the gate of the white picket fence that surrounded the property. When they reached the front door, she knocked.

When Walter came to the door, slightly stooped but still well put together for a man of almost ninety, his hair combed, his face clean-shaven, his short-sleeved blue oxford shirt tucked smartly into his elegant black trousers, Becks smiled warmly. "Rebecca!" he said, brightening.

But when he spotted the other two women, he looked suspicious, pausing in the doorway. "Well . . . come in, I suppose," he said.

Becks stifled her laugh as the women followed him inside. The other reason she wanted this house on tour was because it was so elegantly decorated. With thick oriental rugs, huge, shining crystal chandeliers, and antiques from the early 1900s, it was as authentic to the period in which it was built as any house in Beaufort. Walter's wife, Catherine, had come from money and, as such, spent considerable time traveling the world to furnish her home. She loved to entertain royally, just like Becks. But since her death five years ago, Walter had mostly kept to himself. Becks was privately relieved the house hadn't suffered.

"Walter," Becks started, handing him the basket, "we aren't just here to give you muffins."

He sighed. "I didn't expect that you were."

"We are starting a new fundraiser for the Beaufort Historic Site," Patricia started.

"So you're here for money," Walter said. He scooted toward the edge of the red crushed velvet Victorian sofa on which he was sitting and sighed. "Let me get my checkbook—"

"No sir," Ellen interrupted, somewhat delighted. "You are so generous with the Historic Site already."

He sat back, waiting.

Becks suddenly felt nervous. "Well, you see," Becks began, "many of us around town are going to open our houses for a tour to the public and—"

"Absolutely not," Walter interjected.

Ellen gave Becks an *I told you so* look. "Before you say no," Patricia said, "just think about what a wonderful cause you'd be supporting."

"I already said no," Walter said. "I write my checks. I do my part."

"Certainly," Becks said, getting an idea. "No one could argue that, Walter. You are one of the town's most dedicated philanthropists by far. We only thought it would be such an honor to Catherine if people could really marvel at her beautiful taste in antiques. Give them a sense of appreciation for what goes into the upkeep of a place like this, the preservation of not just the building but also for what's inside it. What makes it not just a house, but a home."

A look of warmth crossed Walter's face. "My Catherine did have beautiful taste."

"She did," Ellen agreed.

"And she loved opening this gorgeous home so much," Patricia chimed in.

Walter was silent for a moment. "I don't know . . ."

"Walter," Becks said, "you have done such a fantastic job preserving what Catherine did here."

He reached into the basket and took a bite of one of Becks's muffins. "Rebecca, this muffin is delightful."

"Well, thank you, Walter. We could have trays of them here if you like, make you a fresh batch for the tour."

"You think a muffin is going to change my mind?" he asked. But the corner of his mouth twitched.

Becks smiled coyly at him. "Not thought, Walter. Only hoped."

He stood up, and Becks, sensing the conversation was over, stood as well.

"Well, you were right. Fine, fine. Put the house on tour. Let me know what I need to do."

Becks hugged him impulsively. "Oh, Walter, thank you!"

"Well, it seems to mean a lot to you girls. Go on, now." He pointed at the other two baskets. "Go swindle your next victims out of their good sense."

They said their goodbyes and, back on the street, Ellen said, "Well, I stand corrected. Townsend was right. Never count Becks Saint James out."

Patricia laughed. "The way to a man's heart is through his stomach. Never fails."

Becks's muffins had saved the day once again. And, with the sun on her face, laughing with her friends to champion her latest cause, she could forget she was sick; she could forget all this goodness was coming to an end. For a moment, basking in the glow of the boats lazing up and down the creek, the children passing by on bicycles, and the neighbors waving from porches, Becks felt like perhaps she wouldn't have to suffer an inelegant ending. She was already in heaven.

Keaton

....

Becks and Townsend Style

Y ou're wearing that?" Harris asks as I walk downstairs in what I have formerly thought is an adorable pink and white linen maxi dress with a tie in the back. He is sitting on the plaid couch in the family room, beer in his hand, as my grandparents' huge antique TV drones in the background.

I cross my arms, and he looks up. "Well I *was* wearing this," I say.

He scrunches his nose. "Don't you think it's a little, I don't know . . . *revealing*?"

I can't help but laugh, mostly because that is such a word our mother would use. "Revealing?" I look down at the dress, which extends to my ankles and up to my collarbone. The back is low, but not super low. "You've lost your mind."

"I just don't want Bowen to get the wrong idea."

"There's no wrong idea. We're going out with, like, a group of people." But then I think about what Anderson said. Is Bowen trying to impress me? Because I'm definitely hoping I impress him.

I sit down beside Harris and pick up the remote, which looks like it could incinerate a human with a single click. "You watch *The Mary Tyler Moore Show*?"

"It seems sort of wrong to watch modern-day programming inside the time capsule."

"When in the seventies do as the seventies do?"

He nods. "Yeah." Then he sighs.

"What now?"

"It's just . . . come on, Keaton. You're barely out of the Jonathan thing and you're just jumping in with the next guy."

"What do you mean? We've never even gone out on a date."

"Fine. But I think you like him. And I think you need to be careful."

I nod resolutely. "I do like him, Harris. And if I discover that he likes me back, I will be thrilled."

He just looks at me.

"I think you're getting a little bit ahead of yourself," I add.

He shakes his head. "Nope. I saw the way he looked at you. And Anderson's no fool. That dad of his is about to make a move."

"God, I hope you're right."

I smile, and Harris sighs again.

I point at the TV screen. "Do you think things were simpler then?" I look around. "Well . . . now?"

We laugh, and it feels nice. There's something about the bond between a brother and sister that can't ever really be broken, something about the person who has been by your side through every single thing you've ever faced. There's a comfort level with Harris I don't have with anyone else, an understanding we share about the lives we've led that no one else could ever get. But it's simple moments like this that I love most.

"I don't think so," he says. "I think they had their own share of problems." He looks down. "Shag carpeting, for starters."

Before I can answer, there's a knock at the front door just a few feet away. I scramble up off the couch, but Harris scrambles faster. He pulls the door open, arms crossed, and appraises Bowen. He is wearing what I intuitively know is a new button-down shirt tucked into his jeans, with very, very nice shoes.

Harris is also looking at the shoes, and despite the grief he's given me, looks begrudgingly impressed.

"Where are you taking my little sister?" he asks. "And what time will you have her home?"

Anderson appears from behind Bowen and says, "Come on, Harris! I'm ready to school you at pool. Does New York City money spend better?"

We all laugh, and I take Bowen's hand to get him out of there before Harris can ask any more obnoxious questions.

The hand holding is kind of a utilitarian move until Bowen doesn't drop my hand. And that makes me feel tingly all over. And I realize I'm actually holding hands with a man I find very attractive. But, I remind myself, this is a regular night with our regular group, and I'm turning it into something it isn't.

"Have you had a good day?" I ask. Bowen nods and smiles at me, heading down the boardwalk.

He is a man of few words, and I'm trying not to let that make me nervous. He turns his head to me. "You are beautiful," he says.

Not I *look* beautiful. But I *am*. It is a small distinction that makes me blush. I don't know how to answer. Returning the compliment seems forced. Saying thank you seems like I agree with him. So I just pull closer to him as we walk.

"You don't smell like fish. Not even a little," I say.

He laughs.

"It's kind of unsettling, actually."

We walk down one of the private docks and I spot a Carolina blue and white boat. The R/V *Capricorn*, which belongs to UNC

Marine Sciences. Bowen points to it and says, "Our vessel for the evening."

I feel myself brighten. "Really? This is awesome. I haven't gotten to see Beaufort by water yet."

He helps me step onto the boat, and I'm instantly glad I wore flat sandals. A man is inside the pilothouse, and Bowen waves. "That's Captain Ron."

I raise my eyebrows. "You aren't captaining?"

He shakes his head. "Not tonight."

I smile and call, "Nice to meet you, Ron!" He waves but doesn't come out, and I get the feeling he's trying to stay out of the way.

"Where is everyone else?" I ask.

Bowen looks disappointed. "Well, I thought maybe I could take you on the boat for a little bit and then we'd meet up with them. Is that okay?"

I smile, surprised and delighted. And I'm laughing on the inside too, because . . . was he too nervous to ask me out? He had to, like, spring a date on me? "Oh, well, I mean, yeah. Yes. That sounds perfect."

Bowen walks into the pilothouse and reappears with a bottle of white wine tucked under his arm, two glasses, stems between his fingers, and a charcuterie board that I know Black Sheep let him take to go. I wonder if this is his go-to move. But then I remember Anderson saying that Bowen doesn't really date, and I feel instantly better. Ron pulls the boat away from the dock, and I marvel at the gorgeous sunset. The entire blue sky has turned hot pink and vibrant orange. Bowen hands me a glass of wine and I take a sip, the cold, crisp Sancerre the perfect antidote to this warm, still evening. Bowen sits, and I lean beside him. He points to a cluster of wild horses grazing on the Rachel Carson Reserve as we ride by.

"Two distinct species of horse live on that island," he says. "And they have never interbred. Not once since they got here hundreds of years ago."

"Wow," I say.

A group of egrets sits patiently, stalking fish in a patch of marsh grass. "I'll take you kayaking in there later if you want," he says, pointing toward the marsh.

I smile and nod, loving that we've just gotten here, and he's already seeing a next time. But I remind myself to take it slow. Because even though this feels like a date—and Bowen is definitely wearing a date shirt and date shoes—I'm still not totally positive it is one. I don't want to jinx it, so I'm going with the flow.

"Do you think you'll always live here?" I ask Bowen, studying him, noticing how comfortable he seems.

He nods. "I really do. It's a great place for me to work, but more than that, it's got great people. I always know that Anderson has someone to keep an eye on him. I have friends here, family, your meddling buddies."

I smile. "They really are something, aren't they?"

"What about you?"

I shake my head. "I love it here, but I don't have a job or the hope of finding one imminently. I'm squatting at my grandparents', but once that sells, I won't have a place to live. It's beautiful, and I love feeling like I'm a part of something. But I have to be realistic that it probably isn't a fit long-term."

He makes a perfect cracker with jam, cheese, and soppressata and hands it to me. We both half sit, half lean against the side of the boat. "Don't people basically work remotely now?"

I nod. "I guess. But New York has been my home for so long now and . . . I don't know. I know all the reasons I shouldn't go back to All Welcome, but you were there. You heard Allison's offer. It's incredible."

Bowen rolls his eyes, and I hit him lightly with the back of my hand. "You can't be serious, Keaton. Allison? She's just so . . ." He trails off, but I can fill in the adjectives he's searching for.

"I know. But, I mean, you've only seen this one, admittedly kind of vapid side of her. Sure, she *is* a little selfish, but she's also totally brilliant, and she's believed in me and encouraged me in a way I can't express. She always makes a big deal out of my ideas—"

"It's because they're good ideas," Bowen interrupts.

I laugh. "You have no idea if they're good."

"I know they're good because they're your ideas."

Well now, that is sweet. My face flushes. "I'm just saying, most CEOs aren't promoting women in their early thirties to the head of their company. She can be tough, but she's also kind, and she really does want to help people. And I want that too, so it makes sense."

"Sure, I get that," Bowen says. "But there are plenty of ways for you to help people right here in Beaufort."

A pair of dolphins jumps up right by the boat, as if to say, *See how great it is here?* "I love it," I admit. "It's paradise. But there's no reason for me to stay."

"No?" he asks, turning toward me. "No reason at all?"

"Well, I mean, I have to finish the house. And I love the Dames. And I have made some friends here." He's looking at me intently, and I hear myself babbling. Suddenly, my palms are sweating, and I'm aware of how quickly my heart is beating.

Bowen stands and takes one of my sweaty hands in his, pulling me up. He seems so calm, in contrast to me, whose pulse is pounding wildly. And, by the way he's looking at me, I think maybe, just maybe, this attraction I feel isn't one-sided.

"What are you doing?" I ask, stupidly, my mouth suddenly dry.

He studies my face, as if reading it, and puts his hand under my chin. "Giving you a reason to stay."

Butterflies explode in my chest as his lips meet mine, as he wraps his arms around me. In his kiss, I feel all the things he hasn't been able to say to me. I don't want to stop kissing him, but he pulls away, and I look up at him. "You make a compelling argument," I say, realizing how breathless I am.

"I want you to stay."

I nod, unable to form words.

He kisses me again so softly that my knees literally go weak—as though, if he weren't holding me up, I might just slide right down onto the deck. He kisses me tentatively and then longer, deeper.

I actually forget that we are on the water, and I feel disoriented.

He breaks the kiss and grins at me, lightening the intensity. "See," he says, "Anderson has just gotten really attached to you, and I'm afraid of how he might feel if you leave."

I laugh. "Anderson, huh?"

He nods and kisses me again.

I take a sip of wine. "Well, Anderson and I have time to get to know each other a little better and figure things out before I make my next career move."

Bowen eyes me. "Sounds like you're getting a little too cozy with my son."

I smack him on the leg, and he laughs, putting his arm around me.

I can't help but think of my grandparents, of their instant connection—at least, if my grandfather's journals are to be believed. Is there a chance that Bowen is my Townsend? Could it really be that easy? I don't know Becks's side of the story, but there's just something about the way she preserved all her entertaining details, her recipes, her secrets, that makes me feel confident she was truly happy in life. The more I delve into trying on her day-to-day for size, the more I under-stand why. I want to know more. I want to *do* more. I want to carry on this legacy that she began.

"Hey," I say, suddenly getting an idea. "I found this notebook of my grandmother's where she kept these super-detailed lists of her dinner party guests and menus and all sorts of other things, like what the guests had in common and questions she planned to ask to keep the conversation flowing."

"I'm doing well if I can find a clean shirt."

I smile. "Well, in the spirit of honoring her memory, I was think-ing about hosting a party for the ladies and their husbands and Harris, of course, after the Old Homes Tour. Want to come?"

"I'd love it. And how about if I get Anderson to keep Salt at our house so you can focus on getting ready?"

"Can he do that? Stay home alone, I mean?"

Bowen nods. "Well, I mean, we're right next door."

"Okay. Well, if you're sure."

By the time we've had dinner and dessert, I am practically float-ing. I feel a little guilty about not meeting our friends tonight, but I don't want to break the spell. As we walk down the dock heading home, I am light-headed and full-on smitten.

Bowen walks me up my front steps, lit only by the moon, and takes me in his arms, kissing me for what feels like the hundredth time tonight, and also the first. I want to take him inside, upstairs, but before I can, the front porch light flips on. "I will kill him," I say. Harris's face appears in one door pane, and I pull away when I see Anderson's in another.

"Do you think they saw us?" Bowen whispers. "Or can we still sneak over to my house?"

We both laugh, because we are not inconspicuous in the least.

"Tonight was perfect," I say. "I'm sorry it has to end."

He nods.

As Harris opens the door, Bowen asks, "What should I do to help you get ready for the tour after-party?"

"How about if you come up with the questions?"

"Questions for what?" Harris asks.

"You know how I was telling you about Becks's party notebook?"

"Yeah."

"We are having a good, old-fashioned dinner party," I say. "Becks and Townsend style, complete with one of her menus and table-wide conversation, just how she liked it."

"I want to come," Harris says.

"Me too," Anderson chimes in.

"You are going to dog-sit Salt at our house," Bowen says.

Anderson looks up at me excitedly. "Really?"

I nod.

"Awesome!"

"And you," I say to Harris, "are going to help me cook."

He shakes his head. "I don't know how."

"He's lying," I say. "He went to the Culinary Institute of America for a semester while he was finding himself."

"I was hoping you'd forgotten about that."

Bowen shakes his head. "Someone's going to have to help her. She doesn't know how to cream butter."

I look at him, aghast. "They *told* you about that?"

Bowen just smiles, and Harris says, "Fine. I'll cook."

"But we're cooking things from Becks's notebook," I add.

When Anderson has run home and Harris has gone upstairs, Bowen and I sneak one more kiss under the stars, and everything inside me feels soft and puddly with how much I adore him. He makes me think that maybe I *could* stay here, that maybe I could make a new life, a happier life.

I know tomorrow is going to be really busy with the tour, and I want this table set like it's ready for one of Becks's famous dinner parties when people walk in the door. So after Bowen leaves, in my dreamy wine-and-kiss-fueled glee, I put a record on my grandparents' old hi-fi, wondering what it must have felt like living in this beautiful house when my grandparents were here. I pull a large linen tablecloth out of the closet and spread it delicately on the wooden table, which I have polished to perfection. As I pull my grandmother's chargers out of the corner cupboard and set one at each place, I think of the friends she must have had around this table, the friends I have made here in such a short time. I open a box that holds the most delicate, beautiful mother-of-pearl-handled dessert forks and knives and decide to use these beside the dessert plates. And, as the Carpenters sing the opening lines of "We've Only Just Begun," I think of who will be sitting beside me at this table. *Bowen.* This man who needs me in his life. This man who, although we've only just begun, wants me to stay.

A Fate Worse Than Death

FRIDAY, AUGUST 20, 1976

Tip: In much the same way that lust is not love and rhinestone is not diamond, paper is not a napkin. Linen is a napkin. In all manners of life, Virginia, find the real thing. Never settle for less.

Becks placed the mother-of-pearl-handled dessert forks in the fork holder beside the stack of plates, smiling at the Rothschild birds hand-painted on them. She loved to examine each of the twelve pairs of birds, thinking of the story of how Baroness Rothschild lost her pearl necklace in the garden and, later, the gardener found pairs of birds playing with it in a tree.

It was such a lovely story, almost as lovely as the idea that the twelve pairs of birds were all ones who mated for life, who were destined to be together until the end, as were she and Townsend. Becks had a rousing thought: Perhaps she would be one of the lucky ones who outlived their doctor's predictions. Perhaps she could carry on as usual for a long, long time, be there to see her children marry and have children of their own. Stay with Townsend until it came time for them both.

Heartened by the thought and by her beautiful table, Becks felt pride shoot through her. Finally, the kickoff party for the First Annual Beaufort Historic Site Old Homes Tour was here! She had made sure to put "First Annual" in the title. She felt it made it more likely that the tradition would continue. And, looking back on her time in Beaufort, Becks felt even prouder that after the rocky start she had had here, she was now making her mark on the town she loved—the town that, she felt certain, finally loved her back.

Townsend and Becks had moved to Beaufort as soon as they married, forty years ago now—just like he had always dreamed. When his grandparents passed away, they left the house to Townsend, the first grandson, as was family tradition.

The first time Townsend drove Becks over the drawbridge, she fell in love with Beaufort's beautiful clapboard houses, its history, and its main attraction—the water. She adored Noe's Hardware and F. R. Bell's soda fountain. She bought fresh bread from Betts Bakery, met Townsend for sandwiches at the KozyNook Luncheonette, and enjoyed movie nights at the Seabreeze Theater. She loved the way she could walk up and down the boardwalk, practically surrounded by water, and that Townsend had Friday night boxing shows, Sunday skeet shooting at Noe Skeet Field, and his fellow sportsmen at the Edgewater Lodge to keep him entertained.

Yes, Becks loved the town. Only, the town didn't quite love her back when she arrived, which she found endlessly frustrating. She wasn't from there, which she learned quickly made the locals distrust her.

Becks was unfathomably grateful when Sarah, who had remained a dear friend, made it her mission to show Becks around and introduce her to everyone, heritage be damned. She was by Becks's side as she participated in the First Annual Carteret Tennis Tournament and served on the altar guild at St. Paul's Episcopal Church—where she had, despite believing it would be impossible, found a home church again. She and Townsend even took first prize at the Casino by the Seas' Tacky Party, where their unattractive attire stole the show. (Jimmie Livingston and the NBC Orchestra were astonishing.) Oh, how she tried. But despite her best efforts to befriend them, the rest of the women were merely polite to Becks. They never quite *warmed* to her.

But then everything changed. When Becks and Townsend sat in their living room and listened to President Roosevelt say, "the American people in their righteous might will win through to absolute victory," Becks believed with all her heart—as her hands moved faster on her cross-stitch—that her husband would be spared from battle. He was the town's only physician, after all. Which is why she was so shocked when he came home three and a half months later and announced, with bravado in his voice, "Becks. I've been accepted."

"Accepted for what?"

"I've been chosen as one of forty-five hundred men who will enter the Army Air Forces Flying Training Command."

Becks blinked at him rapidly, in disbelief. "I'm sorry. You're a thirty-five-year-old doctor. Wouldn't you be better able to serve your country by taking care of patients? Preferably at home?"

He shook his head. "Nah, Becks. They need able-bodied men over there, and it seems they have enough doctors. Plus, I can hire a new partner for here." She didn't know what to say and, suddenly, her mouth was so dry she couldn't speak anyway. "Yup," he told his wife, whistling proudly, "eighteen weeks of training, and I'll be up in the skies, fighting the bad guys." He paused. "You know how much I've always wanted to fly."

Becks had gone pale. "In the skies? Where you could be shot down?"

He had shaken his head. "Nah, not up there. On the ground—now that's where I'd be shot down. But up in the air, I can dodge them."

Becks didn't point out how disastrously flawed this thinking was, especially from a man who had never been in a cockpit, from a man who would be going to war with a paltry eighteen weeks of training. "Why would you volunteer?" Becks asked, her voice catching. "You might never have been drafted at all!"

Townsend looked at her adoringly, like she was silly to believe such a thing. "This way, darling, I get to choose what I do. And I can't stay home while everyone else fights for our country. Would you want to be married to a man like that?"

It was the first time in their six years of marriage that Becks had felt truly angry at Townsend. How could he leave her? And willingly so?

It was the hardest time of her life, bar none, being without Townsend. But it bonded her to the women of Beaufort. Becks's neighbor Ellen, the optometrist's wife, had always been cordial, but with both their husbands gone, they had come to count on each other quite a bit more for evening porch sitting company. One night, during one of their chats, Becks had an idea. "Ellen," she said. "My mother used to have the most spectacular dinner parties. If I could pull one together, could you invite some of the other ladies?"

Ellen had been thrilled by the prospect, and Becks knew that if Ellen helped host—she was very popular in town—the women would come. They all needed something to take their mind off the war and their beloved husbands away fighting.

It was nearly impossible to pull off a dinner party in those days, what with the sugar rations, the meat rations, the dairy rations, and the oil rations. But Becks saved her stamps, ate from her garden for weeks, and, when she was certain she could pull together a meager but suitable meal, invited ten women to sit at her table with Ellen's help. She borrowed the menu from Mrs. Josephine Culbertson, the famous bridge hostess who was often featured in the newspaper with wartime meal tips and recipes. She prepared pork and beans and Mexican-style brown bread and butter sandwiches, baked apple rings, jellied perfection salad, and, for dessert, made brownies. It was a different sort of menu for her, but, with the war on, what wasn't? The women raved about the hearty meal, and they bonded over missing their husbands, registering the serial numbers of their tires with the government, and being suddenly, fiercely alone.

She would later write to Townsend: *Tonight taught me something: We can be from different socioeconomic backgrounds, different parts of the world, have differing political and religious views, but, if one thing binds us—just one—that is enough to start a friendship. That is what has happened here. Strangers have become friends. If that's the one good thing that comes out of this dreadful war, then I suppose I will take it.*

The dinner parties continued, morphing into something that more accurately resembled potluck—something Becks's mother would have despised. But Becks had no way to feed people on her own rations alone. So they all chipped in and week after week, laughing over cups of coffee, soups, and stews, twelve women who had been acquaintances found more than common ground: they found a family. And Becks realized that something as simple as a dinner party could bond women into lifelong friendship, that something as small as a laugh with people who understood your plight could spark joy. Those parties gave her not only her larger circle but also her tight, true friendships with Ellen, Sarah, and Laura. And, for that, she would always be grateful.

Becks mused now, as she folded a linen napkin in the large stack that would serve dozens of guests at this cocktail reception, that these parties had changed her life. When she was younger, she had imagined being the family hostess, having her mother and father, children and, one day, grandchildren gathered around her table when it was time for celebrations. She hadn't gotten that, but she liked to think she had made lemonade out of lemons. She had made family out of strangers. She had made celebrations out of summer suppers.

The napkin in her hand was starched and pressed to perfection. She folded it in half, then fourths, running her fingers down the creases, making crisp straight lines so the corners would meet. She smiled at her monogram, tracing her finger over it.

Townsend entered the room and kissed her. But even as she smiled, he frowned slightly and pulled away, examining her. "Becks, your eyes. They're yellow. When did that start?"

Becks studied him.

"Do you feel all right?" Townsend asked, prodding her.

She could tell by the way he was looking at her, with such fresh shock, that Townsend had no memory of asking her about her jaundiced eyes a few weeks ago. He had no memory that he had worried about her before.

She pulled her husband close. "I am fine, darling. As long as I have you, I am fine."

The fear over her husband's health was replaced by a surge of joy at the remembrance her children were here as Virginia called, "Mom! Can you come up here please?" Oh, how she loved having her children home. The doorbell rang, and Becks knew the time for hosting had begun.

Becks had invited more than one hundred people to celebrate their hard work in making the Old Homes Tour a success—the

docents, the ticket takers, the homeowners, the Historic Site tour vol-
unteers, and more. And now they were arriving. Such fun! "You get
that," she said to Townsend, rolling her shoulders back. "I'm going to
go help Virginia, and then I'll be right down."

When she entered her daughter's room upstairs, Virginia turned
to her and smiled in her usual way. Becks was so happy to have her
daughter here to celebrate this occasion that already meant so much
to her. She hoped she had started something that her daughter would
take over one day, that this event would connect them even after her
death. Virginia's long brown hair was in loose, flowy waves down her
back, and she was wearing a red crocheted dress that hugged her lithe
body. Becks put her hand to her heart. "You look too beautiful," she
said.

Virginia scrunched her nose. "Are you sure? Because I have another dress I could wear if you think this one is inappropriate for
the occasion." Becks shook her head, and, suddenly, she was overwhelmed, light-headed with dread, anger, and fear. How could she
leave this daughter who needed her? It wasn't fair. It was too soon.
This wasn't how it was supposed to be.

Becks heard voices downstairs. Her party guests were arriving.
How many more parties would she host? Panic enveloped her. She
needed to compose herself. "Sweetheart, I'm going to grab some air,"
she said as normally as she could muster. Even still, she could hear the
quaver in her voice. "Please make sure there is a fresh bar of hand soap
and a fresh roll of toilet tissue in every bathroom."

Virginia looked concerned. "Sure, Mother."

Finding herself quite out of words, Becks hurried down the
back steps and out the kitchen door. It was very unlike her, and it
went against all her rules as a hostess. But, for once, she couldn't put
her feelings aside. Her breath was coming in fast gulps. It was like

everything she had kept inside since she'd found out she was dying was bubbling up in her like hot, boiling lava.

She tried the door on the detached garage, which was, blessedly, unlocked. It was far enough from the house that no one would hear her. Becks opened the door, closed it, and let out a blood-curdling, howling, guttural scream that she only now realized had been building up inside her ever since that visit to Daniel's office where he gave her the news that her life wasn't going to turn out like she'd planned. Then, her body, feeling as though it was no longer hers, broke into gasping sobs. She sank down between the lawn mower and a forgotten tricycle, unable to keep it in any longer.

She was crying so hard that she didn't hear the door open. It was only when she looked up and saw a strange man that she realized she wasn't alone. She screamed again, in earnest. She recognized him immediately. The new neighbor who had leered at her so creepily. She didn't want to be alone with him. But he put his hand up, so as not to startle her more. "Are you okay?" She could tell he was trying to remain calm. And that was when she realized how devastatingly handsome he was. "I was taking out the garbage when I heard a scream."

Becks tried to wipe her eyes, tried to compose herself, but a dam had burst inside her, and for a reason she could not explain, she found herself pouring out to this complete stranger: "I'm going to leave them all, and they need me. My husband, my daughter, my son. It is my job to take care of them. That's what I do. I take care of all of them. And they can't do it without me."

She knew the task of taking care of Townsend—even if his memory wasn't failing, the man could barely pour his own milk—would fall to Virginia. To ask her to take care of a father, a potential new husband, and new babies who might come along all at once was unthinkable. And she wouldn't be there to help.

This very handsome stranger knelt down in front of her. He nodded. "I understand. I do. I've recently had some changes that have made my world feel like it was burning down."

Becks cocked her head, still unable to stop her tears, to catch her breath. She was a good listener. People had always told her their stories. She wanted to know more about this man and his past, and she knew enough to know that if she was quiet, he would likely tell her.

"I lost everything," he continued. "My job. My income. My fiancée. But I'm starting over. I'm making a new life." He paused. "Losing someone we love is unthinkable, but that's what people do. They start over."

Something about this story seemed familiar, but she couldn't figure out why. Her eyes adjusted to the light and focused on his. They were a blue she'd never seen before. *The color of ice crystals. The clearest blue I've ever seen.* It was Virginia who had said that. But about a man from D.C. Not North Carolina. Becks shook off her nerves. What was wrong with her lately? That man was back in Kansas. Was it the medicine making her so jumpy? Or the thought that her end was drawing near? She couldn't be sure, but, either way, it was unsettling.

He blew a breath out of his perfectly formed mouth. Becks was suddenly very calm as he studied her face and, almost comically, pulled a pin light out of his pocket and shone it in her eyes. "What kind of cancer do you have?"

"Pancreatic," she whispered.

He winced, and Becks's tears flowed anew, though her sobs had calmed now. "They can't live the end with me," she continued. "They aren't strong enough." She wouldn't have been able to express the desperation she felt in words. But it suddenly consumed her. This man looked as if he was thinking, and her mind strayed enough from her own troubles to realize something. "You're the new doctor in town," she said. "That's how you see that I have cancer."

He nodded. "Yes. I'm Peter. I'm here to practice with Dr. Walker. Do you know him?"

He stood and Becks, calming, suddenly realized how much it smelled like gasoline and fresh yard clippings in there. She wiped her eyes and composed herself. "Dr. Walker is, in fact, my dearest friend besides his wife." As if remembering herself—who she was, what she did—she said, "I'm Rebecca Saint James."

Becks heard the fireworks she had planned as a surprise for her partygoers exploding on the dock. They were nothing compared to the volcano that had just erupted inside her. That ever-calm facade had cracked—and in front of a total stranger of all people. She couldn't believe what a fool she'd made of herself.

Peter nodded. "I hope I can help you," he said. "I'd like very much to try."

Becks felt warm inside at this stranger's kindness. She nodded, realizing that her initial instinct, the one that made shivers run down her spine, had been all wrong. Maybe it was the medicine that had ruined her internal barometer. But then Peter reached his hand down to help her up, and she noticed the scar on his hand. Unavoidable, totally distinct: a bat. In an instant, she knew exactly who he was. And everything inside her went white-hot with panic.

Alone at Last

I graduated top of my class from college. I helped build one of the most successful companies in the country from the ground up. But never have I felt as proud of myself as I do right now, when I see that all the hard work I've put into my grandparents' showplace of a house has paid off. It's still a museum of the seventies, obviously. I didn't change the decor. But it looks fantastic, maybe even Becks-worthy, as groups of people mill from room to room taking in the original molding, the floors repurposed from an eighteenth-century church that caught fire, and, of course, the appliances of yesteryear.

"War generals and presidents alike are rumored to have eaten at this very dining table," I hear Betty saying from the room beside me. It is my cue that the next group is coming my way. Harris, who has begrudgingly joined me as co-docent in the library, looks exhaustedly at me and sighs. I can't believe the ladies roped him into this. My brother being a docent for his grandparents' house? I never thought I'd see the day.

"You'd better get the biggest offer and hugest chunk of commission ever on this place," Harris whispers.

I smile that he would do this for me. As a fresh group of tourists and locals appear, Harris says, for at least the hundredth time today, "The bookshelves in my grandfather's library are made from reclaimed wood from a ship that crashed right off the tip of the Rachel Carson Reserve in the early seventeen hundreds."

"The bookshelves," I add, "contain more than two thousand volumes from our grandparents' collection, including an entire set of Hemingway books personalized to our grandfather."

The crowd gasps. "They were old fishing buddies," Harris adds.

I wonder if this is stretching the truth, but I guess if fishing together once makes people buddies, then so be it. Plus, as Harris pointed out, they could have fished together a hundred times—it wasn't like our grandfather wrote in his journal every day. There is so much we don't know. So much I want to know. And I plan to try to get as many answers as I possibly can tonight after this is all over, at the dinner party I will be hosting for the ladies and their spouses. And Bowen.

When the group exits, Harris says, "How's the work situation?"

I have asked Allison for more time to make my decision, and she has agreed to give me until August, which means I can stay here a little longer, see if this thing with Bowen might be real. I can fix the house up, see the sale through. Then, if Bowen and I do work out . . . well, I don't know what happens then. And I think that is why I am avoiding making a decision.

I'm mad at myself for not being mad at Allison. I'm mad at myself for even considering this. I'm mad at myself for knowing that, in spite of it all, I am still kind of excited by the idea of returning to the job I loved for so long. No matter what I choose, I will lose something.

It's like Harris can hear my thoughts. "Keat, please don't tell me you're basing yet another career decision on some guy."

"I didn't say that." I say it so defensively that I'm sure it affirms his fears. "Besides, he isn't just *some guy.*"

"Neither was Jonathan," Harris says.

I cross my arms. "Harris, you and Mom always do this. You're so critical. You've dated the entire Victoria's Secret catalog, and I don't see anyone jumping all over you about it." Just then, another group walks in.

Harris starts in on his docent commentary, seamlessly: "The leatherbound first editions were all acquired from the Vanderbilts' personal library."

I shoot him a look because that is a total lie, and, furthermore, Biltmore's entire original library is intact. He grins at me devilishly. "Wow," one tourist says. "Yup," Harris agrees, pointing vaguely to the top shelf. "That's the actual book George Vanderbilt was holding when he died."

I give him a withering look as the group passes into the next room. Harris picks up as if our conversation was never interrupted. "At least I'm not rearranging my life around the women I date."

"Which is just so healthy," I say sarcastically.

"You could just come work for me," he says. "Skip out on All Welcome and get your life in New York back."

I shake my head. "I don't want to work for my brother."

He throws his hands up in the air. "What if I need your help?"

"What if I don't need yours?" He rolls his eyes. "Okay," I say. "You have to admit that being the VP of All Welcome is an insane opportunity."

Harris shakes his head. "I know. I know it is."

"Only . . ."

"Only what."

"Only sometimes I wonder if maybe it's time for me to have something of my own. Maybe spend my life building something that's mine, not breaking my neck for something that's Allison's."

Harris leans against Townsend's desk. "I don't know. I mean, not that you have to do what I do, but I've spent my entire life building other people's brands, making their movies happen and their protein powders sell, their egomaniacal memoirs hit bestseller lists. And I actually find it quite fulfilling."

I shake my head. "But it's fulfilling because while you're doing that, you're building your own company, your own reputation. It's *yours.*"

He nods. "I guess you're right. But if I've learned anything from Rebecca and Townsend Saint James, it's that living a life that serves other people isn't the worst thing. Look, Keat, I just want you to be happy. If going back to All Welcome makes you happy, fine. If staying in Beaufort is your North Star, great." He pauses. "On a brother-worried-about-his-sister's-feelings level, I have concerns about All Welcome. But, from a business standpoint, I know that if you go back there as VP, you'll be every headhunter's dream." He shrugs. "You just have to ask yourself: Is what you're getting worth what you're giving up?"

It's a question that echoes in my mind three hours later as I do one last fluff of the flowers on the table, as I breeze by Bowen and squeeze his arm as he pulls a baking dish of brown rice out of the oven. Not, like, the healthy kind of brown rice. A kind of brown rice from Becks's notebook made with butter and French onion soup and beef consommé that smells so good my mouth is watering. I walk toward the sink, and he grabs my wrist. I turn, and he wraps his arms around me, kissing me. Not just in a passing way, but like he means it.

When I turn back toward the sink to start the dishes, a smile on my face, I see Anderson out the window, throwing the ball at Salt. I adore that child. There are no words. "How does someone just walk away from that sweet little boy?" I wonder out loud. I turn, putting my hand to my mouth. This isn't really my business. "Sorry," I whisper.

"Don't be sorry," Bowen says. "I'll never totally understand why Kerry left, or how she could walk away from us so easily. But she did, and that's that."

"She was just gone, and you never heard from her again?"

"No, I heard from her," he says. "She'd call a few times a year, send a present for Anderson's birthday. When he was very young, she'd visit a couple times a year out of the blue . . ." He trails off. "Anderson doesn't remember, but that was the worst part. I spent years thinking she would come back, that we would be a family. How pathetic is that?"

I squeeze his shoulder. "Not pathetic at all. Hope is the most courageous act there is. At least, I've always thought so."

He looks out the window. "She showed up at his fifth birthday party saying that she wanted to come back, that she wanted to be back in our lives for good." I can feel his anger rising. "I knew I couldn't trust her, but I wanted a family for Anderson so badly."

I can feel how much he wanted her to come back, for them to be a family, to raise their son together, maybe have more children. I feel it because I have wanted those very same things. And, sometimes, after a relationship is over, it feels impossible to keep the faith that it will happen one day. I imagine it must be a million times more painful to have that and then watch it slip through your fingers.

"She was here a month, maybe six weeks. Long enough for Anderson to get attached, to want her back in his life, to be devastated when she disappeared. I told her then that that was the last time, that she couldn't keep doing this to him." He shook his head. "And, for five years, she listened. But now she's here again," he says, shocking me so much I almost stab my finger with the knife I'm wiping.

"Wait. What? Here? What do you mean, here? Does Anderson know?"

He rolls his eyes, but I can tell it's out of annoyance at her, not me. "She showed up a few days ago. She's staying in Morehead City and she wants to see Anderson, to prove she's changed, that she's here to stay. But I just don't know. I get that she wants to see him, that she wants to make up for the past, but I don't think it's fair to him to get jerked around by her." He pauses. "I don't love the idea of her being just a couple of miles over the bridge."

My heart is racing uncomfortably at the idea of her being here, of wanting both Anderson and Bowen back. I stare at him, not knowing quite what to say.

"I'm sorry I haven't told you," he says. "You've just been so busy that I figured I'd wait until after the tour to tell you."

I'm somewhat bothered that he hasn't told me until now, but things are very new between us, and, well, this isn't about me. It's about Anderson. So I swallow my annoyance. "I get it, and I'm sure this has been impossible. But maybe she's changed?"

"She has not changed," he says, irritation rising in his voice.

"Well, not everyone has the mother gene," I say, more matter-of-factly than I mean to.

Bowen raises his eyebrows. "From your tone I feel like maybe this is a sore subject?"

I try to laugh, but it doesn't quite take. "I think we're getting in a little too deep." But I can't help but think of my mom right now.

He opens the fridge, grabs a beer and a bottle of champagne and fills one of Becks's crystal coupes, which are all ready and waiting. "We've got fresh drinks and nowhere to be. Hit me with it." He hands me the glass.

I hesitate. "I don't know. It's just that my mom wasn't really around much when we were kids. I mean, we lived in the same house. We ate dinner together a couple times a week." I sigh. "I realize this sounds nothing like your situation with Kerry. By all accounts I had an idyllic childhood. My mom just wasn't really interested in mothering. We were, like, the thing she did if it suited her, if a new family wasn't coming into the domestic violence shelter she started. There's an irony there because she was so interested in building families. Just not her own."

Bowen takes a sip of beer and nods at me, but says nothing.

"But I'm fine, you know? And honestly, my mom and I are good too." I pause. "I know she did the best she could. She taught us how to be independent, how not to need anyone else to get through life. And being here has given me so much insight into why she is the way she is. It must have been really difficult for her to get close to people after she lost her parents all at once like that."

When Bowen doesn't respond, I add, "So, I think that's my long way of saying that sometimes we don't always get the mothers we want, but maybe that's okay." I pause and squeeze his arm. "We can't really know how Kerry's presence is going to affect Anderson. But what I do know is that whatever decision you make about whether she's in his life is going to be the right one."

"Anderson is so lucky to have such a village around him taking Kerry's place," Bowen says. "Including you. But I still get the feeling that sometimes he feels what you feel. Neglected by his mom. And I hate that."

"Then maybe this is your time to let her back into his life." I shrug. "Maybe this is the time she stays. But, either way, Anderson is going to be fine because he has you."

Bowen is quiet, fiddling with his beer label, and I decide to let him be alone with his thoughts. But as I step toward the sink, he turns toward me. "Don't leave," he says suddenly.

I smile at him. "What do you mean? I have to fill the water glasses eventually."

"No," he says, pulling me into him, kissing me again. "I know you got an amazing job offer, and I know I'm supposed to be supportive and smile and tell you to go, to live your best life. And I was going to. I was planning on it. But I'm selfish, and I don't want you to go back to New York because I can't go to New York. I have a ten-year-old in school, and I can't just pick him up and move his life."

"But there are all those great marine biology positions in New York," I joke.

He smiles sadly then shakes his head. "Forgive me. It isn't fair, and it's way too soon. But I hate the idea of never knowing if there's something real here. Anderson and I—"

The timer on the stove dings, and he turns it off. I am worried about my perfect roast chickens. Well, okay, Harris's perfect roast chickens. But I helped. Kind of. "I'm coming!" Harris calls from upstairs. "Don't touch my chickens!"

"I'm kind of shocked," I say.

"That you didn't ruin the chickens?"

"No, because that was the kind of honest conversation I'm not really used to. And when I'm with a guy I think is really honest, like Jonathan, he's busy impregnating his ex."

He laughs. "Well, I'm definitely not busy doing that. But I am being selfish. Because I have no idea what the future holds. But I'll never forgive myself if I don't at least ask you to stay."

I don't know what the future holds either. None of us do. But standing with Bowen in this kitchen in Beaufort, I can imagine a future in this quirky town with these warm, loving people. And that future, I have to admit, looks impossibly bright.

Becks

....

Wholly Irreplaceable

TUESDAY, AUGUST 24, 1976

Tip: In parties, in life—in everything, really—never shout when you can whisper. A gentle prod is almost always more effective than a forceful hand. In the same way, a delicate, well-planned event is almost always more memorable and enjoyable than a large, splashy affair. Your job is to entertain your guests, not impress them.

The Old Homes Tour had been a rousing success. Becks was so pleased that she had gathered Ellen, Patricia, Laura, and Sarah to celebrate over a round of bridge at the Coral Bay Club. Over the bridge in Atlantic Beach, the club was perfect for those days when one needed an ocean view and a lovely saltwater breeze.

Between rounds, as a server refilled their champagne coupes, Becks shared a look with Patricia. They had been hatching a plan all morning, and it was time to enact it.

"Ladies," she said, raising her glass, "cheers to the most successful fundraiser Beaufort has ever seen."

They all clinked glasses, and Becks said, casually, "We raised so much that Patricia and I were thinking that maybe we could hire someone part-time to be in charge of these events in the future. We've spoken with the rest of the board and they agree. It's really too much for a volunteer position."

"You can say that again," Ellen said, lighting a cigarette. "I think we ran all the board members into the ground to the point they were begging for an employee."

"The only problem is," Patricia started, coyly, "it's going to be nearly impossible to find someone who knows Beaufort and all the homeowners well enough *and* who has the good taste to put these events together." She sighed dejectedly.

"Yes," Becks chimed in. "Who do we know who even has the social skills to take it on?"

Patricia and Becks had discussed many times over the past few months that Sarah and her husband, Tim, seemed to be having a hard time. It started with whispers around St. Paul's that their tithe had dropped. (Anyone who had believed the donations to actually be kept secret was sorely disappointed.) Then their house desperately needed painting but nothing had been done about it. The bank where Tim served as president had suffered when the larger chains came to town, but Patricia and Becks thought perhaps it had suffered a little more than they let on.

"Sarah, darling," Becks started. "Your kids are out of the house now . . ."

"And no one is a better party planner than you!" Patricia enthused.

Ellen, who wasn't even a part of this plan, brought it home: "Sarah! You should take the job. It's just part-time. It'd be the perfect fit."

Sarah sipped her champagne, but Becks could see she was trying to contain her enthusiasm. "Well, I don't know if Tim would approve of a working wife."

Becks had, obviously, expected to have to convince Sarah. Sarah wouldn't be able to seem eager for this job, of course. It would be below her station to do so.

"But it would take so little of your time, and I think we could pull together a fairly nice salary," Patricia said. "Not that that would even factor into your consideration process." She and Becks shared a knowing look.

"No one would be better, Sarah. We all know that," Becks said.

Sarah sipped her champagne again and then smiled. "Well, why not. It's 1976, for goodness' sake. A woman's place is no longer in the home. It's out in the world!"

"Cheers to that!" Ellen said, raising her glass again.

Sarah clapped her hands together. "My darling Suzanne and her husband, Wade, are moving back to town in a few months. I couldn't wait to tell you, but this makes it even better." She put her hand to her heart. "My daughter and I can be on the committee together."

Laura smiled. "Oh my goodness. What if all our daughters are on the committee one day?"

"Can you imagine," Sarah said, "if Suzanne, Betty, Arlene, and Virginia all took up the mantle?"

Becks's eyes unwittingly filled with tears. Oh, how she hoped that would be the case. Oh, how she wished she would live to see it.

But she composed herself because she had met her goal. The Old Homes Tour would have a future, meaning the Historic Site would have the income it needed to survive. That was one thing checked off Becks's list. Soon, she would be able to die a happy woman, knowing she had left everything and everyone in her life in the best possible hands. Well, the second-best, anyway. Because anyone who knew Rebecca Saint James knew no one would ever be able to replace a woman so wholly irreplacable.

Keaton

....

Conspiracy Theorist

The Old Homes Tour was a gigantic success, to say the least. And, around the table tonight, I can't help but think of my grandparents—people I never knew, but who through their memories and notebooks, through the stories I have heard about them, I feel like I am getting to know better and better, so much so that I feel sort of homesick for them. I can't turn back the clock, I can't make them reappear. But, as crazy as it seems, that's my greatest wish right now. My whole Beaufort crew is here. Violet and her husband, Arlene, Betty, Suzanne and her husband Wade, Amy, Alex, Jimmy, and Clayton. Harris and, of course, Bowen. It strikes me how much I wish my mom and dad were here. And, if I'm wishing for things, I wish I could have known Betty's and Arlene's late husbands, who I have heard so many stories about. But, otherwise, the night is perfect.

Everyone is laughing as Violet is saying, "And then Becks comes out with this hideous Jell-O mold—the absolute peak of seventies cooking but the antithesis of everything she stood for—loaded with candles and plops it in front of Townsend. And he says, 'Now, see. That's a proper birthday cake.'"

Her husband picks up a mother-of-pearl dessert fork. "Let me tell you, eating fruit-filled Jell-O with these antique forks felt wrong on so many levels."

"Do you remember the fondue night?" Arlene asks, giggling into her napkin.

They all laugh again. "Keaton," Suzanne says, "your grandmother always included us in her parties when we were home from college and in our early twenties. But, let me tell you: Rebecca Saint James was not a fondue type of girl."

"So what kind of girl was she?" I ask.

"Townsend and Becks were a movie couple," Violet interrupts.

Suzanne nods. "Yes. They were Bogie and Bacall. This larger-than-life pair of beautiful people who seemed to have a love story that surpassed anything we'd ever known."

I smile at Harris, and he smiles back at me. It's nice to hear these things about them.

"Everyone wanted to be like Becks," Arlene continues. "So proper but also so warm. So effortless but so beautiful. The way she walked through the world was magnificent."

"No one questioned why Townsend hung on her every word, her every movement," Dr. Scott, Violet's husband, adds. "Everyone who'd ever met Becks was just a little bit in love with her."

Betty shakes her head. "None of us could have imagined they would have come to such a tragic end. It didn't seem fair. It still doesn't. They were our golden couple."

I'm surprised when Harris says, "I've read all those articles. What do you think happened to them? A car crash, really?"

My five protectors—Bowen, Violet, Betty, Suzanne, and Arlene—all swivel to look at me. It's almost comical. "Oh, I'm dying to know," I say.

"I never bought that it was a random car crash," Suzanne says, wincing. "I'm sorry. I hate to be a conspiracy theorist. But while I know the curve of Sunset Lane is sharp on that end and you could easily drive right into the water with one wrong move—especially when the tide is as high as it was that night—I still can't believe the car was found but literally no trace of Becks and Townsend."

Harris and I look at each other. "The newspapers made it seem like their bodies were in the car," Harris says.

The thought makes me shiver.

They all turn to Dr. Scott—I guess for a scientific perspective. He winces. "Don't make me say what could have happened to their bodies. It's needlessly gruesome."

Bowen squeezes my knee.

Betty crosses her arms. "There is no way. I know all sorts of things live out in that waterway but there is no way they could just get eaten without a trace. I'm sorry."

"And Becks always wore her seat belt," Arlene adds.

"Wouldn't that make it worse?" Harris says. "Harder to get out of the car?"

"The seat belt wasn't buckled," Suzanne says. "We went to look at the car. We tried to find them; the whole town formed a search party. Neither seat belt was buckled. So they must have gotten out of the car somehow."

Dr. Scott closes his eyes, opens them, and says, "But, Suzanne, you have to remember: when it's pitch dark outside, especially when you're out on the water, it's hard to tell which way is up and which way down. So even if they got out and tried to swim . . ."

My stomach sinks.

"Well, I'm with Betty," Arlene says. "I always thought they would have found *something*. A shoe. Townsend's glasses. Something."

"Yeah, but this was 1976," Bowen chimes in. "Search and rescue wasn't quite like it is now. It was pretty easy to dispose of a body in the ocean and know it would never be found."

He takes a bite of his dessert and, fork in his mouth, stops cold. It's like all the air has been sucked out of the room and all the eyes around the table are on him.

"Holy shit," Harris whispers. "You think they were murdered?"

"No! No!" Bowen amends, his mouth full. "It was an analogy. I was just saying . . ." He trails off, and Harris says, "What about the rest of the table?"

Everyone is silent, which is the only answer I need.

"Oh, you know small towns," Violet says, breaking the silence. "We can't let scandals like these die. So, instead of just accepting that they're at peace somewhere, we continue to theorize."

"Right. But what would make you think that?" Harris asks.

Suzanne gets brave first. "Your mother told the police she was afraid they had been murdered. That Becks knew something she shouldn't have known."

"What?" Dr. Scott scoffs. "Becks was so clean-cut and wholesome. What could she have possibly known that would have gotten her killed? This is *Beaufort*, for heaven's sake. It's pretty much the same sleepy town now as it was then."

Arlene adds quietly, "My mom, her best friend Patricia, confided in me once that she thought Virginia might have been right, that Becks had confronted a suspected murderer about his crimes right before they disappeared."

Violet rolls her eyes. "That is ridiculous. Don't spread that gossip."

My heart races with the idea that maybe they *could* have been murdered. I think of that blood-tinged samurai sword. "Poor Mom and Uncle Lon," I say, suddenly understanding them both so much more. How could they possibly have come back to this place when it holds so much heartache and, if Mom really believed her parents were murdered, so much fear? I wouldn't be able to face it either.

I feel like my entire childhood is being washed away—every moment of annoyance when my mom wasn't able to move forward, every time she couldn't show up to be the mother I wanted her to be, every time she couldn't talk about my grandparents, is being replaced with this deep, poignant empathy. "They must be so haunted."

I feel chilled to my bones, but I also decide that Becks would not be proud of the vibe at my first dinner party. So I stand up to clear the dishes. As much as I've wanted to solve this mystery, now that we're talking about it, I'm ready for this conversation to be over. Then what Violet says soothes me: "At least they were together in the end. Either of them living in a world without the other would have been inconceivable. So at least they never had to face that reality."

I nod. "Well, that's the silver lining, I guess. So let's finish our non-Jell-O dessert, have another drink, and make the most of the night while we still can." Still standing, I raise my glass. "To Becks and Townsend, wherever they are."

"To Becks and Townsend," the table repeats.

"All I know, my darling, is that Rebecca Saint James would be awfully proud of her granddaughter right now," Arlene says. "You have thrown one heck of a dinner party!" She obviously understands I'm trying to change the subject.

"And, Keaton," Arlene adds. "The Old Homes Tour committee was always such a big deal to our mothers that we felt like we had to follow in their footsteps. We were always really sad that your mother wasn't a part of it." She is tearing up.

Betty takes over for her. "If there is anything that Becks would have loved more than her daughter being a part of her Old Homes

Tour, it's that her granddaughter is." She raises her glass to me, and, still standing, I raise mine to her and take another sip, feeling like my chest might burst with pride. I had worried that the things Becks loved—her traditions, her committees, her parties—are fading away. But now that I am here I can make sure they continue. I love the idea of this one small thing keeping Becks's memory alive.

"In that case," I say, "you're stuck with me. Even if I'm back in New York, every June I'll be here with all of you."

That's all it takes for the joyous tone of the evening to return.

Later, after the ladies have left, I wonder if I will ever have a love like Becks and Townsend's. Harris has gone to get Anderson and walk Salt while Bowen and I take care of the dishes, which is very kind of him. And, as I fill the sink with soap and water, I'm shocked to realize that his true intention might have been to give me time alone with Bowen, which is not only thoughtful but also a vote of confidence I hadn't expected. As I lower each crystal goblet into the water, Bowen wraps his arms around my waist and kisses my neck. "Are we finally, really alone at last?"

Butterflies stir in my stomach. I have dreamt of the lengthy kisses we've been able to steal turning into something more. "I think we might be." I turn around and kiss him, wrapping my wrists around his neck, soap bubbles dripping on the floor behind him.

"Can the dishes wait?" he whispers, never taking his lips off mine.

I nod, and he reaches behind me to turn off the tap. I separate from him long enough to grab the last piece of crystal to put in the sink. I am imagining what happens next, finally touching the skin under that shirt, testing out this connection I feel so clearly between us. Bowen takes a step back, and I hear the door fly open. "Keat!" Harris yells, shaking a notebook in his hands. "Have you read this?"

I don't know if it's the adrenaline that shoots through me or my wet hands, but, either way, the glass slips out of my soapy fingers. I watch it fall, as if in slow motion. Bowen lunges for it, but it's too late. The glass lands, not on the floor, but on my bare foot. I see the blood spurt out of the top before I feel the pain.

Becks

....

Whatever It Takes

FRIDAY, AUGUST 27, 1976

Tip: In entertaining, just like in flying, operating, etc., a checklist is your best friend. My checklist is at the front of my notebook, as you well know, but, darling, feel free to create your own. It is the only surefire way to ensure consistency in your events each week and not leave anything to chance.

Becks had always known that life was about taking the good with the bad, and she had certainly had plenty of both of those lately. Almost a week later, everyone in town was still talking about what a smashing success the first Old Homes Tour was, and the thank-you notes and gifts were still piling up at her door. But she could also feel herself fading, the pain seeping in despite the pain injections, the naps she had to take to get through the day getting longer and more frequent. A new anxiety, however, had joined her increasing worry that she would soon be forced to tell Townsend the truth. She simply could not get her encounter with her neighbor Peter off her mind—and couldn't shake the fear she'd felt in seeing those eyes and that distinctive scar.

But she was making this bigger in her mind, wasn't she? Perhaps it was the feeling that her days were numbered that was making her so delusional. He was, certainly, a little brooding. But that wasn't so unusual for a man, was it? And, in the days that had passed since, Daniel had mentioned several times how impressed he was by Peter's skills as a doctor and his way with patients. He felt he had found the perfect new partner. And the women were certainly swooning over his good looks already, lining up for flu shots early this year. Word got around fast in a small town with few eligible bachelors.

Becks reasoned that everyone cooing about his greatness couldn't be wrong. And she hadn't even welcomed him to the neighborhood properly. Which is why she had set about making her famous homemade chicken potpie at five thirty this morning. She made sure to double the recipe so she could freeze one for Townsend. She had been doing that as much as possible, freezing extras to help ease the transition when she was too sick to cook and then . . . gone. Of course, Evelyn would be there to help, but Becks's chicken potpie was Townsend's favorite dish—and her traditional welcome-to-the-neighborhood offering. She inhaled the scent of it now, the cooling crust, the hearty gravy, basking in the warmth of the oven. She was cold all the time now, despite the stifling August heat.

When the pie had cooled sufficiently, Becks walked through her side gate and, steeling her nerves, knocked on her neighbor's side door. There was no reason to be nervous. It was the steroids that were making her jittery.

Peter came to the door, in his bathrobe, bleary-eyed. Becks was shocked. She had waited until 8 a.m. to come over. Surely he was awake?

"Good morning," he said sheepishly, opening the door. "Aren't you an early bird?"

She smiled and handed him the pie. "Just a little welcome-to-the-neighborhood."

She studied the hand that reached out to take it. Because it couldn't be, could it? But, yet, there it was, the scar. And it was, unmistakably, a bat. How bizarre. She forced herself to look back at his face, into those clear blue eyes.

"Farming accident," he said, clearly noticing the way she stared at his hand. She hoped he didn't see her shiver. Just a coincidence. Of course.

Peter inhaled the scent of the pie. "My mom makes pie just like this."

"She must be southern," Becks said, smiling, sure now that this had all been in her head. The killer wasn't from the South.

"Kansas." She froze as he continued, "It was my job to get the eggs, and it was always worth it when it meant pie crust."

He motioned for her to come in as Becks murmured, under her breath, "It *is* you."

"What?"

It was only then that she noticed how spartan the house was. Why, there was only one chair in the whole family room. It was strange enough that an eligible doctor was unmarried and renting a house, but the fact that he had no furniture, had brought none with him? What kind of doctor had no belongings? A doctor on the run, that's who.

Becks didn't know what came over her, but she said, "You should be ashamed of yourself."

He looked puzzled. "For what?"

"Does Daniel even know?"

She thought a look of suspicion passed over him, but she couldn't be sure. He was trying very hard to stay relaxed, it seemed.

"That you killed your patient!" she added in a whisper-shout.

Peter peered at her. "I don't know what you're talking about."

"You don't? Because see, I'm sure in your estimation you were running away, but honey, the past always follows you." Becks should know. She wanted to tell him that she knew his fiancée, but she didn't want to implicate Virginia in some way.

"Mrs. Saint James, with all due respect, you have no idea what you are talking about."

She felt her blood pressure rise. "Does. Daniel. Know?"

Peter's face turned to stone. "He does not because there is nothing to know."

His expression scared her. That was when Becks realized she had made a big mistake. What had gotten into her? This was none of her business. None at all.

"Mrs. Saint James," Peter said, his voice as icy as his eyes, "you have no idea what you're talking about, but I can tell you this: I will do whatever it takes to make sure Dr. Walker never has to hear this unfounded gossip." He paused. "*Whatever* it takes."

Becks nearly tripped over the threshold on her way as she ran out, his words echoing through her mind. Was that a threat? Or was she just being paranoid? To most people, *whatever it takes* might mean very little. But to a murderer, whatever it takes was an entirely different proposition indeed.

Keaton

....

A Single Secret

I'm no doctor, but I'm fairly aware that blood should not spurt from bodies in the way it is spurting from my foot right now. "Oh my God!" Harris says, running to me. "Keaton! I'm so sorry!" He looks at Bowen. "Let's get her in the car. I can drive to the hospital."

Bowen picks me up in a fireman's carry, and I think that maybe we should wrap my foot until I see a giant shard of crystal sticking out of it. He runs out the door and down the street, and I cling to his neck as he jogs. "Where are you going?" Harris calls as he hurries behind him, breathless.

My foot is throbbing, and I realize as Bowen turns down the side street closest to my house that he's going to Violet and Dr. Scott's. "Isn't he kind of old?" I ask.

"What?" Bowen asks, racing up the steps.

Harris bangs on the door.

"Isn't Dr. Scott kind of old?" I'm getting light-headed. I haven't lost enough blood yet for that, I reason, so this must be panic.

"He's eighty-two," Bowen says, "but he still practices."

"Even sliced in half she has *a lot* of opinions," Harris chimes in.

He's trying to lighten the mood, I know, because we can all see the blood dripping from my foot onto the porch.

"I'm sure I'm fine," I say, as Dr. Scott, in his Brooks Brothers pajamas and bathrobe, opens the door.

I can see in his face that a switch has flipped. "Take her into the kitchen," he says. "Put her on one stool and her foot on another." He walks confidently through the house and calls, "Violet! Please bring my sewing kit."

"Sewing kit?" I squeak.

Bowen follows Dr. Scott and sets me down where he has instructed, and Harris extends his hand for me to squeeze.

Dr. Scott appears with a stack of towels and a crystal glass, which, frankly, I've had enough of tonight. He holds one of the cloths in his hand and hands me the glass. "Drink this," he says.

I take a big gulp and sputter. "It's vodka!" I choke out a moment before I scream. In one swift movement, Dr. Scott has pulled the glass out of my foot and is applying pressure with a towel.

Violet appears in a robe with a zipper, pink foam rollers in her hair, and with what I presume is the "sewing kit." It definitely looks higher tech than I am expecting, thank goodness. She stands beside him, taking over the pressure on my foot without Dr. Scott saying a single word as he rummages through the case. Despite the pain I'm in, I know I am witnessing something that they have done together many times. Dr. Scott produces a needle and what can only be described as thread. I've had stitches before but I've never been in a position to watch the process.

I feel myself start to panic. The pain is setting in now, and I'm realizing he is going to try to sew my skin together right here in his kitchen. I scream again.

Harris holds the vodka to my lips, and I manage to eke out, "Is this for real? Are we doing kitchen surgery?"

"We can triage this and get you to the ER," Dr. Scott says. "But it's just a few stitches. I can take care of them, no problem. Help you avoid the waiting room. But it's up to you." He pulls out a syringe.

"Please tell me that's something to numb my foot."

Dr. Scott laughs. "Of course it is."

Bowen pulls the top part of my body firmly close to him. I realize that, while it's partly an act of comfort, it's really an act of not letting me jump out of my skin as Violet takes the pressure off just long enough for Dr. Scott to give me the shot in my foot.

Then sweet numbing relief washes over me. Maybe this won't be so bad after all. "If you have the supplies, I'd love it if you'd just do it here."

"Oh, sweetie," Violet clucks. "Did you think he was just going to dig in there with no numbing?"

I wince, and Dr. Scott chuckles. "Stitches with no anesthesia? This isn't the battlefield."

"Well, you did give me vodka," I say.

Violet wipes down my foot with a brown liquid—Betadine, according to the label on the bottle—and Dr. Scott begins his work. I am starting to calm down, which is when I realize how sweaty I am. I look up at Bowen. This was not exactly what I had pictured for tonight. As if he's reading my mind he says, "This is exactly the romantic evening I had planned."

We all laugh, and I try not to wince—or look—as I feel the needle going in and out. It's unnerving to see a needle and thread coming at one's body. It doesn't hurt necessarily, but I can definitely feel it. "How's our patient?" Dr. Scott asks, still sewing.

"Our patient is impressed," I say, truthfully. "You just jumped right in there without a second thought."

"Still pretty quick for an old man, huh?" he asks.

I'm ashamed that I had been so judgy. Here he is cleaning up my mess when he could have been snuggled in bed beside Violet and her curlers.

Violet cleans the area one more time and then Dr. Scott puts Polysporin on the stitches. "Brave like her grandmother," Dr. Scott muses as he works. "Half-dead from pancreatic cancer and just kept going."

I'm grateful the stitches are in because the doctor is obviously senile.

"Our grandmother died in a car accident or whatever," I say gently. "Remember? We talked about it at dinner?"

Dr. Scott shares a look with Violet, but he can't hide the surprise written all over his face. "Well, yes, I know," he says. "But surely you know she had pancreatic cancer?"

Violet swats his arm. "To my knowledge, she never even told Townsend that she had it. How would her granddaughter know?"

Dr. Scott backs away, admiring his handiwork. "Well, apologies for dropping the bomb. But to be honest, I always thought that whatever fate she met was kinder than the next month or two would have been for her. She had been sick for quite a while when she died."

"And she didn't tell our grandfather?" I ask Violet.

"I feel guilty speaking of the dead when they aren't here to defend themselves—and I can't know for sure. I only heard about it through the rumor mill."

"She didn't want him to worry about her," Dr. Scott adds.

I put my hand to my heart. "That is really sad and really sweet," I say.

Dr. Scott nods, looking down at my foot. "You, my dear, are as good as new. Swing by the kitchen—or the office—in four weeks or so, and I'll get those stitches out."

Four weeks. Harris looks at me questioningly, and I know he's wondering the same thing I am. Will I even be here in four weeks? But I can discuss that with Dr. Scott later. "I need to pay you," I say.

"You fed me tonight. That is plenty payment enough." He pauses. "No, on second thought, the real payment is putting that house on tour. It's all Violet has been able to talk about."

He kisses his wife's cheek, which I can tell by the smell is slathered in Oil of Olay.

"Well, that is very nice," I say, taking one last sip of vodka for good measure. "I owe you."

Harris and Bowen help me down from the stool. "Need me to carry you back?" Bowen asks.

"Need or want?" I ask, the vodka kicking in.

He laughs, and I shake my head. "No. I'll be fine. Thank you again, Dr. Scott."

Violet sees us to the door, and as we make our way to the street, I say, "If I was a painter, I would paint this." I gesture to the view before us.

"I bet you could paint it," Bowen says. "I have a feeling you can do anything you want."

I smile and he squeezes my arm. "You were a trooper in there."

"I had someone helping me to be brave."

"She means me," Harris says, and we all laugh.

As we walk back to my grandparents' house, the trees make a canopy over the street and through them is a perfect view of the moon dancing over the water. I don't pause enough to realize how beautiful it is here, but sometimes, on nights like tonight, it hits me all at once.

"This place is going to be hard to leave," Harris says. I wonder if he means for me or for him.

I have one arm around his shoulders and the other around Bowen's, and they are helping me hobble. "Hey, Keat, do you think Mom knew Becks was sick?"

"My gut is telling me that she had no idea."

He nods. "Mine too."

"You sure are a secretive family," Bowen says.

Harris laughs. "Buddy, you have no idea."

"Everybody has their secrets." Bowen has an unreadable expression on his face. I don't love the way he says it, like he has so many. But, then again, I guess we all do. He squeezes my hand, and I realize I want to know all of his. And, what's more, there's not a single secret he could tell me that would make me want to walk away.

Becks

....

The Difference

SATURDAY, AUGUST 28, 1976

Tip: Tea—hot or iced—requires its own spoon. Shrimp requires its own utensil, too. And "saving your fork" for the next course is for hospital cafeterias and jails. Your guests are neither patients nor prisoners. (God willing.)

Becks was jittery and distracted all day. She tried to forget, to ignore that tonight marked the end of an era, that it would surely be the last summer supper of her life. She tried to be positive, to think that maybe there would be a miracle—maybe she would live to see one more season. But, well, she was too tired for all that. And so she mourned privately, despite the fact that, outwardly, she whistled in the kitchen, baked brownies, and drank coffee on the front porch with her family, waving to the neighbors as they walked down the street. Yes, by all accounts, today was a normal day in the Saint James world. Only Becks knew that tonight would be the last night of normalcy for their family.

She had decided, since both of her children were home, that she would tell Townsend about the cancer after the party, giving them the opportunity to tell Virginia and Lon together before the children left town tomorrow. Then they would have enough time to prepare for her death and mourn before she was gone—but not too much. Becks had given this a great deal of thought.

Chef Evelyn, Charles, and the other servers arrived one by one to get ready for supper, just like always. Becks reflected on her own preparations. Her beloved Historic Site was in good hands. Her funeral plans—and Townsend's, whenever he may need them—were fully detailed in her notebook, so Virginia would have little to do besides make the phone calls. Her will had been updated. The freezer was full of enough food to last her dear husband for months, and she had already asked Chef Evelyn to increase her hours. And now, before she was too ill to continue, there was one final matter she had to attend to. "Charles, dear, could you please join me in the library?"

If Charles, her chief waiter, wearing his usual perfectly pressed blazer with matching slacks, was alarmed, he didn't let on. He only followed his boss into the library and sat in the chair when she gestured toward it.

"Charles, how long have we been together?" Becks asked. She walked to Townsend's bar and removed a cigarette from the sterling holder. Charles fumbled in his pocket and offered her a light, which she gladly accepted. The surprise at her smoking showed on his face, but he didn't mention it.

"Oh, almost thirty I believe, Mrs. Saint James."

Becks nodded. "And you are still employed at the deli during the day."

"Yes ma'am," he said.

She wanted to tell him that he could drop the formalities. But at a time like this, the formalities soothed her nerves. Or maybe it was the cigarette. Becks couldn't quite say.

Becks stopped pacing and stood in front of the man she had known for so long but, due to his unwavering professionalism, knew very little about. "Charles, if I needed you full time, would you be willing to give that job up?"

He nodded. "Of course, Mrs. Saint James. But what would you need me for full time?"

Becks studied Charles's face, the kind lines around his eyes and mouth, the crinkle in his forehead, the way his brown eyes sparkled. She had never asked his age straight out—it would have been rude— but she'd put him in his late fifties or so. Still strong, still agile, still nimble. The perfect man for the job.

"Well, Charles, as you know, Mr. Saint James is getting older. And it would take a great burden off me for him to have a companion. Someone to accompany him on the boat, drive him in the car, just be a watchful friend when Daniel or the other men can't be around." She paused. "I want to be clear that I'm not suggesting you take on nursing or caregiving duties. Nothing like that. I just feel it might be time for him to spend less time alone."

Charles nodded, and Becks could tell he was suspicious. But he didn't press her for details. "Of course, Mrs. Saint James."

"And Charles," she said gently. "You might have to insist. Because Townsend is not a man to lose his independence easily."

He nodded.

"So you will insist?" she asked. "For me?"

He smiled. "For both of you, Mrs. Saint James." He stood and looked intently down at her. "Don't worry. I'll take care of everything."

The kindness in his face combined with the relief she felt caused tears to spring to her eyes. "Thank you, Charles." She cleared her throat. "I am ever so grateful."

Two hours later, as she sat at her vanity applying moisturizer to begin getting ready for the night's festivities, Becks mused that her affairs really were in order. What a gift she had been given, this time to make sure her great loves were cared for after she was gone. Of course, she did feel her dear Virginia could use more time with her. But, well, Becks had given her the tools she needed in her notebook, if not the will to use them. She was confident that, when tested, her girl could and would stand on her own two feet.

Becks ran her finger over the only picture she had of her wedding with Townsend, the one she looked at every morning as she applied her makeup. *Coming face-to-face with one's own demise does cause a person to get somewhat nostalgic,* Becks realized.

Admittedly, it wasn't the wedding she had envisioned having when she was a girl, with her father officiating while throngs of family members and friends looked on. She wore a simple white suit and a pillbox hat instead of a frothy confection of a gown with a trailing veil. The twelve members of the congregation were virtual strangers, women and their husbands who had refused to allow Becks and Townsend to marry with no one who loved them there to witness it. She had no attendants, where she imagined she would have at least a dozen, and Townsend's best man was his brother, not his father. A kind and generous man—but, again, a relative stranger—stood between them at the altar rail of St. Paul's Episcopal Church in Beaufort announcing his intention to make one flesh out of two.

And yet, Becks had never felt happier. Because the only thing that mattered about that day was that she was marrying Townsend Saint James. His hands were the hands holding hers. His voice was the one promising to love her forever. And she knew he would. She knew that, come what may, Townsend was her future.

Becks couldn't say what had made her enter the double doors of the simple, austerely beautiful church on Ann Street a few weeks before. She had to think now that it was God. Or, perhaps, the blessed Virgin Mary, who had factored so little into Becks's spiritual life growing up but now, as she sought to understand her fiancé's faith more, seemed increasingly important. Because who would understand the predicament Becks found herself in—choosing her great love over her family—more than another woman?

Either way, Becks opened the church door, which was unlocked twenty-four hours a day for those looking for prayer or solace or, at more desperate times, simple shelter. The church was silent and empty, and sunlight shone through the stained glass windows. The church had a simplicity about it, yet, to Becks's mind, also seemed more ornate than the Methodist church of her youth.

As she sat down on the straight-backed wooden front pew, looking at an altar that was both foreign and familiar, she barely even noticed a man in a black shirt with a white clerical collar slide in beside her.

The man didn't look at her, and Becks didn't know what prompted her—an often-silent sufferer—to say "I shouldn't be here."

"And why is that?" the man asked, still not looking at her.

"I'm not Episcopalian. I'm a Methodist minister's daughter, and I'm in love with a Catholic man, and I killed my father."

That was the phrase that finally elicited a head turn.

Becks turned her head too. The priest peered at her. "I'm very intrigued by this story, but I have to say that the killing of your father interests me most right now."

Becks realized what she had said and laughed in spite of herself. "I'm sorry," she said. "My father died right after he found out I was engaged to a Catholic. Heart attack. I didn't run him over with my car or stab him with a turkey knife."

The priest put his hand to his chest and exhaled loudly. "Whew. It's not every day that a man comes face-to-face with a confessed murderess." He paused. "And I have to think that maybe your father died because it was his time."

Becks shrugged, tears coming to her eyes. "My mother doesn't seem to think so." She looked into the hazel eyes of this middle-aged stranger. "Am I crazy to still want to marry Townsend? After all of this?"

"Townsend Saint James?" he asked.

She nodded.

He smiled. "Townsend Saint James is a fine fellow."

Becks's stomach rolled. She felt so guilty. She looked down at her hands. "How could I choose him over my family? What kind of person would do that?"

The priest patted her arm. "One who knows her heart, I think."

It seemed so simple when he said it.

"These marriages can be tricky, but we've had quite a few success stories here, people who have found common ground between their faiths in the pews of this church, at this altar rail. If we can find love between us, we can work the rest out."

Becks felt a surge of warmth wash over her. And all at once, she knew she had found the place where she and Townsend could bridge their one difference. She didn't want to convert to Catholicism—fearing that, even if she did, she would never truly be welcome. And the catechism of her youth was so very different from Townsend's. The Episcopal church was a bridge between the two, technically Protestant, but maintaining many tenets of the Catholic faith that the Methodist church did not. Namely, transubstantiation, the belief that the bread and wine blessed by a priest transformed into the body and blood of Christ during Communion, and that marriage was a sacrament. Becks couldn't help but smile thinking that Townsend's mother would at least be happy about that.

"So we would be accepted here?" she asked, although she felt, looking into his kind eyes, she already knew the answer.

"Everyone is accepted here," he responded. "And if you and Townsend feel this church could help you bridge a gap, I'd be more than happy to help you join us."

Becks looked at the photograph again, taken in that church where she felt she belonged for the first time in a long time, thinking of the special day when she promised to love Townsend Saint James for better or worse, forsaking all others. *Until we are parted by death.*

The memory of those words took her breath away, and it finally hit her that death, that thing that seemed so impossible back then, was coming for her soon. They would be parted. It would be over.

"Hello, my beautiful mother," a male voice—one she loved equally as much as Townsend's—called from the door, bursting the bubble of her thoughts. She could see Lon, her precious baby boy who had arrived last night, entering her room in the reflection of the mirror. She stood up from her vanity to hug him. He squeezed her tight. "What can I do to help?"

"Your being here is all the help I could possibly ask for," she said.

"Mother, you look sensational," he said, kissing her cheeks. She appreciated the effort even though she knew it wasn't true. Underneath her A-line dress she was painfully thin, and even several layers of foundation barely hid her positively gray pallor. But she was glad to know she was pulling it off.

She squeezed her son's arms, and she couldn't help but say, "Do you know how proud I am of you?"

He smiled at her. "I do now." He paused. "But, yes, Mom, of course. I've always known. I suspect you'd like some grandchildren out of me, but otherwise, I think you're proud."

She shook her head. "Those things can't be rushed. People assumed your father would never settle down, and look how well that worked out."

"Yes, but there aren't other women like you, Mom. And that's the difference. That's the problem. I just haven't found anyone who's as perfect for me as you are for Dad."

Oh, her precious boy. He always knew the right thing to say. With his dark hair and dazzling eyes, Townsend's height and chiseled physique—combined with that velvet tongue of his—she knew he had broken more than a few hearts. But not hers. Never hers. And she would never have to share him with a daughter-in-law, never face a day where she was second best. Would she have traded that fate? In a minute. But since she could not, it was a small bonus.

Townsend entered the room now, slapping his son on the back. And there they were, the two men in her life, the ones who felt like the very blood that coursed through her veins.

"Why don't you two go off and have some fun before dinner?" Becks said. That was all she wanted for them, after all. She wanted them to be happy.

"Boat or plane?" Lon asked, looking at his father excitedly. It was like going back in time. These two had been partners in crime, best buddies, united by a love of sport, game, and adventure from seemingly the moment Lon came into the world.

"The boat's out front," Townsend said.

They each leaned down to kiss one of Becks's cheeks.

"Thanks, Mom!"

She watched them leave, her dearest, darling loves. "I have loved you with everything inside of me," she whispered when they were out of earshot. "I always will."

Until we are parted by death.

Catch and Release

No, Keaton, you don't understand," Anderson is saying anima-
tedly as Bowen and I walk with him down the brick boardwalk in downtown Morehead City alongside docks teeming with
huge, beautiful fishing boats, just a bridge away from Beaufort. I am
limping ever so slightly, but between the Advil and my bandage's perfect pressure, I'm shocked that my foot barely hurts. It has been almost a week since my injury, and I'm getting a little better every day.
"You've never seen a fish this big. It's insane."

Bowen smiles down at me, and I can't help but laugh. Anderson
is so, so excited about seeing the fish caught at the Big Rock Tournament this year. "Did Dad tell you that we are fishing in the Big Rock
Kids Tournament?" he asks.

I feel a warmth wash over me with the knowledge that Bowen
hasn't given having me here with his son a second thought. There's
no awkwardness, no push-pull. Anderson is the one who introduced
us after all, and while it isn't like we've told him we're seeing each
other, he's a smart kid. I bet he's figured it out. But maybe this is how
it should be. Easy.

"What do you fish for in the Big Rock Kids?" I ask.

"Same stuff," he says as we pass a row of food trucks. "Billfish, like sailfish, blue marlin, and white marlin. There's a game fish category where you fish for dolphin—"

"Dolphin!" I exclaim, stopping in my tracks.

Anderson rolls his eyes and laughs. "Keaton, dolphin is mahi-mahi."

I put my hand to my heart in relief. "Then why didn't you just say that?"

"Dolphinfish is the scientific name," Bowen clarifies.

"Marine biologist showoff," I joke.

I see the Big Rock Landing off in the distance and can already make out the huge fish hanging from the weigh station. It turns my stomach. "Do you kill them?" I whisper.

"The Big Rock Kids is a catch-and-release tournament—well, for the billfish. We keep the game fish because we eat them," Anderson says, totally in his element. "I caught my first sailfish last year. We even won the whole first-day prize."

"What's the first-day prize?" I ask. I expect him to say, like, a gift certificate to the Sanitary Fish Market, the county's oldest restaurant, or Chasin' Tails, his favorite tackle shop.

"Last year it was thirteen thousand dollars," Anderson says nonchalantly.

My jaw drops. I look up at Bowen. "Seriously? Thirteen thousand dollars for a fish? That you released? What does a nine-year-old do with thirteen thousand dollars?"

Anderson rolls his eyes. "*Someone* made me save it for college."

I laugh as we make our way to the landing, where people are gathered around what is apparently a seven-hundred-pound blue marlin. I think of my grandfather, of how much he loved this sport. The rush of catching a fish is something I have never actually experienced, but

I can appreciate. I get that same incredible adrenaline rush when I'm working on a huge project or closing a big deal.

"This fish," Bowen says, pointing, "if it doesn't get beat by a bigger one, will bring in more than a million dollars."

"What? A million-dollar fish?"

"More if it wins more than one category," Anderson says.

"Well this is just insane!" I exclaim. "I thought people won bragging rights and, like, a case of local beer or something. No wonder everyone is so darn serious about this tournament."

"It's pretty expensive to enter because of that. It costs like fifty thousand dollars," Anderson says knowingly. "Right, Dad?"

"Well, depending on which categories you enter. But yes. Thereabouts. Big entry, but big reward."

"So this isn't like, 'Hey, I'm on vacation. I'm entering a fishing contest,' " I say.

"No." Bowen shakes his head. "This is serious fishermen and women only."

"You should come with us when we fish the Kids," Anderson says.

Bowen smiles down at me. "You don't get seasick, do you?"

I shake my head, but I have no idea. I've never been offshore fishing, which now seems like a shame. I suddenly feel annoyed at my mother. I know she is scarred and damaged, but she had this incredible life here that she never let Harris and me be a part of. It seems kind of selfish. On the other hand, if she truly believes her parents were murdered . . . I have to physically shake off the feeling of fear that washes over me.

"Do I have to pay a bajillion dollars to go to the Kids?" I ask.

"Nah," Anderson says. "The Kids is less. And Dad and I will cover you."

I raise my eyebrows at Bowen. "How nice for your kid to offer to pay my way."

Two fishermen are being interviewed beside their catches as another boat backs up to the landing. They are unloading maybe the biggest mahi-mahi—*dolphinfish*—I have ever seen. "Tacos for everyone!" one of them says, and the crowd cheers. I love fish. I love fish tacos even more. But I don't really need to see how the sausage gets made, you know? I like it better when it just appears on my plate.

Anderson points over at a group of boys on the boardwalk beside the tents. "I'm going over there!" he says, running off. I watch as he joins his friends. One of them hands him a Gatorade. One sort of sideways shoves into him and he sideways shoves him back. I've learned in the past few weeks that boys are like puppies. They're always wrestling, pushing, messing with each other.

"You've done such a good job with him," I say.

Bowen smiles. "Thanks."

"No, I mean it. It couldn't have been easy, being a single dad all these years." He leans over on the wooden railing, and I lean beside him.

He shakes his head. "No, it wasn't. But I think it was easier that he was a boy. Not that I wouldn't love to be a girl dad. I totally would. But we've always liked the same things. All he's wanted to do is fish since he was like three years old."

"And you both like pizza," I say seriously.

He laughs. "Exactly. And I bet one day when he's old enough we'll both like beer."

I nod at him. "Twins."

"What about you?" he asks. "Do you want kids?"

I try to read his face. My answer is my answer no matter how he feels about it, but I have to wonder how he would feel, starting all over again from scratch when he has this almost fully baked kid over there. "More than anything," I say honestly.

Out in the daylight, surrounded by all these people, isn't necessarily the best place for a heart-to-heart. But I guess it's as good as any. "I really want a family," I continue. "The irony is that I'm starting to realize that my job has always been less important to me than creating a family and yet, somehow, I've found all this success in my career and none in my personal life."

"Not *none* I hope," Bowen says, smiling. He really is so cute.

We're quiet for a minute. Then I ask him the question I've been afraid to until now. "What about you? Do you want more kids?"

He nods. "Oh, yeah. I never believed that would happen for me, but maybe the tide is turning." He winks at me.

I don't want to ask. I've been avoiding asking because I want to be cooler than this. But I can't help but say, in the most awkward voice imaginable, "And how did your coffee go with Kerry? Have you decided what you're going to do?"

"I think I'm going to let her see Anderson. As much as I don't like it, and as scared as I am that she'll come back into his life and then bail on him again, I also think it's wrong to keep my kid from his mom." He leans over and kisses me lightly, appearing somewhat amused by my tone. "Kerry is here for Anderson, not for me. And even if she was here for me, that ship sailed a long, long time ago. Plus, I am smart enough to know when I have a good thing going. I wouldn't do anything to mess that up."

He kisses me again and then strolls off in Anderson's direction. I wonder if he knows that I can't help but watch him as he goes.

In fact, I'm staring at him so intently that I'm a little embarrassed when Dr. Scott comes up behind me, wearing a Hawaiian print shirt, cargo shorts, and oversize glasses that look like the ones they give you when you have cataract surgery. I can't believe Violet let him out of the house in any of it.

"Well, hey," I say.

"Hey, yourself," he says.

I look around. "Where's your bride?"

"She's at home. Fishing tournaments aren't really her thing." He looks down. "Hey, how's the foot?"

I give him a thumbs-up. "A really talented doctor did a beautiful job on it."

He smiles and then looks around, as if making sure no one is listening. "Could we talk for a minute?"

He's suddenly serious, and I'm worried. He leads me to a secluded two-person wooden swing in a frame overlooking the water. "Is Violet okay?" I ask.

He nods. "Yes. She's fine. This isn't about her." He looks up at me, and I can see the concern written all over his face.

He doesn't speak, and I realize it's because Bowen has come up behind me. He touches my shoulder. "Hey, I need to run," he says. "Want me to drop you off at home?"

I shake my head. "Dr. Scott can take me back." He nods in agreement.

Bowen looks confused. "Are you sure?"

I nod.

"Um," he says nervously, "Kerry's here."

My eyes go wide. He points to Anderson, and I see a tall brunette in a pink sundress standing about ten feet away from him, watching him laugh with his friends. Honestly, I wanted her to be less pretty. I'm just saying. "Do you want me to keep Anderson?"

He sighs. "She kind of ambushed me. She knew we'd be here. But now that Anderson has seen her, I'll just take him home with me."

I smile encouragingly. "Good luck. I'll check on you later."

As Bowen walks away, I watch him, my stomach filling with anxiety for both him and Anderson. I hope they're both okay.

"So she's back, huh?" Dr. Scott says. "That should be interesting."

I resist the urge to run after Bowen and turn to Dr. Scott. "Should I be worried about this?"

"She tends to come back every few years, blow up Bowen's and Anderson's lives, and leave. So, yeah, we should all be worried."

I can feel how incredulous I look, and he laughs and pats my hand. "Oh, but for your relationship, no. Bowen is totally smitten with you."

Well, that's somewhat of a relief, anyway. "So, what did you want to talk about?"

"Keaton," Dr. Scott says, "I think this is one of those things Violet would think was inappropriate." Oh, good Lord. Is he coming onto me? But then he continues, "I know you're about to put your grandparents' house on the market, and I was just wondering . . . well . . . Do you think your mom and uncle would be willing to sell their plane?"

"Their plane?" I repeat.

He nods. "Yeah. Townsend had this gorgeous Beechcraft Bonanza. Brand new. Or, well, it was. I think it was a 1973. It was his pride and joy. And, I thought if it was just sitting there in their hangar . . ."

He seems weirdly nervous. "What in the world would you do with a plane from 1973?"

He laughs. "Oh, with a GPS and a few tweaks, that plane would be up and running again in no time."

I shrug. "It never occurred to me that they might still have the plane. I have no idea where it would be, but I am happy to ask my mom and Lon if they have it." I pause. "It seems likely since they still have the house. And a boat."

Dr. Scott laughs. "Okay. Well, maybe don't tell Violet I asked? She'll think it's rude."

Sweet Violet. It strikes me how funny it is that my grandparents loved to fly and now Harris does, too. I wonder if my grandmother and I have any similarities like that. Well, I mean, I know we both like champagne. And, as I know now, we're both pretty darn good at the Old Homes Tour. But maybe there's more. And I smile because, if I hadn't taken this big chance, I'd never have had the opportunity to find out.

Keaton

....

A Really Great Catch

D r. Scott and I hung around at the Big Rock Landing for an-other forty-five minutes or so, chatting with friends and buying matching tournament T-shirts for the Dames and me. By the time he drops me off at home, my curiosity about my grandparents' plane has fully transitioned to anxiety about the beautiful woman who followed my boyfriend and their son about an hour ago. My boyfriend. Is he my boyfriend? I mean, when a man asks you not to move away, he's your boyfriend by default, right? Ordinarily, I would say it was way too soon to call him that, but these were extraordinary circumstances.

I walk toward Bowen's house, the smell of gardenias lingering in the heat, when I see Anderson in the driveway. He looks . . . still. Which is somewhat terrifying in that I've never seen him stand still before. "Hey, bud," I call. "You okay?"

He walks slowly down the driveway and, when he reaches me, he whispers, "Kerry is in there."

"And you don't really know her, so this must be really hard and confusing for you."

"I don't want her here," he says solemnly. "We were doing fine without her."

I take his clammy hands in mine and nod. I know I'm not a parent, but I'm kind of judging Bowen, wherever he is, for leaving his only son out in the driveway to have an emotional crisis alone.

"She left us, Keaton. I don't think I should have to get to know her now," he continues. "And I don't want to."

I squeeze his hands. "I get that, buddy. I totally do. But sometimes we don't know the whole story, you know? Like, maybe there's a reason she left. And maybe there's a reason she came back."

He rolls his eyes.

"I don't know your mom," I say, "but do you know what I know about your dad?"

He shakes his head. "I know that your dad loves you more than anything in the entire world, and that he isn't going to let anyone into your life who he doesn't think is good for you." My heart swells because *I* am in Anderson's life. So Bowen must think I'm good for him.

"Don't call her my mom," he says obstinantly.

"Noted."

"Can you at least go see if she's nice?"

I bite my lip. "Well, buddy, I'm not sure it's my place to go—"

"Please, Keaton. Please. I found priceless Hemingways for you. I think you owe me."

I smile because he's right. I owe him. Plus, I mean, I'm super curious about her too, and this gives me an excuse to see what she's about. "Okay," I say. "You stay here, and I'll report back."

I don't know what to do when I reach the side door of the house. Do I knock? Do I walk in? I'm worried for Anderson, yes, but also, I've got some claim to stake here. Kerry left Bowen ten years ago. I'm here now.

But as I open the door, deciding knocking is weird, I realize that maybe I'm wrong. Her hand is on Bowen's cheek, and he is saying,

"For years, I dreamed about this moment, of you coming back here to be with us—"

My gasp must be very loud because they both turn to look at me. Bowen and this *Kerry*, who is, obviously, *not* old news. I am thrust back to that conference room, to Jonathan cheating on me with Allison, choosing her, having a family with her. How could I have been so blind? Again.

"Keaton!" Bowen says.

I don't know I'm crying until I choke out, in a half laugh, half sob, "If you can't be with the one you love, love the one you're with, right?"

Bowen rushes toward me. "It's not what you think!"

But I shake my head and say, sadly, "It never is, Bowen. It never is."

As I back out of the doorway calling, "Don't follow me!" I hear how immature it sounds. But I feel like the wind has been knocked out of me, and all I want is to get out of there. I hear Bowen calling after me, but I don't turn. I wipe my eyes as I walk, hoping Anderson won't notice my tears.

"So?" Anderson asks when I reach him.

I want to say she seems like a skanky tramp, that she doesn't deserve Bowen and she sure as hell doesn't deserve Anderson. I want to tell him to run far away because if she hurt him once, she'll hurt him again. But he is a child. And she is his mother. "I didn't really get to talk to her." It takes every ounce of self-control I have not to start crying again.

He looks skeptical. "But does she seem cool?"

I don't want to lie because *no. No, she does not.* So I just say, "I bet she's caught a blue marlin before."

"Really?"

I shake my head. "Nah. Doubt it."

He laughs, and I notice a group of his friends on bikes coming down the sidewalk. "Anderson, let's go!" one of them calls.

I smile encouragingly. "Go play. Don't worry." But as he turns, I grab his arm and wrap him in a hug. He hugs me back. "You're a great kid," I say. "Don't forget it." He pulls away with a question on his face, but I wave him off with a quick smile before marching back to my house as fast as my feet can carry me.

I feel like I'm in a fog as I walk inside. The last thing I expect to see is Harris standing in the living room with a suitcase. "Where are you going?" I ask.

"Oh, Keaton, I was about to call you. I have to go back to New York. Work emergency."

I look up at him. "Perfect. I'm coming with you."

"I'm flying . . ." he says skeptically. My biggest fear.

I cross my arms, pushing away the swirling panic that washes over me. "Fine." One look at my face tells him not to ask any more questions. He's my brother. He's known me since the day I was born. And, maybe most important of all, he's the only man in the world who has never let me down.

Becks

....

Takes the Cake

SATURDAY, AUGUST 28, 1976

Tip: Always keep white pie boxes and grosgrain ribbon on hand because a box lunch can turn a picnic on the beach, a day on the boat, a walk in the park into an event. Fill the box with something simple. My personal favorite is a pimento cheese sandwich, carrots, Ruffles, and oatmeal cookies. (Keep a roll or two of dough frozen and you'll always have the perfect snack on hand!) It's a run-of-the-mill lunch, but it feels special. And that's the secret, Virginia: With gifts and women, lunches and decisions, sometimes presentation is absolutely everything.

Becks picked up the knife by Townsend's plate at his end of the table and shined it on her blouse, making sure all was ready for tonight's summer supper. Her seat at the head was closest to the kitchen so that she could see where the dinner magic was happening and had an easy escape route if the staff needed her.

She was trying to avoid the thought that this was her last summer supper, that the exhilaration of it all would soon be over. Before she had to break the terrible news to Townsend, she was trying to focus on the fact that the weather was beautiful, her children were here, and she would soon be surrounded by her family and friends this one last time, that they would enjoy this life together before she had to ruin it for everyone. It had been so sweet.

Virginia smiled at Becks from the other end of the table, where she was folding napkins, and Becks was grateful that they had the kind of relationship she and her own mother had lost. She wondered what it would take for a woman to hold a grudge so large for so long like her mother had. If it hadn't been so hurtful, it would be impressive.

Virginia shared some of Myra's fire, her fortitude, but she had Becks's sweetness too, and a keen intuiton. She saw in Virginia's smile, in the way it didn't quite meet her eyes, that she knew something was wrong with her mother. Or that she suspected, at least. As hard as Becks had tried to hide it, she knew her clothes were hanging off her frame, her eyes were tinged yellow, her skin was an unmistakable gray. She was surprised that Virginia, who was always very frank with her, hadn't asked her about it straight out. But Becks was grateful she hadn't. She knew that, sometimes, avoidance was easier than facing the truth.

"Do you think you'll ever want all these things?" Becks asked her daughter, gesturing toward the china, silver, and crystal. Virginia only shrugged.

"I don't know, Mom. They're beautiful things, sure. But I don't know if I'll ever need them. I'm really just so focused on my career now."

"I know that, sweetheart. And I'm very proud of you. I want to hear more about the work you're doing." She lay down another knife and said, "I haven't seen you as much this summer. I've missed you."

She knew before the sentence had left her mouth that her daughter would take this as a criticism. "I'm sorry, Mom," she said. Becks noted a tiny bit of huffiness in her tone as she added, more quietly, "Not all of us have husbands to work while we flit off to the beach for the summer."

Becks thought about letting this go, because she knew her daughter was feeling the pressure to move into this next stage of her life. All her friends were getting married and having babies. But Becks also knew the times she would have with this daughter of hers were getting fewer and farther between, and she didn't want to leave this earth with her daughter having unrealistic visions of what her life had been like—or unrealistic expectations for her own. "You know, Virginia," she said, inspecting a crystal goblet, "it hasn't all been butterflies and flowers. Your father and I have been through a lot together. Families disowning us, death, war and the separation because of it. My life has been lovely, but there have been real rough patches. And that's normal; that's okay. Sometimes the valleys make us appreciate the peaks."

"I know, Mom. I'm sorry," Virginia sighed. "It isn't you. Robert and I had a disagreement earlier, and it's put me in a bad mood."

"Ah, well. I'm certain he is to blame." Becks smiled.

Virginia couldn't help but smile too. "I think we both know that is not the case."

Becks wasn't one to pry, so she changed the subject. "How is work treating you?"

"It's fine," she said. "Purposeful."

Virginia worked for a feminist arts organization, and she acted as though doing their clerical work was akin to curing cancer. Not that Becks didn't support her daughter's work or the organization. She did, wholeheartedly.

Virginia looked up at her mother. She asked, gently, "Did you ever wish you did something more, Mother?"

Becks knew what her daughter meant. She had read *The Feminine Mystique*, for heaven's sake. She felt anger welling up in her, but for the sake of keeping the peace, she quelled it. "No, Virginia. I have been perfectly happy. I was a teacher in my youth. I was a teacher during the war. I was a teacher to my children, a partner to my husband, and I spent every summer weekend of my adult life creating friends out of strangers, serving people in the best way I knew how. So, no, I did not ever want more. I have been supremely, incredibly happy."

Virginia shook her head. "I'm not trying to offend you. I'm just wondering. You're so smart and so good with people. You could have done anything."

Did her daughter not hear her? She did exactly what she wanted to with her one precious life. How many people could say that? How many people could claim they had lived a life they felt was truly meant for them? Becks didn't think many. "It was a different time, darling," was all she said.

Chef Evelyn walked into the dining room, cutting the conversation—which Becks was, quite frankly, tired of—short. Who was her daughter to question her choices? Who was she to act as though Becks's contributions to society didn't have merit? "Mrs. Saint James, would you like to taste the bouillabaisse?" Evelyn asked.

"I'll run up and change while you do that, Mom," Virginia said.

Becks smiled, grateful for the distraction, and smoothed her full skirt. "Why, Evelyn, that would be lovely."

The bouillabaisse was a rich, gorgeous dish, full of the local seafood that the area was known for. And, much to Becks's delight, there wasn't one trendy, store-bought, distinctly 1970s dish on the entire menu for the evening. It was all fresh, all thoughtful. It was the perfect last supper.

Becks was about to walk upstairs to get dressed when she heard "Mom!" ringing through the foyer. She walked in to see her beautiful daughter, wearing the cutest hot pink and yellow bell-sleeved floral print dress. Becks had bought it for her a few months ago and she was pleased to see Virginia had liked it enough to wear it tonight. She was holding the arm of a dark-haired man in a tan suit with a striped tie. He looked nervous. He was handsome—but not *too* handsome, she was happy to note, as young men who depended on their looks to get by were often unpleasant company. "Mom, this is Robert," Virginia said proudly.

"What a pleasure to meet you, Robert," Becks said, smiling. He waited for her to extend her hand before taking it. "The pleasure is all mine, Mrs. Saint James."

Becks's heart swelled. She had wanted this Robert to be wonderful, of course. But her motherly instinct told her right away that he was. Confident, but not full of himself, charming but not smarmy. And anyone could see that he couldn't take his eyes off Virginia.

She was glad for a moment of small talk before Townsend entered. Fathers could be intimidating.

As Townsend entered, he looked from Robert to Becks to Virginia with a puzzled expression. "And who is this?"

Virginia laughed as if her father was obviously kidding. Becks, knowing he wasn't, tried to join in, to cover his gaffe. But, when Townsend didn't instantly recover from his mistake, panic gripped her throat and the laugh wouldn't quite come. They had talked about meeting Virginia's new fellow for days, had been positively giddy— and even a little nervous—about it.

The young man said kindly, "I'm Robert Smith, sir. Thank you for having me."

Townsend shook Robert's hand tentatively, then turned to his daughter. "Virginia, could I talk to you for a moment? Excuse us," he said to Robert, pulling Virginia aside into the other room. He started whispering loudly—Becks could hear him, and she was quite sure Robert could too.

"You know your mother doesn't like strangers at her summer suppers," he started to scold. "And especially not at her birthday dinner."

Becks coughed loudly, trying to cover the sound of his words. "We just couldn't be more thrilled to have you," she said to Robert with as much cheer as she could muster. "Do tell me all about this cousin of yours who is getting married."

As Robert talked, clearly uncomfortable, Becks could barely hear him as the pulse in her neck thrummed loudly. When Virginia and Townsend returned to the foyer, Virginia gave her mother a look of terror that Becks was certain she returned. But Virginia, like her mother, knew how to play the part. "Daddy," Virginia said gently, to a still-frowning Townsend, "this is my boyfriend, Robert. The one I have been telling you about. The one we invited for Mom's birthday dinner?"

It was then that fear flooded Townsend's face too. He put his hand to his forehead and tried to laugh it off. "Oh, *Robert*, of course. Forgive me. It has been a long day on the water, and I must be dehydrated." Then he said the thing he had said to Becks weeks earlier. "Plus, you know fathers always want to forget their daughter's boyfriends."

Townsend shook Robert's hand heartily, the moment of anxiety over, and Becks would hand it to him: Robert hid the discomfort he must be bathing in quite well and clapped Townsend on the shoulder. "I can imagine that might be the case." Virginia shot her mother another concerned look. But Becks thought it best to smooth this over for now. She knew she needed to address the situation, but what would she even say?

"Darlings, we need to get ready," she said. "Virginia, why don't you show Robert the boat while Daddy and I get dressed?"

She and Townsend made their way up the stairs.

"Well that was embarrassing," Townsend said.

Becks squeezed his hand. "It's okay, sweetheart. We all have our moments." But she knew this was more than a moment. This was a lapse in memory too big for her to ignore or brush off. This was a sure sign of the decline she had feared most. And, if she was noticing it this much, she knew Townsend had to be noticing it even more, fighting a daily battle without telling her about it. It broke her heart that he was in this alone, that she soon wouldn't be there to help. As they reached their room, Townsend wrapped Becks in his arms, and leaned down to kiss her. As always, his touch soothed her. She felt her heart rate return to normal. She could not control what came next. It was all going to be okay because it had to be.

Two hours later, while her favorite James Taylor album lazed out of the fabulous high-fidelity record player, four servers swept into the room, all wearing matching black double-breasted blazers and shiny shoes to serve the dozen guests around the table, refill wineglasses, and whisk away bread plates. Although Becks was still shaken from what had happened earlier, she now had guests to attend to and focus on—a distraction for which she couldn't be more grateful. This was Becks's favorite part. The pomp and circumstance of it all, so different from those first parties during the war, when they had made suppers out of whatever they could find, when the women had poured their own wine—if they could even get their hands on any. Life had been very different then. But the worst part? Townsend hadn't been there.

She smiled at him at the other end of the table. All these years later, he was still so handsome. Selfishly, she was glad she would always see him as confident, capable, and sure. As if James Taylor knew what she was thinking, he began singing, "How sweet it is to be loved by you."

She thought of the pages after the dinner party list in her summer supper bible. Behind the guest list, the menu, the questions for the evening, were four pages she had worked on all summer, which included her hospice contacts and plans, Townsend's long-term-care plans, and both their funeral arrangements.

She had thought of it all. From the prayers to be prayed to the twenty-one-gun salute for Townsend, a true war hero, to the jewelry she wanted to be wearing when she was buried (just her wedding band), she had planned everything. Her children would still have plenty to contend with, but this should make it easier. If only Lon had married already. Daughters-in-law tended to be good at these things. Caring yet less attached. It was a good combination.

Becks smiled again at Townsend, then Patricia and Daniel, Ellen and Milton, Virginia and Robert, Lon and Jamie—his date who, she was quite sure, was not daughter-in-law material. The man who was supposed to be Violet's date was running late, and so, while Becks was irritated that she had an uneven table, she was not upset in the least that she didn't yet have a stranger at her last summer supper.

Just as everyone had been served, there was a knock at the door. Becks and Townsend shared a look that told him what he needed to know: He would attend to their latecomer. Becks was annoyed that this stranger had arrived at all—and certainly that he had arrived late. But she would never let it show. As her husband went to answer the door, Becks began the formalities of the evening's conversation. "Well, friends, as another summer draws to a close—I can scarcely believe it, really—I can't help but think of the Labor Day Bonfire on Harkers Point, of the children running free, the fireworks, the sparklers, the feeling that, yes, we might be leaving summer behind, but there is still so much good left to come."

That's how she wanted to feel now. There was good left to come. Wasn't there? She was very glad she hadn't picked up her glass to toast because, if she had, she was quite sure she would have dropped it when she saw the man who walked into her dining room. Becks froze. Was he here to confront her?

Before she could say anything, Virginia started: "Peter?"

He laughed easily, not seeming at all uncomfortable. How did he manage that? "Virginia! What a small world."

Only Becks noticed Virginia's slight recoil as Peter kissed her on the cheek. Becks was terrified. Why was he here? As Peter and Violet were introduced, Virginia said, in a halting voice, "Violet, Peter and I met in Washington, D.C."

"And now," Becks added, with a look to her daughter, "he's our next-door neighbor."

"Oh, how lovely!" Violet said demurely. Virginia shot her mother a wide-eyed expression, and Becks put the pieces together: Peter wasn't here for her—he was here for Violet. He was the date Patricia was setting Violet up with. She tried to convey back that she knew what her daughter was trying to tell her, that she knew who Peter was, as he said, "It really is shocking how small the world can be."

As he sat, Becks realized that while he seemed to find plenty of warm smiles for the rest of the table, they turned to icy glares when directed her way. Well, no matter. The show must go on.

"It really is such a small world," Becks echoed, hoping her tone wasn't as strained as it felt.

Townsend's look at her from the other end of the table revealed that, unfortunately, it probably was. Well practiced in the art of keeping the peace, Townsend raised his glass. "Well, now that we are all here, I must propose a toast to my beautiful wife, the light of my life since the moment we met, on the occasion of her birthday. To Becks."

"To Becks!" everyone chimed in.

"Thank you so very much," said Becks, raising her own glass now. "And I have to propose a toast to summer, to my favorite season, where the days are long, the water is warm, and the feeling of freedom and expectation is almost overwhelming." She cleared her throat to keep herself from getting choked up. "I will always look back on the days on the beach with my children, eating sandy pimento cheese sandwiches and jumping in the surf, as the best days of my life. And so I wanted to know from everyone else: What are your favorite summer memories?"

Becks diverted her gaze from her neighbor's piercing eyes to, as was her custom, begin a conversation that everyone could share in, including the man in question. She wondered what it must be like to be in Peter's head right now, to think that you could outrun your past in a sleepy seaside town, only to find it had caught up with you.

"Mother, your beautiful beach picnics for us were the highlight of every summer when we were growing up," Virginia said, seeming not at all ruffled by Peter's presence even though Becks knew she must be.

"Oh, yes!" Lon said. "And, Mom, I loved how when we were little you used to wake us at midnight every full moon to lie on the roof and look at the stars." Her darling son. Her precious boy. Her heart felt like it was cracking in two and oozing out just thinking of becoming a part of those stars one day soon, of not being here with him.

But, goodness, she had been blessed with these children. In 1949, at thirty-six years old, after fourteen years of marriage, Becks had come to terms with the fact that she would never be a mother. But just as she and Townsend had made peace with never becoming parents, Townsend confirmed in his own office that his wife was pregnant with his first child. Then, four years later, when Becks was nearly forty years old, their little girl arrived. They had the family Becks had always dreamed of, the family Townsend had always wanted to give Becks. Their miracles.

And now, twenty-three years later, they were here, all of them, under the same roof of the happy home they had shared for so long. All of them, that is, except Becks's mother, who never forgave her, never acquiesced. She had never even met her grandchildren, Becks was sorry to say.

"Hey," Townsend interjected. "Was I there for any of these summers?"

They all laughed, and Becks knew this was the memory she would like to end on. She didn't want what came next. The end of the summer. The end of the road.

As Patricia began, "The Fourth of July dance at the club always takes the cake for me—especially when one Mrs. Rebecca Saint James is in charge." Becks smiled at her best friend. "What about when we are in charge together?"

"Then the real magic happens," Daniel said.

"Stay out of their way!" Townsend added.

"I have a lot left to learn from you, Mom," Virginia said, with a soft smile. Becks knew she was trying to apologize for the moment of tension between them earlier.

But Becks didn't have time left to teach Virginia, and, besides, she didn't need to. By the time she was eight years old, Virginia could plan a menu, arrange fresh flowers, order a perfect invitation. No, Becks had imparted all her hostess wisdom to her daughter. She had mothered her for twenty-three years by example and left reminders behind in her notebook. She had nothing left to to give.

Yes, she thought as the conversation rolled on, as laughter filled the room, if only she could control the timing of her own demise, she would choose tonight. She locked eyes with Townsend. If only God would let them go together. She knew that's what Townsend would choose too. If only they could be so lucky. Just like that, Becks thought of the cake waiting patiently in the kitchen. And she knew exactly what her birthday wish this year would be.

Keaton

....

Running Away

My mom and I are the only people in our family who don't have our pilot's licenses. When Harris started getting celebrity clients with big scandals and even bigger retainers and making real money in New York, the first thing he did was buy a small plane. He didn't own a car or an apartment for years longer than he could have because all he really wanted was to fly. "Planes are freedom," he says now as we sit on the runway at the tiny Beaufort airport. Salt barks from behind me as if in agreement. He is the cutest thing ever. He is buckled into one of the passenger seats of this sleek, shiny four-seater Cessna like it's where he belongs. I snap his picture, wishing he had goggles and a scarf. That would really complete the look.

"Feels more like a claustrophobic death trap to me." My mouth is dry, my palms are wet, and my heart is beating out of my chest.

"Don't you want to learn to fly?" he asks.

I'm so terrified that my answer should be an obvious no. But then I think of Becks—of how, all those years ago, she learned to fly. I look down at the ring on my finger, the sparkling diamond that still feels like an interloper on my hand. I came here for a getaway, thinking that my heart would heal and that maybe I'd even find some answers about the grandparents I never knew. But I'm leaving with yet another broken heart and even more questions than I started with.

Harris fiddles with some knobs and dials and the plane buzzes to life, vibrating just a little. It's like it hits me all at once what is happening here—that I am running away from the place and the people I have come to love so much, *and* I am doing so in a tin can that is likely to cause my demise—as the plane begins to roll down the runway.

"I think it would give you a sense of control and make you less afraid of being in the air," Harris continues.

"Nope!" I squeal.

"Geez. Okay. You don't have to learn."

"No!" I shriek. "I mean, I have to get out. I can't do this."

Harris grabs my wrist. "Keaton, you aren't getting out. Chill out. You're fine. Have I ever let anything bad happen to you?"

I shake my head and he lets go of my wrist to take the yoke. Then, what feels like seconds later, the plane picks up speed and soars into the air. I squeeze the seat so tightly my knuckles turn white.

"Deep breaths," he says. "You're fine. Everything's fine."

I take a deep breath. "I actually wanted to leave so badly I got on this plane," I say, laughing through my panic in disbelief.

"Want to tell me why you're running away?"

"Swallow so your ears don't pop, Salt." I know he doesn't know what I'm saying, but he barks, which makes me feel like he does. I close my eyes so I don't have to see the clouds we're flying through, and Harris says, "Just pretend you're on the boat. There are some waves and it's a little choppy."

I gulp a breath. "Anderson's mom came back," I say, "and I overheard Bowen telling her how he'd dreamed of this day for years."

"Yikes," Harris says. "You sure know how to pick 'em, Keat. What are the chances that two in a row would go back to their baby mamas?"

I roll my eyes, annoyed enough that I momentarily forget I'm suspended in midair. "You don't have to kick me while I'm down. I know, I get it, and I'd just like to move on."

He squeezes my shoulder. "You can stay with me as long as you like." He clears his throat. "Until Miss December returns my DMs, that is."

I elbow him.

He groans. "I'm kidding." He pauses. "How about I fully vet someone and just bring you home a husband?"

I nod and lean back in my seat, closing my eyes. "That would be great."

After learning more about them, I can truly say I want what my grandparents had. Finding it was just a little harder than I had imagined.

"Keat," Harris says. "Look, I'm no expert, but shouldn't you at least hear the guy out? You could be walking away from something great because of a misunderstanding."

"Interesting," I say, "that for the last couple of weeks you've made this relationship as hard as possible on me and now you want me to hear him out?"

"If you'll recall, I am your *brother*. My job is to keep guys away from you."

"That was your job when we were kids. Now your job is to be supportive and caring."

"Look," he says, "I just don't want you running away from him or your old-lady friends or the house and that big commission without getting the whole story. I think you're being hasty."

I turn to look at him. "Right now, I'd like to go home. If I change my mind, my handsome, brave big brother will fly me back."

"You are a total pain in the ass."

"But I'm so worth it." I look over at Harris, who is so comfortable at the helm of this plane, one that he worked hard for. I'm proud of him. And I feel myself relax. Because I have always been safe with him. "It's funny to think they left out of that very same airport every single week, isn't it?"

I think Harris might ask who, but he doesn't. "Yeah," he says. "It's sort of weird, actually. Like history repeating itself or something, like we're living out the part of their life they loved most."

"Hey, I forgot to tell you. Dr. Scott asked me about Becks and Townsend's plane. Has mom ever said anything about it to you?"

Harris shakes his head. "Nah, but that's not surprising. Surely they at least sold that, right?"

I shrug. "I have no idea. Honestly, I wouldn't put anything past them. I still don't get how you walk away from a house and never come back. I mean, all their stuff is there. All their memories."

"Oh my gosh, Keaton! Speaking of memories!" He's so excited, I forget for a moment that we're in the air—but only for a moment. "I can't believe I forgot to tell you. I was running into the kitchen the night of the foot injury—"

"You mean the night I almost died of blood loss," I amend.

He rolls his eyes. "You lived. You can quit being so dramatic."

"I think I get at least six months' free rent for that."

"Uh-huh," he says. "Because you were going to pay me rent."

I obviously wasn't but this gave me an excuse. "Okay, sorry. Continue."

Harris reaches into the bag behind him and starts rustling around.

"Umm, do you need something?" I ask nervously. "I could get it for you and maybe keep you from, like, crashing the plane you're supposed to be flying."

But he retrieves one of Townsend's journals and hands it to me. "Read the last entry. This is what I was trying to show you that night."

Townsend

....

In My Head

AUGUST 14, 1976

I'd been trying to avoid the reality for months. At first, it was only in my head, little things. Forgetting where I'd left my keys, why I'd gotten in the car, a date Becks and I had had on the calendar for months. Had I eaten lunch? But those things were just a normal part of aging, weren't they?

But then, little by little, I could feel Becks beginning to notice too. When I'd ask why she was dressing up, who was coming to dinner. When I forgot the name of our daughter's boyfriend. And then, worst of all, scariest of all, when I got in the plane and, for just a moment, a beat of a beat, I forgot the checklist. That was when the panic set in. I immediately began to sweat, my heart racing. But then Becks, in her soft and sweet way, got me back on track as though it was normal for me to forget a part of my life as automatic as breathing.

Last week, I got in the car to go see Daniel. And, as I pulled onto the road, for just a moment, I couldn't remember where to turn. The office I had spent my entire career in, in a town where I had spent the majority of my life. I nearly broke down right then and there. When

I got my wits about me and made my way to the office, Daniel confirmed that I do, indeed, have the signs and symptoms of Alzheimer's disease. I can barely stomach writing that because I know what it means. It's early yet, but the idea of losing my faculties, my memories, the names of my children, of waking up beside my dearest Becks and not knowing who she is . . . It's too awful to bear. Daniel has asked me to quit flying by the end of the summer, which pains me in the depths of my soul. Being in the sky is a part of who I am. I do not want to live when I cannot fly, but, alas, it is not my choice to make.

I've begun writing myself notes, making detailed plans in my calendar, creating routines that are more rote. I know I will have to tell Becks soon. Even though she is too caring to push me on it, I know she senses something is wrong—and when she needs me most. She hasn't told me yet that she is unwell, but of course I know. She is trying to protect me, and so I'm willing to wait. I need to be strong for her. Especially now. And so I will wait as long as I can to confess the one thing I hoped would never become true.

The idea of forgetting the love of my life is too much to bear. But I have to think that somewhere deep down in my soul I will always feel her, always know her. That no matter what happens to my memories, her heart will forever remain a part of mine. As it always has been.

Wormhole

A sick feeling has lodged itself in my throat. I can't imagine feeling that way, knowing my demise was coming—and that it wasn't going to be pretty. "I sort of wish I'd never read that," I say.

"Sorry," Harris says. "I guess it made me feel better. If they were both dying, maybe their death was less tragic? Made it less painful for them in the long run?"

I shake my head. "I don't know. I just can't imagine being Mom and Lon and never finding this stuff out."

Harris looks over at me. "Yeah, but if they really thought their parents were murdered maybe they were too scared to come back."

"That's just so creepy," I whisper.

Harris shakes his head. "I don't think the murder theory holds up. The only thing even remotely sketchy about their disappearance is that, in the newspaper interviews from when it happened, Lon said there was a bunch of cash missing from a secret hiding spot. But then there were no signs of a break-in or foul play, so I think they just wrote it off as a coincidence—or figured Becks and Townsend had taken the cash at some point."

My eyes widen. I didn't know about that. I still haven't been able to bring myself to read the articles. "What if they took the money, faked their deaths, and created a new life for themselves?"

"Maybe," Harris says with a small chuckle. "But Becks was dying of pancreatic cancer."

"Was she?" I ask excitedly. "The town doctor was their best friend. Maybe they made it all up so they could disappear. They could have been living a secret double life that no one knew about."

"I want to say you've been reading too many books, but I actually really love that. They moved away, faked their deaths, changed their names."

"Ruined their children's lives and never met their grandchildren."

"Damn, Keaton. Now you've ruined it. You are no fun at all."

I flick his shoulder hard enough that I know it will sting but not so hard that he will crash the plane. Just thinking about that brings the eerie feeling back.

"Maybe they were on their plane and they got sucked through a wormhole and are living a perfectly fine life in, like, 2057 or something," Harris offers.

"Yes! Then we could meet our grandparents one day!" I smile. "Well, whatever happened to them, I'm glad we got to know them a little better through all this."

He smiles. "I know. I feel like I know my grandfather now. It's crazy."

"Nothing will give you insight into a person's mind quite like reading their innermost thoughts," I say.

He looks down at me. "We got to know our grandparents *and* you got that rock."

I nod, wiggling my fingers. "Truth. How much you want to bet Mom changes her mind about wanting this when she sees it on my hand?"

"Oh, one hundred percent," Harris says. "She'll pry it off your finger with butter when you're sleeping if she has to."

"That's what I figured." I pause. "Do you know what's funny?"

He looks over at me. "What?"

"It seems like Becks lived this quiet life where her main goal was just to make everyone around her happy. At the time, it was so personal and intimate, but now I feel like she would have a couple hundred thousand Instagram followers hanging on her every recipe and entertaining tip. Like, she'd get a cookbook deal and have a coffee table book and a show or something."

"Oh my gosh, Keaton. You're a genius! She still could."

The man has lost his mind. The altitude is getting to him. "Harris, I know we're running pretty deep on the conspiracy theories, but I think it's safe to say the woman is dead."

He is grinning so widely. "But her granddaughter isn't."

I shake my head. "Are you crazy? I can't even cream butter."

"Couldn't!" he says. "You couldn't! But now you can. And that's the genius of the thing. That's the story. Granddaughter pieces together her grandmother's life and finds new passions and talent along the way. It's so feel-good."

I snort. "You've been in PR too long. That is the most ridiculous thing I've ever heard. Fly the plane. I need a nap."

I close my eyes, but I can't sleep. Because I'm thinking about the early days of starting Allison's All Welcome Instagram account—and all the fun posts I could do as @rebeccasaintjames.

A little over an hour later, we're making our descent into Teterboro, New Jersey, and the notion of somehow reincarnating my grandmother through her entertaining has all but left me. It's time to focus on reality. "Thanks, bro," I say when Harris has safely parked the plane. "You really took my mind off things."

"Oh, you're repaying me. I'm borrowing your dog tomorrow to help me get a client out of a mess."

"Great," I say.

My phone beeps and I will it to be Bowen. But it's my mother.

I gasp.

"What?" Harris says, taking my phone. He reads out loud, *Coming to see you and Harris tomorrow night. Miss you both and decided you're right. I should say goodbye to the house.*

Goodbye to the house. That means, I realize, I'm going to have to say goodbye to it too. Goodbye to the house and Beaufort and Violet and Arlene and Betty and Suzanne. Because when will I ever see them again once the house is sold? And Bowen. How could I have been so wrong about this one? That is all hard, but the idea of saying goodbye to Anderson is what brings tears to my eyes.

We're actually just landing at Teterboro, I text Mom as we hop out of the plane.

The phone rings in my hand instantly.

"You *flew*?" Mom asks. "Seriously? Like, in an airplane?"

My entire body feels jittery. "I know. Can you believe it? As it turns out, I trust my brother."

Harris leans over and says, "Mom, if you want to go to the house I'll fly us all back tomorrow." He raises an eyebrow at me and I nod my consent.

I put the phone on speaker.

"Darling, I love you, but I do not fly on single-engine planes."

Harris rolls his eyes. "Keaton did it, and she survived. Salt too."

"Love you both, but I already have a plane ticket to fly on a big airplane out of a regular airport. And Lon is going to join us later in the day. I'll see you tomorrow!"

A car is waiting for us, and, as we leave New Jersey and make our way into the hustle and bustle of Manhattan, I feel so far away from Beaufort I can almost forget I was ever there.

But then Harris sighs contentedly. "Ah. There's no place like home."

And I feel that tug, deep down in my belly, for the smell of the ocean, the breeze off the water, the smiling faces, and the cheerful waves of a place that I haven't realized until this minute really has begun to feel like home.

Becks

....

All Your Dreams

SATURDAY, AUGUST 28, 1976

Tip: You cannot control the manners of the people around your table, but you can control your own. As hostess, you are the example. When you are met with someone impolite, be even more well-mannered. If you are faced with someone grumpy, be as chipper and charming as ever. When someone else is sad, your warm smile might be all it takes to change their day. The same goes for your children too: though, as my child, I presume you would very much not like to admit it.

Becks Saint James would never leave the table for a long stretch of time during dinner—a fact that headwaiter Charles would know better than anyone. So when Becks heard the knock at the side door, she barely considered it, knowing that Charles, who was in the kitchen, would handle the matter posthaste.

She was more than a little surprised when Charles whispered in her ear, "Ma'am, you have a visitor."

She shook her head, smiling as the rest of the group conversed, their cutlery clinking against their plates.

"But, ma'am," Charles murmured under his breath, "the woman says it's urgent."

"I don't care if it's urgent. It's rude," she hissed through gritted teeth, the smile never leaving her face.

"Ma'am," Charles tried one last time, "she says she's your mother."

Townsend studied Becks from the other end of the table, and she met his eye as she put her finger up and silently conveyed that he was to take over. She was positive it wasn't her mother visiting. Her mother hadn't visited in forty-one years, had never once stepped foot inside her home. But the idea that someone would lie about that piqued her interest so fully that she had to get up and break all her rules—all her mother's rules—to see what was going on.

Charles gestured to the library, and when Becks entered, the woman sitting in the dimly lit room, swallowed by Townsend's favorite chair, was, in fact, Myra Bonner. Becks had come to terms with the fact that, after their last encounter, she would never see her mother again. She had never expected her to show up here.

"Hello, Mother," Becks said tentatively. Nervous butterflies formed in her stomach.

To her surprise, she only said, "Happy birthday, darling." It was a tone of voice so opposite from the threatening one she had last heard come out of her mouth that it startled her, unsettled her. Had she ever seen her high-strung mother this calm?

Becks's heart pounded. She didn't know what to say to the woman who hadn't wished her happy birthday in forty birthdays, who had ripped her heart out only a few weeks ago. So Becks did what Becks did best. She acted as that impenetrable woman she had always been.

"Well, thank you, Mother."

"Have you had a good night?"

Becks glanced over her shoulder into the kitchen at Evelyn and Charles as the other servers fussed over the giant flower-covered cake that would mark her last birthday. "I have had an excellent night. I love hosting dinner parties," Becks said.

"And you came out to see me in the midst of hostessing?" her mother scolded. "Didn't I teach you better than that?"

Becks hid her laugh of disbelief. *Why are you here, Mother?* she wanted to ask. But she didn't because she didn't want this conversation to end.

"Well, the visitor was you," Becks said softly.

Her mother cleared her throat, which made her know—or remember, rather—that she was getting choked up. "Rebecca, I've never told you this—I never wanted you to have the fear or worry of it hanging over your head—but you almost didn't live when you were born."

Becks's eyes went wide. "What? What do you mean?"

"You were born in my own bedroom at thirty-one-weeks' gestation, weighing barely three pounds. Your eyes were only partially open, you were less than sixteen inches long, and your lungs were weak. The doctor said you wouldn't make it; they wouldn't even let me see you. Your father thought it was best."

The idea made Becks's stomach flip. "That's awful, Mother."

Myra nodded. "We had a nurse at the house and, without telling me, she burned a fire in the hearth and wrapped you in our thickest blankets—even though it was August—and with your father's help, fed you drops of Dextri-Maltose as often as you would take them. Five days later you had beaten the odds. You were still alive. And the nurse brought you to me and said, 'Mrs. Bonner, do you want to hold your baby?' "

Becks wasn't sure where her mother was going with this, but she was rapt with attention all the same.

"I was nearly delirious with grief and lack of sleep, and I thought I was hallucinating. But then she handed you to me, and you wrapped your little hand around my finger, and I knew you were real.

"You were so brave, such a fighter," Myra continued, her eyes sparkling. "And the woman who saved you, well, we had to name you after her; it was only right. And it was destiny because Rebecca, of course, means 'determined.' And you certainly were."

Still am, she wanted to say. But was she? She felt so defeated now.

Myra leaned forward and took Becks's hands. "What I came here to tell you was that, during that time, those days when you were your father's secret, he bonded to you in a way that I can't quite describe. He always admired your determination; he was proud of you for following your own path."

Becks blew out her breath. "Well, Mother, he wasn't proud one big time. That's for sure."

Myra shook her head. "That's what I came here to say. Your father woke up for a few minutes in the hospital when you and Townsend were in the waiting room," she said, "and he told me he was wrong. How could he stand behind the pulpit each week and preach about tolerance and forgiveness and loving your neighbor as yourself and then cast out his own daughter because the man she loved was of a slightly different faith? Then, of course, he slipped away from me and well . . . that was that."

Becks wondered—stupidly, inconsequentially—whether if she hadn't carried this massive stress she would be dying now. Could stress give people cancer? She didn't know, but she felt that the place it was growing inside of her was where she carried her biggest burden. And now it was killing her. If her mother had told her this forty years ago, would it have made a difference?

Then she had a thought. "Mother, are you lying?"

"I'm not lying." She sighed. "I'm truly not."

"So then why the dramatics? Why did you tell me my entire adult life that I was responsible for killing my father? Why did you disown me?" *Do you know what that has done to me?*

"I was so angry, Becks, and, somehow, it was easier to put my anger on you than your father or God or anyone or anything else. And over the years, that anger—the lie I told myself—started to feel like it was justified, like the lie was true. I was too proud to tell you I was wrong. But I'm here now. I was wrong. I was so very, very wrong."

Becks understood then how different she and her mother were. She understood that her mother was a small, sad woman who would rather give her pain to her child than carry it herself. But Becks couldn't be sorry because that was perhaps why she was the exact opposite.

"Thank you for telling me that, Mother. You can't know how much it means to me to hear that. This is the best birthday present you could have given me."

For a split second, Becks wondered if she should tell her mother that she was dying. She wondered if she should prepare her for the inevitable. But she reaffirmed to herself that telling her mother before Townsend would be a betrayal.

"Happy birthday, sweetheart," her mother said. "I hope all your dreams come true."

Becks nodded. It was a little late for that, she well knew.

"Oh, and Becks, maybe you could come visit some time? If you aren't too busy?"

"Sure, Mother," Becks said. She knew she was close to losing the strength and energy to do so, but to be asked felt like absolution.

She walked through the kitchen, guiding her mother to the side door. "Mom, would you like to stay?" she asked. "I'm worried about you driving alone."

Myra patted Becks's arm. "Don't worry, sweetheart. I won't disrupt your evening any more than I already have. Besides, I always carry a gun in my glove compartment."

Becks's eyes widened. That didn't seem safe at all. But she had let go of the care and keeping of this mother long ago. She had had to. Becks's eyes filled when her mother hugged her goodbye. "I love you, Rebecca," Myra whispered. "I always have."

"I love you too, Mom." It felt like the very last thing she needed before she could leave this earth, happy and content.

Becks wiped her eyes, closed the door, and turned to Charles, who was waiting with a question in his eye. The show must go on. "Once I get back to the table, it will be time for the cake," she said firmly. He gave her a short nod and headed back to the kitchen.

Peter walked by—on his way, she presumed, to the restroom off the library. It unsettled her that he was in her house. It clearly unsettled Virginia too. But maybe she was being dramatic. Maybe her daughter got it all wrong. He could just be a quiet man at the mercy of the gossip mill—a perfect match (presuming he was not, in fact, a murderer) for gregarious Violet, who talked up a storm and ran the show.

As Peter walked by again, Becks felt the skin prick on the back of her neck. But then she thought of her children; she thought of how deeply she wished she could pardon them right now from the news she would have to deliver soon. Peter unnerved her, yes. But, all the same, she had a suspicion he was exactly who she needed right now.

Double Zero

Waking up in Harris's apartment is startling. For the first time in weeks, I am not in 1976 when I open my eyes. His home is so beautiful that it should be in *Architectural Digest*. Yes, it is a little cold. But it is the perfect Manhattan bachelor pad for a young(ish) executive. I click a button on the nightstand, and the shades roll up, revealing a sliver of sunlight and a beautiful city view. I push the weighted blanket, impossibly soft duvet, and gazillion-thread-count sheets off and sink my feet into the fluffy rug that overlays the dark hardwood. *I could get used to living here*, I think as I turn the handle of the glass-enclosed shower that somehow never has a single water stain.

How long is too long for a grown woman to live with her brother? I wonder as I melt into the hottest, steamiest shower with the most perfect water pressure. I complained the night before that Harris's leaving for the gym at five was going to wake me up. I was wrong. Here in heaven, the walls are so well insulated that you can't hear anyone else around you. I should have known. Harris took Salt with him to work, which made me nervous, but he's promised to return him in perfect condition and reward his service with chicken. He's trying to repair the reputation of an actress who's under scrutiny for some questionable comments she made about her costar in a new film, and he thinks having a fluffy, cute puppy will help soften her image.

As I inhale the steam, I almost don't want to leave New York. I don't want to go back and face Bowen—who hasn't even called me to apologize, so that's a pretty clear sign of how he feels about me. But I have promised my uncle and my mother that I will finish the job I started. Mom says she only wants to stay in Beaufort a night or two, so after she and Lon pick any pieces they want to take, I have the Salvation Army coming for the furniture no one else wants, and have procured a storage unit for all the sentimental or valuable items I know we'll want to save. My ladies, who I called when I learned Mom was coming, have promised to help me. Harris has promised to be a Bowen buffer. And then I can finally complete my checklists. If we really focus, I think we should be able to have the house cleared out and on the market in a week or so.

If the house doesn't sell in a month (which is short by usual standards, but long considering this hot market) we will renovate. But I'm hoping that, cleaned and emptied, a buyer with vision and deep pockets will scoop it up. It makes me sad to think that my only physical connection to my grandparents—and many generations of my family before that—will soon be gone.

Thinking of leaving Beaufort causes a wave of sadness to wash over me. I scold myself for the tears that combine with the warm water of the shower, thinking of never again visiting the Dockhouse Dames. Anderson. Bowen. Really, I'm crying for all of it. The life that could have been mine. I tell myself it will be good to get back here. I have a plan to enact today and, if it goes my way, I think I'll feel more secure in my choice.

I get out of the shower, wrap myself in a thick towel, and text Harris. *You'll meet me here at 11 or at the airport?*

The plan is for him to meet me here, but—as I told him last night—I want a minute to gather myself before Mom gets to the house, and we could be cutting it close if we hit traffic. Mom will be in Beaufort at four, and Arlene, Betty, Violet, and Suzanne will be there for emotional support, and this is my subtle way of reminding him that I think I'm right without being overly annoying.

I will meet you there and we won't be late. Quit nagging me.

At 7:50, I have drunk one of the fresh-pressed juices Harris has delivered weekly, eaten some sort of homemade granola that is supposedly gluten- and refined-sugar-free but tastes like the best dessert I've ever had, and my suitcase is sitting by Harris's door so that I am ready to run out when he arrives later.

I text him: *When I stay with you, will the meal plan cost extra?*

Meal plan is double.

Double of zero is still zero, so right in my budget.

I was planning on calling my realtor friend, Stephanie, last night to go apartment hunting, but first things first. I'm going to need a paycheck again before I commit to a place to live.

I'm a little bit nervous as I hail a cab. All Welcome is only ten blocks away, but I don't want to mess up my freshly fixed hair or get that sweaty street smell that is pretty common in the summer. Although, if this cab smell sticks to me, I think to myself as I slide inside, that could potentially be worse. I momentarily have the horrifying thought that Allison could turn me away. But, no. She came all the way to Beaufort to ask me to come back. My visit will be a surprise but not a shock.

When the cab stops in front of the All Welcome building, I step out into the steamy morning, savoring the hustle and bustle of the city all around me. I tell myself that I'm going to love being back in the place that has been my home for more than a decade. Beaufort could have been home, but it wasn't meant to be.

I sigh, put on my game face, and walk into the glass-and-chrome skyscraper. Eddie, the security guard, who's sitting behind the front desk in his uniform, raises his eyebrows when he sees me.

"What kind of welcome back is that for the woman who brought you your favorite latte twice a week?"

He stands up. "Welcome back?" he asks.

I shrug. "Well, not officially. I'm here to talk to Allison, but she'll be happy to see me."

"Uh-huh," he says warily.

I can tell he doesn't believe me. "Eddie, this is cold. After all we've been through?"

"I'm just going to have to call up to her office. You understand. Policy."

As he dials, he motions to me, and I'm a little incensed even though I know he needs my ID. I hand him my license as he puts the phone down and smiles. "Go on up."

I give him a smug smile and walk through the silver turnstile. In some ways, it's like I've never left. Except, of course, I wouldn't have been a tenth this nervous on a usual workday. As I ride up, I consider that Allison said she'd give me anything I wanted. But she couldn't possibly have imagined what I'm going to ask for. The elevator doors open and as I walk through them, I run right smack into . . . Jonathan. Who else?

"Keaton!" he says, obviously shocked to see me. He lunges at me and wraps me in a hug, his whole upper body going half-limp, in what I realize instantly is a reflexive action of pure relief. I laugh as he pulls away awkwardly, saying, "Oh, uh. Sorry. I think I'm just really glad to see you."

I nod and pat his shoulder. I can't *quite* tell him it's good to see him too. But there's something nice about seeing a familiar face. And being surrounded by the scent of geranium essential oils and the softest, loveliest lighting ever to appear in an office setting.

"I know I texted you," Jonathan says, "but I want you to know that I really am sorry. I acted badly, and I'm ashamed."

I nod. "I know. All is forgiven." I'm shocked to realize that I mean it. Then I spot Allison bustling down the hall in a sleeveless white-and-yellow print dress that makes her look like a pregnant fertility goddess. She squeals and runs over to embrace me, kissing both my cheeks rapturously.

"You're back!" She gives me a once-over. "You look great. Rested."

I laugh. "Well, yeah. Unemployment will do that to a person."

She slips her arm through mine, not even acknowledging Jonathan's presence. "Want to see your new office?"

Now I really do have butterflies. A new office sounds promising. But, no. I have conditions. "Actually, can we go to your office and talk first? I want to be really clear on what we're doing here."

She eyes me but walks toward her office. She opens the door and lets me in first. I sit down across from her desk, admiring the view from her floor-to-ceiling windows.

"This is your new view too!" she says, smiling.

"It's magnificent," I say.

"I just want you to know how much I value you, Keaton. I know how instrumental you have been in turning a person—well, me, obviously—into a brand. I wouldn't be here without you," Allison says. I smile because it's like she's reading my mind. "I'm so glad you're here. And I hope I haven't made things harder for you, but when you really want something you have to fight for it, you know?"

It's like an alarm starts ringing in my head. *When you really want something, you have to fight for it.* I instantly think of Kerry, her hand on Bowen's cheek. Was I right to walk away? To have given up on Beaufort so quickly? Should I have fought harder?

I think of Becks. What would have happened if she hadn't fought for Townsend? If she had let him walk away for good, taken the easier path? And what if Townsend hadn't forged ahead and decided to live in Beaufort—the place that became his home, even though it wasn't the most obvious choice?

"Sure," I say, my mind reeling with new uncertainty. "And I appreciate that. We've fought a lot of fights together, and I think we can continue to do so."

She nods. "So, lay it on me, Keaton. You know what I'm offering. What else do you need from me?"

I'm trying to stay focused, but all I can think about is the way I feel being in Beaufort. Bowen was a part of that, sure. But it was bigger than that. And I'm not sure I'm ready to walk away.

I see Allison noticing my distraction, so I clear my throat and say, "I can't sign more than a one-year contract, but I'd like the option of a second year."

She nods. "Totally understandable."

"And if I leave after that first year, I will give you notice and train my replacement."

She smiles. "I will try to make this job so good that you could never walk away, but okay."

This is when it hits me: I walked away from Bowen. Things got a tiny bit convoluted, and I bolted. Just like Kerry. It was the absolute wrong thing to do. He might not even consider taking me back after that. But I have to try. I need to get back to Beaufort, back to Bowen. I need to apologize; I need to fight for him. I am prepared to lose, but as it stands now, I've lost anyway. What's the harm in really laying my cards out on the table?

"Keaton?"

I snap back to Allison. "Right. Sorry."

And then I'm met with sudden clarity. I realize I would rather go back to Beaufort, start something new—something all my own, something that honors the past that could redefine my future—than stay here. And, yes, I think I'd like to talk things through with Bowen before throwing this relationship away. That said, I need a job.

So, with a new plan suddenly forming, I say, "I know I need to be in the office some. But, if we can work it out, I'd like to be mostly remote, at least for the first year."

She nods and stands. I stand too. I smile. Maybe I'm giving up a tiny piece of my self-respect by coming back here. But I'm getting some things I really want too.

"Going back to Beaufort?" she asks.

"I think I am."

She raises her eyebrows. "How's hot neighbor?"

I just shrug, and she laughs. "Well, I have so much to debrief you on. *Growing with Grace* was a huge success thanks to you, and I decided to push the launch of our next title to the fall, hoping and praying that you would come back to work your magic again and—"

"Allison?" I cut her off.

"Yeah."

"Speaking of our forthcoming titles . . . I need one more thing from you." This part of the plan hasn't changed.

As I tell her what I've been thinking, about this desire I have to preserve my grandmother's way of life, her eyes go wide. "Keaton, I don't know . . . Are you sure?"

I nod. "Yeah. I think I'm sure."

She shakes her head, and I think she's going to say no. But then she puts out her hand. "We have a deal. I'll have a contract sent your way by next week."

And that, I think, is how you negotiate. Uncle Lon would be so proud.

Becks

....

Born a Fighter

SATURDAY, AUGUST 28, 1976

Tip: Your instincts, Virginia, are your best gift. When creating a guest list, always trust your gut. This, of course, also goes for choosing friends. And husbands. Your head gets so tangled with all its important thoughts. But somewhere, deep inside, an answer already exists. When you find it, you will know.

As Becks gazed at her birthday cake, trying to digest what had just happened with her mother, she wondered, for the first time, if her mother had never properly bonded with her. If the fear of losing her daughter as an infant—accepting that reality—made it easier for her to exile her after her husband died, to blame her for things that could never be her fault.

But, no. That couldn't be. People bonded with children who weren't biologically theirs all the time, loved them like their own. Becks had even heard tales of whales adopting dolphins, lambs being raised by dogs. But no matter. Her mother had ultimately forgiven her, come to terms with the truth and shared that truth with her daugher. And that was more than she could have hoped for.

Becks looked at herself in the mirror in the restroom off the library. Dim light had been her friend these last few weeks, but now even that couldn't hide her gray pallor and complexion. She felt weak down to her bones. And she knew she didn't have much longer. Even the pain injections and the steroids were having a hard time keeping her going now.

She walked back into the library and was surprised to see that the door leading to the kitchen was closed. She hadn't closed it, had she? She heard a noise—one she recognized—coming from Townsend's chair, and jumped as she saw Peter sitting in Townsend's favorite spot by the fireplace. He was holding one of a pair of antique samurai swords that Townsend's father had acquired on a trip to Japan. The noise she recognized was that of the sword being removed from its sheath. How many times had she scolded Lon as a child—who had been mesmerized by the swords—for doing that very thing? The blades were, as they were meant to be, deathly sharp. The smallest contact with flesh could draw blood.

Becks's heart was already racing from the surprise of seeing Peter, but it practically galloped now that he was sitting there with a sword in his hand, slipping it ominously in and out of the case, almost dazed by the motion. They hadn't exactly left things on polite terms. Never a good place to be with a cold-blooded killer.

The sword still in his hand, Peter said, "I didn't like the way we left things yesterday morning."

"I, um, I didn't either," Becks stuttered, never taking her eyes off the knife. She could scream if he moved any closer. But was there time? Silent patients couldn't testify.

"Like I said, I'm really trying to make a fresh start. It's why I came to Beaufort."

Becks could feel her pulse pounding in her throat. Peter was so close that she knew he could take her out with one movement. She didn't know what made her brave enough to say: "Okay. I get that. But, Peter, how do I know you won't do this again, take another life? And then won't that be on me?"

"Would you like to know why I'm not in jail, Mrs. Saint James? Why I didn't lose my medical license?"

She closed her eyes for just a moment, trying to compose herself. It didn't work. She didn't answer, but he continued. "I'm not in jail because no one could prove what happened."

Oh, God. This was it for her. This was the end. "But it wouldn't have mattered because my patient's family was so grateful. They didn't want to see him suffer anymore. He was in the most pitiful shape I'd ever seen a human being, and—"

A picture was starting to form to Becks now. "Wait, your patient was dying?"

He nodded. "Days from death." He paused. "What I did only hastened the process ever so slightly. I couldn't bear to see a human in the state he was in. He was begging to be released from the hell he was living in; he was in so much pain. After I was convinced he was of entirely sound mind, if not body, I helped him. I helped them all. The family gave us their blessing."

Becks did feel a tiny bit better. But, then again, she was dying too, so who was to say he wouldn't kill her right here to save his reputation? "That doesn't matter, Peter," she said sternly. "It goes against everything the medical community stands for. Do you not remember the Hippocratic oath?"

She glanced down at the sword, gleaming in the light, still in his hand. Her temples were throbbing.

"I understand your opinion, but, with all due respect, you don't actually know what you would do until you are in the position to make that decision." He paused. "And I know it's hard to keep a secret like this. But have you ever needed a fresh start, Mrs. Saint James?"

She nodded, only realizing when her head moved that she was back against the door.

"So maybe you could keep my secret for me?"

With another step toward her, Peter was so close she could see the blood vessels around those crystal eyes of his. Becks almost emitted a scream; this was the end. "Yes, yes," she said hastily. "I'll keep your secret."

Just as her panic reached its peak, Peter, evidently noticing her alarm, hastily moved back toward Townsend's chair and grabbed the case, attempting to slip the sword back inside. But the knife slipped just a centimeter. Peter didn't even notice the blood coming from his hand until the sword was back inside the case.

He swore under his breath and put the cut to his mouth. Becks, realizing how silly she was being, took Peter's arm and led him into the bathroom off the library. She turned on the cold tap and ran Peter's hand underneath to stop the bleeding. Their eyes caught in the mirror.

Becks thought back to the letter she had written Townsend decades earlier. *If just one thing binds us . . . just one . . .* That gave Becks an idea. Peter had a secret he needed kept. And it was becoming increasingly apparent to Becks that perhaps she needed someone to keep a secret for her as well.

"Peter," Becks said, "you obviously understand the value of keeping quiet about things."

Peter looked confused but said, "Well . . . yes ma'am. I suppose that's true."

"If I needed a favor from you, what would you say to that?"

"I suppose this would be a case of us helping each other?" He raised his eyebrow.

Becks smiled affirmatively. He was getting it.

"Mrs. Saint James," he said, "I know you are nearing the end. I'm not totally comfortable accelerating that for you, but when you get to that point—if that is what you're asking me—I would consider—"

Becks laughed, cutting him off. "No, darling. What I need is for you to sink Townsend's convertible." She paused. "And, um, make it look like an accident."

Peter shook his head. "Oh, I don't think I could be involved in an insurance scheme," he said. "I've already had to duck one set of troubles this year."

"Oh, Peter. Not an insurance scheme. I'll never file a claim on the car. That I can promise you. I just need the car gone."

"Might I ask why?"

Without skipping a beat, Becks said, walking back into the library, "Peter, it appears to me that Townsend's mental faculties are going downhill. I can't be the one to tell him he can't drive his beloved convertible. So were it gone, ruined, submerged in Taylor Creek, it would make the whole thing much more palatable."

He scrunched his nose. "Couldn't we act like it was stolen? Crash it into a tree? Disassemble the carburetor? I know how to do that, you know."

Becks's voice was satin calm as she said, "I'm sure you do, Peter. But, no, this is what I need done. I need the car submerged. Tonight. In the middle of the night when no one will see, of course." She paused. "And I need how and why it got that way to be our secret."

Becks could read the confusion written all over Peter's face. She sensed he wanted to say no, but, then again, how could he? Becks knew his secret. Becks could ruin his life. Not that she ever *would*. But Peter didn't know that.

Thinking of his current situation, Becks thought she might have something that could sway Peter. She and Townsend survived the Great Depression. They knew what hard times looked like. As such, they always kept a few thousand in cash stashed in the house for emergencies. And this was that, wasn't it?

Becks ran her fingers along the shelf until she came to the book she was searching for. *The Call of the Wild.* She handed the book to Peter. He tried to hand it back to her. "Mrs. Saint James, I don't understand."

"Open the cover, Peter."

He did as she said and his eyes went wide. "This isn't about money," he started. As if he hadn't spoken at all, Becks rose on her tiptoes and took down a copy of *Antigone* and handed it to him.

"Peter, darling, you told me yourself that you needed a fresh start. Your empty house told me that you could use a leg up toward that end. All I need you to do is sink our car in the creek, and I'll pay you well for it. You're a brilliant doctor, a capable and ruddy farm boy. How hard could that possibly be?"

"It happens, I've heard," he whispered. "Around the curve of Sunset Lane. Cars do lose control. They do wind up in the creek."

Becks nodded. "And when the tops are down, convertibles sink so very quickly."

Peter hadn't actually agreed, but Becks, in her Becks way, thanked him as if he had, in a manner that affirmed no one ever said no to Becks Saint James. "Thank you, Peter. I have something to discuss with my husband now." She paused. She knew Townsend Saint James better than she knew herself. But she was aware that the medication she was on and the thought of her impending death had made her less astute than usual. There was a chance that Townsend would disagree with her. She needed a contingency plan for that. "Peter," she said. "Please check the windshield wipers before you sink it. If I change my mind, I'll leave a note under one of them."

Peter looked mystified but nodded his agreement. Then Becks said something Peter wouldn't understand until decades later, something that he would keep secret for the rest of his natural life. "Thank you, dear. I just can't bear the thought of our children being afraid to fly."

Becks had been born a fighter. She had been born with a keen understanding of who she was, what she wanted, and what she was willing to do to get there. She had learned to recognize those same qualities in other people as well. Consequently, in one of her last actions on earth, Rebecca Saint James had, once again, chosen the right man for the job.

....

Copilot

I am so antsy, I'm practically wearing a hole in the dark wood of Harris's pristine apartment floor. I have been practicing what I'm going to say to Bowen when we get back to Beaufort, how I'm going to tell him that I know he and Kerry have a past, but that we could have a future. When my phone rings in my hand I'm positive it's him. I've manifested him! Just like Allison would say. Crazy Allison. And crazy me for going back. But it isn't Bowen. I sigh. "Hi, Uncle Lon."

"Keaton, Keaton, Keaton, remind me to never doubt you again!"

I love the cheeriness of his tone, but I'm confused. "Oh, I will. Don't you worry. But why are we never doubting me again?"

"We got an offer on the house this morning, out of the blue! One of the attendees of your Old Homes Tour found my name and number on the deed and made me an offer. And, Keaton, it's a winner. We're in high cotton, dear niece of mine!"

My heart sinks. The house is going to be gone. "Well, great. Then I guess it's a good thing Mom is coming for a final walk-through."

"I think so. So proud of you, Keaton! You deserve that commission."

I tell him thanks and drop my phone in my bag, feeling so many emotions at once. On the bright side, I'll have a nice big commission check. On the other bright side, I'm no longer unemployed. I think I just got so swept up in the moment in Allison's office that I forgot Beaufort was always meant to be temporary. This is good; this is right. Mom and I will get this finished, and I can walk away.

On that note, I'm about to text Harris to ask where he is when there's a knock at the door, right by my head, and I jump. I open it. "Two minutes early. I'm so proud."

But when I look up, it isn't Harris. It's Bowen. He's wearing a rumpled linen button-down with jeans and has this two-day beard that I find irresistible. I have to fight back tears when I see him—though of joy or sadness, I can't really say.

So many things are fighting for top position in my mind that I can't think of where to start. So I blurt out, stupidly, "Did you miss shark tagging for this?"

I hear a voice I positively adore say, "We'll do anything for the people we love." I rush into the hall to wrap Anderson in a hug and kiss his cheek. I can't help it. I begin to cry with relief. "You're so tall," I say.

He looks at me like I'm nuts. "Keaton, you saw me yesterday. I couldn't have grown that much."

I wipe my eyes. "Maybe it's just that you look older in New York."

He shrugs like that's a good possibility.

"How did you find me?" I ask Bowen. But I know before he answers.

"Violet," Bowen and Anderson say simultaneously.

Harris flies around the corner. "I know. I know. It's eleven oh one." Salt yanks away from him and I lean down so he can smother me with kisses. I instantly feel better. Harris stops dead in his tracks when he sees Bowen and Anderson. "But I guess . . . why go to Beaufort when Beaufort can come to you?"

He looks at me questioningly, then looks down at Anderson. "I've always felt eleven oh one is the ideal time for an ice cream sandwich."

Anderson nods and follows him inside, and I turn and gesture for Bowen to do the same. Harris guides Anderson to the kitchen while Bowen and I sit on Harris's white couch under the huge picture window. Salt jumps up beside me, which is not technically allowed, but I'm in crisis here. Bowen looks around. "Wow," he says. "This is like a TV show apartment."

Suddenly, all my resolve to tell him how I feel is replaced with anger that he put me through the last twenty-four hours without so much as a text. And fear that he is here to tell me he is getting back together with Kerry in person, that I'm too late. "Why are you here?" I ask. "Did Kerry turn you down? Bail already? Because I'm super disinterested in being your second choice."

"Keaton, if you had let me explain instead of just running off, I think we would be in a different place right now."

"There's nothing to explain," I say. "You dreamed of her coming back for a decade, and she came. I'm happy for you," I lie. "I'm happy for Anderson." That part is true. "I get it. I've been the third wheel in one family already this year. Now I'm the fourth in yours."

This is not the speech I have practiced, but I'm so raw, so emotional that I realize my pride won't let me fight for him. Not without knowing first that he is willing to fight for me.

Bowen is staring at me. "Are you finished?"

I feel a stabbing pain in my heart, remembering the way he looked at her. But I nod anyway because I'm afraid if I talk, I'll cry.

"Keaton, I told you I had decided years ago that things were over for good between Kerry and me. She might feel like she's finally ready to be in Anderson's and my lives, but I have heard that from her before.

And even if she ends up being mother of the year and getting a trophy for it, she is only ever going to be Anderson's mom to me."

"But you said—"

"I know what I said," he interrupts. "And if you had bothered to let me explain, you would know that Kerry said she had been thinking and she wanted to start over, try for us to be a family." My eyes widen, and my heart sinks. "But if you had stayed, like, two seconds longer, you would have heard me respond that I dreamed of her coming back for the first couple years after she left. But then I realized we weren't right for each other, that I deserved someone who was all in, who was sure. That Anderson deserved that too. You would have heard me say that I never even wanted to try with another woman—*until I met you.* And for the first time since she walked out the door, I had this sense, way down deep inside, that maybe Anderson and I could let someone else into our family after all."

"Oh," I said, looking down at my hands, trying to hide my smile. "Well that's nice to hear."

I'm starting to feel better until he says, "I almost didn't come here." There's an agitation in his voice, and I can see we've switched places. I want to be indignant, but, really, he has reason to be upset with me too.

I look up and see the hurt in his eyes. "But then I realized how easily the situation could be misinterpreted, and I realized that you must have thought history was repeating itself—that I was going to get back with Kerry just like Allison got back with Jonathan. And I know that must have brought out the urge to flee, and so I'm giving you the benefit of the doubt here and assuming that leaving without so much as a goodbye is not your typical go-to move. So I guess I packed my kid up and flew here to allow you to explain."

I look into his blue eyes, which seem grayer against Harris's cool walls, and reach my hand up to touch the stubble on his cheek. I bite my lip. "I'm sorry, Bowen. I really am. And, just so you know, my bags are packed by the door because I was champing at the bit to get back to Beaufort to apologize to you, to see if I was wrong, and there was the possibility of a future between us. I know she hurt you by running away, and I did the same thing. Even if it was hard, I should have at least given you the courtesy of a real conversation."

My eyes fill with tears. "I didn't realize until this morning that leaving you with no warning would be the worst thing I could do to you—and to Anderson too. That it would bring back all your fears and all your hurts and could end up breaking us for good."

He looks up, asking an unsaid question.

I shake my head. "I shouldn't have left like that. I should have been more sensitive. It's just that I really, truly thought you had chosen her."

He nods. "I get it. It's a wound for you. But, Keaton, I do need to be up front about the fact that while I am not romantically interested in her, Kerry is always going to be in my life—and Anderson's—in some way, shape, or form, whether she's physically present or not. Do I prefer it when she disappears for years on end? Yup. I sure do. But the reality is that I can't control her, and she is Anderson's mother."

I feel really embarrassed that he feels he has to even say that. "Oh my gosh, Bowen. Of *course* she is. I know that. I hope for Anderson that she is a huge part of his life in a really positive way." I smile. "But even if she's not, I know she's in your life. And I know she'll always be a part of your heart. She gave you the coolest kid on earth. I just needed to know that the romantic part of your relationship is in the past."

"Definitely, one hundred percent, all the way, in the past." He pauses. "And maybe all this was for the best, actually."

"How so?"

"Because it wasn't until Kerry told me that she still loved me that I realized I was in love with someone else."

I scoot closer to him. "This person you love. Do I know her?"

He nods. "And what I'm hoping is that maybe, one day, she might learn to love me too."

My turn to look down at my feet. I shake my head. "She won't learn to love you." Then I look back up, and I see the pain in his eyes. "Because she already does."

He stares at me for a long moment, as if he is taking in my face, memorizing it, like it's new.

"Bowen?"

"Yeah?"

"I know you're out of practice, but this is when you kiss me."

He laughs and pulls me close, kissing my lips, then my cheeks, then my neck. Harris calls from the kitchen, "Is it safe to come out? If we're going to beat Mom to Beaufort, we've got to get going."

Harris and Anderson trail out of the kitchen. Harris looks around at the small group sitting in his apartment—all of whom have to get back to North Carolina—and sighs. "Bowen and Anderson can come with us. Will be better in the long run than having everyone here eating my granola."

"Can I be copilot?" Anderson asks, looking up at Harris.

"Obviously," Harris says. "You think these two could do it?" They both shake their heads skeptically.

An hour later, Bowen and I are in the back two seats of the plane, Salt between us, his leash looped through my seat belt. Bowen looks over the dog and kisses my hand. *I love you*, he mouths.

And I believe him. I truly do. For the first time in a long time, I think I might have made the right choice. I think I might be right where I'm supposed to be. "This is absolutely awesome!" Anderson says as we take off. I'm so happy to be beside Bowen that I am panicking far less than usual. And . . . the single Xanax I found in the bottom of my purse has helped ever so slightly too. Even still, I realize I'm squeezing Salt to me way too tightly. But he just rests his head on my chest, not seeming to mind. I swear he knows when I'm scared. And I suddenly get the whole emotional support animal thing.

"Do you know there's no minimum age to learn to fly in North Carolina?" Harris asks.

Bowen shoots me a panicked look as Anderson cheers, "That's awesome! Will you teach me to fly?"

"Maybe when you're sixteen!" Bowen chimes in.

Harris winks at Anderson, and it's the first time I've ever considered what Harris might be like as a father. It's the first time I've considered that, if this all goes well, I might be someone's stepmother.

It's the best thought I've had in quite some time.

My stomach drops as we pull up to the house. It is only three thirty—half an hour before Mom is supposed to arrive—but she is sitting on the front steps, looking bewildered. "I told you we needed to leave earlier," I say to Harris, who is driving my Bronco.

"Oh, yes," Harris says sarcastically. "I can see why you would blame this on me. The confession of love in my living room was all my fault."

"Well, if you had come home earlier—"

"Do you guys do this a lot?" Anderson asks. He doesn't sound accusatory. Just curious.

"Ah, the life of an only child," Harris says. "You have no idea what you're missing, buddy."

Bowen eyes me over Salt, and I wonder if he's thinking what I'm thinking, if he is imagining a world and a future in which maybe Anderson isn't an only child forever. But I know I'm getting way ahead of myself.

As Harris pulls into the driveway, I take a deep breath. "I don't feel emotionally equipped to deal with this," I say.

"Me neither," Harris agrees.

"Well," says Bowen, "Anderson and I would love to take Salt for the evening while you attempt to handle the crisis with your mother."

I sigh, and Harris looks at me over the seat. "Now or never."

As we get out of the car and walk slowly to the front porch, I feel like it's a march to the executioner. But then I notice that Mom isn't on the porch alone. She's with a pirate. My favorite pirate. Alex. He has her laughing at something. Instead of us having to go over to comfort Mom, she jumps off the step.

"My babies!" she exclaims.

"Hi, Mom." I give her a big hug and kiss, suddenly feeling guilty that I didn't want to deal with her impending meltdown. She is my mother, and dealing with meltdowns is what daughters do. I don't realize how very much I've missed her until I sink into her hug. She would hate hearing this; she raised me to be stronger than this. But I need her here. I realize I don't know how to finish clearing out the house without her.

"You two look sensational," Mom says, pulling back. Then she gasps, and I see the Dockhouse Dames entering the front gate. They are carrying trashbags and Post-it Notes, and I love them for being here to help—not just with the physical load but also with the emotional one.

Mom hugs them one by one as they file onto the porch, then takes a deep breath. "Okay. Let's do this."

Harris and I exchange a glance, and I know we're thinking the same thing: We haven't expected her to be so level-headed.

I smile gratefully at Alex. He pulls me to the side. "Your mom's cool," he says. "Oh, and don't go on the back porch. I painted the floor today."

I give him a thumbs-up. "Thank you, Alex. You're a lifesaver."

He shrugs. "It's just porch paint."

I was talking about the way he handled my mom, but I let it go. He's a lifesaver either way.

I let Mom be the one to put the key in the front door, the one I struggled with when I first got here. She opens it instantly, and it breaks my heart a little to think that this home of hers, where she can still open the tricky door, has become a burden and a sadness for her. It breaks my heart that this place that has felt so much like home is going to be gone. But I have to think it will be a relief for my mom. So that's a good thing.

Her chin quivers as she leans over the threshold. I realize that she is laughing, not crying. "It's exactly the same," she says. She hugs me. "You really didn't change a thing."

"Well, not anything I didn't have to."

Mom walks from room to room as if in a trance, and we follow her. Upstairs into her parents' bedroom, Lon's room, the guest rooms, her childhood room, down the back stairs, and into the library. She runs her fingers along the spines of her parents' books and says out loud, "What happened to you two?"

I haven't said one word to her about any of the things I've discovered, any of the mystery I've unraveled—not that it has led me to any answers. But this question is all it takes for me to know that she isn't convinced of the car wreck story either. I'm not quite brave enough to ask her yet if it's true that she thought Becks and Townsend were murdered—or why.

Harris pulls a notebook out of his back pocket and slides it back in place on the bookshelf. "This was Townsend's last journal," he says. "I've read them all. And no hint of what happened. The last entry I read was that he knew Becks was sick but she hadn't confided in him, and it was eating him alive."

Mom whirls around. "What? Mom was sick?"

"She didn't know," Harris and I say to each other at the same time.

She shakes her head. Then she pauses. "Well, okay. I was worried about her. But I thought she was just aging quickly, not sick."

My four friends are pretending to busy themselves in the kitchen, but I know they're listening.

"And if his journals are to be believed," Harris adds, "Townsend had early-onset Alzheimer's, and his doctor had told him he shouldn't fly anymore." He paused. "But he hadn't told Becks either."

Mom puts her hand to her heart. "Poor Daddy. Flying was his favorite thing. He always used to say he didn't want to live when he couldn't fly."

I don't know why, but all the hairs on the back of my neck stand when she says that. Maybe because flying always gets me so worked up. But I had done it *twice* in two days. I was really maturing.

"If Daddy wrote about the disappearance, if he had any idea what was coming, he might have hidden it," she says. I'm not sure what this means. She stands on her tiptoes and grabs *Call of the Wild*. She opens the cover, which reveals an empty hollow inside. She hands the book to me and grabs *Antigone*. Also empty. She appears to be searching and finds *Sense and Sensibility* and then *Heart of Darkness*. She lifts the covers to reveal a perfectly bound stack of cash in each. "Huh. There's still some cash here. I just assumed all of it was gone."

Harris mouths to me, *Faked their deaths.*

I roll my eyes, and Harris chuckles.

"What?" Mom asks.

"They were so clever." He holds up the spines of the books: "C, A, S, H. Cash."

I laugh. "That *is* clever."

"It was Mom's idea," Mom says. "So Lon and I would remember which books had money in them." Her voice quavers, but she doesn't break down.

"Well, this was a really good hiding spot," I say. "I wiped those books down and never noticed they weren't real." I pause. "Anderson would never have let that slide because he was really good about inspecting the insides of all his books. I was a little less detailed . . ." I perk up, thinking of something. "Wait. Why didn't you come back for the money after they died?"

Mom squints at me. "Honey, I don't know quite how to express this, but I never walked through the front door again. Lon came to look in the library, and when he realized the cash was gone from the first two books, he got spooked and ran. After that, we didn't even come back for the things in our rooms."

She walks over to Townsend's credenza, kneels down, fiddles with what looks like the foot and, in one motion, slips a latch to reveal a hidden drawer underneath.

I gasp. "Mom, were you ever going to tell me about any of this stuff? What if I had just sold this house with all the cash and . . ." I pick something up from the hidden drawer of the credenza. "Gold?" I question.

Mom nods. "Gold."

"Why do they have gold? Maybe pirates got them!" Harris says. I shake my head sternly at him.

By the way Mom rustles around in the drawer I can tell these coins and bars aren't what she is looking for. "My parents lived through the Great Depression, a world war, a cold war, the Vietnam War, and more social and economic unrest than you can imagine. They were always prepared for the worst."

"Clearly," I say.

"It looks like it's all here . . ." she muses more to herself than to us.

"Where are the guns and liquor?" Harris asks.

"In the basement," Mom says absentmindedly.

"Seriously?" I squeak.

She smiles up at me. "Come on, Keat. We're at sea level. A basement would be underwater."

Oh. Right, right.

Mom unearths what she has clearly been searching for: a journal that matches all the others, with *TSJ* embossed on the leather cover. She hands it to Harris. "I don't think Dad had any deep dark secrets to leave behind. But if he did, they'd be in here."

I look at Harris. "This would have saved us so much time."

Harris nods. "Forty years' worth of reading." He pauses. "Although I wouldn't take back a single page. I feel like I know my grandfather now."

"Me too," I say. "And my grandmother."

Mom shakes her head. "You know your grandmother through your grandfather's eyes. He thought she could do no wrong."

"I like the image of her I have through his eyes," I say.

Mom smiles. "Me too."

She lies down on the oriental rug, seeming almost out of breath.

"So, we're taking a short break?" I ask.

That's when Mom finally notices and grabs my hand. "Whoa," she says. "I'd forgotten how beautiful this ring was."

I start to slip it off, but she stops me. "No. You wear it so well. Mom would have wanted you to have it."

As much as I don't want to part with this ring I've come to love so much, I know Mom isn't quite right. "Becks left the ring for you," I say. "I know she did. Because she left it with the letter." I pause, trying to read Mom's expression, but she doesn't seem to have one. "I can go upstairs and get it if you—"

"No," Mom says. "Please don't. Baby steps."

I nod. She has tackled more in the past hour than I thought she'd make it through in days. It's as if she's possessed by the spirit of something or someone else. My heart swells with pride for her. She looks over at Harris, who is rifling through Townsend's journal. "So, what have you figured out?"

He looks up at both of us, wide-eyed. "I think I might have figured out what happened to Rebecca and Townsend Saint James."

I look down at Mom, who is still lying on the floor as if she's in savasana pose.

"We can talk about it later," Harris says.

"It has been almost fifty years," Mom says. "I think it's time I knew the truth."

I have no idea what my brother has just read. As he fills us in, I have the sinking suspicion that whatever it says might be a version of events. But I highly doubt it's the whole truth.

Townsend

....

Jump

AUGUST 28, 1976

In 1943, after the first two weeks of basic arms and military training at Maxwell Air Force Base in Alabama, I finally caught the thrill I had been chasing. Growing up as the son and grandson of avid hunters, I knew how to handle firearms with care, caution, and, most of all, precision. So the previous two weeks were a chance for me to shine and stand out more than anything. But this final test was what I had come for; this was my moment.

At twenty-two and a half feet long, with a thirty-foot wingspan, the Ryan PT-20 we used for primary pilot training—the "Recruit," as we named her—wasn't huge. But as I climbed up the wing and sat in the captain's seat with my trainer behind me, it felt like it was capable of carrying all my dreams, no matter its size. Even with my helmet on, the propeller was loud enough to drown out my fears and my thoughts as I placed my feet on the military-green pedals. The open-air craft was all metal inside, utilitarian, the seat offering nothing in the way of comfort, and it contained little more than a fire extinguisher for safety. But it was the most beautiful thing I'd ever seen. As I caught speed and took off, up into the air, I realized that all my anxieties about whether this was a good idea were unfounded. I knew at once that I was made to be a pilot, born to be a part of the sky. I would excel at this; I would defend my country.

And I vowed that, when I got home, I would teach my Becks to fly so that she too could experience this feeling, so that she could know what it was like to lift off into the air and leave all her earthly problems on the ground. From then on, the plane would be where we left all our worries behind.

It was a memory I never wanted to forget, that I always assumed I would remember. And flying was still the place where I would leave all my worries behind. It was there I could forget the horrifying Alzheimer's diagnosis Daniel had given me. For long stretches of time even. Not in an I'm-losing-my-faculties kind of way. In a blissful, best-moments-are-in-the-sky kind of way. It was the same with fishing. I remembered everything out on the water. During our most recent fishing trip I mentioned this to Daniel and he responded, "Well, of course. Fishing has never been about a list or the mind. Fishing is about instinct."

We hadn't mentioned my condition since he diagnosed me in his office three weeks ago. But now he said, "Towns, as long as I am able, as long as we can walk on and off this boat, I will bring you out here. I promise. You might not know me or the boat or your name, but I have zero doubt in my mind that you will still know these fish. You will still know this water. You will still be the best damn fisherman I've ever had the pleasure of knowing."

That's a good friend. One who will stand by you even knowing what's ahead for you, one who will make promises you know he will keep. I looked over at him. Maybe it wasn't time for rhapsodies yet. But who knew how much time we had? "Daniel," I said, clearing my throat, "you're the best damn friend I've ever had the pleasure of knowing."

He teared up, and it occurred to me how impossible it must have felt for him to tell me, his best friend, that I was going to face a terrible fate, all while knowing that he would be powerless to do anything about it. Any soldier could tell you that once you have lost a brother in arms, you are never the same.

Men our age had lost so much, so many. I hope the next generation never has to see what we have seen. But I knew I could not control that any more than I could control the fate coming for me. What Daniel said next is part of that fate, a part I had both entirely expected and not expected in the least.

"Daniel, as your best friend, there's something I need to ask you. Is Becks . . ."

I trailed off. I couldn't ask him. I already knew the answer. But if I hadn't, it was there in the quiver of his chin. I loved Becks in a way that split me wide open, in a way that was all-consuming and terrifying. But Daniel loved her too. He loved her hard.

"Is she dying, Daniel?"

He cleared his throat. "You know I can't tell you that, Townsend. I can't tell a patient about another patient, even when it's my best friends." Even still, his eyes filled with tears. And that told me all I needed to know.

I shook my head. "I've spent forty-one years of my life with her. I can tell when my own wife is dying. I just don't want it to be true."

I was surprised how stoic I was when I said it. Maybe it was because I knew I was dying too. Knowing that I would slowly lose all my memories, my sense of self, somehow made it easier to accept. Once Becks was gone in body, she would also be gone in my mind. A small kindness from a brutal disease.

"I'm so sorry, Townsend. I would have done anything to save her if I could have. You know that."

I nodded, unable to find the words.

"How have you resisted the urge to intervene?" he asked.

I shrugged. "Becks is the smartest person I know. And she's the most steadfast. So whatever she decided about her illness was what would happen. I couldn't change her mind anyway."

"Will you tell her?" Daniel asked. "About you?"

I shook my head. "I can't increase her burden by telling her," I said. "She'll just be worried about me instead of herself."

Daniel nodded. "I know. No reason to make her final weeks even worse."

I wasn't sure why I wasn't crying, wailing, flinging myself over the side of the boat. That's how I knew that, somewhere deep down, I had already come to terms with Becks's death. "When she goes, can you take me too?"

"I'm sorry, my friend. I can't. I just can't. I'm going to need you when she's gone."

That was when the tears finally came for both of us. "I'm going to need you too," I whispered.

"At least the kids are grown," he offered.

The kids. It panged me anew that their mother wouldn't be at their weddings. Wouldn't see her grandchildren, should some come along. Lon and Virginia would miss me, sure. But not like they would miss her. She was their mother, the blood that ran through their veins, the fierce protector of their dreams and hearts. Mine too. Becks was the thread that wove through our family. She would be gone. Life without Becks. No. Living without Becks. There was no life without her.

"I could just go ahead and jump," I said, gesturing to the ocean surrounding us. "Sink to the bottom. Let the sharks have their way with me."

"You could jump." Daniel nodded seriously. "But then you'd ruin Becks's dinner party."

I paused as if considering. "Yes. And not just any dinner party."

"The last dinner party of summer," Daniel said, "which we all know is the most important."

Her last dinner party ever.

"Shall we get this to the chef?" he asked, gesturing toward our cooler of fish.

"Can you imagine if we're late?" I asked.

We both laughed, and Daniel turned the boat toward home. For years, Becks had lamented that with our age difference she would likely have to live without me. I had never, not once, considered that I might have to exist in a world without her.

I used to dream of flying when I was younger—not in a plane, but of my own accord, zipping through the night sky, swimming among stars and the bright silver moon. I would wake with the feeling that this was what awaited me on the other side. Oh, how I hope that's true. Oh, how I long for a day when Becks and I can float among the stars together. If I could choose our time and place, I know just when and where it would be.

As Daniel drove on, I turned to see it, the spot where light blue and dark blue collide, where the white of the clouds and the white of the surf merge. No land. No people. I'm grateful that Daniel sped on so he couldn't hear the sob that caught in my throat as we pulled away from the place most special to my girl and me. If we could go together, choose our time, I would pick that enchanted merging for the two of us to spend eternity: where the sky meets the sea.

....

Cake for Dinner

M y mouth is so dry I cannot speak. "You think he wanted them to die together?" I finally eke out.

"I think he planned it," Harris says grimly.

My mother is motionless, still lying on the floor. For a second, I worry she is dead. But then she says, "They never would have planned it. They were way too religious to risk eternal damnation." She sighs. Hard. "Well, I guess the fact that they were both dying makes their murder a little less tragic. I was still robbed of months or years of my parents' lives, but I guess this is some comfort."

"Mom, why would someone want to kill your parents?" I ask.

"We had this really sketchy neighbor who had done something illegal. Mom knew about it, and in true Mom fashion, she confronted him. And, well, I don't think he took kindly to that." She sighs again, her voice cracking, "And I was the reason she knew. I was the one who told her. My parents were murdered because of me."

Harris and I share a disbelieving look. And I know we're thinking the same thing: *Murder* seems a little extreme. "I don't know, Mom. It seems to me like maybe Townsend planned it," Harris says.

She finally sits up, her face stricken. "You don't understand Catholic guilt, Harris." She shakes her head. "Plus, if they had planned it, they would have left me a clue or *something*. I just can't believe no one ever found them. All these years."

I remember what Bowen said last week. "Search and rescue teams weren't as well equipped then as they are now," I say gently. I want to remind her that her mother *left her a letter* that could have a clue, but I feel like she is teetering on the edge of losing it so it doesn't seem like the right time.

She nods. "Well, that is true."

"I just can't imagine being that brave," Harris says. "I'm serious. To be like, okay, I'm going to end it."

I hear a light rap behind me and see Violet peek her head in. "Y'all okay in here?"

Mom says, "Dad made some comments in his journal about how he wished he and Mom could die together, and now Sherlock Holmes and Nancy Drew have decided that they did."

"He did hide the journal after he wrote that," I chime in. I'm not convinced he planned his and Becks's deaths; that wasn't really what he said at all. He was more musing that it would be nice.

"Or *someone* hid it," Mom says under her breath.

Harris and I share a look. She really believes someone killed her parents.

Violet nods and looks from one of us to the other. She takes a deep breath, and I just know she's going to soothe us all with her wonderful Violet wisdom. Instead, she claps her hands together. "So, wine."

Harris pulls Mom up off the floor, and she says, "If by wine you mean martinis, then yes!"

"Ladies," I say to a very antsy Betty, Arlene, and Suzanne, who have all materialized behind Violet at the word *wine*, "I think we're going to have to wait on the cleaning out for today."

"But the Salvation Army is scheduled for—" Betty starts.

Arlene elbows her. "We can reschedule the pickup for another time. We're here for whatever you need, whenever you need."

She hugs Mom and mouths over her shoulder, *Whenever you need us.* I'm waiting for the other shoe to drop, for Mom's sadness or panic or *something* to take over. I know the ladies are too. But maybe, given how strong she's been today, we've underestimated my mother's capacity for handling hard things.

As Violet makes her way toward the front door along with the other Dames, I follow her, grabbing Becks's notebook off the kitchen counter on the way. On the front porch, I say, "Can you decipher this for me?"

I open the notebook to the very last page, where there is a list but no description:

1. #687 "A Mighty Fortress Is Our God"

2. "Ave Maria" (soloist)

3. #355 "Give Rest, O Christ"

4. Isaiah 61:1–3

5. Job 19: 21–27a

6. White roses, lilies—not too fragrant!! And NOT with the food—hydrangeas if in season. Call Rider's in Kinston. They will deliver for an extra fee, and they'll know the exact arrangements I'd want.

7. Reception at home, not the Parish Hall. Ladies of the church will make dishes.

8. Please use good silver and nothing disposable, for heaven's sake.

9. Black dress with rosettes around the collar.

Violet covers her mouth, and I can see her laughing despite her efforts to conceal it.

"What?"

She shakes her head. "Only Becks Saint James would have planned her own funeral."

Now I laugh too, but then I stop suddenly, something occurring to me. "Did they ever have a funeral?"

Violet laughs. "They did. I'm sorry to say hydrangeas were not in season. But Patricia immediately jumped into action after Becks and Townsend were declared dead to plan the funeral. I don't know if she knew about the notebook, but she at least had the good sense to have the reception at her home. Can you imagine if it had been at the Parish Hall? Becks would have haunted us forever."

We both laugh, and I shush Violet when I see Mom coming.

"What's so funny?" she asks.

"Nothing," I say, which is true because this is not, should not be funny.

After the ladies leave, Mom, Harris, and I decide to stroll down the boardwalk to take in the setting sun—a vivid hot pink against the blue sky—and the yachts and fishing boats from all over the world. It's like a new place every day, and I love how there's always something different to see. An egret lands on the dock and stares at us.

Sometimes I wonder if the birds we see are really Becks or Townsend, just here to check in.

The bird reminds me: "Mom, I don't know if this is a bad time, but a neighbor wanted to know if he could potentially buy Townsend's plane if you still had it."

Her head swivels toward me. "What?" Her reaction seems too big for what I have asked, but I'm sure her emotions are all over the place right now.

"So you don't still have it?" Harris asks, interpreting her response.

"No, we still have it. It's in the same hangar it has always been in."

Harris stops walking. "Mom, are you serious? Do you know how hard I worked to save up for my plane? And you could have just given me Townsend's?"

She sighs. "All right, Harris. I'm a terrible mother. But, honestly, the plane was maybe even worse than the house for me. All the memories of sunset flights and quick trips. When I think of my dad, I think of him at the helm of that plane. He was so proud of it. Part of me wanted to leave it there for him, just in case he ever came back."

Sadness washes over me anew. If their bodies were never found, Mom probably always wondered if maybe they were still alive somewhere. The thought turns my stomach. "Well, yeah," Harris says. "I'm sure it was an awesome plane."

Mom tears up, and I elbow Harris.

She is obviously finished talking about the plane because she says briskly, "Well, this is tough but it is easier than I thought." Harris and I share a look over her head because, obviously, we agree. "I built up how terrible it was going to be for so long, but now that I'm here it's actually kind of nice to be home."

"What are you in the mood to eat?" Harris asks as she stops and leans on the railing to look at the water. "Should we wait for Uncle Lon?"

Mom is typing something on her phone, and she says, "Cake. I'd like cake for dinner. And maybe a chocolate martini."

Sweets are Mom's stress-eat of choice. She looks up. "Lon won't be here for a few more hours. His flight into New Bern was delayed. Plus, he'll be very judgy about my dinner of cake, and I don't need that right now."

I don't know if we should be worried but, well, it's just a little cake. So we make our way to the end of the boardwalk, turn left onto Queen Street, and cozy up at the bar at Blue Moon Bistro, which I now realize my mother has never been to because it opened after she left. When she was here, it was just a house. It's so weird to think how long it has been since she was last in Beaufort, how much has changed.

"We are here for chocolate martinis and dessert," I announce to the bartender.

She smiles. "Well, you're just in time. I have a new espresso brownie martini on the menu that, in my humble opinion, is the best drink I've ever made."

Mom looks very happy.

"I'm here for an old fashioned and whatever the fish special is," Harris says.

"And I'll start with a salad and a glass of white wine," I whisper, like I'm going to be in trouble with Mom for eating my veggies.

Mom shakes her head like I've betrayed her. Her metabolism is a thing of wonder. "I'd like to start with the beignets."

Then she turns to me. "So, I assume that man with that little boy is your new love interest?"

"Diving right in, aren't we?"

"And why not?" Harris asks. "When it's so fun."

Mom shoots him a look. "Oh, I'll get to you next."

He pretends to hide behind the menu.

"So, is it serious?" Mom asks. "With the man in the rumpled shirt?"

I roll my eyes. His shirt was a little rumpled, I'll admit. But that is part of his charm.

The bartender slides an espresso brownie martini directly into Mom's hand, and she sips. "Ah. Perfect. Thank you."

The bartender winks and hands me my wine. As much as I love a dessert martini, they tend to pair poorly with arugula.

"I actually thought it was over. But then he came to New York to get me."

Mom looks skeptical, and I know how it sounds.

"Anderson's mom came back," Harris clarifies. "First time in five years."

"Thank you," I shoot at him. "You're so helpful."

"Seriously?" Mom says. "This seems like it's your new thing."

She can tell I'm getting perturbed, so she pats my hand and says, "I'm just kidding, honey. Even Harris likes this one."

I'm surprised by this. "You do?"

He stirs his drink. "He's not terrible. Don't let it go to your head." He pauses. "For real, I actually think he seems like a stand-up guy. We've had some talks."

"I can't even imagine what those were like." I put my head in my hands. "And I presume you two were talking about this behind my back?"

Mom nods enthusiastically as Harris says, "Oh, yeah. Totally."

My salad and Mom's beignets arrive. They are piping hot and

melty, and I eat one before my salad. When in Rome. It dissolves in my mouth. I can see why Mom stress-eats sugar.

"So are you going to stay here?" Mom asks between bites.

Harris's fish arrives, and I'm happy he'll have something other than this conversation to occupy himself with.

I shrug. "I think I have to. If I love him, which I do, it's the only choice. He can't upend Anderson's entire life. So if we want to explore this, and we don't want to do long distance—which is never fun—then here is where I shall stay." I take a sip of wine and add, "And as much as I haven't wanted to admit it to myself, I feel like I'm supposed to be here. I love it, and I don't want to leave."

"I can imagine the employment market here is just steaming hot." Mom rolls her eyes.

"Well, at least a job here won't completely disrespect and degrade you like at All Welcome, which would be a step up." Harris obviously wasn't that busy with his fish.

Deciding this isn't the right time to divulge my new life plan, I start on my salad. As I chew, Mom comments, "You know how I feel about moving to a new town for a man. This is your life. Not a Hallmark movie."

I nod. I do know. Mom is not a fan. She says it never ends well. "But, Mom, I wouldn't be moving for him. I'd be moving because I really love living here." I pause. "Plus, who was it that insisted I come here in the first place?" It occurs to me that none of this matters because I don't have a place to live once the house is sold. But that's just a small hurdle, right?

Mom's chocolate cake arrives, and I stick my fork in it immediately. It's real gooey, buttery cake, not that flourless dark thing restaurants usually favor. "Oh my God," Mom says, her mouth full. Harris sticks his fork in too.

His eyes go wide. "That is amazing."

When we're all sufficiently full and verging on tipsy, Mom says, "We should get back. I'm ready to read the letter."

I shake my head. "Mom, I don't know if that's a great idea. Don't you think you should be totally sober for that?"

"If I'm totally sober, I'll never have the guts to do it."

I'm bracing myself for what this is going to be like as we walk down the boardwalk. The setting sun has given way to a clear night sky, and despite my worries, I can't help but be dazzled by the mast lights of the sailboats, the way they combine with the stars to create a glorious light show. And I think about Becks, about the life she had here with the man she loved. With her friends and her dinner parties, her bridge club and volunteer work. What a different life she had. Until this trip, I hadn't known how to do any of the things she did and, even still, I feel sad at the thought of her way of life disappearing. And that is why I want to do my part to save it.

I walk through the front door and up the stairs with Mom, who sits at Becks's dressing table, staring at the monogram on her mother's sterling silver hand mirror that, I am proud to admit, I now know how to polish. Life skills left and right over here.

Mom slides open the top drawer, where I've left the letter, and removes the envelope. She runs her finger over her name. She smiles just a little. "She had perfect penmanship," she says. "She had perfect everything."

She puts the letter down and looks up at me. Harris has gone to Bowen's to check on Salt and, obviously, drink beer, the coward, so it's just the two of us.

I think she's going to say something about the letter as her eyes fill with tears, but instead she says, "Keaton, I have been a terrible mother."

I make a noise of disagreement. Yes, growing up, I wished she was the kind of mom who had my friends over for sleepovers and made pancakes and didn't make me cut my hair short so I could fix it myself. From kindergarten through fifth grade, every single week, I wished and hoped and prayed that the mystery reader who entered our class would be my mom. It never was. But that didn't make her a terrible mother. I always knew I was loved.

Before I can respond she says, "Honey, after my parents died, it took almost twelve years for me to even be able to consider having children. All I could think about was that if I had babies, I could die and leave them alone one day, and that would ruin their lives."

I start to get a pit in my stomach. "That's awful, Mom."

"And when I had you and Harris," she continues, "I battled that terror every day."

A clarity washes over me, and I know what she is going to say before she even says it. Being back in this house, understanding what my mother has gone through, has opened my eyes little by little. In this moment, everything about my childhood suddenly makes perfect sense.

"I know it seems like I pushed you too hard from too young an age, that I made you rely on yourself too much. But my parents did everything for me. Even at twenty-three, my dad was paying my rent, and I couldn't even go to a party without calling to ask Mom what to wear. And then, they were just gone. And I was rudderless. I was totally unprepared for life on my own." She looks me in the eye now and takes my hands. "It broke my heart to make you so independent. But I had to, honey. I had to know that if something happened to me, you would be okay."

I lean down to hug her. "It's okay, Mom. I get it. And look, you did it. I've been able to do everything on my own."

I pull away, and she says, "Keat, when you moved to New York without a second thought and landed an amazing job right away, I felt so proud at first. And then I realized I had done it all wrong. What I should have done is cherished every second in case the worst happened, instead of pushing you to grow up. That wasn't how I saw it at the time. But that's why I wanted to come to New York, why I want to be close to you now. I want to savor every moment with you and Harris that I can. I want to make up for it."

I know she needs some sort of absolution from me, but I don't know how to grant it properly. So instead I say, "You raised an adult, Mom. Sometimes it was hard, but I guess I have to thank you for it, too. Everything I've become I've become because I always had to rely on myself. And that's all thanks to you."

She nods. I don't think I've given her exactly what she wanted, but I've given her what I can. And so I point to the letter. I can only hope that whatever is inside heals what needs to be healed inside of her.

Mom clears her throat. "You haven't read this?" she asks. "Not at all?"

I shake my head. "It was sealed when I found it. It would have felt like defying a dead woman's last wishes."

Mom nods and looks back at the letter. She sighs.

"Why are you so scared to read it?"

"This is it, you know? Once I read this, I never get to hear her say something new again." She scrunches her nose. "And what if they *were* murdered, Keaton? What if this is my fault?"

I take the letter. "You don't have to open it. But if I had a few minutes to hear someone's voice from beyond the grave, I would want to know what they had to say. And, Mom, as long as *you* didn't murder them, it could never be your fault." I pause. "You didn't, did you?" I joke.

She smiles, just a little.

"I can read it for you," I offer.

Before she can answer, we both hear a voice we recognize from downstairs. "Whoa, it's like we never left. It's exactly how I remember it."

I roll my eyes. "Oh, Uncle Lon."

"What did he expect?" Mom asks. "We haven't been here in almost fifty years."

"I'll go get him," I say, backing toward the door.

Mom nods and slides her finger under the flap of the envelope. And I wonder what it must be like to have another moment to hear your dead mother's voice.

I must cherish my mother's voice while I have her, I think. I'm lucky I have more time to say the things I haven't said, mend what needs to be fixed. We're getting there; I feel it. As I turn my head and glimpse my mom removing the piece of paper, I have to feel like the grandmother I never knew is part of that.

In the Shadows

SATURDAY, AUGUST 28, 1976

Tip: The rules are always changing, Virginia. A hostess in my mother's day is not what a hostess is in mine, and certainly is not what it will be in yours. But it has been my experience that returning to those small touchstones—elegant table settings, appropriate serving, thoughtful invitations—those constants create parties that seem extravagant in their undertaking when, really, they are only proper. It is in following the rules that are traditional, classic, unchanging, that something simple seems extraordinary. When in doubt, get back to basics. Some things truly are timeless. They will never lead you astray.

Dear Virginia,

I am so happy to see you happy in your relationship, your job, your life. And I hope you know that I would never want to change you; I am so proud of the woman you are becoming. I know my dinner parties may sometimes seem silly to you. And maybe they are silly. But, you see, over the course of the past three decades or so your father and I have welcomed people into our home and fed them, given them the best of ourselves, turned strangers into friends, a cold new place into a warm and welcoming one. People have fallen in love at our dinner parties, met their spouses, made best friends, gotten new jobs, found a place in this corner of the world we love so much. (I know your life is so very different from mine, but, if, one day, when I am not here, you decide to pick up the mantle, I hope you know that my notebook—a.k.a. my Guide to Entertaining—has everything you need in it!)

No, it isn't curing cancer or marching on Washington, but I'd like to think that, in a small way, I have made a mark on people's lives. But none of that is what really matters. None of that is why I picked up this pen.

What I really wanted to say was that, one day, I will be gone, and when I am, I never want you to look back and say, "Poor Mom and her little life." My little life has made me so terribly happy. It has been more than I deserved. Being a hostess, a southern woman, a church altar guild member, a Historic Site volunteer, a teacher, the support system for a very busy doctor, the mother to two extraordinary children, and the person who made the best damn key lime pie in all of Carteret County? Those things meant something to me. They were everything. They were enough. If I could do it all over again, I wouldn't change a thing.

I would, as I always have, do anything to protect you and Lon, to soothe your pain, to make you smile. I didn't get that with my own mother and, of all the things I have done, what makes me proudest is my relationship with the two of you.

You, my girl, I am sure, will make a mark. A big one. People will read about you in history books and be in awe of how you changed the world. But don't forget, I am the one who brought you into it. Some people cast a bright light while others stand in the shadows. If I had to stand in the shadows so that you could shine, well, so be it. Keep shining, my girl. Keep shining.

All my love,
Mom

1970s Vortex

U ncle Lon!" I say, running to meet him. "You're here! You came!"

"Keaton!" he says, sweeping me up in a hug.

Harris walks up the front steps, Salt in tow. "It's getting real in here. The band is back together."

Uncle Lon claps Harris on the back. "What are you doing here, Harris?"

Harris gestures to me. "I had to make sure this one didn't get swept into a 1970s vortex, turn into the ghost of Becks, and never leave."

Lon nods like that is downright sensible as he walks through the house toward the kitchen, looking around. "Where is my sister? Is she in a heap on the floor somewhere?"

Harris and I share a look. "She's actually doing eerily well," Harris says.

Lon notices my hand. "Whoa," he says, holding it up to admire Becks's ring.

"Oh, um, I found this," I stammer. "But I will pay you your part as soon as I get the commission from selling the house." I pause. I don't want to offer because what if he takes me up on it? But I figure I have to. "Unless you want the ring," I say. "Mom doesn't."

"No, no," he says. "It's just kind of like seeing a ghost. Mother left it in her will for Virginia, anyway. We just assumed she was wearing it when she died. She never took it off. Not even to sleep."

"That's so weird," I say.

"I just think it's surprising that whoever stole their cash didn't find the ring," Lon says. Harris starts to fill Lon in on all we have learned about our grandparents' deaths and Townsend's last journal entry and then adds, "Orrrrr . . . maybe they faked their deaths and took the cash."

I roll my eyes at Lon. "I'm so tired of him saying that." Then I see Bowen at the side door. My head is beginning to hurt with the idea of my mother upstairs having an emotional moment and my uncle here to suck all the air out of every room. But having Bowen here is a balm.

I open the door and kiss him quickly. "I just wanted to check on you," he says. "And, also, I miss you."

I smile at him. "You are welcome to come in if you dare, but I would understand if you didn't . . ."

"I would love to come in, but can you come here first?"

I take his hand and walk down the back steps, laughing as I see Anderson standing beside the cutest yellow bike—just the perfect size for me. It has a little rattan basket and best of all, it's filled with hydrangeas and . . . "A baguette!" I squeal. I kiss Bowen quickly and muss Anderson's hair.

"You guys!" I put my hand to my heart. "I don't know what to say."

Bowen looks at me seriously. "You have to promise you will never try to ride a bike with Salt again."

I put my hand up, as if I'm making a solemn vow.

"Thank you so, so much," I say, climbing onto the seat. I ride toward the street, to the end of the driveway, surprised by how much better I've gotten since my first foray back into bike riding a couple weeks ago.

Bowen and Anderson follow me. When I stop, Bowen clears his throat. "Oh, and, um, I got rid of that other one you tried to ride . . ." I smile at him and his eyes lock on mine. "Sometimes a bike is just a bike, Keaton. And that was just a bike, nothing more."

I get what he means. And it soothes me to hear that.

"Want to ride with me tomorrow?" Anderson asks.

"I want to ride with you always!" I say.

"But right now, I think Keaton needs to be at home," Bowen says to Anderson kindly. He turns to me. "And I need to go meet your uncle."

Anderson takes off on his bike, and I put my kickstand down, leaving mine at the end of the driveway. Bowen and I walk through the gate and up the front steps. "I hope that wasn't bad timing," he says. "I knew this was going to be a hard day, and I thought you might need a little something to cheer you up."

I squeeze his hand. "Perfect timing."

Bowen smiles and walks into the house, presumably to introduce himself to Uncle Lon.

I take a deep breath and turn, looking out over the waterfront. It is so peaceful here. I will miss this beautiful family home. It seems like a shame to sell it, especially when neither Mom nor Lon are particularly hard up for the money. The idea of losing this house makes my heart hurt. But there's nothing I can do about it.

Although . . . maybe I just need to make Mom and Lon remember the magic of this place, wipe away the traces of the horrors they faced here—and the 1970s time warp—and turn it into the beach cottage of their dreams. It would give me an excuse to stay for a little while, to oversee the progress. But only if they agree to it, of course.

Chewing on the idea, I walk inside, through the living room, and toward the voices in the kitchen. I run my finger down Becks's cherished dining room table and smile. Her life's work was important. It mattered. And I'm going to make sure people know it.

The front door opens behind me, and when I turn toward it, I have a clear view of Dr. Scott peeking his head inside. I walk toward him and, in the flash of the light from the chandelier, I realize for the first time how incredibly blue his eyes are. "Is Violet here?" he asks quietly.

I shake my head, but he comes inside anyway, and I hear footsteps behind me. When Dr. Scott sees Harris too, he says, "Hey, any news on that plane?"

Harris nods. "They still have it. Want to go check it out?"

"Oh, that would be fantastic!" says Dr. Scott.

"Want to come with us?" I ask Bowen.

"For sure," he says.

"I'll get my car and drive everyone over," Dr. Scott says.

"I'm going to go leave Anderson a note to get Violet if he needs anything while we're gone," Bowen adds. "I'll meet you outside."

I walk into the kitchen. "Hey, Uncle Lon, do you know where the key to Townsend's hangar is?"

"Oh, yeah."

I follow him toward the pantry. He reaches his hand inside, fumbling for a hook, but comes back empty-handed. He peers inside, and I do too, noticing that the hook he was reaching for is empty. "Huh. This is where Dad always kept the key." He pauses for a moment, squinting. "I went to the hangar the day after they died," he says. "The police wanted to make sure their plane hadn't taken off." He pauses. "Covering their bases." He's looking at me, but I feel like he's basically thinking out loud.

"And?"

"And Mom and Dad hadn't called in a flight plan. They were both sticklers for the checklist, so I knew they hadn't taken off that night, but I just wanted to confirm that no one had seen them. No one had."

"Okay," I say. I'm not sure why this relates to the key.

He closes his eyes, obviously piecing the day together. "I remember driving over to the hangar." He opens his eyes and looks at me. "It was locked."

"But you had the key?" I say, not following.

"I think," he says. "But I can't remember. I'd flown with my parents hundreds of times. We always locked the hangar when we got back."

"Ah," I say. "That's how you knew the plane was inside."

"Maybe I didn't return the key," he muses. "Gosh, did I have the key with me? I wonder what I did with it."

I pat him on the shoulder. "It was forty-seven years ago, Uncle Lon. I wouldn't beat myself up about it."

He nods. "I'll just get the extra from the credenza."

He rifles through it and hands me an old key that was buried under a stack of papers. "Uncle Lon," I say, "are you like Mom? Do you think your parents were murdered?"

He shakes his head. "I love my sister, but honestly I thought she was coming totally undone. No, my parents died in a car crash. We never had any reason to think otherwise."

"So why didn't you ever come back?" Harris asks. "Mom was too scared."

He sighs and runs his hands through his hair. "A lot of reasons. It was too sad. I didn't want to deal with actually admitting they were gone and letting go of the life we had." He sighs. "And, well, honestly, I didn't really think our parents were murdered. But maybe there was enough doubt in my mind that I was a little scared too."

"Oh, but you both sent me here! Thanks!" I say.

He laughs. "No, no. If there was a killer, he's probably dead by now. Or at least moved away. Besides, the whole story was nuts. The man Virginia was afraid of was some new doctor in town or something. I don't even remember the details of her theory." He pauses. "But, you know, Keaton, I think your mom never felt safe again—and I don't just mean in Beaufort; I mean in general. I think that's why she's dedicated her life to creating a safe place for people who, like her, don't feel safe."

The idea makes me physically shudder.

Lon points upstairs. "I'm going to go hug my sister. Let me know how it goes at the hangar."

I walk outside, spotting Dr. Scott's car. Harris climbs in the front seat and Bowen and I slide in the back, and Dr. Scott drives the short distance to Beaufort's teeny private airport. We turn left toward the gated area and Bowen—who has called a friend to get the gate code—enters the numbers from the index card into a key code box, and I hold my breath. The chain link section of fence slides open. We all squint, looking at hangar numbers, until I spot number four and we pull the car right up to it. Harris gets out, turning on his phone flashlight, and Dr. Scott turns the car so the lights shine directly onto the hangar. Harris gets the lock undone relatively quickly. I want to stop Dr. Scott from—at eighty-two years old, mind you—getting out to help Bowen raise the metal garage door. Harris's flashlight is shining on him, and I notice the most unusual scar on his hand. But I don't have time to ask him how he got it. Because before they've gotten the door halfway up, I can see what they can't.

There's nothing there. Townsend and Rebecca Saint James's plane is gone.

Harris and I don't discuss what we will say to Mom and Uncle Lon. But we're brother and sister. We've been winging this stuff for years. We walk in the door, and I follow Harris to the kitchen. It's there I see

Lon holding the piece of paper, the note from the phone pad I have not moved.

There's a place that I know.
It has called out to me.
Where the sea meets the sky,
And the sky meets the sea.

I see Mom walking down the back steps, her eyes puffy with tears, and I run to her. "So?" I ask.

She shrugs. "It was definitely the letter of a woman who knew she was dying." She pauses. "But it wasn't the letter of a woman who knew she was dying that day."

I'm about to ask more when Mom gasps. "Peter?" she whispers. She takes a few steps back and clasps Lon's arm like a life raft.

I look around. *Who's Peter?*

Then I realize that she's looking at Dr. Scott, and I think how funny it is that I hadn't known his first name, just as I hear Violet's "Yoo-hoo!" coming from the front door.

Mom looks like she's seen a ghost. I walk over to put my hand on her arm, and she jumps, her eyes never leaving Peter's.

"What are you doing here?" she asks, breathless.

I am so confused. "Mom, Dr. Scott wanted to look at the plane."

"Why would you want a plane?" Violet interjects. "You don't fly."

Well that *is* odd.

"Wait," Mom says, pointing from Violet to Dr. Scott. "Are you," she gulps, "married?"

I look from Lon to Harris and back to Mom. What is happening here? Why is this so weird?

Violet nods. "Yes. Forty years. We met right here." She adds quietly, "Well, you remember."

"The last dinner party," Lon whispers.

Maybe this is why they're being so weird? That was the last time they saw each other?

"Peter had been engaged to a friend of Virginia's," Violet explains.

Okay, sure. But, well, that was more than forty years ago. *Get it together, Mom.*

Before I can ask anything else or tell Mom what we found—or, well, didn't find, as it were—Lon hands her the paper in his hand. I assume he's trying to diffuse this weirdness.

Mom gasps. She holds up the paper. "This is a poem Daddy and I wrote together when I was in fourth grade." She pauses. "Or, well, maybe fifth. I'm not positive." Harris and I share a *here it comes* look. We've been waiting for a freakout.

Lon pats Mom's arm. "Well, that's great, Ginny. How nice."

"I didn't understand quatrains," Mom says. "And so he wrote this for me."

I don't know what to say, and I look at Bowen, afraid that this real-life, deep-inside glance into my family is going to be too much for him.

"Geez, talk about the favorite child," Lon says. "Letter from Mom, poem from Dad. I'm chopped liver."

I ignore him. "That's interesting that it would be on the phone pad," I say. "Maybe he thought of you and thought of the poem and decided to write it down." I'm about to tell them about the plane.

But before I can, Mom's eyes lock with Peter's, and her voice breaks as she says, "He left it for me. He left this poem for me."

I can see why this makes her emotional, of course, but why is she looking at Peter?

"You knew?" she whispers to him.

He shrugs. "Not until right now. I only guessed."

Her eyes fill with tears. "I'm so sorry, Peter. I thought . . ."

She trails off, and Violet is looking from Mom to Dr. Scott—well, Peter, I guess—and back.

"What are you two talking about?" Violet asks.

To Mom, Dr. Scott says, "It's okay. I understand. I always understood." And to Violet he whispers, "We'll talk about this later."

Mom looks down at the paper again and then back up. "I know where they are." She puts her hand to her mouth. "I know what happened to my parents."

Harris and I share a look. And, without a word, I know we both understand something: We don't need to tell my mom the plane is gone. She already knows.

Kinder Than Home

SATURDAY, AUGUST 28, 1976

Tip: Darling, in the end, entertaining, like life, is all about taking care of the people you love. It is about treating them well, easing their burden, putting something on yourself to make their day a little more palatable, their experience on this earth a little simpler. It is my great wish that, as a hostess, as a friend, as a wife and mother, I have made the right choices. But it is my greatest wish that, in what I have done and what I have not, I have taken some of life's sorrow and fear and pain away from you and your brother. Creating an effortless experience for others is, after all, what being a great hostess is all about.

Becks let the staff go early. They hadn't put away all the dishes yet, and, while she usually liked to leave her kitchen looking like it had been untouched, she had the utmost faith in Virginia's capacity to handle that at a later date. Besides, time was of the essence. The sun had nearly set, and she wanted to see it. From the air.

Becks sat at her dressing table, finishing a letter to Virginia. After dinner, the children were going to Robert's cousin's engagement party at the Coral Bay Club and would be staying over at the beach. She felt a pang of nostalgia thinking of how they would dance to the band, of all the nights she and Townsend had done the same.

"Mom!" Virginia had hissed to her mother when they were finally alone. "That's him! Peter! The doctor who murd—"

Becks had cut her off and rubbed her arms. "I know. I figured it out. I confronted him about it, too."

Virginia's eyes went wide. "Are you insane? You confronted him?"

Becks grimaced. "I know. Maybe not my smartest idea?" She paused. She had come to an understanding with Peter, she thought. "I wouldn't get too tight with that one. I know everyone else seems to love him, but there's something about him that doesn't sit quite right with me."

"Maybe that he's a *murderer*?" Virginia whispered.

"Well, darling," Becks said, wondering how much of Peter's truth to tell, "not everything is as simple as it seems."

"So he told you what happened?"

Becks nodded.

"Mother, the *last* thing you want to have from a murderer is information. You don't want to be guilty by association."

Becks waved her hand like her daughter was being silly.

"And, Mom, what was up with Daddy earlier when he met Robert? Is he okay?"

Becks knew Townsend was very much not okay. But that wasn't important at this particular moment. "He's just fine, darling. Overtired and sunburned is all."

Virginia looked skeptical. "If you say so. I'll be back in the morning. We've got to get to the party now."

"I take it all is well with Robert?" Becks asked Virginia, glad for a change of subject.

She laughed. "Oh, yes. I don't know why I can't be more agreeable," she said. "Why can't I be more like you, Mother?"

Becks smoothed her daughter's hair. "Always be exactly who you are. No apologies. Promise?"

Virginia nodded.

Becks pulled her daughter close so she couldn't see the tears in her eyes. "You are the most exceptional daughter, and I love you more than all the grains of sand on the beach."

"I love you too, Mom." Virginia pulled away and studied her mother. "Are you crying?"

Becks shrugged. "Just thinking about how you will be the most beautiful bride."

"And you will be the most beautiful mother of the bride."

If only . . .

Sitting at her dressing table now, Becks spritzed perfume on her neck, wondering what Townsend was going to say about her idea, questioning whether this would be the last time she sat here, the last time she saw her own reflection. Knowing Virginia's future was all but set, knowing that she had said a lovely goodbye to each of her children, she was surprised at how light she felt. She was pardonir them from an unnecessary season of suffering, and giving herself t gift of choosing her own time, before the shadows began to creep the corners of the room, before she ruined her children's live made everything hard. She could never, would never, be a b God would forgive her for that, certainly. And to think it w who had made her see the light in the end. It was Peter who ing her pull this off by sinking the car, creating the diversi course, had to consider that Townsend wouldn't feel how

she believed in the very marrow of her bones that he would agree this was the solution to all their problems.

But it didn't feel real until Becks slipped her ring off. Her beautiful ring. She had left in her wishes that she wouldn't wear it to be buried. But she had assumed she would be dead when some coroner or her daughter or her husband removed it from her finger. Thinking of that made Becks even sadder. This ring had scarcely left her finger since the day Townsend got down on his knee in front of her in his office. She hated the idea of being without it. But really what she hated was the idea of being without him. And now she'd never have to be.

She walked downstairs, into the library, where he was scribbling in his journal as she had seen him do a million times. She paused to watch him, study him, his brow furrowed, his stare intense. Every single day for the past forty-one years he had been her reason for living. Yes, even when her mother let her down so royally, she still believed in some of the things her mother had taught her. Namely, that her marriage had to come first, that a happy marriage made for happy children. Becks had never forgotten that. And, when it came to marriages, she believed she had had the happiest.

"Darling," Townsend said, looking up, dropping his pen and closing the journal. Becks smiled when she heard his voice.

As Townsend opened the bottom drawer of the credenza to store his journal, Becks gathered all her strength. He sat back down in his chair, and she sat on the ottoman, facing him. She took his hands in hers and he looked at her expectantly. "Townsend, this isn't easy for me to say."

He looked as though he was about to interrupt but stopped himself.

Becks took a deep breath. "Sweetheart," she said. "I'm dying."

She didn't know what to expect, but as Townsend calmly kissed her hand, she knew it wasn't that. "I know," he said.

"You know?"

"I'm a doctor, Becks." His voice broke as he added, "But more important, I'm your husband. You thought I wouldn't know?"

Becks was truly at a loss for words. Maybe he would be okay without her after all. Maybe she had read this all wrong.

Townsend took a deep breath. "Becks, since we're making confessions . . . I have one of my own."

Becks felt a lump rise in her throat. She knew what was coming. But hearing it out loud would make it real. "Daniel believes . . ." He paused. "Well, Becks, it appears I am beginning to get a touch of Alzheimer's."

She squeezed his hand tenderly, her eyes filling with tears. Then she smiled at him encouragingly.

"You aren't surprised," he said.

"I'm your wife. You thought I wouldn't know?"

"Becks," Townsend started. "I don't want to live without you. I don't want to spend the next years of my life in decline. I can't bear the thought of losing you. Physically, of course. But from my mind and heart most of all. I can't stomach the thought of not knowing my children and—" Townsend put his head in his hands. Then he looked up at Becks.

Becks smiled at him reassuringly, realizing that perhaps she had been right all along. Perhaps this plan of hers hadn't been as foolish as she'd believed. "Townsend," she said seriously, looking him straight in the eye. "What if we went together? Tonight."

Becks held her breath for a few long moments. What if Townsend thought she was crazy? What if he wasn't as worried about life without her as she was about life without him?

Townsend stood and pulled Becks up, in a gesture that revealed nothing. He drew Becks into his arms, kissed her, and said simply, "Darling girl, you have, as always, read my mind."

"I have?" she asked, somewhat surprised. But, then again, hadn't she and Townsend always been on the same page?

"Oh yes." He kissed her again. "My very first day of flight school I had this overwhelming feeling that, from then on, up in the air is where we would solve all our problems."

"Together?" she whispered.

"Together," Townsend repeated. "Just like it always has been."

"It's such a nice night for a walk," Becks said. "Would you like to stroll to the airport, maybe catch the last moments of the sunset from the air?"

He paused for a moment, taking her in. "That would be lovely."

As they walked out the door into the cooling summer evening, she said simply, "I'll fly us tonight."

Townsend shook his head. "No, Becks, that isn't fair. This should be on me."

Becks inhaled deeply, savoring the summer scent of jasmine, gardenia, and magnolia that lingered in the southern air. She knew it was the last time she would ever smell this. It broke her heart to turn back and look at her house one last time. What happiness they had had here. Were they making a mistake? She looked at Townsend, who was looking at the house too. "It has been a good life, Becks." Then, as if confirming what she couldn't reason out, he added, "I am so glad we can leave it together, while it's still good."

His statement bolstered her. He was right.

Becks shook her head as they made their way down the street, thinking about Townsend's offer to fly them. Peter wrecking the car would buy a couple days until they were discovered, throw everyone off the scent. But when they were found, Becks didn't want people saying Townsend had lost his faculties and crashed the plane. No, that wouldn't do at all. She would do everything she could to preserve him.

"You can't fly, Townsend," she said as they turned toward the airport, hands clasped and swinging. Passersby would have envisioned them as a couple without a care in the world. Townsend chuckled. "Daniel agrees, but that feels of little consequence now."

"That's not what I mean," she said. "You are a decorated pilot. A hero. I will not have anyone saying that the plane went down because of your mistake."

"And so I'm supposed to let the blame land on you?" He looked at her, stricken.

"I insist on it."

He smiled. "When Rebecca Saint James insists, a smart man knows he has lost the battle."

So that solved it. She would fly.

When they reached the hangar that they knew so well, Townsend leaned over and used his key to unlock it, then slid the door up. Becks stopped for a moment to admire the plane, kept so clean and shining by Townsend. The silver propeller practically gleamed against the aircraft's white paint. The plane's two stripes—one burgundy, one silver—were so shiny she could see her reflection in them. It seemed a shame to waste it. But, well, sometimes these things couldn't be helped.

She looked at Townsend, her heart swelling. She loved him so much. The idea of their being apart was impossible. Becks kissed Townsend and hugged him with all her might. "I love you, Townsend Saint James," she said. "This life with you has been more than anyone deserves."

"I love you too, Rebecca Saint James," he said. "And I refuse to live a moment without you. I cannot, will not do it. I've always wanted to protect you, Becks. To take care of you. Sometimes I forget how very much you have protected me too."

She kissed him hard in affirmation. Townsend helped her up onto the wing of their Bonanza, opening the door on the co-captain side and helping her slide into the captain's seat. Then he climbed out again. As she glided the plane out on the airstrip, he closed the hangar behind him, locking it even though nothing remained inside. *What a nice touch*, she thought. No one was here to see them take off, and no one would suspect they had locked an empty hangar.

As he resumed his place beside her, Becks disregarded the checklist for the first time in her life. She didn't call in their flight plan. It would be obvious what had happened, she knew.

"I left a poem on the counter for Virginia," Townsend said. "She'll know right away what happened, where we are."

Becks just smiled as the plane took off and they rose higher and higher into the sky. She believed in an afterlife. She believed there was a God who painted this sunset a fiery deep yellow and wild pink tonight, her favorite combination. She believed God would see their actions for what they were—an act of great love—and have mercy on them. But, just in case, she at least wanted them to share as many living moments as they could.

Townsend reached over and took Becks's hand as their plane glided effortlessly through the evening sky. She smiled at him.

"I was reading my journal entry from the day we met," Townsend said. "It was the best damn day of my life, Becks. We are so lucky."

"So lucky," Becks said. That they could be in this position and still believe in their own good fortune meant the world to her. She was, indeed, a blessed woman.

"It's heaven up here, isn't it?" he said, looking up. "This has been one of the best parts of my life, being in this plane with you, being a part of the sky."

She nodded. "We've gotten to experience so much," she said. "Together."

"Together," he repeated.

"I have this dream where you and I are flying," Becks said. "Not in a plane, just flying like birds in the night sky, gliding past the moon, dancing among the stars. Where the sky is dark, but it is also so very bright."

Townsend squeezed her hand. "Becks," he whispered, "I have that very same dream."

Becks laughed. "Naturally."

She started to get the tiniest bit nervous as she approached the place she was looking for, where the land disappeared from view, where the clouds began to blend seamlessly with the water below. A flock of birds streaked across the horizon, floating along the air, diving into the deep endless blue. She and Townsend were one of them now. She took a deep breath. "This is the place," she said.

"Hasn't it always been?" He leaned over and kissed her for what she knew would be the last time. He gripped her hand tighter, and she killed the engine. It was smoother than she imagined, peaceful even, like descending a staircase to a place even warmer and kinder than home. In her mind's eye, she saw her daughter's smile, heard her son's laugh, imagined each of them the moment they were born, when the doctor placed them on her chest. She saw Townsend's face in the flickering candlelight the night they married in a ceremony so intimate, so special, that it had carried them through a lifetime.

Becks opened her eyes and saw that Townsend's eyes were fixed on her face. She fixed hers to his, her other half, and now, in these final moments, her last link to life. For a moment, Becks faltered. She could change this; she could correct it. But then she thought of the weeks ahead, of her drowning in a sea of pain that Townsend couldn't soothe, of him facing the blinding tunnel of losing all his memories, all their dreams, and she knew they had made the right choice; she knew they would be forgiven.

The blue of the water, the blue of the sky, the blue of his eyes. Becks and Townsend were suspended for one beautiful, fleeting, silent second in the majesty and mystery of the most spectacular place they had ever known, where now they would get to be together always. Just as it was meant to be. Suspended forever. Lost in time. Reborn into the light.

Where the sky meets the sea.

Keaton

....

On Sunset Lane

ONE YEAR LATER

I t nearly killed Uncle Lon to give up the amazing offer he got on the house. And, well, giving up my commission gave me pause too. But after learning about the choice my grandparents had made, we all decided, as a family, that the house and its memories meant too much to us to sell. It had been the Saint James house for more than two centuries. And, if we had anything to say about it, it would continue to stay in our family for generations to come. Yes, we had lost something precious here, my mom and my uncle especially; but we have all found something here too. Something stronger, something better.

So much of the house on Sunset Lane has changed. But this dining room, Becks's sanctuary, has stayed the same. It has been my respite while the kitchen has been redone, the bathrooms torn out, the shag carpeting removed, and the original floors refinished. It has been my home office and my inspiration as I began working on the book I asked Allison to help me publish, as I started the Instagram account Harris dreamed up. As @rebeccasaintjames grew to a respectable 18,946 followers, as I waded through Becks's notebooks and cookbooks, advice and letters to my mom, and stories from her friends, I started feeling like I was making my grandmother proud. And as I worked side by side with, yes, *Allison* to create the thing that would preserve Becks's legacy, I knew her grand vision and keen understanding of what makes something sell would help make it truly spectacular. *Rebecca Saint James's Guide to Entertaining.* (*How could we possibly call it anything else?* Allison had asked. She was right, as she so often is about these things.) My book—Becks's book, really—was released last Tuesday. A combination of her recipes, her entertaining tips, and my thoughts on how my grandmother's traditional life helped me forge my own, modern path.

I have done eight days of shockingly well-attended signings at independent bookstores in New York, North Carolina, South Carolina, and Georgia—planned by my genius publicist brother, of course. I have heard women's stories about following my account, about laughing at my foibles and feeling seen in my mishaps, like they could approach cooking and entertaining because I was such a mess at it and did it anyway. I think I am flattered? It's resonated with so many people that I have already gotten emails from multiple publishers about another Rebecca Saint James book.

But tonight I can't think about any of that. Tonight, we celebrate and, well, film. Because when you have released a book from your grandmother's point of view about cooking and hosting, it makes sense to stream an actual party for your viewers to see. My family, bless their hearts, is here to support me. They have been by my side every step of the way.

Speaking of family, Mom seems to have found her purpose again doing something she is amazing at: furniture shopping for her new old beach house. After a buddy of Bowen's in search and rescue was able to locate Becks and Townsend's plane at the very spot Mom said, something broke free inside her. She seemed less afraid of the world. I would say she was like her old self, but, of course, I didn't know her in a world with my grandparents.

She and Lon agreed that I could stay here for a year before I needed to start looking for a place of my own. None of us said it out loud, but we were all thinking the same thing: In one year, I'd know if Bowen was the real deal. In one year, I'd know if becoming my grandmother could actually be a job. In one year, I'd know if I'd be happy here. And I am. So happy that I have told Allison that I will not be taking the second year on my contract. Instead, I will be training my replacement. I found my confidence at All Welcome. But it is in tackling the world of Rebecca Saint James that I have found my voice. And I will continue to do so.

Weirdest of all, I finally figured out why I'm so afraid to fly. I have to think that some ancient part of my DNA knew that my grandparents had met their demise in a plane crash. From the minute I knew they planned it, I haven't been afraid to fly. Not once.

As I look around the dining room table at Harris and the shockingly age-appropriate woman he brought here with him, at Mom and Dad, Uncle Lon, Anderson, and, yes, sweet Bowen by my side, I can say, with conviction, that I am happy. Violet and Dr. Scott are also here, as are, of course, Arlene, Suzanne and her husband, Wade, and Betty, who could never miss a party. And would it even be one without them? Amy and Jimmy and Alex and Clayton are here too. We had to get out the extra leaf for the table and pull in chairs from the other rooms and still it is crowded. But it's crowded with people I love, with people who love me and want to celebrate this very exciting moment.

After dinner, we will go to the 1776 Celebration on the Historic Site grounds, to see our neighbors and friends dressed in period costumes to reenact the day we claimed our independence from England.

And then we will all go watch fireworks light up the night sky and Taylor Creek.

I interrupt the chatter around the table, tapping my wineglass. "Friends, family, we are breaking the cardinal rule of a Becks Saint James dinner party!"

"Oh, yes. Group conversation only!" Mom chimes in.

Bowen smiles and takes my hand. "I guess we're rule breakers. But now that you bring it up," he says, playing along, "who is most excited to see Beaufort by air with Pilot Keaton?" Mom and I decided this year that we couldn't be the only two in our family who couldn't fly. So we got our pilot's licenses. Together. It is, hands down, the most fun thing I've ever done with my mom, and I'll remember it for the rest of my life.

I smile at Bowen, and something clicks, something new. I've known that I love him. I've known that we have something special. But it's the first time I feel really deep down inside that we are going to be together forever.

And, goodness knows, the man is patient. Because, between rushing to get this book out, flying back and forth to New York when I needed to be in person at All Welcome, and burning the candle from both ends nonstop, it has been quite a year. The community college student I've paid to film tonight says, "Oh my gosh, you guys. Can we start over? I don't think we were recording."

Everyone laughs. "At least I haven't served the Waldorf salad yet." I had to make at least one dish tonight that my grandfather would have wanted. This is, after all, about honoring his legacy too.

I go back into the kitchen to reenact walking in with the roast that, I might add, I cooked all on my own. As I do, I can't help but smile. I hadn't realized it—not consciously—but not knowing this part of my family history had created this dark hole in my life. Once that was filled, everything started to change for me; once I uncovered the story of my grandparents and figured out who I was, I could actually move forward. I was brave enough to find a job I really enjoy. Strong enough to be with a man I love, whose life isn't simple. And, maybe best of all, I've gotten to know a really special little boy who has lit up my world in ways I never could have imagined.

I hear footsteps in the kitchen behind me. When I turn, I realize it is Bowen. And that he is down on one knee. And he is holding a small velvet box.

I can't say I didn't imagine this moment was coming. But I didn't expect it to be right now. "Yes!" I blurt out without thinking, forgetting all about the roast and the cameras and the live stream and my family and my guests. (This is why, while I might impersonate my grandmother on Instagram and in cookbooks, I will never really *be* her. She would never forget her guests.)

Bowen laughs. "I haven't said anything yet."

"Right. Sorry. Go ahead then. And make sure you are filled with anticipation over what my answer might be."

He shakes his head. "Keaton, I never, ever expected to fall in love with the crazy new neighbor who I was certain was going to turn the house next door into a subdivided Airbnb. But I couldn't help myself. You make it impossible not to love you. You have been the most amazing partner to me, and I think the only person who loves you more than I do is my son." He takes a deep breath. "So, will you marry me?"

He opens the box and holds up a beautiful eternity band as I pretend to ponder. "Well, did you ask Salt's permission?"

He nods seriously. "Salt is very excited by the prospect of being a family dog."

I laugh. "You know I'd do anything for Salt."

"And you know I'd do anything for you."

"Anderson!" I call.

He peeks his head tentatively into the kitchen, and I motion for him. He looks from Bowen—who is still on his knee—to me a little nervously. "Well, did you ask her?"

"I want to make sure this is okay with you," I say. "You are the most important person in the world to me, you know." I mean that. I know without having anything to compare it to that I love this boy as if he were my very own. The idea of things not working out with Bowen and not having Anderson in my life keeps me up at night.

"Keaton," he says so maturely, "I picked out your ring like six months ago." He whispers behind his hand and points at Bowen, "You should have seen the ring *he* wanted to get you." I laugh. "Plus," he adds, "I'm getting really tired of having to walk next door to check on you and Salt all the time."

I look down at Bowen. "Well then, I think it's settled. I think we must get married due to Anderson's busy schedule."

Bowen stands and leans in to kiss me, and, as I wrap my arms around him, as he dips me toward the ground, I'm so excited that I feel like my heart might burst. When he rights me, I look up to see my family, friends, and, of course, Salt, all crammed in the doorway. Bowen spins me around in a circle, kissing me for all the world to see. And I can't help but think about that day a little over a year ago when I walked into All Welcome, asking the universe to give me that promotion or something better. This has definitely been that something better. Well done, universe. Well done.

"Did she say yes?" Mom calls, breathless, from the back of the group.

I want to say, *If I didn't, thanks for making it awkward.*

"She said yes!" Bowen exclaims. Harris pushes through the group and opens the fridge. It's a new Sub-Zero, although I have to say that

I miss the old Kelvinator with all my heart. He pops a bottle of Dom Perignon I haven't even noticed, its cork flying way up in the air and making a joyful noise.

"Oh, Harris! You are so sweet. You got that to celebrate our engagement?"

"Your engagement, my successful *Rebecca Saint James's Guide to Entertaining* launch campaign . . . Tomato, tomahto." Harris pours champagne, and I hug my four Beaufort besties.

"Well, ladies," Violet says, "I think our work here is done."

"Done?" I ask. "So I suppose none of you would be interested in planning a big Beaufort wedding?"

"They don't enjoy things like that," Mom says.

"Nope," Lon agrees. "They're more sit-quietly-in-the-back-seat kind of ladies."

Harris holds up his champagne flute and says, "To my sister, who I love dearly, and whose streak of terrible men and terrible jobs has finally come to an end."

"Hear, hear!" my dad says too loudly.

"To Dad and Keaty!" Anderson cheers, and I wrap him in the biggest hug. He's only a few inches shorter than I am now, a fact I can scarcely believe. Kerry is still in Morehead City, working, which I give her tons of credit for. Anderson ultimately decided that he only wants his mom back in his life in small doses. He isn't ready for overnights or a lot of solo time, and Kerry has received that decision with a lot of grace, taking her cues from Anderson. I don't have much contact with her; I don't feel like it's my place. But, I'm happy to say, Bowen has consulted me on the matter every step of the way.

"Can I taste your champagne?" Anderson asks, looking up at me with those big eyes.

"No!" I say as Bowen says, "Sure." I crinkle my nose. "It's gross. You won't like it." I take a sip. It is decidedly not gross. But he can learn that for himself when he's older.

I smile down at him. The meaning of family has changed for me since I've been here. I feel this deep, almost mystical connection to the people who have come before me, to the previous inhabitants of Sunset Lane. And to Becks and Townsend most of all. Getting to uncover the pieces of their lives, side by side with my brother, mom, and uncle, has given me a new understanding of who I am. Getting to re-create a part of Becks's life, to preserve her memory, means more to me than any job ever could. I hold out my hands, admiring the new eternity band on the left, Becks's diamond on the right. My future and my past.

I am proud that despite the hurt, the perceived failures, the difficult days, I plunged ahead to create the family I always wanted. And this precious little boy has been one of the biggest parts of that.

"Do I get to be your stepmom now?" I ask him, ruffling his hair.

He wrinkles his nose, and I feel my heart fall as he says, "Nah."

But then he continues, "Just my mom. You always say that we choose our family, and so I choose you."

I squeeze him to me again so he doesn't see me wipe my eyes as I kiss his head. Bowen, seeing my face, comes to the other side of Anderson, wrapping us both in a hug. "Anderson sandwich!" Bowen teases, kissing me lightly.

"Our family," Anderson says, his voice muffled against my chest.

There it is again, that word. Family. *Our family.* For better or worse, the people in this room have all shaped each other and will continue to do so as we refine what that word means.

"So is that what's next for the toast of the publishing world?" Harris asks. "*Rebecca Saint James's Guide to Marriage?*"

"If only she'd left that notebook behind," I joke. Only, somehow, within the walls of this house, imprinted on her china, her silver, Townsend's journals, and Becks's words of wisdom, it's like they did leave it behind. Uncovering these people I never knew, this part of my history that was always shrouded in mystery, has led me to this next part of my life and given me the confidence to move forward into what I have always dreamed of. It's big and it's scary but, most of all, it's wonderful.

I smile at Bowen over Anderson's head. He smiles at me. I realize that, sure, I've seen great examples of love and marriage. Even still, this is a chapter of our life story Bowen and I will have to write all on our own. I can't wait to get started.

Acknowledgments

The first time I came to Beaufort, NC, I was nineteen years old. At the crest of the old Grayden Paul Drawbridge, I declared offhandedly, absurdly, "I'm going to live here one day." I am a breathing example of the power of simply putting something out into the universe because roughly a decade later I moved to Beaufort—a town of around forty-five hundred residents—with my husband and our son for "one year." We still haven't left.

Many have probably heard me say that the Peachtree Bluff in my Peachtree Bluff series was based on Beaufort. That is true. But Peachtree Bluff is based on the Beaufort of my weekend trips and slow summers away from the real world.

The Beaufort of *A Happier Life* is the Beaufort of my real life, the one I have come to know in perhaps a truer way while living here year-round. Needless to say, I love it dearly. And researching what Beaufort used to be like—whether in digitized copies of old Carteret County newspapers online or with the microfilm machine at the Beaufort Library (thanks, librarians!), I loved every moment of reading about what this town and its surrounding county used to be like, from the 1930s and beyond. Many of the places and events in this book are real, but, of course, this is fiction, and I did take some liberties as well.

Some might consider the most significant liberty the changing of the date of one of Carteret County's most hallowed events: the Big Rock Tournament, which takes place in June, not July as it is here. (But the Kids Big Rock *is* in July, usually my birthday weekend, in fact!)

Also, notably, our beloved Old Homes Tour & More, hosted each year by the Beaufort Historic Site, led by our fearless leader, the indomitable Patricia Suggs, began in 1961, not in 1976 as I write here. I was looking for an event to connect Becks's life to Keaton's and there are few celebrations in this town that mean as much to me as the Old Homes Tour. Held the last full week of June each year, it is a fabulous combination of home and garden tours, music, luncheons, historic demonstrations, double-decker bus tours, historic site tours, and so much more. If you are ever this way during that time of year, don't miss this wonderful event!

Thank you so much, Patricia and everyone at Beaufort Historical Association, for always being such generous hosts of events for me. Peachtree Bluff Town Takeovers have always been epic, and I can't wait to share Beaufort with readers again in this new way, with this book. This community has embraced my family and me so deeply— even though, like Becks, I am not and will never be a local!—and I am endlessly grateful for the support of this place that we chose. Or, maybe, it chose us. I never can be sure.

Also, for those who know Beaufort, "Sunset Lane" in this book isn't the real Sunset Lane. It's actually Front Street, but I thought that Sunset Lane was a nice metaphor in this story.

And, a little historical detail: the Viking 1 actually entered Martian orbit on June 19, 1976, not June 18. But I was hoping to have a headline that oriented readers to the time period and, well, nothing super exciting happened on June 18, 1976! (And June 19 was a Saturday, so the doctor's office wouldn't be open.)

This novel was inspired by something that happened in my family, long before I was born. My grandmother lost her sister and brother-in-law far too young, and it's a story that has always stuck with me. I do certainly believe their deaths were an accident and, so, little of what I write here is based on the true story. In fact, part of the eventual discovery of where they were came at the hands of a psychic and a group of Boy Scouts, truth that is far stranger than fiction and I knew would never translate realistically on the page. I won't elaborate more here in case someone is reading the acknowledgments before the book. No spoilers! But it seems fitting that I thank my family first because they are so intimately tied to this story and involved in every book I write.

My two Wills, thanks for being my biggest cheerleaders and in-house support squad, for all your fun ideas (and fact-checking!), and for being so willing to share me with these other worlds I create. I love you both so very much! And my first-ever dog, Salt, obviously inspired a thing or two in this book, so thanks to him for being so cute and fluffy and making a dog person out of me, a feat that seemed completely impossible before he was in our world.

Mom and Dad (Paul and Beth Woodson), thank you, as always, for being my tireless support system and for giving me a blissful childhood full of stability—and books! Mom, thanks for always being my first reader and, no matter what, saying it's my best book ever! Same goes for my aunts Nancy Sanders and Cathy Singer, editors extraordinaire, who, no matter how many eyes have been on this book, always manage to find mistakes!

I dedicated this novel to my neighbors and dear friends who are so much more like family, Tricia and Lee Johnson and their three daughters, my "little sisters" Brooke Smith, Alee Halsey, and Ann Rollins Johnson, mainly because I love them and wanted to dedicate a book to them, but also because their house inspired this story, in part. We were neighbors in Salisbury, NC, and when we moved to another neighborhood my parents recruited them to buy the house across the street. Again. But this house was special because, while it was located on a beautiful street in an idyllic neighborhood and had great bones, as they say, the owners had literally walked out the door decades earlier and never came back. Dishes were on the table, toys and baby dolls still mid-play in children's rooms, vines covering the outside. Needless to say, it needed to be completely gutted and redone, which they did beautifully, saving a lovely home. But the memory of how eerie it was to walk inside a house with a turkey petrified on the table, newspaper on the couch like someone was coming back for it, and so much more stayed with me. I always knew I'd incorporate that into a story somehow, but I softened it quite a bit for this novel because both my editor and agent found my original version, based on this actual house, unbelievable. Again, truth is stranger than fiction!

I am also so grateful to B. C. Cone for spending time with me on his actual 1970s Beechcraft Bonanza and helping me get to know what Becks and Townsend's plane might have been like. Thank you so much for sharing so much knowledge with me, B. C.! I am convinced he knows everything about flying, and, for sure, all mistakes are my own.

In *The Summer of Songbirds*, I thanked my *Friends & Fiction* co-hosts and dearest friends Mary Kay Andrews, Kristin Harmel, and Patti Callahan Henry, our managing director, Meg Walker, and podcast partner Ron Block for creating this magical community, one hundred thousand members strong. Less than a year later, I am thanking them for a community that is now nearly two hundred thousand members strong. Wow, wow, wow! Thanks to all of you for your love and support. Lisa Harrison, Brenda Gardner, Annissa Armstrong, Shaun Hettinger, James Way, and Rachel Jensen, thank you for all you do to create this thriving space on the internet. To our darling *Friends & Fiction* ambassadors, who show up online and in person, sharing love and light and confetti (real and virtual!) wherever they go: Amber Prater, Anne Floccari, Barbara Wojcik, Bubba Wilson (the lucky coin queen!), Clare Plaxton, Dallas Strawn, Dawne McCurry, Debby Stone (the countdown queen!), Francene Katzen, Irene Wenner, Jill Mallia, Jodena Pysher, Kathy Saccamano, Laurie Brown, Lesley Bodemann, Linda Burrell, Maria Lew, Marilyn Rumph, Marlene Waters, Mary Vasquez, Meredith D'Agostino, Michelle Marcus, Mindy Ehrlich, Molly Neville, Nicole Fincher, Rhonda Perrett, Robin Klein, Sharon Person, Susan Seligman, Susie Baldwin, and Taylor Lintz, I love each of you to pieces and can't express how your support boosts me all year long—but never more than on a book tour! *Friends & Fiction* members everywhere, you are true treasures!

Speaking of treasures, Elisabeth Weed, you are certainly one. Thanks for the million little things you do for each and every book, from negotiating contracts to hosting epic dinner parties. All I can say is that Rebecca Saint James would want tips from *you*. Molly Gregory, you knew how special this book was to me from the beginning and treated it like your own from day one. Thanks for all your guidance and insight as we made this story the very best version of itself. Lauren Carr, if you're lucky enough to have a publicist who will text you turn-by-turn directions when you find yourself accidentally driving through New York City with no GPS, you're lucky enough. Thanks for your tireless efforts in getting my books out into the world! (And let's hope I never accidentally drive in NYC again . . .) Bianca Salvant, your fresh marketing ideas for each book always inspire me! I'm so grateful! Jennifer Bergstrom, Aimee Bell, Jennifer Long, Sally Marvin, and Eliza Hanson, thank you for each and every page we've published together. You are all such a gift to me! Gabrielle Audet and Sarah Lieberman, listening to the audio versions of my books is always like a new dream come true. I can't possibly thank you enough! Olivia Blaustein, and the whole CAA crew, you guys are simply the best. I'm looking forward to many more projects together in the future!

Kathie and Roy Bennett, Susan Zurenda, and the Magic Time team, thank you for creating incredible tours that bring me so much joy and help spread the word about my stories. Taylor Brightwell, Hannah Lindsley, Crystal Patriarche, and the Booksparks team, thanks for all the creative ways you continue to support my work.

Ashley Edmondson, we love you so much and are so grateful to you for being such an important part of our family! Tamara Welch, what a joy it has been to work with you for so many years. You're amazing in every way. Ashley Hayes, thank you, thank you for all your support, expertise, and friendship. I am so grateful to have you as a part of my team.

I would not be here for this *eleventh* novel were it not for the many, many people who share my work and continue to support me in so many ways! A special shout-out to the amazing JoAnna Garcia Swisher and the Happy Place, Kristy Barrett of A Novel Bee, Stephanie Gray, Zibby Owens, and the Moms Don't Have Time team, Maghon Taylor of All She Wrote Notes, Grace Atwood from The Stripe, Andrea Katz, Cristina Frost, Susan Roberts, Susan Peterson, Ashley Bellman, Susan McBeth, Emmy Griffith, Judy Collins, Meagan Briggs, Ali Albrecht, Amy Wilcox, Courtney Marzilli, Jennifer Clayton, Chase Waskey, Kristin Thorvaldsen, Randi Burton, Melissa Steele-Matovu, and Jess Williams for being by my side and being so supportive!

Independent bookstores and libraries everywhere have long been my heroes, so a huge thank-you to all of you. Another special shout-out to my hometown bookstore, South Main Book Company in Salisbury, NC, for always going above and beyond to celebrate. Oxford Exchange in Tampa, FL, thanks for not only always hosting me but for all your amazing work on this year's *Friends & Fiction* subscription. My tour wasn't set yet when I wrote this, but thank you to each and every store that has hosted me for this book and the ones that came before.

I don't have a group of "Dockhouse Dames" like Keaton—although I do now plan to fervently seek one out—but I do have the best friends anyone could ask for. You know who you are, and I love you dearly!

Last but certainly not least, thank you to every single person who picked up this book. I hope it made you smile or tear up or think about someone special in your life. I hope it reminded you that it's never too late to begin again and that, sometimes, we find our next steps in totally unexpected ways. I get to do what I love because of each of you who read my books, and I never take that for granted.

And never forget to say your most outlandish dreams out loud. You never know who might be listening—or how your life might change in the very best ways.

Recipes

OATMEAL COOKIES

2 sticks of butter, room temperature	1¼ cups all-purpose flour
1 cup brown sugar	½ teaspoon baking soda
1 cup white sugar	1 teaspoon vanilla
2 eggs	3 cups oatmeal (quick cooking)
	1 cup chopped pecans

- In a bowl, cream the butter, then add the sugars and mix well.
- Add the eggs, flour, baking soda, vanilla, oatmeal, and pecans and mix well.
- Roll the dough onto wax paper and wrap in a 1½- to 2-inch-diameter roll.
- Refrigerate the dough overnight.
- Slice the dough into thin rounds and bake at 375 degrees Fahrenheit for 9 to 11 minutes until slightly brown.
- Eat and enjoy!

From the kitchen of my grandmother, Ola Rutledge.

I don't even have to make a batch to be able to taste these absolutely perfect cookies. Some of my fondest memories are in my grandmother's kitchen, making these heavenly bites. Everyone in our family loves cookie dough, and sneaking bites of it from my grandparents' freezer—where Grandmommy always kept rolls and rolls of dough—is another of my earliest memories. These cookies were a part of every holiday and every celebration and are a staple of our beloved family beach trips.

FAVORITE CHICKEN SALAD

1 large fryer (3 pounds or more)
2 ribs celery, cut fine
1 small onion, chopped fine

2–3 tablespoons sweet pickle salad
cubes, drained
mayonnaise

- Place the fryer in a pot with water, cover, and boil until tender.
- When the fryer has cooled, take the meat off the bones, removing the skin.
- Cut the fryer into bite-sized pieces and add salt and pepper to taste.
- In a bowl, mix the celery, onion, salad cubes together with the mayonnaise until just moist.
- Refrigerate the salad until ready to use. It will keep in the refrigerator for three days.

From the kitchen of my grandmother, Hazel Woodson.

Note from Hazel: I do not use hard-boiled eggs, as it takes away from the taste of the chicken. Most people use eggs, but I have found it tastier without them.

My grandmother passed away when I was three, so I don't remember tasting her cooking, but everyone in my family raves about how special it was. This chicken salad recipe might be simple, but, in her practiced hand, it was extraordinary, which goes to show that, sometimes, the chef is more important than the recipe.